this
LULLABY

SARAH DESSEN

Hodder
Children's
Books

A division of Hachette Children's Books

A Catalogue record for this book is available from
the British Library

ISBN-13: 978 0 340 98902 9

Typeset in NewBaskerville by Avon DataSet Ltd,
Bidford-on-Avon, Warwickshire

Printed in Great Britain by
Clays Ltd, St Ives plc

The paper and board used in this paperback are natural
recyclable products made from wood grown in sustainable
forests. The manufacturing processes conform to the
environmental regulations of the country of origin.

Hodder Children's Books
a division of Hachette Children's Books
338 Euston Road, London NW1 3BH
An Hachette UK Company
www.hachette.co.uk

June

1

The name of the song is 'This Lullaby'. At this point, I've probably heard it, oh, about a million times. Approximately.

All my life I've been told about how my father wrote it the day I was born. He was on the road somewhere in Texas, already split from my mom. The story goes that he got word of my birth, sat down with his guitar, and just came up with it, right there in his motel room. An hour of his time, just a few chords, two verses and a chorus. He'd been writing music all his life, but in the end it would be the only song he was known for. Even in death, my father was a one-hit wonder. Or two, I guess, if you count me.

Now, the song was playing overhead as I sat in a plastic chair at the car dealership, in the first week of June. It was warm, everything was blooming, and summer was practically here. Which meant, of course, that it was time for my mother to get married again.

This was her fourth time, fifth if you include my father. I chose not to. But they were, in her eyes, married – if being united in the middle of the desert by someone they'd met at a rest stop only moments before counts as married. It does to my mother. But then, she takes on husbands the way other people change their hair colour: out of boredom, listlessness, or just feeling that this next one will fix everything, once and for all. Back when I was younger, when I asked about my dad and how they'd met, when I was actually still curious, she'd just sigh, waving her hand, and say, 'Oh, Remy, it was the Seventies. You know.'

My mother always thinks I know everything. But she's wrong. All I knew about the Seventies was what I'd learned in school and from the History Channel: Vietnam, President Carter, disco. And all I knew about my father, really, was 'This Lullaby'. Through my life I'd heard it in the backgrounds of commercials and movies, at weddings, dedicated long-distance on radio countdowns. My father may be gone, but the song – schmaltzy, stupid, insipid – goes on. Eventually it will even outlive me.

It was in the middle of the second chorus that Don Davis of Don Davis Motors stuck his head out of his office and saw me. 'Remy, honey, sorry you had to wait. Come on in.'

I got up and followed him. In eight days, Don would become my stepfather, joining a not-so-exclusive group. He was the first car salesman, the second Gemini, the only one with money of his own. He and my mother met right there in his office, when we came in to buy her a new Camry. I'd come along because I know my mother: she'd pay the list price right off the bat, assuming it was set, like she was buying oranges or toilet paper at the grocery store, and of course they'd let her, because my mother is somewhat well known and everyone thinks she is rich.

Our first salesman looked right out of college and almost collapsed when my mother waltzed up to a fully loaded new-year model, then poked her head inside to get a whiff of that new-car smell. She took a deep gulp, smiled, and announced, 'I'll take it!' with characteristic flourish.

'Mom,' I said, trying not to grit my teeth. But she knew better. The entire ride over I'd been prepping her, with specific instructions on what to say, how to act, everything we needed to do to get a good deal. She kept telling me she was listening, even as she kept fiddling with the air-conditioning vents and playing with my automatic windows. I swear that was what had really led to this new-car fever: the fact that I had just got one.

So after she'd blown it, it was up to me to take over. I started asking the salesman direct questions, which made him nervous. He kept glancing past me, at her, as if I was some kind of trained attack dog she could easily put into a sit. I'm used to this. But just as he really started to squirm we were interrupted by Don Davis himself, who made quick work of sweeping us into his office and falling hard for my mother in a matter of about fifteen minutes. They sat there making googly eyes at each other while I haggled him down three thousand bucks and got him to throw in a maintenance plan, a sealant coat, and a changer for the CD player. It had to be the best bargain in Toyota history, not that anyone noticed. It is just expected that I will handle it, whatever it is, because I am my mother's business manager, therapist, handyman, and now, wedding coordinator. Lucky, lucky, me.

'So, Remy,' Don said as we sat down, him in the big swivelling leather throne behind the desk, me in the just-uncomfortable-enough-to-hurry-the-sale chair opposite. Everything at the dealership was manufactured to brainwash customers. Like memos to salesmen encouraging great deals just casually 'strewn' where you could read them, and the way the offices were set up so you could easily 'overhear' your salesman pleading for a good deal with his manager. Plus the fact that the window I was now facing opened up to the part of the lot where people picked up their brand-new cars. Every few minutes, one of the salesmen would walk someone right to the centre of the window, hand them their shiny new keys, and then smile benevolently as they drove off into the sunset, just like in the commercials. What a bunch of shit.

Now, Don shifted in his seat, adjusting his tie. He was a portly guy, with an ample stomach and a bit of a bald spot: the word *doughy* came to mind. But he adored my mother, God help him. 'What do you need from me today?'

'Okay,' I said, reaching into my back pocket for the list I'd brought. 'I double-checked with the tux place and they're expecting you this week for the final fitting. The rehearsal dinner list is pretty much set at seventy-five, and the caterer will need a cheque for the rest of the deposit by Monday.'

'Fine.' He opened a drawer and pulled out the leather binder where he kept his chequebook, then reached into his jacket pocket for a pen. 'How much for the caterer?'

I glanced down at my paper, swallowed, and said, 'Five thousand.'

He nodded and started writing. To Don, five thousand bucks was hardly any money at all. This wedding itself was setting him back a good twenty, and that didn't seem to faze him either. Add to it the renovation that had been done on our house so we could all live together like one happy family, the debt Don was forgiving on my brother's truck, and just the day-to-day maintenance of living with my mother, and he was making quite an investment. But then again, this was his first wedding, first marriage. He was a rookie. My family, however, had long been of pro status.

He ripped out the cheque, slid it across the desk, and smiled. 'What else?' he asked me.

I consulted my list again. 'Okay, just the band, I think. The people at the reception hall were asking . . .'

'It's under control,' he said, waving his hand. 'They'll be there. Tell your mother not to worry.'

I smiled at this, because he expected me to, but we both knew she wasn't worrying at all about this wedding. She'd picked out her dress, decided on flowers, and then pushed the rest off on me, claiming she needed absolutely every free second to work on her latest book. But the truth was, my mother hated details. She loved to plunge into projects, tackle them for about ten minutes, and then lose interest. All around our house were little piles of things that had once held her attention: aromatherapy kits, family tree software, stacks of Japanese cookbooks, an aquarium with four sides covered in algae and one sole survivor, a fat white fish who had eaten all the others.

Most people put off my mother's erratic behaviour to the fact that she was a writer, as if that explained everything. To me that was just an excuse. I mean, brain surgeons can be crazy too, but no one says it's all right. Fortunately for my mother, I am alone in this opinion.

'. . . is so soon!' Don said, tapping his finger on the calendar. 'Can you believe it?'

'No,' I said, wondering what the first part of his sentence had been. I added, 'It's just amazing.'

He smiled at me, then glanced back down at the calendar, where I now saw the wedding day, 10th June, was circled several times in different colours of pen. I guess you couldn't blame him for being excited. Before he met my mother, Don was at the age where most of his friends had given up on him ever getting married. For the last fifteen years he'd lived alone in a condo right off the highway, spending most of his waking hours selling more Toyotas than anyone else in the state. Now, in nine days, he would get not only Barbara Starr, romance novelist extraordinaire, but also, in a package deal, my brother Chris and me. And he was happy about it. It *was* amazing.

Just then the intercom on his desk buzzed, loudly, and a woman's voice came on. 'Don, Jason has an eight fifty-seven on deck, needs your input. Should I send them in?'

Don glanced at me, then pushed down the button and said, 'Sure. Give me five seconds.'

'Eight fifty-seven?' I asked.

'Just dealership lingo,' he said easily, standing up. He smoothed down his hair, covering the small bald spot I only noticed when he was seated. Behind him, on the other side of the window, a ruddy-faced salesman was handing a woman with a toddler the keys to her new car: she took them as the kid tugged on her skirt, trying to get her attention. She didn't seem to notice. 'Hate to push you out, but . . .'

'I'm done,' I told him, tucking the list back in my pocket.

'I really appreciate all you're doing for us, Remy,' he said as he came around the desk. He put one hand on my shoulder, Dad-style, and I tried not to remember all the stepfathers before him that had done the same thing, that same weight, carrying the same meaning. They all thought they were permanent too.

'No problem,' I said as he moved his hand and opened the door for me. Waiting for us out in the hallway was a salesman, standing with what had to be that eight fifty-seven – code for an on-the-fence customer, I assumed – a short woman who was clutching her handbag and wearing a sweatshirt with an appliquéd kitten on it.

'Don,' the salesman said smoothly, 'this is Ruth, and we're trying our hardest to get her into a new Corolla today.'

Ruth looked nervously from Don to me, then back to Don. 'I just–' she sputtered.

'Ruth, Ruth,' Don said soothingly. 'Let's just all sit down for a minute and talk about what we can do for you. Okay?'

'That's right,' the salesman echoed, gently prodding her forward. 'We'll just talk.'

'Okay,' Ruth said, somewhat uncertainly, and started into Don's office. As she passed she glanced at me, as if I were part of this, and it was all I could do not to tell her to run, fast, and not look back.

'Remy,' Don said, quietly, as if he'd noticed this, 'I'll see you later, okay?'

'Okay,' I told them, then watched as Ruth made her way inside. The salesman steered her to the uncomfortable chair, facing the window. Now, an Asian couple was climbing into their new truck. Both of them were smiling as they adjusted the seats, admired the interior: the woman flipped down the visor, checking her reflection in the mirror there. They were both breathing deep, taking in that new-car smell, as the husband stuck the key in the ignition. Then they drove off, waving to their salesman as they went. Cue that sunset.

'Now Ruth,' Don said, settling into his chair. The door was closing on them, and I could barely see his face now. 'What can I do to make you happy?'

I was halfway across the showroom when I remembered that my mother had asked me to please, *please* remind Don about cocktails tonight. Her new editor was in town for the evening, ostensibly just passing through from Atlanta and wanting to stop in and be social. Her true motivation, however, was that my mother owed her publisher a novel, and everyone was starting to get a little antsy about it.

I turned around and walked back down the hallway to Don's office. The door was still closed, and I could hear voices murmuring behind it.

The clock on the opposite wall was the school kind, with big black numbers and a wobbly second hand. It was already one-fifteen. The day after my high school graduation and here I was, not beach bound or sleeping off a hangover like everyone else. I was running wedding errands, like a paid employee, while my mother lay in her king-size Sealy Posturepedic, with the shades drawn tight, getting the sleep she claimed was crucial to her creative process.

And that was all it took to feel it. That slow, simmering burn in my stomach that I always felt when I let myself see how far the scale had tipped in her favour. It was either resentment or what was left of my ulcer, or maybe both. The Muzak overhead was growing louder, as if someone was fiddling with the volume, so that now I was getting blasted with a rendition of some Barbra Streisand song. I crossed one leg over the other and closed my eyes, pressing my fingers into the arms of my chair. Just a few weeks of this, I told myself, and I'm gone.

Just then, someone plopped down hard into the chair on my left, knocking me sideways into the wall; it was jarring, and I hit my elbow on the moulding there, right in the funny bone, which sent a tingly zap all the way up to my fingers. And suddenly, just like that, I was pissed. *Really* pissed. It's amazing how all it takes is one shove to make you furious.

'What the *hell*,' I said, pushing off the wall, ready to take off the head of whatever stupid salesperson had decided to get cosy with me. My elbow was still buzzing, and I could feel a hot flush creeping up my neck: bad signs. I knew my temper.

I turned my head and saw it wasn't a salesman at all. It was a guy with black curly hair, around my age, wearing a bright orange T-shirt. And for some reason he was *smiling*.

'Hey there,' he said cheerfully. 'How's it going?'

'What is your problem?' I snapped, rubbing my elbow.

'Problem?'

'You just slammed me into the wall, asshole.'

He blinked. 'Goodness,' he said finally. 'Such *language*.'

I just looked at him. *Wrong day, buddy*, I thought. *You caught me on the wrong day.*

'The thing is,' he said, as if we'd been discussing the weather or world politics, 'I saw you out in the showroom. I was over by the tyre display?'

I was sure I was glaring at him. But he kept talking.

'I just thought to myself, all of a sudden, that we had something in common. A natural chemistry, if you will. And I had a feeling that something big was going to happen. To both of us. That we were, in fact, meant to be together.'

'You got all this,' I said, clarifying, 'at the tyre display?'

'You didn't feel it?' he asked.

'No. I did, however, feel you slamming me into the wall,' I said evenly.

'That,' he said, lowering his voice and leaning closer to me, 'was an accident. An oversight. Just an unfortunate result of the enthusiasm I felt knowing I was about to talk to you.'

I just looked at him. Overhead, the Muzak was now playing a spirited version of the Don Davis Motors theme song, all plinking and plunking.

'Go away,' I told him.

He smiled again, running a hand through his hair. The Muzak was now building to a crescendo over us, the speaker popping, as if close to short-circuiting. We both glanced up, then at each other.

'You know what?' he said, pointing up at the speaker, which popped again, louder this time, then hissed before resuming the theme song at full blast. 'From now on, forever' – he pointed up again, jabbing with his finger – '*this* will be our song.'

'Oh, Jesus,' I said, and right then I *was* saved, hallelujah, as Don's office door swung open and Ruth, led by her salesman, came out. She was holding a sheaf of papers and wore that stunned, recently-depleted-of-thousands look on her tired face. But she did have the complimentary fake-gold-plated key chain, all hers.

I stood up, and the guy beside me leapt to his feet. 'Wait, I only want—'

'Don?' I called out, ignoring him.

'Just take this,' the guy said, grabbing my hand. He turned it palm up before I could even react, and pulled a pen out of his back pocket, then proceeded – I am not joking – to write a name and phone number in the space between my thumb and forefinger.

'You are insane,' I said, jerking my hand back, which caused the last digits to get smeared and knocked the pen out of his hand. It clattered to the floor, rolling under a nearby gumball machine.

'Yo, Romeo!' someone yelled from the showroom, and there was a burst of laughter. 'Come on man, let's go!'

I looked up at him, still incredulous. Talk about not respecting a person's boundaries. I'd dumped drinks on guys for even brushing against me at a club, much less yanking my hand and actually *writing* on it.

He glanced behind him, then back at me. 'I'll see you soon,' he said, and grinned at me.

'Like hell,' I replied, but then he was already going, dodging the truck and minivan in the showroom and out the front glass door, where a beaten-up white van was idling by the kerb. The back door flung open and he moved to climb in, but then the van jerked forward, making him stumble, before stopping again. He sighed, put his hands on his hips, and looked up at the sky, then grabbed the door handle again and started to pull himself up just as it moved again, this time accompanied by someone beeping the horn. This sequence repeated itself all the way across the parking lot, the salesmen in the showroom chuckling, before someone stuck a hand out the back door, offering him a hand, which he ignored. The fingers on the hand waggled, a little at first, then wildly, and finally he reached up and grabbed hold, hoisting himself in. Then the door slammed, the horn beeped again, and the van chugged out of the lot, bumping its exhaust on the way out.

I looked down at my hand, where in black ink was scrawled 933-54somethingsomething, with one word beneath it. God, his handwriting was sloppy. A big D, a smear on the last letter. And what a stupid name. Dexter.

When I got home, the first thing I noticed was the music. Classical, soaring, filling the house with wailing oboes and flowing violins. Then, the smell of candles, vanilla, just tangy sweet enough to make you wince. And finally, the dead giveaway, a trail of crumpled papers strewn like bread crumbs from the foyer, through the kitchen, and leading to the sunporch.

Thank God, I thought. *She's writing again.*

I dropped my keys on the table by the door and bent down, picking up one balled-up piece of paper by my feet, then uncrumpled it as I walked toward the kitchen. My mother was very superstitious about her work, and only wrote on the beat-up old typewriter she'd once dragged around the country when she did freelance music articles for a newspaper in San Francisco. It was loud, had a clanging bell that sounded whenever she reached the end of a line, and looked like some remnant from the days of the Pony Express. She had a brand-new top-of-the-line computer too, but she only used that to play solitaire.

The page in my hand had a 1 in the upper right-hand corner, and started with my mother's typical gusto.

Melanie had always been the type of woman who loved a challenge. In her career, her loves, her spirit, she lived to find herself up against something that fought her back, tested her resolve, made the winning worthwhile. As she walked into the Plaza Hotel on a cold November day, she pulled the scarf from her hair and shook off the rain. Meeting Brock Dobbin hadn't been in her plans. She hadn't seen him since Prague, when they'd left things as bad as they'd started them. But now, a year later, with her wedding so close, he was back in the city. And she was here to meet him. This time, she would win. She was

She was . . . what? There was only a smear of ink after the last word, trailing all the way down the page, from where it had been ripped from the machine.

I continued picking up discarded papers as I walked, balling them into my hand. They didn't vary much. In one, the setting was in LA, not New York, and in another Brock Dobbin became Dock Brobbin, only to be switched back again. Small details, but it always took a little while for my mother to hit her stride. Once she did, though, watch out. She'd finished her last book in three and a half weeks, and it was big enough to function effectively as a doorstop.

The music, and the clanging of the typewriter, both got louder as I walked into the kitchen, where my brother, Chris, was ironing a shirt on the kitchen table, the salt and pepper shakers and napkin holder all pushed to one side.

'Hey,' he said, brushing his hair out of his face. The iron hissed as he picked it up, then smoothed it over the edge of the collar of the shirt, pressing down hard.

'How long's she been at it?' I asked, pulling the trash can out from under the sink and dumping the papers into it.

He shrugged, letting some steam hiss out and stretching his fingers. 'A couple of hours now, I guess.'

I glanced past him, through the dining room to the sunporch, where I could see my mother hunched over the typewriter, a candle beside her, pounding away. It was always weird to watch her. She really slammed the keys, throwing her whole body into it, as if she couldn't get the words out fast enough. She'd keep it up for hours at a time, finally emerging with her fingers cramped, back aching, and a good fifty pages, which would probably be enough to keep her editor in New York satisfied for the time being.

I sat down at the table and flipped through a stack of mail by the fruit bowl as Chris turned the shirt over, nudging the iron slowly around one cuff. He was a really slow ironer, to the point that more than once I'd just jerked it away, unable to stand how long it took him to do just the collar. The only thing I can't stand more than seeing something done wrong is seeing it done *slowly*.

'Big night tonight?' I asked him. He was leaning close to the shirt now, really focusing on the front pocket.

'Jennifer Anne's having a dinner party,' he said. 'It's smart casual.'

'Smart casual?'

'It means,' he said slowly, still concentrating, 'no jeans, but not quite a sport jacket event either. Ties optional. That kind of thing.'

I rolled my eyes. Six months ago, my brother wouldn't have been able to define *smart* much less *casual*. Ten months earlier, on his twenty-first birthday, Chris had got busted at a party for selling pot. It wasn't his first brush with the law, by any means: during high school he'd racked up a few breaking and enterings (plea-bargained), one drink-driving (dismissed), and one possession of a controlled substance (community service and a big fine, but just by the skin of his teeth). But the party bust did him in, and he did jail time. Only three months, but it scared him enough to shape up and get a job at the local garage, where he'd met Jennifer Anne when she'd brought her car in for a thirty-thousand-mile check-up.

Jennifer Anne was what my mother called 'a piece of work', which meant she wasn't scared of either of us and didn't care if we knew it. She was a small girl with big blonde chair, whip smart – though we hated to admit it – and had done more with my brother in six months than we'd ever managed in twenty-one years. She had him dressing better, working harder, and using proper grammar, including wacky new terms like 'networking' and 'multi-tasking' and 'smart casual.' She worked as a receptionist for a conglomerate of doctors, but referred to herself as an 'office specialist'.

Jennifer Anne could make anything sound better than it was. I'd recently overheard her describing Chris's job as a 'multi-level automotive lubrication expert', which made working at the garage sound on a par with heading up NASA.

Now Chris lifted the shirt off the table and held it up, shaking it slightly as the typewriter bell clanged again from the other room. 'What do you think?'

'Looks okay,' I said. 'You missed a big crease on the right sleeve, though.'

He glanced down at it, then sighed. 'This is so freaking hard,' he said, putting it back on the table. 'I don't see why people bother.'

'I don't see why *you* bother,' I said. 'Since when do you need to be wrinkle free, anyway? You used to consider wearing trousers dressing up.'

'Cute,' he said, making a face at me. 'You wouldn't understand, anyway.'

'Yeah, right. Excuse me, Eggbert, I keep forgetting you're the smart one.'

He straightened the shirt, not looking at me. 'What I mean,' he said slowly, 'is that you'd just have to know what it's like to want to do something nice for somebody else. Out of consideration. Out of *love*.'

'Oh, Jesus,' I said.

'Exactly.' He picked up the shirt again. The wrinkle was still there, not that I was going to point it out now. 'That's exactly what I'm talking about. Compassion. Relationships. Two things you are sadly, and sorely, lacking.'

'I am the queen of relationships,' I said indignantly.

'And hello, I just spent the entire morning planning our mother's wedding. That is so freaking compassionate of me.'

'You,' he said, folding the shirt neatly over one arm, waiter-style, 'have yet to experience any kind of serious commitment . . .'

'What?'

'. . . and you have bitched and moaned so much about the wedding I'd hardly call that compassionate.'

I just stood there, staring at him. There was no reasoning with him lately. It was like he'd been brainwashed by some religious cult. 'Who are you?' I asked him.

'All I'm saying,' he replied, quietly, 'is that I'm really happy. And I wish you could be happy too. Like this.'

'I am happy,' I snapped, and I meant it, although it sounded bitter just because I was so pissed off. 'I am,' I repeated, in a more level voice.

He reached over and patted my shoulder, as if he knew better. 'I'll see you later,' he said, turning and heading up the kitchen stairs to his room. I watched him go, carrying his still-wrinkled shirt, and realised I was clenching my teeth, something I found myself doing too often lately.

Bing! went the typewriter bell from the other room, and my mother started another line. Melanie and Brock Dobbin were probably halfway to heartbreak already, by the sound of it. My mother's novels were the gasping romantic type, spreading across several exotic locales and peopled with characters that had everything and yet nothing. Riches yet poverty of the heart. And so on.

I walked over to the entrance of the sunroom, careful to be quiet, and looked in at her. When she wrote she seemed to be in another world, oblivious of us: even when we were little and screaming and squawking, she'd just lift her hand from where she was sitting, her back to us, the keys still clacking, and say, 'Shhhhhh.' As if that was enough to shut us up, making us see into whatever world she was in at that moment, at the Plaza Hotel or some beach in Capri, where an exquisitely dressed woman was pining for a man she was sure she had lost forever.

When Chris and I were in elementary school, my mom was pretty broke. She hadn't published anything yet except newspaper stuff, and even that had petered out once the bands she was writing about – like my dad's, all 1970s stuff, what they call 'classic rock' now – began to die out or drop off the radio. She got a job teaching writing at the local community college, which paid practically nothing, and we lived in a series of nasty apartment complexes, all with names like Ridgewood Pines and Lakeview Forest, which had no lakes or pines or forests anywhere to be seen. Back then, she wrote at the kitchen table, usually during the evenings or late at night, and some afternoons. Even then, her stories were exotic; she always picked up the free brochures from the local travel agency and fished *Gourmet* magazine out of the stacks at the recycling centre to use as research. While my brother was named after my mother's favourite saint, my name was inspired by an expensive brand of cognac she'd seen advertised in *Harper's Bazaar*. Never mind that we were living on Kraft macaroni and cheese while her characters favoured Cristal and caviar, lounging in Dior trouser suits while we shopped at the thrift store. She always loved glamour, my mother, even if she'd never seen it up close.

Chris and I constantly interrupted her while she was working, which drove her crazy. Finally, at a flea market, she found one of those gypsy curtains, the kind that are made up of long strings of beads, and attached it above the entrance to the kitchen. It became our understood symbol: if the curtain was pulled aside, out of the way, the kitchen was fair game. But if it was hanging there, my mother was working, and we had to find our snacks and entertainment elsewhere.

I was about six then, and I loved to stand there and brush my fingertips over the beads, watching them swish back and forth. They made the softest sound, like little bells. I could peer through them and still see my mother, but now she looked almost exotic, like a fortune-teller or a fairy, a maker of magic. Which was what she was, but I didn't know it then.

Most of the remnants of our apartment years had been long lost or given away, but the beaded curtain had made the trip to the Big New House, as we'd called it when we moved in. It was one of the first things my mother hung up, before even our school pictures or her favourite Picasso print in the living room. There was a nail so it could be pulled back out of sight, but now it was down, a little worse for wear, but still doing the job. I leaned closer, peering in at my mother. She was still hard at work, fingers flying, and I closed my eyes and listened. It was like music I'd heard all my life, even more than 'This Lullaby'. All those keystrokes, all those letters, so many words. I brushed my fingers over the beads and watched as her image rippled, like it was on water, breaking apart gently and shimmering before becoming whole again.

2

It was time to dump Jonathan.

'Tell me again why you're doing this?' Lissa asked me. She was sitting on my bed, flipping through my CDs and smoking a cigarette, which was fast stinking up my room even though she'd sworn it wouldn't, since she had it halfway out the window. Even before I quit I'd hated the stink of smoking, but with Lissa I always let things slide more than I should have. I think everyone has at least one friend like that. 'I mean, I like Jonathan.'

'You like everybody,' I told her, leaning closer to the mirror and examining my lip liner.

'That's not true,' she said, picking up a CD and turning it over to examine the back. 'I never liked Mr Mitchell. He always looked at my boobs when I went up to do theorems on the board. He looked at *everybody's* boobs.'

'Lissa,' I said, 'high school is over. And besides, teachers don't count.'

'I'm just saying,' she said.

'The thing is,' I went on as I lined my lips, turning the pencil slowly, 'that it's summer now, and I'm leaving for school in September. And Jonathan . . . I don't know. He's just not a keeper. He's not worth working my schedule around if we're only going to break up in a few weeks anyway.'

'But you might not break up.'

I leaned back, admiring my handiwork, and smudged a bit along my top lip, evening it out. 'We'll break up,' I said. 'I'm not going to Stanford with any other entanglements than absolutely necessary.'

She bit her lip, then tucked a springy curl behind one ear, ducking her head with the hurt expression she always got lately when we talked about the end of the summer. Lissa's safe zone was the eight weeks left before we all split for different directions, and she hated to think past that. 'Well, of course not,' she said quietly. 'I mean, why would you?'

'Lissa,' I said, sighing. 'I didn't mean you. You know that. I just mean' – I gestured to the bedroom door, slightly ajar, beyond which we could hear my mother's typewriter still clacking, with violins drifting in the background – 'you know.'

She nodded. But in truth I knew she didn't understand. Lissa was the only one of us who was even slightly sentimental about high school being over. She'd actually cried at graduation, great heaving sobs, ensuring that in every picture and video she'd be red-eyed and blotchy, giving her something to complain about for the next twenty years. Meanwhile, me, Jess, and Chloe couldn't wait to get across that stage and grab our diploma, to be free at last, free at last. But Lissa had always felt things too deeply. That was what made us all so protective of her, and why I worried most about leaving her behind. She'd been accepted into the local university with a full scholarship, a deal too good to pass up. It helped that her boyfriend,

Adam, was going there too. Lissa had it all planned out, how they'd go to freshman orientation together, live in dorms that were in close proximity, share a couple of classes. Just like high school, but bigger.

The very thought of it made me itch. But then, I wasn't Lissa. I'd powered through the last two years with my eyes on one thing, which was getting out. Getting gone. Making the grades I needed to finally live a life that was all my own. No wedding planning. No messy romantic entanglements. No revolving door of stepfathers. Just me and the future, finally together. Now there was a happy ending I could believe in.

Lissa reached over and turned up the radio, filling the room with some boppy song with a la-la-la chorus. I walked over to my closet, pulling open the door to examine my options.

'So what do you wear to dump somebody?' she asked me, twirling a lock of hair around one finger. 'Black, for mourning? Or something cheerful and colourful, to distract them from their pain? Or maybe you wear some sort of camouflage, something that will help you disappear quickly in case they don't take it well.'

'Personally,' I told her, pulling out a pair of black trousers and turning them in my hands, 'I'm thinking dark and slimming, a bit of cleavage. And clean underwear.'

'You wear that every night.'

'This is every night,' I replied. I knew I had a clean red shirt I liked somewhere in my closet, but I couldn't find it in the shirt section. Which meant somebody had been in there, picking around. I kept my closet the way I kept everything: neat and tidy. My mother's house was usually in chaos, so my room had always been the only place I could keep the way I chose. Which was in order, perfectly organised, everything where I could easily find it. Okay, so maybe I was a little obsessive. But so what? At least I wasn't a slob.

'Not for Jonathan,' she said, and when I glanced at her she added, 'I mean, this is a big night for him. He's getting dumped. And he doesn't even *know* it yet. He's probably eating a cheeseburger or flossing or picking up his dry cleaning, and he has no idea. No inkling.'

I gave up on the red shirt, pulling out a tank top instead. I didn't even know what to say to her. Yes, it sucked getting dumped. But wasn't it better to just be brutally honest? To admit that your feeling for someone is never going to be powerful enough to justify taking up any more of their time? I was doing him a favour, really. Freeing him up for a better opportunity. In fact, I was practically a saint, if you really thought about it.

Exactly.

A half hour later, when we pulled up to the Quik Zip, Jess was waiting for us. As usual, Chloe was late.

'Hey,' I said, walking over to her. She was leaning against her big tank of a car, an old Chevy with a sagging bumper, and sucking on an Extra Large Zip Coke, our drug of choice. They were the best bargain in town, at $1.59, and served a multitude of uses.

'I'm getting Skittles,' Lissa called out, slamming her door. 'Anybody want anything?'

'Zip Diet,' I told her, and reached for my money, but she shook me off, already heading inside. 'Extra large!'

She nodded as the door swung shut behind her. She even walked perkily, hands jauntily in her pockets as she headed for the candy aisle. Lissa's sweet tooth was infamous: she was the only person I knew who could discern between Raisinets and chocolate-covered raisins. There *was* a difference.

'Where's Chloe?' I asked Jess, but she just shrugged, not even taking her lips off the straw of her Zip Coke. 'Did we not say six sharp?'

She raised an eyebrow at me. 'Calm down, anal retentive,' she said, shaking her drink. The ice rattled around, sloshing in what was left of the liquid. 'It's just six right now.'

I sighed, leaning back against her car. I hated when people were late. But Chloe always ran five minutes behind, on a *good* day. Lissa was usually early, and Jess was Jess: solid as a rock, there right on the dot. She'd been my best friend since the fifth grade, and was the only one I knew I could always depend on.

We'd met because our desks sat side by side, per Mrs Douglas's alphabet system. Mike Schemen the nose picker, then Jess, then me, with Adam Struck, who had bad adenoids, on my other side. It was practically required that we be best friends, seeing as we were surrounded by the bogey twins.

Jess was big, even then. She wasn't fat, exactly, just like she wasn't fat now. More just large, big-boned, tall and wide. Thick. Back then, she was larger than any of the boys in our class, brutal at dodgeball, able to hit you hard enough with one of those red medicine balls before school that it left a mark that lasted through final bell. A lot of people thought Jess was mean, but they were wrong. They didn't know what I knew: that her mom had died that summer, leaving her to raise two little brothers while her dad worked full-time at the power plant. That money was always tight, and Jess didn't get to be a kid any more.

And eight years later, after making it through some hellish middle school and decent high school years, we were still close. Mostly because I did know these things about her, and Jess still kept most stuff to herself. But also because she was one of the only people who just didn't take my shit, and I had to respect that.

'Looky look,' she said now in her flat voice, crossing her arms over her chest. 'The queen has arrived.'

Chloe pulled up beside us, cutting the engine on her Mercedes and flipping down the visor to check her lipstick. Jess sighed, loudly, but I ignored her. This was old news, her and Chloe, like background music. Only if things were really quiet or dull did the rest of us even notice it any more.

Chloe got out, slamming her door, and came over to us. She looked great, as usual: black trousers, blue shirt, cool jacket I hadn't seen before. Her mom was a flight attendant and a compulsive shopper, a deadly combination that resulted in Chloe always having the newest stuff from the best places. Our little trendsetter.

'Hey,' she said, tucking her hair behind her ear. 'Where's Lissa?'

I nodded toward the Quik Zip, where Lissa was now at the counter, chatting up the guy behind the counter as he rang up her candy. We watched as she waved good-bye to him and came out, a bag of Skittles already opened in one hand. 'Who wants one?' she called out, smiling as she saw Chloe. 'Hey! God, great jacket.'

'Thanks,' Chloe said, brushing her fingers over it. 'It's new.'

'Is that surprising?' Jess said sarcastically.

'Is that diet?' Chloe shot back, eyeing the drink in Jess's hand.

'All right, all right,' I said, waving my hand between them. Lissa handed me my Zip Diet, and I took a big sip, savouring the taste. It was the nectar of the gods. Truly. 'What's the plan?'

'I have to meet Adam at Double Burger at six-thirty,' Lissa said, popping another Skittle into her mouth. 'Then we'll catch up with you guys at Bendo or whatever.'

'Who's at Bendo?' Chloe asked, jangling her keys.

'Don't know,' Lissa said. 'Some band. There's also a party we can go to in the Arbors, Matthew Ridgefield has a beer keg somewhere and, oh, and Remy has to dump Jonathan.'

Now, everyone looked at me. 'Not necessarily in that order,' I added.

'So Jonathan's out.' Chloe laughed, pulling a pack of cigarettes out of her jacket pocket. She held them out to me, and I shook my head.

'She quit,' Jess said to her. 'Remember?'

'She's always quitting,' Chloe replied, striking a

match and leaning into it, then shaking it out. 'What'd he do, Remy? Stand you up? Declare undying love?'

I just shook my head, knowing what was coming.

Jess grinned and said, 'He wore a non-matching outfit.'

'Smoked in her car,' Chloe said. 'That's got to be it.'

'Maybe,' Lissa offered, pinching my arm, 'he made a major grammatical error and was fifteen minutes late.'

'Oh, the horror!' Chloe shrieked, and all three of them burst out laughing. I just stood there, taking it, realising not for the first time that they only seemed to get along when ragging on me as a group.

'Funny,' I said finally. Okay, so maybe I did have a bit of history with expecting too much from relationships. But God, at least I had *standards*. Chloe only dated college guys who cheated on her, Jess avoided the issue by never dating anyone, and Lissa – well, Lissa was still with the guy she lost her virginity to, so she hardly counted at all. Not that I was going to point this out. I mean, I was all about the high road.

'Okay, okay,' Jess said finally. 'How are we doing this?'

'Lissa goes to meet Adam,' I said. 'You, me, and Chloe hit the Spot and then go on to Bendo. Okay?'

'Okay,' Lissa said. 'I'll see you guys later.' As she drove off, and Chloe moved her car to the church parking lot next door, Jess lifted up my hand, squinting at it.

'What's this?' she asked me. I glanced down, seeing the black letters, smudged but still there, on my palm. Before leaving the house I'd meant to wash it off, then got distracted. 'A phone number?'

'It's nothing,' I said. 'Just this stupid guy I met today.'

'You heartbreaker,' she said.

We piled into Jess's car, me in front, Chloe in back. She made a face as she pushed aside a laundry hamper full of clothes, a football helmet, and some knee pads of Jess's brothers, but she didn't say anything. Chloe and Jess may have had their differences, but she knew where to draw the line.

'The Spot?' Jess asked me as she cranked the engine. I nodded, and she put the car in reverse, backing up slowly. I reached forward and turned on the radio while Chloe lit another cigarette in the back seat, tossing the match out the window. As we were about to pull out onto the road, Jess nodded toward a big metal trash can by the gas pumps, about twenty feet away.

'Bet me?' she asked, and I craned my neck, judging the distance, then picked up her mostly empty Zip Coke and shook it, feeling its weight.

'Sure,' I said. 'Two bucks.'

'Oh, God,' Chloe said from the back seat, exhaling loudly. 'Now that we're out of high school, can we please move on from this?'

Jess ignored her, picking up the Zip Coke and pressing her hand around it, flexing her wrist, then stuck her arm out the driver's window. She squinted, lifted her chin, and then, in one smooth movement, threw her arm up and released the Zip Coke, sending it arcing over our heads and the car. We watched as it turned end over end in the air, a perfect spiral, before disappearing with a crash, top still on and straw engaged, in the trash can.

'Amazing,' I said to Jess. She smiled at me. 'I never have been able to figure out how you do that.'

'Can we go now?' Chloe asked.

'Like everything else,' Jess said, turning out into traffic, 'it's all in the wrist.'

The Spot, where we always started our night, really belonged to Chloe. When her dad and mom divorced back in the third grade, he'd left town with his new girlfriend, selling off most of the property he'd amassed in town while working as a developer. He only kept one lot, out in the country past our high school, a grassy field with nothing on it but a trampoline he'd bought for Chloe on her seventh birthday. Chloe's mom had banished it quick from the backyard – it didn't match her English garden decor, all sculpted hedges and stone benches – and it ended up out on the land, forgotten until we were all old enough to drive and needed someplace of our own.

We always sat on the trampoline, which was set up in the middle of the pasture, with the best view of the stars and sky. It still had some good bounce to it, enough so that any sudden movement by anybody jostled the rest. Which was good to remember whenever you were pouring something.

'Watch it,' Chloe said to Jess, her arm jerking as she poured some rum into my Zip Coke. It was one of those little airplane bottles, which her mom regularly brought home from work. Their liquor cabinet looked like it was designed for munchkins.

'Oh, settle down,' Jess replied, crossing her legs and leaning back on her palms.

'It's always like this when Lissa isn't here,' Chloe grumbled, opening up another bottle for herself. 'The balance of weight gets all out of whack.'

'Chloe,' I said. 'Give it a rest.' I took a sip of my Zip Coke, now spiked, tasting the rum, and offered it to Jess purely out of politeness. She never drank, never smoked. Always drove. Being a mom for so long to her brothers made it a given she'd be the same to us.

'Nice night,' I said to her now, and she nodded. 'Hard to believe it's all over.'

'Thank God,' Chloe said, wiping her mouth with the back of her hand. 'Not a second too soon, either.'

'Let's drink to that,' I said, and leaned forward to press my cup against her tiny bottle. Then we just sat there, suddenly quiet, no noise except the cicadas starting up in the trees all around us.

'It's so weird,' Chloe said finally, 'that it doesn't feel different now.'

'What?' I asked her.

'Everything,' she said. 'I mean, this is what we've been waiting for, right? High school's over. It's a whole new thing but it feels exactly the same.'

'That's because nothing new has started yet,' Jess told her. She had her face tipped up, eyes on the sky above us. 'By the end of the summer, then things will feel new. Because they will be.'

Chloe pulled another tiny bottle – this time gin – out of her jacket pocket and popped the top. 'It sucks to wait, though,' she said, taking a sip of it. 'I mean, for everything to begin.'

There was the sound of a horn beeping, loud and

then fading out as it passed on the road behind us. That was the nice thing about the Spot: you could hear everything, but no one could see you.

'This is just the in-between time,' I said. 'It goes faster than you think.'

'I hope so,' Chloe said, and I eased back on my elbows, tilting my head back to look up at the sky, which was pinkish, streaked with red. This was the time we knew best, that stretch of day going from dusk to dark. It seemed like we were always waiting for nighttime here. I could feel the trampoline easing up and down, moved by our own breathing, bringing us in small increments up and back from the sky as the colours faded, slowly, and the stars began to show themselves.

By the time we got to Bendo, it was nine o'clock and I had a nice buzz on. We pulled up, parked, and eyed the bouncer standing by the door.

'Perfect,' I said, pulling down the visor to check my make-up. 'It's Rodney.'

'Where's my ID?' Chloe said, digging through her jacket. 'God, I just had it.'

'Is it in your bra?' I asked her, turning around. She blinked, stuck her hand down her shirt, and came up with it. Chloe kept everything in her bra: ID, money, extra hair clips. It was like sleight of hand, the way she just pulled things from it, like coins from your ear, or rabbits out of a hat.

'Bingo,' she said, sticking it in her front pocket.

'So classy,' Jess said.

'Look who's talking,' Chloe shot back. 'At least I *wear* a bra.'

'Well, at least I need one,' Jess replied.

Chloe narrowed her eyes. She was a B cup, and a small one at that, and had always been sensitive about it. 'Well at least—'

'*Stop*,' I said. 'Let's go.'

As we walked up, Rodney eyed us from where he was sitting on a stool propping the door open. Bendo was an eighteen-and-up club, but we'd been coming since sophomore year. You had to be twenty-one to drink, though, and with our fakes Chloe and I usually could get our hand stamped. Especially by Rodney.

'Remy, Remy,' he said as I reached into my pocket, pulling out my fake. My name, my face, my brother's birthday, so I could quote it quick if I had to. 'How's it feel to be a high school graduate?'

'I don't know what you're talking about,' I said, smiling at him. 'You know I'm a junior at the university.'

He hardly glanced at my ID but squeezed my hand, brushing it with his fingers as he stamped it. Disgusting. 'What's your major?'

'English lit,' I said. 'But I'm minoring in business.'

'I got some business for you,' he said, taking Chloe's ID and stamping her hand. She was quick though, pulling back fast, the ink smearing.

'You're an asshole,' Jess told him, but he just shrugged, waving us in, his eyes on the next group of girls coming up the steps.

'I feel so dirty,' Chloe sighed as we walked in.

'You'll feel better after you have a beer.'

Bendo was crowded already. The band hadn't come on yet, but the bar was two deep and the air was full of smoke, thick and mixed with the smell of sweat.

'I'll get a table,' Jess called out to me, and I nodded, heading for the bar with Chloe behind me. We pushed through the crowd, dodging people, until we got a decent spot by the beer taps.

I'd just hoisted myself up on my elbows, trying to wave down the bartender, when I felt someone brush up against me. I tried to pull away, but it was packed where I was standing, so I just drew myself in a bit, pulling my arms against my sides. Then, very quietly, I heard a voice in my ear.

It said, in a weird, cheesy, right-out-of-one-of-my-mother's-novels way, 'Ah. We meet again.'

I turned my head, just slightly, and right there, practically on top of me, was the guy from the car dealership. He was wearing a red Mountain Fresh Detergent T-shirt – NOT JUST FRESH: MOUNTAIN FRESH! it proclaimed – and was smiling at me. 'Oh, God,' I said.

'No, it's Dexter,' he replied, offering me his hand, which I ignored. Instead I glanced around behind me for Chloe, but saw she had been waylaid by a guy in a plaid shirt I didn't recognise.

'Two beers!' I shouted at the bartender, who'd finally seen me.

'Make that three!' this Dexter yelled.

'You are *not* with me,' I said.

'Well, not technically,' he replied, shrugging. 'But that could change.'

'Look,' I said as the bartender dropped three plastic cups in front of me, 'I'm not—'

'I see you still have my number,' he said, interrupting me and grabbing one of the beers. He also slapped a ten down, which redeemed him a bit but not much.

'I haven't had a chance to wash it off.'

'Will you be impressed if I tell you I'm in a band?'

'No.'

'Not at all?' he said, raising his eyebrows. 'God, I thought chicks loved guys in bands.'

'First off, I'm not a chick,' I said, grabbing my beer. 'And second, I have a steadfast rule about musicians.'

'Which is?'

I turned my back to him and started to elbow my way through the crowd, back to Chloe. 'No musicians.'

'I could write you a song,' he offered, following me. I was moving so fast the beers I was carrying kept sloshing, but damn if he didn't keep right up.

'I don't want a song.'

'Everybody wants a song!'

'Not me.' I tapped Chloe on the shoulder and she turned around. She had on her flirting face, all wide-eyed and flushed, and I handed her a beer and said, 'I'm going to find Jess.'

'I'm right behind you,' she replied, waggling her fingers at the guy she'd been talking to. But crazy musician boy kept after me, still talking.

'I think you like me,' he decided as I stepped on somebody's foot, prompting a yelp. I kept moving.

'I really do not,' I said, finally spying Jess in a corner booth, head propped on one elbow, looking bored.

When she saw me she held up both hands, in a what-the-hell gesture, but I just shook my head.

'Who is this guy?' Chloe called out from behind me.

'Nobody,' I said.

'Dexter,' he replied, turning a bit to offer her his hand while still keeping step with me. 'How are you?'

'Fine,' she said, a bit uneasily. 'Remy?'

'Just keep walking,' I called behind me, stepping around two guys in dreadlocks. 'He'll lose interest eventually.'

'Oh, ye of little faith,' he said cheerfully. 'I'm just getting started.'

We arrived at the booth in a pack: me, Dexter the musician, and Chloe. I was out of breath, she looked confused, but he just slid in next to Jess, offering his hand. 'Hi,' he said. 'I'm with them.'

Jess looked at me, but I was too tired to do anything but plop into the booth and suck down a gulp of my beer. 'Well,' she said, '*I'm* with them. But I'm not with you. How is that possible?'

'Well,' he said, 'it's actually an interesting story.'

No one said anything for a minute. Finally I groaned and said, 'God, you guys, now he's going to *tell* it.'

'See,' he began, leaning back into the booth, 'I was at this car dealership today, and I saw this girl. It was an across-a-crowded-room kind of thing. A real moment, you know?'

I rolled my eyes. Chloe said, 'And this would be Remy?'

'Right. Remy,' he said, repeating my name with a smile. Then, as if we were happy honeymooners recounting our story for strangers, he added, 'Do you want to tell the next part?'

'No,' I said flatly.

'So,' he went on, slapping the table for emphasis, making all our drinks jump, 'the fact is that I'm a man of impulse. Of action. So I walked up, plopped down beside her, and introduced myself.'

Chloe looked at me, smiling. 'Really,' she said.

'Could you go away now?' I asked him just as the music overhead cut off and there was a tapping noise from the stage, followed by someone saying 'Check, check.'

'Duty calls,' he said, standing up. He pushed his half-finished beer over to me and said, 'I'll see you later?'

'No.'

'Okay, then! We'll talk later.' And then he pushed off, into the crowd, and was gone. We all just sat there for a second. I finished my beer, then closed my eyes and lifted the cup, pressing it to my temple. How could I already be exhausted?

'Remy,' Chloe said finally in her clever voice. 'You're keeping secrets.'

'I'm not,' I told her. 'It was just this stupid thing. I'd forgotten all about it.'

'He talks too much,' Jess decided.

'I liked his shirt,' Chloe told her. 'Interesting fashion sense.'

Just then Jonathan slid in beside me in the booth. 'Hello, ladies,' he said, sliding his arm around my waist. Then he picked up crazy musician boy's beer, thinking it was mine, and took a big sip. I would have stopped him, but just the fact that he did it was part of our problem. I hated it when guys acted proprietary toward me, and Jonathan had done that from the beginning. He was a senior too, a nice guy, but as soon as we'd started dating he wanted everyone to know it, and slowly began to encroach on my domain. He smoked my cigarettes, when I still smoked. Used my cell phone all the time to make calls, without asking, and got very comfortable in my car, which should have been the ultimate red flag. I cannot abide anyone even changing my station presets or dipping into my ashtray change, but Jonathan charged right past that and insisted on *driving*, even though he had a history of fender benders and speeding tickets as long as my arm. The stupidest part was that I let him, flushed as I was with love (not likely) or lust (more likely), and then he just expected I'd ride shotgun, in my own car, for ever. Which just led to more Ken behaviour – as in ultraboyfriend – like always grabbing onto me in public and drinking, without asking, what he thought was my beer.

'I've got to go back to the house for a sec,' he said now, leaning close to my ear. He moved his hand from around my waist, so it was now cupping my knee. 'Come with me, okay?'

I nodded, and he finished off the beer, slapping the cup down on the table. Jonathan was a big partier, another thing I had trouble dealing with. I mean, I drank too. But he was sloppy about it. A puker. In the six months we'd been together I'd spent a fair amount of time at parties outside the bathroom, waiting for him to finish spewing so we could go home. Not a plus.

He slid out of the booth, moving his hand off my knee and closing his fingers around mine. 'I'll be back,' I said to Jess and Chloe as someone brushed past, and Jonathan finally had to cease contact with me as the crowd separated us.

'Good luck,' Chloe said. 'I can't believe you let him drink that guy's beer.'

I turned and saw Jonathan looking back at me, impatient. 'Dead man walking,' Jess said in a low voice, and Chloe snorted.

'Bye,' I said, and pushed through the crowd, where Jonathan's hand was extended, waiting to take hold of me again.

'Okay, look,' I said, pushing him back. 'We have to talk.'

'Now?'

'Now.'

He sighed, then sat back on the bed, letting his head knock against the wall. 'Okay,' he said, as if he were agreeing to a root canal, 'go ahead.'

I pulled my knees up on the bed, then straightened my tank top. 'Running in for something' had quickly morphed into 'making a few phone calls' and then he was all over me, pushing me back against the pillows before I could even begin my slow easing into the dumpage. But now, I had his attention.

'The thing is,' I began, 'things are really starting to change for me now.'

42

This was my lead-up. I'd learned, over the years, that there was a range of techniques involved in breaking up with someone. You had your types: some guys got all indignant and pissed, some whined and cried, some acted indifferent and cold, as if you couldn't leave fast enough. I had Jonathan pegged as the last, but I couldn't be completely sure.

'So anyway,' I continued, 'I've just been thinking that—'

And then the phone rang, an electronic shriek, and I lost my momentum again. Jonathan grabbed it. 'Hello?' Then there was a bit of umm-hmming, a couple of yeahs, and he stood up, walking across the room and into his bathroom, still mumbling.

I pulled my fingers through my hair, hating that my timing seemed to be off all night long. Still listening to him talking, I closed my eyes and stretched my arms over my head, then curled my fingers down the side of the mattress closest to the wall. And then I felt something.

When Jonathan finally hung up, checked himself in the mirror, and walked back into the bedroom, I was sitting there, cross-legged, with a pair of red satin bikini panties spread out on the bed in front of me. (I'd retrieved them using a Kleenex: like I'd *touch* them.) He came strolling in, all confident, and, seeing them, came to a dead, lurching stop.

'Ummpthz,' he said, or something like that, as he sucked in a breath, surprised, then quickly steadied himself. 'Hey, um, what—'

'What the hell,' I said, my voice level, 'are these?'

'They aren't yours?'

I looked up at the ceiling, shaking my head. Like I'd wear cheap red, polyester panties. I mean, I had standards. Or did I? Look who I'd wasted the last six months on.

'How long,' I said.

'What?'

'How long have you been sleeping with someone else?'

'It wasn't—'

'How long?' I repeated, biting off the words.

'I just don't—'

'*How long?*'

He swallowed, and for a second it was the only sound in the room. Then he said, 'Just a couple of weeks.'

I sat back, pressing my fingers to my temples. God, this was just great. Now not only was I cheated on, but other people had to know it, which made me a victim, which I hated most of all. Poor, poor Remy. I wanted to kill him.

'You're an asshole,' I said. He was all flushed, quaky, and I realised that he might have even been a whiner or weeper, had things gone differently. Amazing. You just never knew.

'Remy. Let me—' He reached forward, touching my arm, but for once, finally, I was able to do what I wanted and yank it back as if he'd burned me.

'Don't touch me,' I snapped. I grabbed my jacket, knotting it around my waist, and headed for the door, feeling him stumbling behind me. I slammed door after door as I moved through the house, finally hitting the front walk with such momentum I was at the mailbox before I even realised it. I could feel him watching me from the front steps as I walked away, but he didn't call out or say anything. Not that I wanted him to, or would have reconsidered. But most guys would have at least had the decency to try.

So now I was walking through this neighbourhood, full-out pissed, with no car, in the middle of a Friday night. My first Friday night as a grown-up, out of high school, in the Real World. Welcome to it.

'Where the hell have you been?' Chloe asked me when I finally got back to Bendo, with the help of City Transit, about twenty minutes later.

'You are not going to believe—' I began.

'Not now.' She took my arm, pulling me through the crowd and back outside, where I saw Jess was in her car, the driver's door open. 'We have a situation.'

When I walked up to the car, I didn't even see Lissa at first. She was balled up in the back seat, clutching a wad of those brown school-restaurant-public-bathroom kind of paper towels. Her face was red and tear streaked, and she was sobbing.

'What the hell happened?' I asked, yanking open the back door and sliding in beside her.

'Adam b-b-broke up with m-m-me,' she said, her voice gulping in air. 'He just *d-d-dumped* me.'

'Oh, my God,' I said as Chloe climbed in the front seat, slamming the door behind her. Jess, already turned around facing us, looked at me and shook her head.

'When?'

Lissa took in another breath, then burst into tears again. 'I can't,' she mumbled, wiping her face with a paper towel. 'I can't e-e-ven . . .'

'Tonight, when she picked him up from work,' Chloe said to me. 'She took him back to his house so he could take a shower and he did it there. No warning. Nothing.'

'I had to walk p-p-past his *p-p-parents*,' Lissa added, sniffling. 'And they knew. They looked at me like I was a kicked d-d-dog.'

'What did he say?' I asked her.

'He told her,' Chloe said, clearly in her spokesperson role, 'that he needed his freedom because it was summer and high school was over and he didn't want either of them to miss any opportunities in college. He wanted to make sure that they—'

'M-m-made the most of our lives,' Lissa finished, wiping her eyes.

'Jerk,' Jess grumbled. 'You're better off.'

'I l-l-love him!' Lissa wailed, and I reached over, sliding my arm around her.

'It's okay,' I said.

'And I had no idea,' she said, taking in a deep breath, which shuddered out, all bumpy, as she tossed aside the paper towel she was holding, letting it fall to the floor. 'How could I not even have known?'

'Lissa, you'll be okay,' Chloe told her, her voice soft.

'It's like I'm Jonathan,' she sobbed, leaning into me. 'We were just living our lives, picking up the dry cleaning . . .'

'What?' Jess said.

'. . . unaware,' Lissa finished, 'that t-t-tonight we'd be *d-d-dumped*.'

'Speaking of,' Chloe said to me, 'how'd that go?'

'Don't ask,' I said.

Lissa was full-out crying now, her face buried in my shoulder. Over Chloe's head I could see Bendo was fully packed, with a line out the door. 'Let's get out of here,' I said to Jess, and she nodded. 'This night has sucked anyway.'

Chloe dropped down into the front passenger seat, punching in the car lighter as Jess cranked the engine. Lissa blew her nose in the paper towel I handed her, then settled into small, quick sobs, curling against me. As we pulled out I patted her head, knowing how much it had to hurt. There is nothing so bad as the first time.

Of course we had to have another round of Zip Drinks. Then Chloe left, and Jess pulled back out into traffic to take me and Lissa to my house.

We were almost to the turnoff to my neighbourhood when Jess suddenly slowed down and said, very quietly, to me, 'There's Adam.'

I cut my eyes to the left, and sure enough, Adam and his friends were standing around in the parking lot in front of the Coffee Shack. What really bugged me was that he was *smiling*. Jerk.

I glanced behind me, but Lissa had her eyes closed, stretched out across the back seat, listening to the radio.

'Pull in,' I said to Jess. I turned around in my seat. 'Hey Liss?'

'Hmmm?' she said.

'Be still, okay? Stay down.'

'Okay,' she said uncertainly.

We chugged along. Jess said, 'You or me?'

'Me,' I told her, taking a last sip of my drink. 'I need this tonight.'

Jess pushed the gas a little harder.

'You ready?' she asked me.

I nodded, my Zip Diet balanced in my hand. Perfect.

Jess gunned it, hard, and we were moving. By the time Adam looked over at us, it was too late.

It wasn't my best. But it wasn't bad either. As we whizzed by, the cup turned end over end in the air, seeming weightless. It hit him square in the back of the head, spilling Diet Coke and ice in a wave down his back.

'Goddammit!' he yelled after us as we blew past. 'Lissa! Dammit! Remy! You bitch!'

He was still yelling when I lost sight of him.

After a sleeve and a half of Oreos, four cigarettes, and enough Kleenex to pad the world, I finally got Lissa to go to sleep. She was out instantly, breathing through her nose, legs tangled around my comforter.

I got a blanket, one pillow, and went into my closet, where I stretched out across the floor. I could see her from where I was, and made sure she was still sleeping soundly as I pushed aside the stack of shoe boxes I kept in the far right corner and pulled out the bundle I kept there, hidden away.

I'd had such a bad night. I didn't do this all the time, but some nights I just needed it. Nobody knew.

I curled up, pulling the blanket over me, and opened the folded towel, taking out my portable CD player and headphones. Then I slipped them on, turned off the light, and skipped to track seven. There was a skylight in my closet, and if I lay just right, the moonlight fell in a square right across me. Sometimes I could even see stars.

The song starts slowly. A bit of guitar, just a few chords. Then a voice, one I knew so well. The words I knew by heart. They did mean something to me. Nobody had to know. But they did.

> *This lullaby is only a few words*
> *A simple run of chords*
> *Quiet here in this spare room*
> *But you can hear it, hear it*
> *Wherever you may go*
> *I will let you down*
> *But this lullaby plays on . . .*

I'd fall asleep to it, to his voice. I always did. Every time.

3

'Aiiiieeeeeee!'

'Mother of pearl!'

'Oh, suuuugggaaarrr!'

In the waiting room, the two ladies on deck for manicures looked at each other, then at me.

'Bikini wax,' I explained.

'Oh,' said one, and went back to her magazine. The other just sat there, ears perked like a hunting hound, waiting for the next shriek. It wasn't long before Mrs Michaels, enduring her monthly appointment, delivered.

'*H-E*-double-hockey-sticks!' Mrs Michaels was the wife of one of the local ministers, and loved God almost as much as having a smooth, hairless body. In the year I'd worked at Joie Salon, I'd heard more cussing from the back room where Talinga worked her wax strips than all the other rooms combined. And that included bad manicures, botched haircuts, and even one woman who was near perturbed about a seaweed body wrap that turned her the colour of key lime pie.

Not that Joie was a bad place. It was just that you couldn't please everyone, especially women, when it came to their looks. That's why Lola, who owned Joie, had just given me a raise in the hopes that maybe, just maybe, I'd turn my back on going to Stanford and stay at her reception desk for ever, keeping people under control.

I'd got the job because I wanted a car. My mother had offered to give me her car, a nice Camry, and buy herself a new one, but it was important to me that I do this on my own. I loved my mother, but I'd learned long ago not to enter into any more agreements with her than I had to. Her whims were legendary, and I could just see her taking the car back when she decided she no longer was happy with her new one.

So I emptied out my savings account – which consisted mostly of baby-sitting and Christmas money I'd hoarded for ever – got out *Consumer Reports*, and did all the research I could on new models before hitting the dealerships. I wrangled and argued and bluffed and put up with so much car-salesman bullshit it almost killed me, but in the end I got the car I wanted, a new Civic with a sunroof and automatic everything, at a price way off the manufacturer's suggested rip-off retail. The day I picked it up, I drove over to Joie and filled out an application, having seen a RECEPTIONIST WANTED sign in their front window a week or so earlier. And just like that, I had a car payment and a job, all before my senior year even began.

Now, the phone rang as Mrs Michaels emerged from the waxing room. At first I'd been startled by how bad people looked right afterward: like war victims, or casualties of a fire. She was walking stiffly – bikini waxes were especially brutal – as she came up to my desk.

'Joie Salon,' I said into the phone. 'Remy speaking.'

'Remy, hello, this is Lauren Baker,' the woman on the other end said in a rushed voice. Mrs Baker was always all wispy sounding and out of breath. 'Oh, you just *have* to fit me in for a manicure today. Carl's got some big client and we're going to La Corolla and this week I restripped the coffee table and my hands are just—'

'One second please,' I said, in my clipped, oh-so-professional voice, and hit the hold button. Above me, Mrs Michaels grimaced as she pulled out her wallet, sliding a gold credit card across to me. 'That's seventy-eight, ma'am.'

She nodded, and I swiped the card, handing it back to her. Her face was so red, the area around her eyebrows practically raw. Ouch. She signed the slip, then glanced at herself in the mirror behind me, making a face.

'Oh, goodness,' she said. 'I guess I can't go to the post office looking like this.'

'Nonsense!' Talinga, the waxer, said as she breezed in, ostensibly for some good reason but actually to make sure Mrs Michaels's tip was big enough and made it into her envelope. 'No one will even notice. I'll see you next month, okay?'

Mrs Michaels waggled her fingers, then walked out the door, still moving stiffly. Once she hit the kerb Talinga grabbed her envelope, leafed through the bills there, and made a *hmmph* kind of noise before flopping down in a chair and crossing her legs to await her next appointment.

'Moving on,' I said, hitting the button for line one. I could hear Mrs Baker panting before I even started talking. 'Let's see, I could squeeze you in at three-thirty, but you have to be here right on the dot, because Amanda's got a firm four o'clock.'

'Three-thirty?' Mrs Baker said. 'Well, you see, earlier would be better, actually, because I have this—'

'Three-thirty,' I repeated, clipping my vowels. 'Take it or leave it.'

There was a pause, some anxious breathing, and then she said, 'I'll be there.'

'Okay. We'll see you then.'

As I hung up the phone, pencilling her in, Talinga looked at me and said, 'Remygirl, you are such a hard-ass.'

I shrugged. The truth was, I could deal with these women because most of them had that used-to-having-everything, me-me-me mentality, in which I was well versed because of my mother. They wanted to bend the rules, to get things for free, to run into other people's appointments and still have everyone love them just *so* much. So I was good at this job, if only because I had a lifetime of previous experience.

In the next hour I got the two women waiting to their manicures, ordered lunch for Lola, did the receipts from the day before, and between two eyebrow waxings and an underarm job I heard every gory detail about Talinga's most recent disastrous blind date. But by two o'clock, things had slowed down a bit, and I was just sitting there at the desk, drinking a Diet Coke and staring out at the parking lot.

Joie was located in a glorified strip mall called Mayor's Village. It was all concrete, right on the highway, but there were some nice landscaped trees and a fountain to make it look more upmarket. To our right was Mayor's Market, which sold expensive organic food. There was also Jump Java, the coffee place, as well as a video store, a bank, and a one-hour photo.

As I was staring out, I saw a beat-up white van pull into the parking lot, taking a space by Gone to the Birds, the speciality bird feeder store. The front and side doors of the van opened and three guys got out, all about my age, all in dress shirts and ties and jeans. They huddled for a second, discussing something, then split up, each heading into a different store. A short guy with red curly hair came toward us, tucking in his shirt as he got closer.

'Oh boy,' I said. 'Here come the Mormons.' Although we had a very nice sign in the window that read PLEASE – NO SOLICITING, I was always having to chase away people selling candy bars or Bibles. I took a sip of my Diet Coke, readying myself as the door chime clanged and he came in.

'Hello,' he said, walking right up. He was mighty freckled, which I guess a lot of red-headed guys are, but his eyes were a nice deep green and he had a decent smile. His dress shirt, upon closer inspection, had a stain on the pocket, however, and looked decidedly thrift store-esque. Plus, the tie was a clip-on. I mean, it was obvious.

'Hello,' I said. 'Can I help you?'

'I was wondering if perhaps you were hiring?'

I looked at him. No men worked at Joie: it wasn't a conscious thing on Lola's part, just that frankly the work didn't appeal to most men. We'd had one male stylist, Eric, but he'd jumped to Sunset Salon, our biggest competition, earlier in the year, taking one of our best manicurists with him. Since then it was all oestrogen, all the time.

'Nope,' I said. 'We're not.'

'You're sure?'

'Positive.'

He didn't seem convinced, but he was still smiling. 'I wonder,' he said, all charming, 'if perhaps I could fill out an application in case an opening became available?'

'Sure,' I said, pulling open the bottom drawer of the desk, where we kept the pad of applications. I ripped one off, handed it to him, along with one of my pens.

'Thanks so much,' he said, taking a seat in the corner by the window. I watched from where I was as he wrote his name across the top in neat block letters, then wrinkled his brow, contemplating the questions.

'Remy,' Lola called out, walking into the waiting area, 'did we ever get that shipment from Redken?'

'Not yet,' I told her. Lola was a big woman who wore tight, bright clothes. She had a huge laugh to match her huge frame and inspired such respect and fear in her clients that no one even came in with a picture or anything when they had a hair appointment: they just let her decide. Now, she glanced over at the guy in the corner.

'Why are you here?' she asked him.

He looked up, hardly startled. I had to admire that. 'Applying for a job,' he told her.

She looked him up and down. 'Is that a clip-on tie?'

'Yes, ma'am,' he said, nodding at her. 'It sure is.'

Lola looked at me, then back at him, then burst into laughter. 'Oh, Lord, look at this boy. And you want to work for me?'

'Yes, ma'am, I sure do.' He was so polite I could see him gaining points, quickly. Lola was big on respect.

'Can you give a manicure?'

He considered this. 'No. But I'm a fast learner.'

'Can you bikini wax?'

'Nope.'

'Cut hair?'

'No, I sure can't.'

She cocked her head to the side, smiling at him. 'Honey,' she said finally, 'you're useless.'

He nodded. 'My mother always said that,' he told her. 'But I'm in this band and we all have to get jobs today, so I'm trying anything.'

Lola laughed again. It sounded like it came all the way from her stomach, bubbling up. 'You're in a band?'

'Yes, ma'am. We just came down from Virginia, for the summer. And we all have to get day jobs, so we came here and split up.'

So they're not Mormons, I thought. *They're musicians. Even worse.*

'What do you play?' Lola asked.

'Drums,' he said.

'Like Ringo?'

'Exactly.' He grinned, then added, in a lower voice, 'You know they always put the redheaded guy in the back. Otherwise all the ladies would be on me.'

Lola exploded in laughter, so loudly that Talinga and one of the manicurists, Amanda, poked their heads around the corner.

'What in the world?' Amanda asked.

'Good God, is that a clip-on tie?' Talinga said.

'Look,' Lola said, catching her breath, 'we've got nothing for you here. But you come down to the coffee place with me and I'll get you a job. That girl owes me a favour.'

'Really?'

She nodded. 'But come on. I don't have all day.'

He leapt up, the pen he was holding clattering to the floor. He bent down to get it, then brought the application back to me. 'Thanks anyway,' he said.

'No problem.'

'Let's go, Ringo!' Lola yelled from the door.

He jumped, grinning, then leaned a little closer and said to me, 'You know, he's still talking about you.'

'Who is?'

'Dexter.'

Of course. Just my luck. He's not just in a band, he's in that band. 'Why?' I said. 'He doesn't even know me.'

'Doesn't matter,' he said, shrugging. 'You're officially a challenge. He'll never give up now.'

I just sat there, shaking my head. Ridiculous.

He didn't seem to notice, instead just patted his hand on the desk, as if we'd made a deal or something, before walking over to Lola.

Once they'd left, Talinga looked at me and said, 'You know him?'

'No,' I said, grabbing the phone as it rang again. Small world, small town. It was just a coincidence. 'I don't.'

In the week since Jonathan and I had split, I'd hardly thought about him or Dexter the musician or anything else other than my mother's wedding. It was a distraction I needed, not that I'd ever have admitted it aloud.

Jonathan had called a bunch, at first, but after a while he just stopped, knowing I'd never get back to him. Chloe pointed out that I'd got what I wanted, really: my freedom. Just not exactly the way I wanted it. But it still burned at me that I'd been cheated on. It was the kind of thing that woke me up at night, pissed, unable to remember anything I'd been dreaming.

Luckily, I had Lissa to deal with too. She'd spent the last week completely in denial, sure Adam would change his mind. It was all we could do to thwart her calling/driving by/going to his work impulse, which we all knew never led to any good in a dumping situation. If he wanted to see her, he'd find her. If he wanted to get back together, she should make him work for it. And so on.

And now, the wedding was here. I got off work early, at five, and drove home to get ready for the rehearsal dinner. As I walked up to the front door, I realised the house was just as I'd left it. In chaos.

'But there's just no way they'll get here in time!' my mother was shrieking as I walked in and dropped my keys on the table. 'They're supposed to be here in an hour or we won't be able to make the dinner!'

'Mom,' I called out, instantly recognising her close-to-meltdown voice. 'Calm down.'

'I understand that,' she said, her voice still shrill. 'But this is my wedding!'

I glanced into the living room, which was empty except for Jennifer Anne, already dressed for the dinner, sitting on the couch reading a book entitled *Making Plans, Making Dreams*, which had a picture of a woman looking pensive on its cover. She glanced up at me, turning a page.

'What's going on?' I said.

'The limo service is having some problems.' She fluffed her hair. 'It seems one of their cars was in an accident and the other is stuck in traffic.'

'That's just not *acceptable*!' my mother yelled.

'Where's Chris?'

She looked up at the ceiling. 'In his room,' she said. 'Apparently, there's been some sort of hatching.' Then she made a face and went back to her book.

My brother bred lizards. Upstairs, next to his room in what had once been a walk-in closet, he kept a row of aquariums in which he raised monitor lizards. They were hard to describe: smaller than iguanas, bigger than geckos. They had snake-like tongues and ate tiny crickets that were forever getting loose in the house, bouncing down the stairs and chirping from where they hid in shoes in the closets. He even had an incubator, which he kept on the floor of his room. When he had eggs in it, it ran in cycles all day, softly clicking to maintain the temperature needed to bring the babies to maturity.

Jennifer Anne hated the lizards. They were, in fact, the one sticking point of her transformation of Chris, the one thing he would not give up for her. As a result, she refused to go anywhere near his room, instead spending her time at our house on the couch, or at the kitchen table, usually reading some motivational self-help book and sighing loud enough for everyone – except Chris, who was usually upstairs, tending to his animals – to hear her.

But now, I had bigger problems.

'I understand that,' my mother said, her voice now wavering close to tears, 'but what you're not hearing is that I have a hundred people that are going to be waiting for me at the Hilton and I will not *be* there!'

'Whoa, whoa, whoa,' I said, coming up behind her and gently closing my hand over the phone. 'Mom. Let me talk to them.'

'It's just ludicrous!' she sputtered, but she let me take it. 'It's—'

'Mom,' I said quietly, 'go finish getting dressed. I'll handle this. Okay?'

She just stood there for a second, blinking. She already had on her dress and was carrying her tights in her hand. No make-up, no jewellery. Which meant another good twenty-five minutes if we were lucky.

'Well, okay,' she said, as if she were doing me a favour. 'I'll be upstairs.'

'Right.' I watched as she walked out of the room, brushing her fingers through her hair. When she was gone, I put the phone to my ear. 'Is this Albert?'

'No,' the voice said, warily. 'This is Thomas.'

'Is Albert there?'

'Hold on.' There was a muffled noise, someone's hand covering the receiver. Then, 'Hello, Albert speaking.'

'Albert, this is Remy Starr.'

'Hey, Remy! Look, this thing with the cars is just messed up, okay?'

'My mother is approaching meltdown, Albert.'

'I know, I know. But look, this is what Thomas was trying to tell her. What we'll do is . . .'

Five minutes later, I went up the stairs and knocked on my mother's door. When I came in, she was sitting in front of her vanity. She looked no different except that she had changed her dress and now sat dabbing at her face with a make-up brush. Ah, progress.

'All fixed,' I told her. 'A car will be here at six. It's a Town Car, not a limo, but we're set for tomorrow and that's what really matters. Okay?'

She sighed, placing one hand over her chest, as if this, finally, calmed her racing heart. 'Wonderful. Thank you.'

I sat down on her bed, kicking off my shoes, and glanced at the clock. It was five-fifteen. I could be ready in eighteen minutes flat, including drying my hair, so I lay back and closed my eyes. I could hear my mother making her getting-ready noises: perfume bottles clinking, brushes dabbing, small containers of face cream and eye gel being moved around on the mirrored tabletop in front of her. My mother was glamorous long before she had reason to be. She'd always been small and wiry, full of energy and prone to dramatic outbursts: she liked to wear lots of bangle bracelets that clanked as she waved her arms around, sweeping the air as she talked. Even when she taught at the community college and most of her students were half asleep after working full days, she dressed for class, with full make-up and perfume and her trademark swishy outfits in bright colours. She kept her hair dyed jet black now that it was greying, and wore it in a short, blunt cut with a thick fringe cut straight across. With her long, flowing skirts and the hair she almost could have been a geisha, except that she was way too noisy.

'Remy, honey,' she said suddenly, and I jerked up, realising I'd almost fallen asleep. 'Can you come do my clasp?'

I stood up and walked over to where she was sitting, taking the necklace she handed to me. 'You look beautiful,' I told her. It was true. Tonight, she was wearing a long red dress with a drop neckline, amethyst earrings, and the big diamond ring Don had given her. She smelled like L'Air du Temps, which, when I was little, I thought was the most wonderful scent in the world. The whole house reeked of it: it clung to the drapes and rugs the way cigarette smoke does, stubbornly and for ever.

'Thank you, sweetheart,' she said as I did the clasp. Looking at us reflected in the mirror I was struck again by how little we resembled each other: me blonde and thin, her darker and more voluptuous. I didn't look like my father, either. I didn't have many early pictures of him, but in the ones I had seen he always looked grizzled, in that 1960s rock kind of way, with a beard and long hair. He also looked permanently stoned, which my mother never disputed when I pointed it out. *Oh, but he had such a beautiful voice*, she'd say, now that he was gone. *One song, and I was a goner*.

Now, she turned around and took my hands in hers. 'Oh, Remy,' she said, smiling, 'can you believe this? We're going to be so *happy*.'

I nodded.

'I mean,' she said, turning around, 'it's not like this is my first time going down the aisle.'

'Nope,' I agreed, smoothing her hair down where it was poking up slightly in the back.

'But it just feels real this time. Permanent. Don't you think?'

I knew what she wanted me to say, but still I hesitated. It seemed like a bad movie, this ritual we'd gone through twice already that I could remember. At this point, the other bridesmaids and myself considered the ceremonies more like class reunions, where we stood off to the side and discussed who had got fat or gone bald since my mother's last wedding. I had no illusions about love any more. It came, it went, it left casualties or it didn't. People weren't meant to be together for ever, regardless of what the songs say. I would have been doing her a favour dragging forth the other wedding albums she kept stacked under her bed and pointing at the pictures, forcing her to take in the same things, the same people, the same cake/champagne toast/first dance poses we'd be seeing again in the next forty-eight hours. Maybe she could forget, push those husbands and memories out of sight and out of mind. But I couldn't.

She was still smiling at me in the mirror. Sometimes I thought if she could read my mind it would kill her. Or both of us.

'Different,' she said, convincing herself. 'It's different this time.'

'Sure, Mom,' I said, putting my hands on her shoulders. They felt small to me, somehow, from where I stood. 'Sure it is.'

On my way down to my room, Chris jumped out at me.

'Remy! You've got to see this.'

I glanced at my watch – five-thirty – and then followed him into the lizard room. It was cramped, and he had to keep it hot all the time, which made being in there feel like a really long elevator ride to nowhere.

'Look,' he said, grabbing my hand and yanking me down beside him, next to the incubator. The top was off and inside there was a small Tupperware container, filled with what looked like moss. On top of it were three little eggs. One was broken open, one kind of mushed, and the other had a little hole in the top.

'Check it out,' Chris whispered, and pointed at the one with the hole.

'Chris,' I said, looking at my watch again. 'I haven't even taken a shower yet.'

'Just wait,' he told me, poking at the egg again. 'This is worth it.'

We crouched there, together. My head was starting to hurt from the heat. And then, just as I was about to get up, the egg stirred. It wobbled a bit, and then something poked out of the hole. A tiny little head, and as the egg tore, it was followed by a body. It was slippery and slimy and so small it could have fitted on the tip of my finger.

'*Varanus tristis orientalis*,' Chris said, as if he was casting a spell. 'Freckled monitor. He's the only one that survived.'

The little lizard still seemed a bit dazed, blinking its eyes and moving in a stuttered kind of way, jerkily. Chris was beaming, as if he'd just single-handedly created the universe.

'Pretty cool, huh?' he said as the lizard moved again on his tiny webbed feet. 'We're the first thing he's ever seen.'

The lizard stared up at us, and we stared back, taking each other in. He was little and defenceless, I felt sorry for him already. This was a screwed-up place he'd just come into. But he didn't have to know that. Not yet, anyway. There in that room, where it was hot and cramped, the world probably still seemed small enough to manage.

4

'And finally, please lift your glasses and toast Barbara's daughter, Remy, who planned and organised this entire event. We couldn't have done it without her. To Remy!'

'To Remy!' everyone echoed, glancing at me before sucking down more champagne.

'And now,' my mother said, smiling at Don, who hadn't stopped grinning since the organist had started the 'Prelude' for the ceremony two hours earlier, 'please, enjoy yourselves!'

The string quartet began playing, my mother and Don kissed, and finally I let out a breath. The salads had been served, everyone seated. Cake: check. Table centrepieces: check. Bartender and liquor: check. This and a million other details completed meant that now, after six months, two days, and approximately four hours, I could relax. At least for a few minutes.

'Okay,' I said to Chloe, '*now* I will have some champagne.'

'Finally!' she said, pushing a glass at me. She and Lissa were past tipsy, red faced and giggly enough to have attracted attention to our table more than once already. Jennifer Anne, who was sitting on my left with Chris, was drinking seltzer water and watching us, a pinched look on her face.

'Great job, Remy,' Chris said, spearing a tomato from his salad and stuffing it in his mouth. 'You really made this a good day for Mom.'

'After this,' I told him, 'she's on her own. Next time, she can go to Vegas and get married by an Elvis impersonator. I'm out.'

Jennifer Anne let her mouth drop open. 'Next time?' she said, shocked. Then she looked over at my mother and Don, who were now at the head table, managing to eat and hold hands concurrently. 'Remy, this is *marriage*. In front of God. It's for ever.'

Chris and I just looked at her. Across the table, Lissa burped.

'Oh my God,' she said as Chloe began snorting with laughter. 'Excuse me.'

Jennifer Anne rolled her eyes, clearly offended at sharing a table with a bunch of peasants and cynics. 'Christopher,' she said, and she was the only one who ever called him that, 'let's get some air.'

'But I'm eating my salad,' Chris said. He had dressing on his chin.

Jennifer Anne just picked up her napkin, folding it delicately. She'd finished her salad already and left her utensils in that neat cross in the middle, signalling to the server that she was done.

'Sure,' Chris said, standing up. 'Air. Let's go.'

Once they were gone, Chloe hopped over two seats, with Lissa following along behind her clumsily. Jess was missing, having had to stay home with her little brother when he came down with a sudden case of strep throat. Quiet as she was, I always felt things were out of balance when she wasn't around, as if Lissa and Chloe were too much for me to handle alone.

'Man,' Lissa said as Jennifer Anne led Chris out into the lobby, talking the whole way, 'she hates us.'

'No,' I said, taking another gulp of my champagne, 'she just hates me.'

'Oh, stop,' Chloe said, picking through her salad.

'Why would she hate you?' Lissa asked as she tipped up her glass again. Her lipstick was smudged, but in a cute way.

'Because she thinks I'm a bad person,' I told her. 'I go against everything she believes in.'

'But that's not true!' she said, offended. 'You're a *wonderful* person, Remy.'

Chloe snorted. 'Now, let's not get crazy.'

'She is!' Lissa said, loud enough so that a couple of people at the next table – Don's dealership co-workers – glanced over at us.

'I'm not wonderful,' I said, squeezing Lissa's arm. 'But I am a bit better than I used to be.'

'That,' Chloe said, tossing her napkin down on her plate, 'I can agree with. I mean, you don't smoke any more.'

'Right,' I agreed. 'And I hardly get falling down drunk at all.'

Lissa nodded. 'That's true too.'

'And finally,' I said, finishing my drink, 'I don't sleep around *nearly* as much as I used to.'

'Here, here,' Chloe said, lifting up her glass so I could tap mine against it. 'Watch out Stanford,' she said, smiling at me. 'Remy's practically a saint now.'

'St Remy,' I said, trying it out. 'I think I like that.'

The dinner was good. No one else seemed to think the chicken was a little rubbery besides me, but then I'd lobbied hard for the beef and lost, so I might have just been sore. Jennifer Anne and Chris never returned to our table; later, on my way to the rest room, I saw they'd defected to one where I'd put several of the local bigwigs Don was friendly with from the chamber of commerce. Jennifer Anne was talking away to the town manager, waving her fork as she made a point, while Chris sat beside her, a stain now on his tie, shovelling food in his mouth. When he saw me he smiled, apologetically, and just shrugged, as if this, like so many other things, was completely out of his hands.

Meanwhile, at our table, the champagne was flowing. One of Don's nephews, who went to Princeton, was busy hitting on Chloe, while Lissa, in the ten minutes I'd been gone, had crossed over from happily buzzing to completely maudlin, and was now well on her way to flat-out weepy drunk.

'The thing is,' she said, leaning into me, 'I really thought that Adam and I would get married. I mean, I did.'

'I know,' I said, feeling relieved as I saw Jess, in one of her few dresses, heading toward us. She looked uncomfortable, as she always did in anything but jeans, and as she sat down she made a face.

'Tights,' she grumbled. 'Stupid things cost me four bucks and feel like freaking sandpaper.'

'Well, if it isn't Jessica,' Chloe said, her voice

high and giggly. 'Don't you own any dresses from this decade?'

'Bite me,' Jess told her, and Don's nephew raised his eyebrows. Chloe, hardly bothered, went back to her champagne and some long story she'd been telling about herself.

'Jess,' Lissa whispered, falling off my shoulder and onto hers, her head nudging Jess's ear, 'I'm drunk.'

'I see that,' Jess said flatly, pushing her back to me. 'Gosh,' she said brightly, 'I'm so glad I came!'

'Don't be like that,' I told her. 'Are you hungry?'

'I had some tuna fish at home,' she said, squinting at the centrepiece.

'Stay here.' I stood up, easing Lissa back against her own chair. 'I'll be right back.'

I was just on my way back to the table, plate of chicken and asparagus and pilaf in hand, when I heard the microphone up front crackle, a few guitar chords jangling behind it.

'Hi everyone,' a voice said as I ducked between two tables, sidestepping a server clearing plates, 'we're the G Flats, and we'd like to wish Don and Barbara the best of happiness together!'

As everyone applauded this, I stopped where I was standing, then turned my head. Don had insisted on handling the band, claiming he knew someone who owed him a favour. But now, I wished more than anything that I'd just hired the local Motown group, even if they had played two of my mother's previous receptions.

Because of course it was Dexter, the musician boy,

standing in front of the microphone in a black suit that looked a size too big. He said, 'What do you say, folks? Let's get this party going!'

'Oh, my God,' I said, as the band – a guitar player, someone on keyboards, and in the back, the red-haired Ringo I'd met the day before – burst into a rousing rendition of 'Get Ready'. They were all wearing thrift shop suits, Ringo in the same clip-on tie. But already people were crowding onto the dance floor, shuffling and shimmying, my mother and Don in the middle of it all, whooping it up.

I went back to the table and gave Jess her plate, then flopped down into my seat. Lissa, as I'd expected, was now teary-eyed, dabbing at her face with a napkin while Jess patted her leg, mechanically. Chloe and the nephew were gone.

'I don't believe this,' I said.

'Believe what?' Jess asked, picking up her fork. 'Man, this smells *great*.'

'The band—' I began, but that was as far as I got before Jennifer Anne appeared beside me, Chris in tow.

'Mom's asking for you,' Chris said.

'What?'

'You're supposed to be dancing,' Jennifer Anne, queen of etiquette, informed me, gently nudging me out of my seat. 'The rest of the wedding party is already up there.'

'Oh, come on,' I said, looking at the dance floor, where of course my mother was now staring right at me, smiling beatifically and waggling her fingers in that come-here-now kind of way. So I grabbed Lissa up with one arm – damned if I was going out there alone – and dragged her with me, through the maze of tables, and into the crowd.

'I don't feel like dancing,' she sniffled.

'Neither do I,' I snapped.

'Oh, Remy, Lissa!' my mother shrieked as we came closer, reaching out her arms to pull us both in close. Her skin was warm, the fabric of her dress slippery and smooth as she brushed against me. 'Isn't this just so *fun*?'

We were right in the middle of the crowd, people dancing all around us. The band segued cleanly into 'Shout', accompanied by a whoop from someone behind me. Don, who had been dipping my mother wildly, now grabbed my arm and spun me out, hurling me into a couple doing the bump. I almost felt my arm disconnect from my body before he yanked me back, gyrating his pelvis wildly.

'Oh, Lord,' Lissa said from behind me, having seen this. But then I was flying out again, this time in the opposite direction. Don danced with such vigour I feared for the rest of us. I kept trying to send him back to my mother, but she was distracted dancing with one of Don's little nephews.

'Help me,' I hissed at Lissa as I whizzed past her, Don's hand still clamping my wrist. Then he pulled me close for a weird, jitterbug kind of hopping that made my teeth knock together, but not enough to distract me from seeing Chloe, who was standing off to the side of the dance floor, laughing hysterically.

'You're a great dancer!' Don said, pulling me in close and dipping me wildly. I was sure my cleavage would bust out of my dress – the fittings, while many, had not quite done the trick – but then he pulled me back up, lickety-split, and I got a mean head rush. 'I love to dance,' Don yelled at me, throwing me out into another spin. 'I don't get to do it enough!'

'I think you do,' I grumbled, as the song finally began to wind down.

'What's that?' he said, cupping his hand over his ear.

'I said,' I told him, 'that you really can move.'

He laughed, wiping his face. 'You too,' he said, as the band finished up with a crashing of cymbals. 'You too.'

I escaped as everyone was applauding, pushing my way to the bar, where my brother was standing nibbling on a piece of bread, alone for once.

'What was that?' he said, laughing. 'God, it looked like some wild tribal ritual.'

'Shut up,' I said.

'And now, folks,' I heard Dexter say from the stage as the lights dimmed a bit, 'for your listening pleasure . . . a little slow song.'

The opening strains of 'Our Love Is Here to Stay' began, a bit clumsily, and people who'd been avoiding the dance floor during the faster numbers started getting up from their chairs and pairing off. Jennifer Anne appeared next to me, smelling of hand soap, and slid her fingers over Chris's, dislodging the bread he was holding.

'Come on,' she murmured, tactfully dropping the bread onto a nearby table. Whatever I felt for her personally, I had to admire her technique. *Nothing* stopped this girl. 'Let's dance.'

'Absolutely,' Chris agreed, and wiped his mouth as he followed her, glancing back at me as they reached the floor. 'You okay?'

I nodded. 'Fine,' I said. The room had grown quieter as the music did, people's voices more hushed as they moved together, cheek to cheek. Onstage, Dexter sang on while the keyboardist looked bored, glancing at his watch. I could relate.

What was it about slow dancing, anyway? Even in junior high I'd hated the moment the music stalled, screeching to a halt so that someone could press their sweaty body to yours. At least with real dancing you weren't trapped, forced to rock back and forth with a total stranger who now, simply because of proximity, felt it was perfectly all right to grab your ass and anything else within reach. What a bunch of crap.

And it was crap. Totally. Because all slow dancing was really only about getting close to someone you wanted close or being forced to be close to someone you wished was far, far away. Okay, so my brother and Jennifer Anne looked totally smitten, and yeah, okay, the words to the song were nice and romantic. I mean, it wasn't a bad song or anything. It just wasn't my thing.

I grabbed a glass of champagne off a passing tray, taking a sip and wincing as the bubbles worked their way up my nose. I was fighting off a coughing fit when

I felt someone come up beside me. I glanced over to see a girl who worked with Don – her name was Marty, or Patty, something with a middle *t*. She had long, permed hair, a big fringe, and was wearing too much perfume. She smiled at me.

'I love this song,' she said, taking a sip of her drink and sighing. 'Don't you?'

I shrugged. 'I guess,' I said as Dexter leaned into the microphone, closing his eyes.

'They look so happy,' she went on, and I followed her gaze to my mother and Don, who were laughing and doing dips as the song wound down. She sniffled, and I realised she was near tears. How weird that weddings do that to some people. 'He's really happy, isn't he?'

'Yeah,' I said, 'he is.'

She wiped her eyes, then waved her hand at me apologetically, shaking her head. 'Oh, dear,' she said, 'forgive me. I just—'

'I know,' I said, if only to save her from whatever she was about to say. I'd had all the sentimental stuff I could handle for one day.

Finally the last verse came to an end. Marty/Patty took a deep breath, blinking as the lights came up again. Under closer scrutiny I could see she was actually crying: red eyes, face red, the whole deal. Her mascara, which I could not help but notice was applied a bit too plentifully, was beginning to streak.

'I should . . .' she said shakily, touching her face. 'I need to freshen up.'

'Good to see you,' I told her, the same way I'd told

everyone who I was forced to talk to all night long, in the same cheery hey-wedding-ho! voice.

'You, too,' she said, with less enthusiasm, and then she was gone, bumping against a chair on her way out.

Enough, I thought. *I need a break*.

I walked past the cake table and out a side door to the parking lot, where a couple of guys in waiter's jackets were smoking cigarettes and picking at some leftover cheese puffs.

'Hey,' I said to them, 'can I bum one?'

'Sure.' The taller guy, whose hair was kind of model-poofy, shook a cigarette out of his pack, handing it to me. He pulled out a lighter and held it for me as I leaned into it, taking a few puffs. He lowered his voice and said, 'What's your name?'

'Chloe,' I said, pulling back from him. 'Thanks.' I eased away around the corner, even as he was calling after me, finding a spot by the Dumpsters on the wall. I kicked off my shoes, then looked down at the cigarette in my hand. I'd done so well: eighteen days. It didn't even taste that good, really. Just a weak crutch on a bad night. So I tossed it down, watching it smoulder, and leaned back on my palms, stretching out my back.

Inside, the band stopped playing, to scattered applause. Then the canned hotel music came on, and a few seconds later a door farther down the wall banged open and out came the G Flats, their voices loud.

'This totally *sucks*' the guitar player said, pulling a pack of cigarettes from his pocket and shaking one out. 'After this, no more weddings. I'm serious.'

'It's money,' Ringo the drummer said, taking a sip of a bottled water he was holding.

'Not this one,' the keyboard guy muttered. 'This is a gimme.'

'No,' Dexter said, running a hand through his hair. 'This is the bail money. Or have we all forgotten that? We owed Don, remember?'

There was a grumbling acquiescence, followed by silence. 'I hate doing covers,' the guitarist said finally. 'I don't see why we can't do our own stuff.'

'For this crowd?' Dexter said. 'Be serious. I don't think Uncle Miltie from Saginaw wants to dance to your various versions of "The Potato Song".'

'It's not called that,' Ted snapped. 'And you know it.'

'Settle,' the redheaded drummer said, waving his arm in a peacemaking gesture I recognised. 'It's only a couple more hours, okay? Let's just make the best of it. At least we get to eat.'

'We get to eat?' the keyboardist said, perking up. 'Seriously?'

'That's what Don said,' the drummer replied. 'If there's enough left over. How much longer of a break do we have?'

Dexter glanced at his watch. 'Ten minutes.'

The keyboardist looked at the drummer, then the guitarist. 'I say food. Food?'

'Food,' they replied in unison. The keyboardist said, 'You in, Dexter?'

'Nah. Just nab me some bread or something.'

'Okay, Gandhi,' Ringo said, and somebody snorted. 'We'll see you in there.'

The guitarist tossed down his cigarette, Ringo threw his water bottle toward the Dumpster – and missed – and then they went inside, the door slamming shut behind them.

I sat there, watching him, knowing for once he couldn't see me first. He wasn't smoking, instead just sitting there on the wall, drumming his fingers. I'd always been a sucker for dark-headed boys, and from a distance his suit didn't look so tacky: he was almost cute. And tall. Tall was good.

I stood up and brushed my hands through my hair. Okay, so maybe he was really annoying. And I hated the way he'd bumped me against the wall. But I was here now, and it seemed only fitting that I take a few steps toward him, show myself, if only to throw him off a bit.

I was about to come around the Dumpster and into full sight when the door opened again and two girls – daughters of some cousin of Don's – came out. They were younger than me, by a couple of years, and lived in Ohio.

'I told you he'd be out here!' one of them, the blonde, said to the other. Then they both giggled. The taller one was hanging back, hand on the door, but her sister walked right up, plopping down beside Dexter. 'We were looking for you.'

'Really,' Dexter said, and smiled politely. 'Well, hello.'

'Hello yourself,' the blonde said, and I made a face, in the dark. 'You got a cigarette?'

Dexter patted his pockets. 'Nope,' he said. 'Don't smoke.'

'No way!' the blonde said, hitting him in the leg. 'I thought all guys in bands smoked.' The taller girl, still by the door, glanced back behind her, her face nervous. 'I smoke,' the blonde said, 'but my mother would kill me if she knew. *Kill* me.'

'Hmmm,' Dexter replied, as if this was actually interesting.

'Do you have a girlfriend?' the blonde said abruptly.

'Meghan!' her sister hissed. 'God!'

'I'm just asking,' Meghan said, sliding a little closer to Dexter. 'It's just a question.'

'Well,' Dexter said, 'actually . . .'

And at that, I turned around and headed back the way I'd come, already pissed at myself. I'd come close to doing something really stupid – way lowering my standards, which judging by Jonathan were rock bottom already. This was the way the old me worked, living just for the next second, hour, wanting only to have a boy want me for a night, no more. I'd changed. I'd quit that, along with smoking – okay, with one lapse – and drinking – for the most part. But the sleeping around thing, that I'd held true to. Completely. And I'd been ready to throw it away, or at least bend it a bit, for a Frank Sinatra wanna-be who would have easily settled for Meghan from Ohio. *God*.

Back inside, the cake was out on the dance floor, with my mother and Don posing beside it, their hands intertwined over the cake knife as the photographer moved all around them, flash popping. I stood on the edge of the crowd, watching as Don fed my mother a

79

piece, carefully easing it into her mouth. Another flash popped, capturing the moment. Ah, love.

The rest of the night went pretty much as I expected. My mother and Don left in a shower of birdseed and bubbles (with much of the hotel cleaning staff standing by looking hostile), Chloe ended up making out with Don's nephew in the lobby, and Jess and I got stuck in the bathroom, holding Lissa's head while she alternately puked up her fifteen-dollar-a-head dinner and moaned about Adam.

'Don't you just love weddings?' Jess asked me, passing over another wad of wet paper towels, which I pressed against Lissa's forehead as she stood up.

'I do,' Lissa wailed, missing the sarcasm. She patted the towels to her face. 'I really, really, do.'

Jess rolled her eyes at me, but I just shook my head as I led Lissa out of the stall and to the sinks. She looked in the mirror at herself – smeared make-up, hair wild and curly, dress with a questionable brown stain on the sleeve – and sniffled. 'This has to be the worst time of my life,' she moaned, blinking at herself.

'Now, now,' I told her, taking her hand, 'you'll feel better tomorrow.'

'No, you won't,' Jess said, getting the door. 'Tomorrow, you'll have a wicked hangover and feel even worse.'

'Jess,' I said.

'But the next day,' she went on, patting Lissa's shoulder, 'the next day you'll feel much better. You'll see.'

So we were a bedraggled bunch as we made our way out into the lobby, with Lissa held up between us. It was one in the morning, my hair was flat, and my feet hurt. The end of a wedding reception is always so goddamn depressing, I thought to myself. And only the bride and groom are spared, jetting off into the sunset while the rest of us wake up the next morning to just another day.

'Where's Chloe?' I asked Jess as we struggled through the revolving doors. Lissa was already falling asleep, even as her feet were moving.

'No idea. Last I saw her she was all over what's-his-bucket back there by the piano.'

I glanced behind me into the lobby, but no Chloe. She always seemed to be elsewhere when anyone else was puking. It was like she had a sixth sense or something.

'She's a big girl,' Jess told me. 'She'll be fine.'

We were hoisting Lissa into Jess's front seat when there was a rattling noise, and the white van I now recognised as belonging to Dexter's band pulled up in front of the hotel. The back doors popped open and out jumped Ringo, now without the clip-on tie, with the guitarist hopping out from the driver's seat and following him. Then they disappeared inside, leaving the engine running.

'You need a ride?' Jess asked me.

'Nope. Chris is in there waiting for me.' I shut the door, closing Lissa in. 'Thanks for this.'

'No problem.' She pulled her keys out of her pocket, jangling them. 'It went okay, don't you think?'

I shrugged. 'It's over,' I said. 'That's all that matters.'

As she drove off, beeping the horn once, I started

back to the hotel to find my brother. When I passed the white van, Ringo and the keyboardist were coming back out, hauling equipment and bickering.

'Ted never helps,' the keyboardist said, hoisting some big speaker into the back of the van, where it landed with a crash. 'This vanishing act is getting *old*, you know?'

'Let's just get out of here,' Ringo replied. 'Where's Dexter?'

'They get five minutes,' the keyboardist said. 'Then they can walk.' Then he reached in the open driver's window and planted his palm on the horn, letting it blare out, loud, for a good five seconds.

'Oh, good,' Ringo said sarcastically. '*That'll* go over well.'

A few seconds later the guitarist – the elusive Ted – came out the revolving doors, looking irritated.

'Nice,' he yelled, coming around the van. 'Real classy.'

'Get in or walk home,' the keyboardist snapped. 'I mean it.'

Ted got in, the horn sounded one more time, and then they waited. No Dexter. Finally, after what seemed like a bit of bickering from the front seats, the van chugged away, taking a right onto the main road. The turn signal, of course, was busted.

Back in the hotel, the cleaning crew was at work on the reception hall, clearing glasses and pulling off tablecloths. My mother's bouquet – eighty bucks of flowers – sat abandoned on a tray table, still as fresh as when she'd first picked it up at the church over nine hours earlier.

'They left you,' I heard someone say. I turned around. Dexter. God help me. He was sitting at a table next to the ice sculpture – two swans intertwined and quickly melting – a plate in front of him.

'Who did?' I asked.

'Chris and Jennifer Anne,' he replied, as if he'd known them forever. Then he picked up a fork, taking a bite of whatever he was having. It looked like wedding cake, from where I was.

'What?' I said. 'They left?'

'They were tired.' He chewed for a second, then swallowed. 'Jennifer Anne said she had to go because she had an early seminar tomorrow at the convention centre. Something about achievement. She's very bright, that girl. She thinks I might have a future in the corporate and private leisure activity sector. Whatever that means.'

I just looked at him.

'Anyway,' he went on, 'I said it was fine, because when you showed up we'd just give you a ride.'

'We,' I repeated.

'Me and the guys.'

I considered this. And I'd been so close to being scot-free, home by now care of Jess. Great. 'They're gone too,' I said finally.

He looked up, his fork midway to his mouth. 'They what?'

'They left,' I repeated slowly. 'They beeped the horn first.'

'Oh, man, I *thought* I heard the horn,' he said, shaking his head. 'Typical.'

I looked around the mostly empty room, as if a solution to this and all my other problems might be lurking behind, say, a potted plant. No luck. So I did what seemed, by now, inevitable. I walked over to the table where he was sitting, pulled out a chair, and sat down.

'Ah,' he said, with a smile. 'Finally, she comes around.'

'Don't get too excited,' I said, dropping my bag onto the table. I felt tired in every part of my body, as if I'd been stretched thin. 'I'm just getting the energy up to call a cab.'

'You should try some of this cake first.' He pushed the plate at me. 'Here.'

'I don't want any cake.'

'It's really good. It doesn't taste chalky at all.'

'I'm sure it doesn't,' I said, 'but I'm fine.'

'You probably didn't even get any, right?' He wiggled the fork at me. 'Just try it.'

'No,' I said flatly.

'Come on.'

'No.'

'Mmmm.' He poked at it with the fork, gently. 'So tasty.'

'You,' I said finally, 'are *really* pissing me off.'

He shrugged, as if he'd heard this before, then pulled the plate back toward himself, dipping the fork in for another bite. The cleaning crew was chattering away in the front of the room, stacking chairs. One woman with her hair in a long braid picked up my mother's bouquet, cradling it in her arms.

'Da-da-da-dum,' she said, and laughed when one of

84

her co-workers yelled at her to stop dreaming and get back to work.

Dexter put down the fork, the tasty, non-chalklike cake gone, and pushed the plate away. 'So,' he said, looking at me, 'this your mom's first remarriage?'

'Fourth,' I said. 'She's made a career of it.'

'Got you beat,' he told me. 'My mom's on her fifth.'

I had to admit, I was impressed. So far I'd never met anyone with more ex-steps than me. 'Really.'

He nodded. 'But you know,' he said sarcastically, 'I really think *this* one's going to last.'

'Hope springs eternal.'

He sighed. 'Especially in my mom's house.'

'Dexter, honey,' someone called out from behind me, 'did you get enough to eat?'

He sat up, then raised his voice and said, 'Yes, ma'am, I sure did. Thank you.'

'There's a bit more of this chicken dish left.'

'No, Linda. I'm full. Really.'

'Okay then.'

I looked at him. 'Do you know *everybody*?'

He shrugged. 'Not everybody,' he said. 'I just bond easily. It's part of the whole repeating-stepfather thing. It makes you more mellow.'

'Yeah, right,' I said.

'Because you have to just go with the flow. Your life is not your own, with people coming in and out all the time. You get mellow because you have to. I mean, you know exactly what I'm saying, I bet.'

'Oh yes,' I said flatly, 'I am just so easy-going. That is precisely the word that describes me.'

85

'Isn't it?'

'No,' I told him. 'It isn't.' And then I stood up and got my bag, feeling my feet ache as they settled into my shoes. 'I have to go home now.'

He got to his feet, taking his jacket off the back of the chair. 'Share a cab?'

'I don't think so.'

'All right,' he said, shrugging. 'Suit yourself.'

I walked to the door, thinking he'd be behind me, but when I glanced back he was across the room, going out the other way. I had to admit I was surprised, after such intense pursuit, that he had given up already. The drummer had been right, I supposed. The conquest – getting me alone – was all that mattered, and once he saw me up close I wasn't so special after all. But I, of course, knew that already.

There was a cab parked out front, the driver dozing. I climbed into the back seat, sliding off my shoes. It was, by the green numbers on the dashboard, exactly 2 AM. At the Thunderbird Hotel across town, my mother was most likely fast asleep, dreaming of the next week she'd spend in St Bart's. She'd come home to finish her novel, to move her new husband into the house, to take another stab at being a Mrs Somebody, sure that this time, indeed, it would be different.

As the cab turned onto the main road, I saw a glint of something through the park, over to my right. It was Dexter, on foot, turning into a neighbourhood, and in his white shirt he stood out, almost as if he were glowing. He was walking down the middle of the street, the houses dark on either side of him, quiet in sleep. And watching him head home, for a second it was like he was the only one awake or even alive in all the world right then, except for me.

5

'Remy, really. He's just wonderful.'

'Lola, please.'

'I know what you're thinking. I do. But this is different. I wouldn't do you like that. Don't you trust me?'

I put down the stack of cheques I'd been counting and looked up at her. She was leaning on her elbow, chin cupped in her hand. One of her earrings, a huge gold hoop, was swinging back and forth, catching the sunlight streaming through the front window.

'I don't do blind dates,' I told her, again.

'It isn't blind, honey, I know him,' she explained, as if this made some kind of difference. 'A nice boy. He's got great hands too.'

'What?' I said.

She held up her hands – impeccably manicured, naturally – as if I needed a visual aid for this basic part of human anatomy. 'Hands. I noticed it the other day, when he came to pick his mother up from her sea salt scrub. Beautiful hands. He's bilingual.'

I blinked, trying to process the connection between these two characteristics. Nope. Nothing.

'Lola?' a voice called out tentatively from inside the salon. 'My scalp is burning?'

'That's just the dye working, sugar,' Lola called back,

not even turning her head. 'Anyway, Remy, I really talked you up. And since his mother is coming back this afternoon for her pedicure—'

'No,' I said flatly. 'Forget it.'

'But he's perfect!'

'Nobody,' I told her, going back to the cheques, 'is perfect.'

'Lola?' Now the voice sounded more nervous, less polite. 'It's really hurting . . .'

'You want to find love, Remy?'

'No.'

'I don't understand you, girl! You're about to make a big mistake.' Lola always got loud when she felt passionate about something: now, her voice was booming around the small waiting room, rattling the sample nail polishes on the shelf above my head. A few more active vowels and I'd be concussed, and as quick to sue as the woman whose hair was burning off, ignored, in the next room.

'Lola!' The woman, now shrieking, sounded like she was on the verge of tears. 'I think I smell burning hair—'

'Oh, for God's sake!' Lola bellowed, angry at both of us, and whirled around, stomping out of the room. As a purple nail polish crashed onto my desk, missing me by inches, I sighed, flipping open the calendar. It was Monday. My mother and Don would be back from St Bart's in three days. I turned another page, running my finger down past the days, to count again how many weeks I had before I left for school.

Stanford. Three thousand miles away from here, almost a direct shot across the country. An incredible school, my top choice, and I'd been accepted by five out of the six others I'd chosen to apply to. All my hard work, advanced placement classes, honours seminars. Finally it meant something.

Freshman year, when such decisions are made, my teachers had me pegged for the state party school, if I was lucky – someplace where I could do an easy major, like psych, with a minor in frat parties and make-up. As if just because I was, okay, blonde and somewhat attractive with an active social life (and, okay, not the best of reputations) and didn't do the student council/debate team/cheerleader thing, I was destined for the sub-par. Grouped with the burn-outs and the barely graduating, where just making it down from the parking lot after lunch was far exceeding expectations.

But I'd proved them wrong. I used my own money to pay for a tutor in physics, the class that almost killed me, as well as a prep class for the SAT, which I took three times. I was the only one of my friends in AP classes except for Lissa, who as the daughter of two PhDs had always been expected to be brilliant. But I always worked harder when I was up against something, or when someone assumed I couldn't succeed. That's what drove me, all those nights studying. The fact that so many figured I couldn't do it.

I was the only one from our graduating class going to Stanford. Which meant I could begin my life again, fresh and new, so far from home. All the money I had left from my salon paycheque after my car payment I'd stuck in my savings account, to cover the dorm fees and books and living expenses. The tuition I'd got out of my part of the trust left to me and Chris in our father's estate. It had been set aside, by some lawyer who I wished I could thank personally, until we were twenty-five or for school, which meant that even during the lean times my mother couldn't touch it. It also meant that no matter how she burned through her own money, my four years in college were safe. And all because each time 'This Lullaby' (written by Thomas Custer, all rights reserved) played in the background of a commercial, or on lite radio, or was performed by some lounge singer in Vegas, it bought me another day of my future.

The chimes over the door sounded and the UPS man came in, carrying a box, which he put down on the desk in front of me. 'Package for you, Remy,' he said, whipping out his clipboard.

I signed on the screen, then took the box. 'Thanks, Jacob.'

'Oh, and this too,' he said, handing me an envelope. 'See you tomorrow.'

'Okay,' I said. The envelope wasn't stamped – weird – or sealed. I opened the flap and reached in, pulling out a stack of three pictures. They were all of the same couple, both in their seventies, probably, posing in some seaside setting. The man had on a baseball hat and a T-shirt that read WILL GOLF FOR FOOD. The woman had a camera strapped to her belt and was wearing sensible shoes. They had their arms around each other and looked wildly happy: in the first picture they were smiling, the next laughing, the third kissing, sweetly, their lips barely touching. Like any couple you'd see on vacation who would ask you to take a picture, please, of the two of us.

Which was all fine and dandy, except who the hell were they? And what was this supposed to *mean*, anyway? I stood up, looking outside for the UPS truck, but it was already gone. Was I supposed to know these people, or something? I glanced back at the pictures, but the couple just grinned back at me, caught in their tropical moment, offering no explanation.

'Remy, honey, get me some cold water, would you?' Lola yelled from the other room, and I could tell by her voice – cheerful but *loud* – she meant do it now, stat. 'And some of that Neosporin from the cabinet beneath the cash drawer?'

'Sure thing!' I yelled back just as cheerfully, shoving the pictures into my bag.

I yanked the Neosporin out of the cabinet, adding some gauze and a few bandages, which from previous experiences, I thought we might need. Hair emergencies happened all the time, and the truth was, you just knew to be prepared.

Three hours later, when the drama had finally subsided and Lola's customer had left with a bandaged scalp, a hefty gift certificate, and a written promise of eyebrow waxing for life, I finally got to lock the cash drawer, get my bag, and walk outside.

It finally felt like summer. Heavy heat, totally humid, and everything just smelled kind of smoky and thick, as if close to boiling. Lola kept the salon ice cold, so walking outside was like leaving an arctic freeze. I always got goose bumps as I walked to my car.

I got in, cranked the engine, and turned the AC on full blast to get it going. Then I picked up my cell phone and checked my messages. One from Chloe, asking what we were doing tonight. One from Lissa saying she was fine, just fine, but sounding all sniffly, which she knew I was getting sick of by now. And lastly my brother, Chris, reminding me that Jennifer Anne was cooking us dinner tonight, six sharp, don't be late.

I deleted this last message with an angry jab of my finger. I was never late. And he knew it. Further evidence of brainwashing by Jennifer Anne, who, unlike my brother, knew me not at all. I mean, *I* was the one who got him up each morning when he started for that garage job, otherwise, he would have slept through all three of his alarms, which he had set in various positions around the room, all requiring him to get up out of the bed to hit the snooze button. I made sure he wasn't late, didn't get fired, was out the door by 8:35 at the latest, in case he hit traffic down main street, which he always—

I was interrupted, suddenly, by a thwacking sound as something hit my windscreen. Not hard: more like a slap. I looked up, heart jumping, and saw yet another snapshot of the old vacationing couple. Same WILL GOLF FOR FOOD T-shirt, same crinkly smiles. Now staring down at me, pressed against the glass, held there by someone's hand.

And I knew. It was ridiculous I hadn't figured it out earlier.

I hit the button for my window and it went down. Standing there, right by my side mirror, was Dexter. He took his hand off the windscreen and the picture slid down the glass, lodging itself under one of my wipers.

'Hi there,' he said. He was wearing a white T-shirt under a uniform I recognised: polyester shirt, green with black piping. Right over the front pocket was neatly stitched FLASH CAMERA, the name of the one-hour photo place directly across the street from the salon.

'You're stalking me,' I told him.

'What?' he said. 'You didn't like the pictures?'

'Will Golf for Food? How stupid is that?' I said, putting my car in reverse. 'Is it supposed to mean something?'

'No musicians, no golfers,' he said, ticking these off on his fingers. 'What's left? Lion tamers? Accountants?'

I just looked at him, then put my foot on the gas. He had to jump out of the way to avoid my tyre flattening his foot.

'Wait,' he said, putting his hand on my open window, 'in all seriousness. Can you give me a ride?' I must have looked sceptical, because he added quickly, 'We have a band meeting in fifteen minutes. And we instituted this new policy, so the repercussions for being late are brutal. Seriously.'

'I'm late too,' I said, which was a lie, but I wasn't a freaking taxi service.

'Please.' He squatted down, so we were eye to eye. Then he lifted up his other hand, exposing a grease-stained bag from Double Burger. 'I'll share my fries with you.'

'No thanks,' I said, hitting the button to put up my window. 'Besides, I have a no-food policy in my car. Repercussions are brutal.'

He smiled at this, stopping the window with his hand. 'I'll behave,' he said. 'I promise.' And then, he started around the front of the car as if I had said yes, grabbing the picture off my windscreen and tucking it into his back pocket. The next thing I knew he was sliding in beside me, settling into the seat, the door swinging shut behind him.

What was it about this guy? Resistance was futile. Or maybe I was just too tired and hot to pursue another argument.

'One ride,' I told him in my stern voice. 'That's it. And if you get even a speck of food in this car you're out. And I won't slow down to do it, either.'

'Oh, please,' he said, reaching for his seat belt, 'you don't have to coddle me, really. Be blunt. Don't hold back.'

I ignored this as I pulled out of the shopping centre and onto the road. We weren't half a block when I caught him sneaking a French fry. He thought he was being slick, cupping it in his hand and faking a yawn, but I was a pro at this. Lissa was always testing my limits.

'What did I say about food?' I said, hitting the brake for a red light.

'I'm hmphrgy,' he mumbled, then swallowed. 'I'm hungry,' he repeated.

'I don't care. No food in the car, full stop. I'm trying to keep it nice.'

He turned around, glancing at the back seat, then at the dashboard and floor mats. 'Nice?' he said. 'This thing is like a museum. It still smells new.'

'Exactly,' I said as the light changed.

'Take this left here.' He pointed, and I changed lanes, glancing behind me. 'I bet you're a real control freak.'

'Wrong.'

'You are, I can tell.' He ran a finger across the dash, then glanced at it. 'No dust,' he reported. 'And you've cleaned this windscreen from the inside, haven't you?'

'Not lately.'

'Hah!' he hooted. 'I bet it would drive you crazy if something was out of place.'

'Wrong,' I told him.

'Let's see.' He reached into the bag, carefully withdrawing a French fry. It was long and rubbery looking, bending as he held it between two fingers. 'In the interest of science,' he said, waving it at me, 'a little experiment.'

'No food in the car,' I repeated, like a mantra. God, how far away was his house? We were back over near the hotel where we'd had the reception, so it had to be close.

'Left here,' he said, and I hooked us onto the street,

scaring a couple of squirrels into the trees. When I next glanced over at him, his hands were empty and the French fry, now straightened, was lying on the gearshift console. 'Now, don't panic,' he said, putting his hand on my arm. 'Breathe. And just appreciate, for a minute, the freedom in this chaos.'

I moved my arm out from under his hand. 'Which house is yours?'

'It's not messy at all, see? It's beautiful. It's nature in all its simplicity . . .'

Then I saw it: the white van, parked crookedly in the front yard of a little yellow house about a hundred feet up. The porch light was on, even though it was broad daylight, and I could see the redheaded drummer, Ringo, coffee shop employee, sitting on the front steps with a dog beside him. He was reading a newspaper; the dog was just panting, its tongue out.

'. . . the natural state of things, which is, in fact, utter imperfection,' he finished as we jerked into the driveway, spraying gravel. The French fry slid off the console, leaving a grease trail like a slug, and landed in my lap. 'Whoops,' he said, grabbing it. 'Now, see? That was a first, good step in conquering . . .'

I looked at him, then moved my hand, hitting the automatic lock: click, and the button on his door shot up.

'. . . your problem,' he finished. He opened the door and got out, taking his bag o' grease with him. Then he bent down, poking his head back in quickly, so that we were almost face-to-face. 'Thanks for the ride. Really.'

'Sure,' I said. He didn't move for a second, which threw me off: just us, there together, eye to eye. Then he blinked and pulled away, ducking out of the car and shutting the door. I watched as the dog on the porch suddenly got up and made its way down the steps, tail wagging wildly, when it saw Dexter coming. Meanwhile, I was noticing that my car now stank of grease, another bonus. I put down the window, hoping the air freshener hanging from my rearview was up to the job.

'Finally,' the drummer said, folding his newspaper. I put the car in reverse, then made sure Dexter's back was still turned before brushing my finger over the gearshift console, checking for grease. My dirty little secret.

'It's not six yet,' Dexter said, reaching down to pet the dog, who was now circling him, tail thwacking against the back of his legs. He had a white muzzle and moved kind of creakily, in that old-dog way.

'Yeah, but I don't have my key,' the drummer said, standing up.

'Neither do I,' Dexter told him. I started to back out then had to stop to let a bunch of cars pass. 'What about the back door?'

'Locked. Plus you know Ted moved that bookcase in front of it last night.'

Dexter stuck his hands in his pockets, pulling them out. Nothing. 'Well, I guess we just have to break a window.'

'What?' the drummer said.

'Don't panic,' Dexter said in that offhand way I

already recognised. 'We'll pick a small one. Then you can wriggle through it.'

'No way,' the drummer said, crossing his arms over his chest as Dexter started up the steps, moving to check out the windows on the front side of the house. 'Why do I always have to do the stupid shit, anyway?'

'Because you're a redhead,' Dexter told him, and the drummer made a face, 'plus, you have slim hips.'

'What?'

By now I wasn't even waiting for a gap in traffic any more. Instead I was watching as Dexter found a rock around the side of the house, then came back and squatted down in front of a small window on the far end of the porch. He studied it, then the rock, readying his technique while the dog sat down beside him, licking his ear. The drummer stood behind, still looking miffed, his hands in his pockets.

Call it rampant control issues, but I couldn't stand to watch this. Which was why I found myself pulling back up the driveway, getting out of my car, and walking up the steps just as Dexter was pulling his arm back, rock in hand, to break the window.

'One,' he was saying, 'two . . .'

'Wait,' I called out, and he stopped, the rock tumbling from his hand and landing on the porch with a thunk. The dog jumped back, startled, with a yelp.

'I thought you left,' Dexter said. 'Couldn't do it, could you?'

'Do you have a credit card?' I asked him.

He and the drummer exchanged looks. Then Dexter

said, 'Do I look like I have a credit card? And what, exactly, do you need purchased?'

'It's to unlock the door, idiot,' I told him, reaching into my own pocket. But my wallet was in the back seat, buried in my bag.

'I have one,' the drummer said slowly, 'but I'm only supposed to use it for emergencies.'

We looked at him, and then Dexter reached up and smacked him on the back of the head, Three Stooges style. 'John Miller, you're a moron. Just give it to her.'

John Miller – his real name, although to me he was still somehow Ringo – handed over a Visa. I opened the screen door, then took the card and slid it between the lock and the doorjamb, wiggling it around. I could feel them behind me, watching.

Every door is different, and the weight of the lock and the thickness of the card are all factors. This skill, like the perfect toss of an Extra Large Diet Zip, was acquired over time, with lots of practice. Never to break and enter, always just to get into my own house, or Jess's, when keys were lost. My brother, who had used it for evil at times, had taught me this when I was fourteen.

A few pulls to the left, then the right, and I felt the lock give. Bingo. We were in. I handed John Miller back his card.

'Impressive,' he said, smiling at me in that way guys do when you surprise them. 'What's your name again?'

'Remy,' I told him.

'She's with me,' Dexter explained, and I just sighed at this and walked off the porch, the dog now trailing along behind me. I bent down and petted him, scratching his ears. He had cloudy white eyes, and horrible breath, but I'd always had a soft spot for dogs. My mother, of course, was a cat person. The only pets I'd ever had were a long line of big, fluffy Himalayans with various health problems and nasty temperaments who loved my mother and left hair everywhere.

'That's Monkey,' Dexter called. 'Him and me, we're a package deal.'

'Too bad for Monkey,' I replied, and stood up, walking to my car.

'You're a bad ass, Miss Remy,' he said. 'But you're intrigued now. You'll be back.'

'Don't count on it.'

He didn't answer this, instead just stood there, leaning against a porch post as I pulled out of the driveway. Monkey was sitting next to him, and together they watched me drive away.

6

Chris opened the door to Jennifer Anne's apartment. He was wearing a tie.

'Late,' he said flatly.

I glanced at my watch. It was 6:03, which, according to Chloe and Lissa and everyone else who had always made *me* wait, meant I was well within the bounds of the official within-five-minutes-doesn't-count-as-late rule. But something told me maybe I shouldn't point this out just now.

'She's here!' Chris called out over his shoulder, then shot me the stink eye as I walked in, shutting the door behind me.

'I'll be right out,' Jennifer Anne replied, her voice light. 'Offer her something to drink, would you, Christopher?'

'This way.' Chris started into the living room. As we walked, our shoes made swishy noises on the carpet. It was the first time I'd been to Jennifer Anne's, but I wasn't surprised by the decor. The sofa and the love seat were both a little threadbare and matched the border of the wallpaper. Her diploma from the community college hung on the wall in a thick gold frame. And the coffee table was piled with thick, pretty books about Provence, Paris, and Venice, places I knew she'd never been, arranged with great care to look as though they were stacked casually.

I sat down on the couch, and Chris brought me a ginger ale, which he knew I hated but thought I deserved. Then we sat down, him on the couch, me on the love seat. Across from us, over the fake fireplace, a clock was ticking.

'I didn't realise this was a formal occasion,' I said, nodding at his tie.

'Obviously,' he replied.

I glanced down at myself: I had on jeans, a white T-shirt, with a sweater tied around my waist. I looked fine, and he knew it. There was a clang from the kitchen, which sounded like an oven closing, and then the door swung open and Jennifer Anne emerged, smoothing her skirt with her hands.

'Remy,' she said, coming over and bending down to kiss my cheek. This was new. It was all I could do not to pull back, if only from surprise, but I stayed put, not wanting another dirty look from my brother. Jennifer Anne settled down beside him on the couch, crossing her legs. 'I'm so glad you could join us. Brie?'

'Excuse me?'

'Brie,' she repeated, lifting a small glass tray from the end table and extending it toward me. 'It's a soft cheese, from France.'

'Oh, right,' I said. I just hadn't heard her, but now she looked very pleased with herself, as if she actually thought she'd brought some foreign culture into my life. 'Thank you.'

We were not given the opportunity to see if the conversation would progress naturally. Jennifer Anne clearly had a list of talking points she had culled from the newspaper or CNN she believed would allow us to converse on a level she deemed acceptable. This had to be a business tactic she'd picked up from one of her self-improvement books, none of which, I noticed, were shelved in the living room on public display.

'So,' she said, after we'd all had a cracker or two, 'what do you think about what's happening with the elections in Europe, Remy?'

I was taking a sip of my ginger ale, and glad of it. But finally I had to reply. I said, 'I haven't been following the news lately, actually.'

'Oh, it's fascinating,' she told me. 'Christopher and I were just discussing how the outcome could affect our global economy, weren't we, honey?'

My brother swallowed the cracker he'd been eating, cleared his throat, and said, 'Yes.'

And so it went. In the next fifteen minutes, we had equally fascinating discussions about genetic engineering, global warming, the possibility of books being completely obsolete in a few years because of computers, and the arrival at the local zoo of a new family of exotic, nearly extinct Australian birds. By the time we finally sat down for dinner, I was exhausted.

'Great chicken, sweetheart,' my brother said as we all dug into our plates. Jennifer Anne had prepared some complicated-looking recipe involving chicken breasts stuffed with sweet potatoes topped with a vegetable glaze. They looked perfect, but it was the kind of dish where you just knew someone had to have been pawing at your food for a long while to get it just right, their fingers all in what now you were having to stick in your mouth.

'Thank you,' Jennifer replied, reaching over to pat his hand. 'More rice?'

'Please.' Chris smiled at her as she dished food onto his plate, and I realised, not for the first time, that I hardly recognised my brother any more. He was sitting there as if this was the life he was used to, as if all he'd ever known was wearing a tie to dinner and having someone fix him exotic meals on what clearly were the good plates. But I knew differently. We'd shared the same childhood, were raised by the same woman, whose idea of a home-cooked meal involved Kraft dinner, Pillsbury biscuits, and a pea-and-carrot combo from a can. My mother couldn't even make toast without setting off the smoke detector. It was amazing we'd even made it past grade school without getting scurvy. But you wouldn't know that now. The transformation of Chris, my stoner brother with a police record, to Christopher, man of culture, ironing, and established career of lubrication specialist, was almost complete. There were only a few more kinks to work out, like the lizards. And me.

'So your mother and Don get back Friday, correct?' Jennifer Anne asked me.

'Yep,' I said, nodding. And maybe it was those meticulously made chicken rolls, or the fakeness of the entire evening thus far, but something suddenly kicked up my evil side. I turned to Chris and said, 'So we haven't done it yet, you know.'

He blinked at me, his mouth full of rice. Then he swallowed and said, 'What?'

'The wager.' I waited for him to catch up, but either he didn't or was pretending not to.

'What wager?' Jennifer Anne asked, gamely allowing this divergence from her scripted dinner conversation.

'It's nothing,' Chris mumbled. He was trying to kick me under the table, but hit a leg instead, rattling Jennifer Anne's butter dish.

'Years ago,' I said to Jennifer Anne, as he took another swipe, barely nicking the sole of my shoe, 'when my mother married for the second time, Chris and I started a tradition of laying bets on how long it would last.'

'This bread is just great,' Chris said quickly to Jennifer Anne. 'Really.'

'Chris was ten, and I must have been six or so,' I continued. 'This was when she married Harold, the professor? The day they left for the honeymoon, we each sat down with a pad of paper and calculated how long we thought they'd stay together. And then, we folded up our guesses and sealed them in an envelope, which I kept in my closet until the day my mother sat us down to tell us Harold was moving out.'

'Remy,' Chris said in a low voice, 'this isn't funny.'

'He's just mad,' I told her, 'because he's never won yet. I always do. Because it's like blackjack: you can't go over. Whoever comes closest to the actual day wins. And we've had to really be specific about the rules over the years. Like it's the day she tells us it's over, not the official separation day. We had to establish that because when she and Martin split Chris tried to cheat.'

Now, Chris was just glaring at me. Sore loser.

'Well, I think,' Jennifer Anne said, her voice high, 'that is just horrible. Just *horrible*.' She put down her fork carefully and pressed her napkin to her lips, closing her eyes. 'What an awful way to look at a marriage.'

'We were just kids,' Chris said quickly, putting his arm around her.

'I'm just saying,' I said, shrugging, 'it's like a family tradition.'

Jennifer Anne pushed out her chair and picked up the chicken dish. 'I just think that your mother deserves better,' she snapped, 'than for you to have so little faith in her.' And then she walked into the kitchen, the door swinging shut behind her.

Chris was across the table at me so quickly I didn't even have time to put down my fork: he almost pierced his own eyeball. 'What are you *doing*?' he hissed at me. 'What the hell is wrong with you, Remy?'

'Gosh, *Christopher*,' I said. 'Such language. You better not let her hear you, she'll make you stay after school and write a report on those Australian blue-footed boobies.'

He sat back down in his chair, getting out of my face at least. 'Look,' he said, spitting out the words, 'I can't help it if you're a bitter, angry bitch. But I love Jennifer Anne and I won't let you play your little games with her. Do you hear me?'

I just looked at him.

'Do you?' he snapped. 'Because dammit, Remy, you make it really hard to love you sometimes. You know that? You really do.' And then he pushed out his chair, threw his napkin down, and pushed through the door into the kitchen.

I sat there. I honestly felt like I'd been slapped: my face even felt red and hot. I'd just been messing around with him, and God, he'd just freaked. All these years Chris was the only one who'd ever shared my sick, cynical view on love. We'd always told each other how we'd never get married, no way, shoot me if I do it. But now, he'd turned his back on everything. What a chump.

I could hear them in the kitchen, her voice quiet and tremulous, his soothing. On my plate my food was cold, just like my hard, hard heart. You would have thought I'd feel brittle too, being such a bitter, angry bitch. But I didn't. I felt nothing, really, just the sense that now the circle I'd always kept small was a little smaller. Maybe Chris could be saved that easily. But not me. Never me.

After much whispered discussion in the kitchen, an uneasy peace was negotiated. I apologised to Jennifer Anne, trying to make it sound genuine, and suffered through some more talking points over chocolate soufflé before finally being allowed to leave. Chris still wasn't really speaking to me, and didn't even try to make it sound like he wasn't slamming the door at my back when I left. I shouldn't even have been surprised, actually, that he'd caved so easily to love. That was why he'd lost our marriage bet every time: his guess was always over, way over, the last time by a full six months.

I got in my car and drove. Going home seemed depressing, with just me there, so I cut across town, into Lissa's neighbourhood. I slowed down in front of her house, turning off my lights and idling by the mailbox. Through the front window I could see into the dining room, where she and her parents were eating dinner. I thought about going up and ringing the bell – Lissa's mom was always quick to pull a chair and another plate up to the table – but I wasn't in the mood for parental talk about college, or the future. In fact, I felt like I was primed for a little backsliding. So I went to Chloe's.

She answered the door holding a wooden spoon, her brow furrowed. 'My mom's due home in forty-five minutes,' she informed me, holding the door open so I could come in. 'You can stay thirty, okay?'

I nodded. Chloe's mom, Natasha, had a strict policy of no uninvited guests, which meant that as long as I'd known Chloe there'd always been a set time limit of how long we could hang out at her house. Her mom just didn't seem to like people that much. I figured this was either a really bad reason to choose a career as a flight attendant or a natural reaction to having become one. Either way, we hardly ever saw her.

'How was dinner?' she asked me over her shoulder as I followed her into the kitchen, where I could hear something sizzling on the stove.

'Uneventful,' I told her. I wasn't lying as much as I

just didn't feel like getting into it. 'Can I score a couple of minibottles from you?'

She turned around from the stove, where she was stirring something in the pan. It smelled like seafood. 'Is that why you came over?'

'Partially.' That was the thing about Chloe: I could always shoot it straight with her. In fact, she preferred it that way. Like me, she wasn't into bullshitting around.

She rolled her eyes. 'Help yourself.'

I pulled a stool over and stepped up, opening the cabinet. Ah, the mother lode. Tiny bottles her mom had filched from the drink cart lined the shelf, arranged neatly by height and category: clear liquors on the left, dessert brandies on the right. I grabbed two Bacardis from the back, readjusted the rows, then glanced at Chloe to make sure it looked okay. She nodded, then handed me a glass of Coke, into which I dumped the contents of one bottle, shaking it around with some ice cubes. Then I took a sip. It was strong, and burned going down, and I felt this weird twinge, like I knew this wasn't the way to react to what had happened at Jennifer Anne's. It passed, though. That was the bad thing. It always passed.

'Want a sip?' I asked Chloe, holding out my glass. 'It's good.'

She shook her head. 'Yeah,' she said, adjusting the flame under the pan, 'that's just what I need. She comes home to my first tuition bill *and* I smell like rum.'

'Where's she been this time?'

'Zurich, I think.' She leaned closer to the pan, sniffing it. 'With a layover in London. Or Milan.'

I took another sip of my drink. 'So,' I said, after a few seconds of quiet, 'I'm an angry, bitter bitch. Right?'

'Right,' she said, without turning around.

I nodded. Point proved. I supposed. I drew in the dampness left by my glass on the black countertop, stretching out the edges.

'And you bring this up,' Chloe said, turning around and leaning against the stove, 'because . . .'

'Because,' I told her, 'Chris suddenly believes in love and I don't and therefore, I am a terrible person.'

She considered this. 'Not altogether terrible,' she said. 'You have some good points.'

I waited, raising my eyebrows.

'Such as,' she said, 'you have really nice clothes.'

'Piss off,' I told her, and she laughed, putting her hand over her mouth, so I laughed too. Really, I don't know what I'd expected. I would have said the same thing to her.

She wouldn't let me drive when I left. She moved my car around the corner – if it was parked out front her mom would be pissed – then drove me to Bendo, where I had to swear I would only have one more beer and then call Jess for a ride home. I promised. Then I went inside, had two beers, and decided not to bug Jess just yet. Instead I set myself up at the bar, with a decent view of the room, and decided to stew for a while.

I don't know how long it was before I saw her. One minute I was arguing with the bartender, a tall, gangly guy named Nathan, about classic rock guitarists, and the next I turned my head and caught a glimpse of her in the mirror behind the bar. Her hair was flat, her face a little sweaty. She looked drunk, but I would have known her anywhere. It was everybody else who always liked to think she was gone for good.

I wiped off my face, ran my fingers through my hair, trying to give it some life. She stared back at me as I did this, knowing as well as I that these were just smoke and mirrors, little tricks. Behind her and me the crowd was thickening, and I could feel people pressing up against me, leaning forward for drinks. And the sick thing? In a way, I was almost happy to see her. The worst part of me, out in the flesh. Blinking back at me in the dim light, daring me to call her a name other than my own.

Truth be told, I used to be worse. Much worse.

I hardly ever drank much any more. Or smoked pot. Or went off with guys I didn't know that well into dark corners, or dark cars, or dark rooms. Weird how it never worked in the daylight, when you could actually see the topography of someone's face, the lines and bumps, the scars. In the dark everyone felt the same: the edges blurred. When I think of myself then, what I was like two years ago, I feel like a wound in a bad place, prone to be bumped on corners or edges. Never able to heal.

It wasn't the drinking or the smoking that was really the problem. It was the other thing, the one harder to admit out loud. Nice girls didn't do what I did. Nice girls waited. But even before it happened, I'd never counted myself as a nice girl.

It was sophomore year, and Lissa's next-door neighbour Albert, a senior, was having a party. Lissa's parents were out of town, and we were all sleeping over, sneaking into their liquor cabinet and mixing anything we found together, then chasing it with Diet Coke: rum, vodka, peppermint schnapps. To this day I couldn't stomach cherry brandy, not even in the torts my mother loved from Milton's Market. The smell of it alone made me gag.

We never would have been invited to Albert's, being sophomores, and weren't bold enough to even consider crashing. But we did go out on Lissa's back porch with our spiked Diet Cokes and sneaked cigarettes we'd stolen from Chloe's grandmother, who smoked menthols. (Which also, to this day, made me gag.) Some guy, who was already drunk and slurring, waved us over. After a bit of whispered conferring, which consisted of Lissa saying we couldn't and me and Chloe overruling her, we went.

That was the first night I ever got really drunk. It was a bad start with the cherry brandy, and an hour later I found myself making my way across Albert's living room, clutching an easy chair for support. Everything was spinning, and I could see Lissa and Chloe and Jess sitting on a couch in the living room, where some girl was teaching them how to play quarters. The music was really loud, and someone had broken a vase in the foyer. It was blue, and the pieces were still scattered everywhere, strewn across the lime carpet. I remember thinking, in my blurry state, that it looked like sea glass.

It was one of Albert's friends, a really popular senior guy, who I bumped into on the stairs. He'd been flirting with me all night, pulling me into his lap while we played shithead, and I'd liked it, felt vindicated, like it proved I wasn't just some stupid sophomore. When he said we should hang out and talk, alone, I knew where we were going and why. Even then, I wasn't new to this.

We went into Albert's bedroom and started kissing, there in the dark, as he fumbled for a light switch. Once he found it I could make out a Pink Floyd poster, stacks of CDs, Elle McPherson on the wall with December beneath her. He was easing me back, toward the bed, and then we were lying down, all so quick.

I'd always prided myself on having the upper hand. I had my patented moves, the push offs and casual squirm, easily utilised to slow things down. But this time, they weren't working. Every time I moved one of his hands another seemed to be on me, and it seemed like all my strength had seeped down to my toes. It didn't help that I was so drunk that my balance was off, my equilibrium shot. And it had felt so good, for a while.

God. The rest comes in bursts when I do reach that far back, always these crazy sharp details: how fast it was all happening, the way I kept coming in and out of it, one second vivid, the next lost. He was on me and everything was spinning and all I could feel was this weight, heavy, pushing me backward until I feel like Alice, being sucked into the rabbit hole. It was not how I wanted my first time to be.

When it was over, I told him I felt sick and ran for the bathroom, locking the door with my hands shaking, unable at first to perform even that easiest of operations. Then I gripped the sink, gasping hard into it, my own breath coming back at me, amplified, rattling my ears. When I lifted my head up and looked in the mirror, it was her face I saw then. Drunk. Pale. Easy. And scared, unsteady, still gasping as she looked back at me, wondering what she had done.

'Nope.' The bartender shook his head, plunking a cup of coffee in front of me. 'She's cut off.'

I wiped my face with my hand and looked at the guy beside me, shrugging. 'I'm fine,' I said. Or slurred. Maybe. 'I only had a couple.'

'I know. They don't know anything.' We'd been talking for about an hour now, and this was what I knew: his name was Sherman, he was a junior at some college I'd never heard of in Minnesota, and in the last ten minutes he'd progressively slid his leg closer and closer to mine while trying to pass it off as just the crowd jostling him. Now he shook a cigarette out of the pack in his hand, then offered it to me. I shook my head and he lit it, sucking down smoke and then blowing it straight up in the air. 'So,' he said, 'a girl like you must have a boyfriend.'

'Nope,' I said, poking at my coffee with the spoon.

'I don't believe you,' he said, picking up his drink. 'Are you lying to me?'

I sighed. This entire scenario was like the default talk-to-a-girl-at-a-bar script, and I was only playing along because I wasn't entirely sure I could get off my bar stool without stumbling. At least Jess was coming. I'd called her. Hadn't I?

'It's the truth,' I told him. 'I'm really just such a bitch.'

He looked surprised at this, but not necessarily in a bad way. In fact, he looked kind of intrigued, as if I'd just admitted I wore leather panties or was double-jointed. 'Now, who told you that?'

'Everyone,' I said.

'I've got something that'll cheer you up,' he said.

'I bet you do.'

'No, really.' He raised his eyebrows at me, then pantomimed holding a joint between two fingers. 'Out in the car. Come with me and I'll show you.'

I shook my head. Like I was that stupid. Any more. 'Nope. I'm waiting for a ride.'

He leaned closer to me: he smelled like aftershave, something strong. 'I'll make sure you get home. Come on.' And then he put his hand on my arm, curling his fingers around my elbow.

'Let go,' I said, trying to tug my arm back.

'Don't be like that,' he said, almost affectionately.

'I'm serious,' I told him, jerking my elbow. He held on. 'Let go.'

'Oh come on, Emmy,' he said, finishing his drink. He couldn't even get my stupid name right. 'I don't bite.'

Then he started to tug me off my stool, which normally I would have made more difficult, but again, my balance wasn't exactly right on just then. Before I knew it I was on my feet, then getting yanked through the crowd.

'I said let go, you stupid asshole!' I pulled my arm loose, hard, and it flew up, smacking him in the face and sending him stumbling, just slightly, backward. Now people were looking at us, in that mildly-interesting-at-least-until-the-music-starts-again kind of way. How had I let this happen? One nasty remark from Chris and I'm bar trash, fighting in public with some guy named Sherman? I could feel the shame rising up in me, flushing my face. Everyone was looking at me.

'Okay, okay, what's going on here?' That was Adrian, the bouncer, too late as usual for the real commotion but always up for a chance to throw his little bit of power around.

'We're just talking at the bar and we go to go outside and she freaks,' Sherman said, pulling at his collar. 'Crazy bitch. She *hit* me.'

I was standing there, rubbing my arm, hating myself. I knew if I turned around I'd see that girl again, so weak and screwed up. She'd go to the parking lot, no problem. After that night at the party, she'd got a reputation for it. I hated her for that. So much I could feel a lump rising in my throat, which I pressed down because I was better than that, much better. I wasn't Lissa: I didn't trot my pain out to show around. I kept it better hidden than anyone. I did.

'God, this is swelling,' Sherman whined, rubbing his eye. What a wuss. If I'd hit him on purpose, well, then that would have been different. But it was an accident. I didn't even really have my arm in it.

'You want me to call the police?' Adrian asked.

I was suddenly so hot, and I could feel my shirt sticking to my back with sweat. The room tilted, just a bit, and I closed my eyes.

'Oh, man,' I heard someone say, and suddenly there was a hand enclosing mine, squeezing slightly. 'There you are! I'm only fifteen minutes late, honey, no need to cause a commotion.'

I opened my eyes to see Dexter standing beside me. Holding my hand. I would have yanked it away, but honestly I thought better of it, after what had just happened.

'This doesn't concern you,' Adrian said to Dexter.

'It's my fault, though,' Dexter replied in that quick, cheery way of his, as if we were all friends who met coincidentally on a street corner. 'It is. See, I was late. And that makes my sweetums so foul tempered.'

'God,' I said under my breath.

'Sweetums?' Sherman repeated.

'She clocked him,' Adrian told Dexter. 'Might have to call the cops.'

Dexter looked at me, then at Sherman. 'She hit you?'

Now Sherman didn't seem so sure, instead pulling at his collar and glancing around. 'Well, not exactly.'

'Honey!' Dexter looked at me. 'Did you really? But she's just a little thing.'

'Watch it,' I said under my breath.

'You want to get arrested?' he said back, just as low. Then, back in cheery mode, he added, 'I mean, I've

118

seen her get mad before, but hit somebody? My Remy? She's not even ninety pounds soaking wet.'

'Either I call the cops or I don't,' Adrian said. 'But I got to get back to the door.'

'Forget it,' Sherman told him. 'I'm out of here.' And then he slunk off, but not before I noticed that yes, his eye was swelling. Wimp.

'You.' Adrian pointed at me. 'Go home. Now.'

'Done,' Dexter said. 'And thank you so much for your cordial, professional handling of this situation.'

We left Adrian there, mulling over whether he'd been insulted. As soon as we were outside, I yanked my hand loose from Dexter's and started down the stairs, toward the pay phone.

'What, no thank-you?' he asked me.

'I can take care of myself,' I told him. 'I'm not some weak woman who needs to be saved.'

'Obviously,' he said. 'You just almost got arrested for assault.'

I kept walking.

'And,' he continued, darting ahead of me and walking backward so I had no choice but to look at him, 'I saved your butt. So you, Remy, should be a little more grateful. Are you drunk?'

'No,' I snapped, although I may or may not have just tripped over something. 'I'm fine. I just want to call for a ride and go home, okay? I had a really shitty night.'

He dropped back beside me, sticking his hands in his pockets. 'Really.'

'Yes.'

We were at the phone now. I reached into my pockets: no change. And suddenly it just seemed to hit me all at once – the argument with Chris, the fight in the bar, my own pity party, and, right on the tails of that, all the drinks I'd consumed in the last few hours. My head hurt, I was deadly thirsty, and now I was stuck. I put my hand over my eyes and took a few good, deep breaths to steady myself.

Don't cry, for God's sakes, I told myself. *This isn't you. Not any more. Breathe.*

But it wasn't working. Nothing was working tonight.

'Come on,' he said quietly. 'Tell me what's wrong.'

'No,' I sniffled, and hated the way it sounded. Weak. 'Go away.'

'Remy,' he replied. 'Tell me.'

I shook my head. How did I know this would be any different? The story could have been the same, easily: me drunk, in a deserted place. Someone there, reaching out for me. It had happened before. Who could blame me for my cold, hard heart?

And that did it. I was crying, so angry at myself, but I couldn't stop. The only time I ever allowed myself to be this weak was at home, in my closet, staring up at those stars with my father's voice filling my ears. And I wished so much that he was here, even though I knew it was stupid, that he didn't even know me to save me. He'd said it himself, in the song: he'd let me down. But still.

'Remy,' Dexter said quietly. He wasn't touching me, but his voice was very close, and very soft. 'It's okay. Don't cry.'

Later, it would take me a minute to remember how exactly it happened. If I turned around and moved forward first, or he did. I just knew we didn't meet halfway. It was just a short distance really, not worth squabbling over. And maybe it didn't matter so much whether he took the step or I did. All I knew was that he was there.

7

I woke up with my mouth dry, my head pounding, and the sound of guitar music coming from the direction of the door across the room. It was dark, but there was a slant of light stretching right to where I was, falling across the end of a bed in which I had apparently, up until now, been sleeping.

I sat up quick, and my head spun. God. This was familiar. Not the place but this feeling, waking up in a strange bed, completely discombobulated. Moments like this, I was just glad no one was there to witness my absolute shame as I verified that yes, my trousers were still on and yes, I was still wearing a bra and yes, okay, nothing major had happened because, well, girls just know.

Jesus. I closed my eyes, taking a deep breath.

Okay, okay, I told myself, *just think for a second*. I looked around me for any distinguishing details that might clarify what, exactly, had happened since the last thing I remembered, which was me and Dexter at the phone booth. There was a window to my left, along the sill of which there was what appeared to be a series of snow globes. A chair across the room was covered with clothes, and there was a bunch of CDs stacked in piles beside the door. Finally, at the end of the bed, in a pile, were my sandals, the sweater I'd been wearing around my waist, and my money and ID. Had I put them there? No way. Even drunk, I would have folded them. I mean, please.

Suddenly I heard someone laugh, and then a few guitar chords, playing softly.

'*You gave me a potato*,' someone sang, as there was another snort of laughter, '*but I wanted a kumquat . . . I asked you for lovin'* . . . *You said* – hey, wait, is that my cottage cheese?'

'I'm hungry,' someone protested. 'And the only other thing in here is relish.'

'Then eat the relish,' another voice said. 'The cottage cheese is *off limits*.'

'What's your problem, man?'

'House rules, John Miller. You don't buy food, you don't eat. Full stop.'

A refrigerator door slammed, there was a second of silence, and then the guitar started up again. 'He's such a baby,' someone said. 'Okay. So where were we?'

'Kumquat.' This time I recognised the voice. It was Dexter.

'Kumquat,' the other voice repeated. 'So . . .'

'*I asked you for lovin'*,' Dexter sang. '*You said, do what?*'

I pushed off the blankets that were covering me, got out of the bed, then put on my shoes. For some reason, this made me feel better, more in control. Then I stuck my ID back in my pocket, slipped on my sweater, and sat down to think.

First off: the time. No clock, but I could see what looked like a tangled phone cord poking out from under the bed, half buried under a couple of shirts.

This place was a mess. I dialled the time and temperature number, listened to the five-day forecast, and then found out it was, at the tone, 12:22 AM. Beep.

It was really bothering me that the bed wasn't made. But it wasn't my problem. I needed to get home.

I dialled Jess's number and bit my pinky nail, awaiting the inevitable wrath.

'Mmmpht.'

'Jess?'

'Remy Starr. I am *so* going to kick your ass.'

'Hey, okay, but listen—'

'Where the hell are you?' She was wide awake now, managing to sound totally pissed off and keep her voice down at the same time. Jess was multi-talented. 'Do you know that Chloe has been on me for the entire night about you? She said she dropped you at Bendo for one beer at eight-thirty, for God's sake.'

'Well, see, I ended up staying a little bit longer.'

'Clearly. And I ended up driving there to look for you, hearing that you were not only drunk but also in a fight and, to top it off, had left with some guy and completely disappeared. What the hell are you thinking, Remy?'

'I understand that you're mad, okay? But right now I just need to—'

'Do you think I enjoy repeated phone calls from Chloe telling how if you're dead or something it's my fault because, obviously, I was supposed to have some kind of psychic connection that would enable me to know I was supposed to pick you up without the benefit of a phone call?'

This time, I was quiet.

'Well?' she snapped.

'Look,' I said, whispering. 'I screwed up. Big time. But right now I'm at this guy's house and I need out and please can you just help me?'

'Tell me where you are.'

I did. 'Jess, I really—'

Click. Okay, well, now we could both be pissed at me. But at least I was getting home.

I walked to the door and leaned against it. The guitar music was still going, and I could hear Dexter singing that line about the potato and kumquat, again and again, as if waiting for inspiration to strike. I inched the door open a little more, then peered through the crack. I could see right into the house's kitchen, where there was a beat-up Formica table with a bunch of mismatched chairs, a fridge covered with pictures, and a brown-and-green-striped couch pulled up against the back window. Dexter and the guy I recognised as Ted, the guitarist, were sitting at the table, a couple of cans of beer between them. The dog I'd met earlier, Monkey, was asleep on the couch.

'Maybe *kumquat* isn't the right word,' Dexter said, leaning back in his chair – a wooden one painted yellow – exactly the way your teachers in school always told you not to, balancing on the back legs. 'Maybe we need another kind of fruit.'

Ted picked at the guitar's strings. 'Such as?'

'Well, I don't know.' Dexter sighed, pulling both hands through his hair. It was so curly this just added volume, springing loose as he let his arms drop. 'What about pomegranate?'

'Too long.'

'Nectarines?'

Ted cocked his head to the side, then strummed another chord. '*You gave me potato but I wanted a nectarine . . .*'

They looked at each other. 'Terrible,' Dexter decided.

'Yup.'

I shut the door back, wincing as it made a tiny click. It would have been bad enough to face Dexter after what had – or hadn't – happened. But the thought of there being someone else there was enough to make a full-on window escape necessary.

I crawled up on the bed and pushed the snow globes – God, who over the age of ten collected snow globes? – aside, then undid the latch. It stuck at first, but I put some shoulder in it and up it went, rattling slightly. Not much space, but enough.

One arm through, about to start wriggling, I had a small but noticeable pang of guilt. I mean, he had got me to a safe place. And, judging by the taste in my mouth and past experience, it was highly likely that I had puked at some point. Since I didn't remember getting there, he must have had to drag me. Or carry me. Oh, the shame.

I dropped back down on the bed. I had to do something decent here. But Jess was on her way and I didn't have many options. I looked around me: not enough time to straighten up the room, even though my fast cleaning skills were legendary. If I left a note, that was an open invitation to get back in touch with me, and honestly I wasn't sure I wanted that. There was nothing else to do but make the bed. Which I did, quickly and thoroughly, with hospital corners and the pillow trick that was my trade secret. Even at the Four Seasons they couldn't do better.

So it was with a less heavy conscience that I pushed myself through the (small) window, trying to be stealthy, and pretty much succeeding until I kicked the back of the house on my dismount, leaving a scuff mark by the electric meter. No biggie. Then I cut through the side yard to find Jess.

There was a time when I'd been famous for my window escapes. It was my preferred way to exit, always, even if I had a mostly clear path to the door. Maybe it was a shame thing, a punishment I chose to inflict upon myself because I knew, in my heart, that what I had done was bad. It was my penance.

Two streets over, on Caldwell, I stepped off the kerb by the stop sign and held up my hand, squinting in Jess's headlights as she came closer. She reached over, pushed open the passenger door, and then stared straight ahead, impassive, as I got in.

'Just like old times,' she said flatly. 'How was it?'

I sighed. It was too late to go into details, even with her. 'Old,' I said.

She turned up the radio and we cut through a side street, then passed Dexter's house on our way out of the neighbourhood. The front door was open, the porch dark, but from the light inside I could see Monkey sitting there, his nose pressed against the screen. Dexter probably didn't even know I was gone yet. But just in case, I slid down, dropping out of sight, although I knew in the dark, and at this speed, he couldn't have found me if he tried.

This time, I awoke to tapping.

Not normal tapping: tapping in a rhythm that I recognised. A song. It sounded, in fact, like 'Oh, Tannenbaum'.

I opened one eye, then looked around me. I was in my room, my bed. Everything in place, the floor clean, my universe just as I liked it. Except for the tapping.

I rolled over, burying my face in my pillow, assuming it was one of my mother's cats, which were all having minor breakdowns in her absence, attacking my door in an effort to get me to feed them more Fancy Feast, which they devoured by the case.

'Go away,' I mumbled into my pillow. 'I mean it.'

And then, just then, the window right over my bed suddenly opened. Slid up, smooth as silk, scaring me to death, but not quite as much as Dexter shooting through it, head first, limbs flailing. One of his feet hit my bedside table, sending my clock flying across the room to crash into a closet door with a bang, while his elbow clocked me right in the gut. The only thing slightly redeeming about any of this was that he had so much momentum behind him he missed the bed entirely, instead landing with a thunk, belly-flop style, on the throw rug by my bureau. The whole commotion, while seemingly complicated, was over in a matter of seconds.

Then it was very quiet.

Dexter lifted up his head, glanced around, then put it back on the carpet. He still seemed a little stunned by the impact. I knew how he felt: I had a first-floor window, and climbing in off the trellis, as I had many times, was a bitch. 'You could at least,' he said, eyes closed, 'have said good-bye.'

I sat up, pulling my blanket up to my chest. It was so surreal, him splayed out on my carpet like he was. I wasn't even sure how he'd found my house. In fact, the entire trajectory of our relationship, all the way back to the day we'd met, was like one long dream, bumpy and strange, full of things that should have made sense but didn't. What had he said to me that first day? Something about natural chemistry. He claimed he'd noticed it right from the start, and maybe it was an explanation, of sorts, of why we kept coming together, again and again. Or maybe he was just too damn persistent. Either way, I felt that we were at a crossroads. A choice had to be made.

He sat up, rubbing his face with one hand. Not much the worse for wear: at least nothing was broken. Then he looked at me, as if now it was my turn to say or do something.

'You don't want to get involved with me,' I told him. 'You really don't.'

He stood up then, wincing a bit, and walked over to the bed, sitting down. Then he leaned in to me, sliding his hand up my arm around the back of my neck, pulling me nearer to him, and for a second we just stayed like that, looking at each other. And I had a sudden flash of the night before, a part of memory opening up and falling into my hands again, where I could see it clearly. It was like a picture, a snapshot: a girl and boy standing in front of a phone booth. The girl had her hands over her eyes. The boy stood in front of her, watching. He was speaking, softly. And then, all of a sudden, the girl stepped forward, pressing her face into his chest as he lifted his hands to stroke her hair.

So it had been me. Maybe I'd known that all along, and that was why I had run. Because I didn't show weakness: I didn't depend on anyone. And if he'd been like the others, and just let me go, I would have been fine. It would have been easy to go on conveniently forgetting as I kept my heart clenched tight, away from where anyone could get to it.

Now, Dexter sat as close to me as I could remember him being. It seemed like this day could go in so many directions, like a spiderweb shooting out toward endless possibilities. Whenever you made a choice, especially one you'd been resisting, it always affected everything else, some in big ways, like a tremor beneath your feet, others in so tiny a shift you hardly noticed a change at all. But it was happening.

And so, while the rest of the world went on unaware, drinking their coffee, reading the sports page, and picking up their dry cleaning, I leaned forward and kissed Dexter, making a choice that would change everything. Maybe somewhere there was a ripple, a bit of a jump, some small shift in the universe, barely noticeable. I didn't feel it then. I felt only him kissing me back, easing me into the sunlight as I lost myself in the taste of him and felt the world go on, just as it always had, all around us.

July

8

'*Don't you give me no rotten tomato, 'cause all I ever wanted was your sweet potato.*' Dexter stopped as the music did. Now, all we could hear was the fridge rattling and Monkey snoring. 'Okay, so what else rhymes with *potato*?'

Ted strummed his guitar, looking at the ceiling. On the couch by the refrigerator, John Miller rolled over, his red head banging the wall.

'Anybody?' Dexter asked.

'Well,' Lucas said, crossing his legs, 'it depends on if you want a real rhyme, or a pseudo rhyme.'

Dexter looked at him. 'Pseudo rhyme,' he repeated.

'A real rhyme,' Lucas began, in what I already recognised as his eggbert voice, 'is tomato. But you could easily tack an *o* onto another word and make a rhyme of it, even if it's not grammatically correct. Like, say, relate-o. Or abate-o.'

'*Don't you give me no rotten tomato,*' Dexter sang, '*just 'cause to your crazy shit I cannot relate-o.*'

Silence. Ted plucked out another chord, then tightened a string.

'Needs work,' Lucas said. 'But I think we're getting somewhere.'

'Can you all just please shut up,' John Miller moaned from the couch, his voice muffled. 'I'm trying to *sleep*.'

'It's two in the afternoon, and this is the kitchen,' Ted told him. 'Go someplace else or quit bitching.'

'Boys, boys,' Dexter said.

Ted sighed. 'People, we need to focus on this. I want "The Potato Opus" to be ready for that show next week.'

' "The Potato Opus"?' Lucas said. 'Is that what it's called now?'

'Can you think of something better?'

Lucas was quiet for a second. 'Nope,' he said finally. 'Sure can't.'

'Then shut the hell up.' Ted picked up the guitar. 'From the top, first verse, with feeling.'

And so it went. Another day at the yellow house, where I'd been spending a fair amount of my free time lately. Not that I liked the setting, particularly; the place was a total dump, mostly because four guys lived there and none of them had ever been introduced formally to a bottle of bleach. There was rotting food in the fridge, something black and mildewy growing on the shower tiles, and some sort of unidentifiable rank smell coming from beneath the back deck. Only Dexter's room was decent, and that was because I had my limits. When I found dirty underwear under a couch cushion, or had to fight the fruit flies in the kitchen that were always swarming the garbage can, I at least could take comfort in the fact that his bed was made, his CDs stacked alphabetically, and the plug-in air freshener was working its pink, rose-shaped little heart out. All of this work on my part was a small price to pay, I figured, for my sanity.

Which, in truth, had been sorely tested lately, ever since my mother had returned from her honeymoon and set up her new marriage under our shared roof. All through the spring we'd had workmen passing through, hauling drywall and windows and tracking sawdust across the floors. They'd knocked out the wall of the old den, extending it into the backyard, and added a new master suite, complete with a new bathroom featuring a sunken tub and side-by-side sinks separated by blocks of coloured glass. Crossing over the threshold into what Chris and I had named 'the new wing' was like entering an entirely different house, which was pretty much my mother's intention. It was her matched set, with a new bedroom, a new husband, and new carpet. Her life was perfect. But as was often the case, the rest of us were still adjusting.

One problem was Don's stuff. Being a lifelong bachelor, he had certain objects that he'd grown attached to, very little of which fitted my mother's decorating scheme for the new wing. The only thing that even remotely reflected Don's taste in their bedroom, in fact, was a large Moroccan tapestry depicting various biblical tableaux. It was enormous and took up most of a wall, but it did match the carpet almost perfectly, and therefore constituted a compromise of taste that my mother could live with. The remainder of his belongings were exiled to the rest of the house, which meant that Chris and I had to adjust to living with Don's decor.

The first piece I noticed, a couple of days after their return, was a framed print by some Renaissance painter of a hugely buxom woman posing in a garden. Her fingers were big, pudgy, and white, and she was stretched across a couch, buck naked. She had huge breasts, which were hanging down off the couch, and she was eating grapes, a fistful in one hand, another about to drop into her mouth. It might have been art – a flexible term, in my opinion – but it was disgusting. Especially hanging on the wall over our kitchen table, where I had no choice but to look at it while I ate breakfast.

'Man,' Chris said to me the first morning it was there, about two days after Don had moved in. He was eating cereal, already dressed in his garage uniform. 'How much you think a woman like that weighed?'

I took a bite of my muffin, trying to concentrate on the newspaper in front of me. 'I have no idea,' I said.

'At least two-fifty,' Chris decided, slurping down another spoonful. 'Those breasts alone have to be five pounds. Maybe even seven.'

'Do we have to talk about this?'

'How can you not?' he said. 'God. It's right there. It's like trying to ignore the sun or something.'

And it wasn't just the picture. It was the modern art statue that now stood in the foyer that looked, frankly, like a big penis. (Was there a theme here? I'd never pegged Don for that type, but now I was starting to wonder.) Add to that the fancy set of Calphalon pots that now hung over our kitchen island and the red leather sofa in the living room, which just screamed Single Man on the Make to me, and it was no wonder I was feeling a little out of place. But then again, this house wasn't really mine to claim any more. Don was now permanent – supposedly – while I was of temporary status, gone come fall. For once, *I* was the one with an expiration date, and I was finding I didn't like it much.

Which explained, in some ways, why I was over at Dexter's so much. But there was another reason, one I wasn't so quick to admit. Even to myself.

For as long as I'd been dating, I'd had a mental flow chart, a schedule, of how things usually went. Relationships always started with that heady, swoonish period, where the other person is like some new invention that suddenly solves all life's worst problems, like losing socks in the dryer or toasting bagels without burning the edges. At this phase, which usually lasts about six weeks max, the other person is perfect. But at six weeks and two days, the cracks begin to show; not real structural damage yet, but little things that niggle and nag. Like the way they always assume you'll pay for your own movie, just because you did once, or how they use the dashboard of their car as an imaginary keyboard at long stoplights. Once, you might have thought this was cute, or endearing. Now, it annoys you, but not enough to change anything. Come week eight, though, the strain is starting to show. This person is, in fact, human, and here's where most relationships splinter and die. Because either you can stick around and deal with these problems, or ease out gracefully, knowing that at some point in the not-too-distant future, there will emerge another perfect person, who will fix everything, at least for six weeks.

I knew this pattern even before my first real boyfriend, because I'd seen my mother go through it several times already. With marriages, the pattern is stretched out, adjusted, like working with dog years: the six weeks becomes a year, sometimes two. But it's the same. That was why it was always so easy to figure out how long my stepfathers would last. It all comes down to maths.

If I did the maths with Dexter, on paper it was perfect. We'd come in well under the three-month mark, with me leaving for college just as the shine was wearing off. But the problem was that Dexter wasn't cooperating. If my theories of relationships were plotted geographically, Dexter wasn't even left of centre or far out in right field. He was on another map altogether, rapidly approaching the distant corner and headed into the unknown.

First, he was very gangly. I'd never liked gangly guys, and Dexter was clumsy, skinny, and always in motion. It was not surprising to me now that our relationship had started with him crashing into me in various ways, since I now knew he moved through the world with a series of flying elbows, banged knees, and flailing limbs. In the short time we'd been together, he'd already broken my alarm clock, crushed one of my beaded necklaces underfoot, and managed, somehow, to leave a huge scuff mark on my ceiling. I am not joking. He was always jiggling his knees, or drumming his fingers, as if revving up, just waiting for the chequered flag to drop so he could spin out at full speed. I found myself constantly reaching over and trying to quiet him, covering his knee or fingers with my hand, thinking it would silence them, when instead I would be caught up in it with him, jangling along, as if whatever current charged him was now flowing through me.

Point two: he was a slob. His shirt-tail was always out, his tie usually had a stain, his hair, while curly and thick, sprung out from his head wildly in a mad-scientist sort of fashion. Also, his shoelaces were continually untied. He was all loose ends, and I hated loose ends. If I could ever have got him to stand still long enough, I knew I would have been unable to resist tucking, tying, smoothing, organising, as if he were a particularly messy closet just screaming for my attention. But instead I found myself gritting my teeth, riding the wave of my natural anxiety, because this wasn't permanent, me and him, and to think so would only hurt both of us.

Which led to point three: he really liked me. Not in an only-until-the-end-of-the-summer way, which was safest. In fact, he never talked about the future at all, as if we had so much time, and there wasn't a definite end point to our relationship. I, of course, wanted to make things clear from the start: that I was leaving, no attachments, the standard spiel I repeated in my head finally spoken aloud. But whenever I tried to do this, he evaded so easily that it was as if he could read my mind, see what was coming, and for once move gracefully to sidestep the issue entirely.

Now, as work on 'The Potato Song' broke up so that Ted could go to work, Dexter came over and stood in front of me, stretching his arms over his head. 'Total turn-on seeing a real band at work, isn't it?'

'*Relate-o* is a lame rhyme,' I said, 'pseudo or not.'

He winced, then smiled. 'It's a work in progress,' he explained.

I put down my crossword puzzle – I'd finished about half of it – and he picked it up, glancing at what I'd finished. 'Impressive,' he said. 'And of course, Miss Remy does her crosswords in ink. What, you don't make mistakes?'

'Nope.'

'You're here, though,' he said.

'Okay,' I admitted, 'maybe one.'

He grinned again. We'd only been seeing each other for a few weeks now, but this easy give-and-take still surprised me. From that very first day in my room, I felt like we'd somehow skipped the formalities of the Beginning of a Relationship: those awkward moments when you're not all over each other and are still feeling out the other person's boundaries and limits. Maybe this was because we'd been circling each other for a while before he finally catapulted through my window. But if I let myself think about it much – and I didn't – I had flashes of realising that I'd been comfortable with him even at the very start. Clearly, he'd been comfortable with me, grabbing my hand as he had that first day. As if he knew, even then, that we'd be here now.

'I bet you,' he said to me, 'that I can name more states by the time that woman comes out of the dry cleaners than you can.'

I looked at him. We were sitting outside of Joie, both of us on our lunch break, me drinking a Diet Coke, him snarfing down a sleeve of Fig Newtons. 'Dexter,' I said, 'it's hot.'

'Come on,' he said, sliding his hand over my leg. 'I'll bet you.'

'No.'

'Scared?'

'Again, no.'

He cocked his head to the side, then squeezed my knee. His foot, of course, was tapping. 'Let's go. She's about to walk in. When the door shuts behind her, time's on.'

'Oh, God.' I said. 'What's the bet?'

'Five bucks.'

'Boring. And too easy.'

'Ten bucks.'

'Okay. And you have to buy dinner.'

'Done.'

We watched as the woman, who was wearing pink shorts and a T-shirt and carrying an armful of wrinkled dress shirts, pulled open the door to the cleaners. As it swung shut, I said, 'Maine.'

'North Dakota.'

'Florida.'

'Virginia.'

'California.'

'Delaware.' I was keeping track on my fingers: he'd been known to cheat but denied it with great vehemence, so I always had to have proof. Challenges, to Dexter, were like those duels in the old movies, where men in white suits smacked each other across the face with gloves, and all honour was at stake. So far, I hadn't won them all, but I hadn't backed down either. I was, after all, still new at this.

Dexter's challenges, apparently, were legendary. The first one I'd seen had been between him and John Miller. It was a couple of days after Dexter and I had got together, one of the first times I'd gone over to the yellow house with him. We found John Miller sitting at the kitchen table in his pyjamas, eating a banana. There was a big bunch of them on the table in front of him, seemingly out of place in a kitchen where I now knew the major food groups consisted of Slurpees and beer.

'What's up with the bananas?' Dexter asked him, pulling out a chair and sitting down.

John Miller, who still looked half asleep, glanced up and said, 'Fruit of the Month Club. My nana gave it to me for my birthday.'

'Potassium,' Dexter said. 'You need that every day, you know.'

John Miller yawned, as if used to this kind of stupid information. Then he went back to his banana.

'I bet,' Dexter said suddenly, in the voice I later would come to recognise as the one that always preceded a challenge, deep and game show host-like, 'that you can't eat ten bananas.'

John Miller finished chewing the bite in his mouth, then swallowed. 'I bet,' he replied, 'that you're right.'

'It's a challenge,' Dexter said. Then he nudged out a chair, with a knee that was already jiggling, for me, and said, in the same low, slow voice, 'Will you take it?'

'Are you crazy?'

'For ten bucks.'

'I am not eating ten bananas for ten bucks,' John Miller said indignantly.

'It's a dollar a banana!' Dexter said.

'And furthermore,' John Miller went on, tossing the now-empty peel at an overflowing garbage can by the back door, and missing, 'this double-dare shit of yours is getting old, Dexter. You can't just go around throwing down challenges whenever you feel like it.'

'Are you passing on the challenge?'

'Will you stop using that voice?'

'Twenty bucks,' Dexter said. 'Twenty bucks . . .'

'No,' John Miller told him.

'. . . and I'll clean the bathroom.'

This, clearly, changed things. John Miller looked at the bananas, then at Dexter. Then at the bananas again. 'Does the one I just ate count as one?'

'No.'

John Miller slapped the table. 'What? It's not even to my stomach yet, for godsakes!'

Dexter thought for a second. 'Okay. We'll let Remy call this one.'

'What?' I said. They were both looking at me.

'You're an unbiased view,' Dexter explained.

'She's your girlfriend,' John Miller complained. 'That's not unbiased!'

'She is not my girlfriend.' Dexter looked at me, as if this might upset me, which was evidence that he didn't know me at all. He said, 'What I mean is, we may be

145

seeing each other' – and here he paused, as if waiting for me to chime in with something, which I didn't, so he went on – 'but you are your own person with your opinions and convictions. Correct?'

'I'm not his girlfriend,' I told John Miller.

'She loves me,' Dexter said to him, as an aside, and I felt my face flame. 'Anyway,' he said, moving on breezily, 'Remy? What do you think? Does it count or not?'

'Well,' I said, 'I think it should count somehow. Perhaps as half.'

'Half!' Dexter looked at me as if he was just so pleased, as if he had carved me out of clay himself. 'Perfect. So, if you choose to accept this challenge, you must eat nine and a half bananas.'

John Miller thought about this for a second. Later, I would learn that money was always scarce at the yellow house, and these challenges provided some balance of cash flow from one person to another. Twenty bucks was food and beer money for at least a couple of days. And it was really only nine bananas. And a half.

'Okay,' John Miller said. And they shook on it.

Before the challenge could happen, witnesses had to be gathered. Ted was brought in from the back deck, along with a girl he'd been seeing, introduced to me as Scary Mary (I chose not to ask), and, after a futile search for the keyboardist, Lucas, Dexter's dog Monkey was agreed upon as a suitable replacement. We all gathered around the table, or on the long, ugly brown couch that was next to the refrigerator, while

John Miller did some deep breathing and stretching, as if preparing for a fifty-yard dash.

'Okay,' Ted, the only one with a working watch and therefore timekeeper, said, 'Go!'

If you've never seen someone take on a food challenge, as I had not at that point, you might expect it to actually be exciting. Except that the challenge was not to eat nine and a half bananas quickly: it was just to eat nine and a half bananas. So by banana four or so, boredom set in, and Ted and Scary Mary went to the Waffle House, leaving me, Dexter, and Monkey to wait out the next five and a half bananas. It turned out we didn't have to: John Miller conceded defeat in the middle of banana six, then carefully got to his feet and went to the bathroom.

'I hope you didn't kill him,' I told Dexter as the door shut behind him, the lock clicking.

'No way,' he said easily, stretching back in his chair. 'You should have seen him last month, when he ate fifteen eggs in a row. Then we were worried. He turned bright red.'

'You know,' I said, 'funny how it's never *you* having to eat vast quantities of things.'

'Not true. I just moved on after completing the master of all challenges back in April.'

I hated to even ask what would earn such a title, but curiosity got the better of me. 'Which was?'

'Thirty-two ounces of Miracle Whip,' he said. 'In twenty minutes flat.'

Just the thought of this made my stomach twist. I hated mayonnaise, and any derivation thereof:

egg salad, tuna salad, even devilled eggs. 'That's disgusting.'

'I know.' He said it proudly. 'I could never top it, even if I tried.'

I had to wonder what kind of person got such satisfaction from constant competitiveness. And Dexter would make challenges about anything, whether it was in his control or not. Some recent favourites included I Bet You a Quarter the Next Car That Passes Is Either Blue or Green, Five Bucks Says I Can Make Something Edible Out of the Canned Corn, French-Fried Potato Sticks, and Mustard in the Pantry, and, of course, How Many States Can You Name While That Woman Picks Up Her Dry Cleaning?

I, personally, was up to twenty. Dexter was at nineteen and experiencing a bit of a brain cramp.

'California,' he said finally, casting a nervous look at the front of the cleaners, where we could see the woman talking to someone behind the counter.

'Already said it,' I told him.

'Wisconsin.'

'Montana.'

'South Carolina.'

The door opened: it was her. 'Game over,' I said. 'I win.'

'You do not!'

I held up my fingers, where I'd been keeping track. 'I win by one,' I said. 'Pay up.'

He started to reach into his pockets, sighing, then instead pulled me closer, spreading his fingers around my waist, burying his face in my neck.

'Nope,' I said, putting my hands on his chest, 'won't work.'

'I'll be your slave,' he said into my ear, and I felt a chill run up my back, then cast it off just as quickly, reminding myself again that I always had a boyfriend in summer, someone that caught my eye after school was finished and usually lasted right up until the beach trip my family took each August. The only difference this time was that I was going west instead of east. And I liked being able to think about it that way, in terms of a compass, something set in stone that would remain, unchanged, long after I was gone.

Besides, I knew already we would never work long-term. He was so imperfect already, his cracks and fissures apparent. I could only imagine what structural damage lay beneath, deep in the foundations. But still, it was hard to keep my head clear as he kissed me there, in July, with another challenge behind me. After all, I was up now, and it still seemed like we had time.

'The question is, has he been given The Speech yet?' Jess asked.

'No,' Chloe told her. 'The question is, have you slept with him yet?'

They all looked at me. It wasn't rude for them to ask, of course: usually this was common knowledge – once, common assumption. But now I hesitated, which was unnerving.

'No,' I said finally. There was a quick intake of breath – shock! – from somebody, then silence.

'Wow,' Lissa said finally. 'You *like* him.'

'It's not a big deal,' I said, not refuting this exactly, which set off another round of silence and exchanged looks. Out at the Spot, with the sun going down, I felt the trampoline bounce lightly beneath me and leaned back, spreading my fingers over the cool metal of the springs.

'No Speech, no sex,' Jess said, summing up. 'This is dangerous.'

'Maybe he's different,' Lissa offered, stirring her drink with one finger.

'Nobody's different,' Chloe told her. 'Remy knows that better than any of us.'

It says something about my absolute adherence to a plan concerning relationships that my best friends had terms, like outline headings, detailing my actions. The Speech usually came right as the heady, romantic, fun-new-boyfriend phase was boiling to full steam. It was my way of hitting the brakes, slowly downshifting, and usually involved me pulling whatever Ken was in my life at that time aside to say something like: hey, I really like you and we're having fun, but you know, I can't get too serious because I'm going to the beach/really going to focus on school come fall/just getting over someone and not up to anything long-term. This was the summer speech: the winter/holiday one was pretty much the same, except you inserted I'm going skiing/really going to have to rally until graduation/dealing with a lot of family crap for the last part. And usually, guys took it one of two ways. If they *really* liked me, as in wear-my-class-ring-love-me-always, they bolted, which was just as well. If they liked me but were willing to slow down, to see boundaries, they nodded and saved face by saying they felt the same way. And then I was free to proceed to the next step, which – and I'm not proud – usually involved sleeping with them.

But not right away. Never right away, not any more. I liked to have enough time invested to see a few cracks and get rid of anyone whose failings I knew I couldn't deal with in the long term, i.e., more than the six weeks that usually encompassed the fun-new-boyfriend phase.

Once, I was easy. Now, I was choosy. See? Big difference.

And besides, something was different about Dexter. Whenever I tried to revert to my set outline, something stopped me. I could give him the talk, and he'd probably be fine with it. I could sleep with him, and he'd be fine – more than fine – with that too. But somewhere, deep in my conscious mind, something niggled me that maybe he wouldn't, that maybe he'd think less of me, or something. I knew it was stupid.

And besides, I'd just been busy. That was probably it, really.

Chloe opened her bottled water, took a swig, then chased it with a sip from the tiny bottle of bourbon in her hand. 'What are you doing?' she asked me, point blank.

'I'm just having fun,' I replied, taking a swig of my Diet Zip. It seemed easy to say this, having just run through it in my head. 'He's leaving at the end of the summer too, you know.'

'Then why haven't you given him The Speech?' Jess asked.

'I just . . .' I said, and then shook my cup, stalling. 'I haven't thought about it, to be honest.'

They looked at one another, considering the implications of this. Lissa said, 'I think he's really nice, Remy. He's sweet.'

'He's clumsy,' Jess grumbled. 'He keeps stepping on my feet.'

'Maybe,' Chloe said, as if it was just occurring to her, 'you just have big feet.'

'Maybe,' Jess replied, 'you should shut up.'

Lissa sighed, closing her eyes. 'You guys. Please. We're talking about Remy.'

'We don't have to talk about Remy,' I said. 'We really don't. Let's talk about somebody else.'

There was silence for a second: I sucked down some more of my drink, Lissa lit a cigarette. Finally Chloe said, 'You know, the other night Dexter said he'd give me ten bucks if I could stand on my head for twenty minutes. What the hell does that mean?'

They all looked at me. I said, 'Just ignore him. Next?'

'I think Adam's seeing someone else,' Lissa said suddenly.

'Okay,' I said. 'Now, *see*, this is interesting.'

Lissa ran her finger over the rim of her cup, her head down, one curl bouncing slightly with the movement. It had been about a month since Adam had dumped her, and she'd moved through her weepy stage to just kind of sad all the time, with occasional moments when I actually heard her laugh out loud, then stop, as if she'd forgotten she wasn't supposed to be happy.

'Who is she?' Chloe asked.

'I don't know. She drives a red Mazda.'

Jess looked at me, shaking her head. I said, 'Lissa, have you been driving by his house?'

'No,' she said, and then looked up at us. We, of course, were all staring back at her, knowing she was lying. 'No! But the other day there was construction on Willow and then I—'

'Do you want him to think you're weak?' Jess asked her. 'Do you want to give him that satisfaction?'

'How can he already be with somebody else?' Lissa asked her, and Jess just sighed, shaking her head. 'I'm not even totally okay yet, and he's with someone else? How can that *be*?'

'Because he's a jerk,' I told her.

'Because he's a guy,' Chloe added. 'And guys don't get attached, guys don't ever give themselves over completely, and guys lie. That's why they should be handled with great trepidation, not trusted, and held at arm's length whenever possible. Right, Remy?'

I looked at her, and there it was again: that shifting of her eyes that meant she'd seen something in me lately she didn't recognise, and it worried her. Because if I wasn't cold, hard Remy, then she couldn't be the Chloe she was, either.

'Right,' I said, and smiled at Lissa. I had to lead the way here, of course. She'd never make it out otherwise. 'Absolutely.'

* * *

The band wasn't called the G Flats at all. That was just their wedding persona, the one they had been forced to take on because of an incident involving the van, some authorities in Pennsylvania, and Don's brother Michael, who was an attorney there. Apparently playing at my mother's wedding had been some kind of payback, but it had also seemed like the right time to relocate, as the band – whose real name was Truth Squad – did every summer.

For the past two years, they'd worked their way across the country, always following the same process: find a town with a decent local music scene, rent a cheap apartment, and start playing the clubs. In the first week they all got day jobs, preferably at the same place, since they shared one mode of transportation. (So now, Dexter and Lucas worked at Flash Camera, while John Miller fixed lattes at Jump Java, and Ted bagged groceries at Mayor's Market.) Although most of the guys had some college, or, in Ted's case, a diploma, they always got easy jobs that didn't require much overtime or thinking. Then they'd hit the local club scene, hoping to land a regular weekly gig, as they had at Bendo. Tuesday nights, which were the slowest there, were now all theirs.

They'd only been in town for a couple of days when I'd first met Dexter at Don's Motors: they were sleeping in the van then, in the city park, until they found the yellow house. Now it seemed they'd stick around until they were run out of town for owing money or small legal infractions (it had happened before) or just got bored. Everything was planned to be transitory: they boasted that they could pack up and be gone in an hour flat, already drawing a finger across the wrinkled map in the van's glove box, seeking out a new destination.

So maybe that was what kept me from giving The Speech, this idea that his life was just as impermanent at this moment as mine. I didn't want to be like other girls that were probably in other towns, listening to Truth Squad bootlegs and pining for Dexter Jones, born in Washington, D.C., a Pisces, lead singer, thrower of challenges, permanent address unknown. His history was as murky as mine was clear, with his dog seeming to be the only family in which he had interest. I was soon to be Remy Starr, formerly of Lakeview, now of Stanford, undecided major, leaning toward economics. We were only converging for a few weeks, fleeting. No need to follow protocol.

That night me, Chloe, Jess, and Lissa got to Bendo around nine. Truth Squad was already playing, and the crowd was thin but enthusiastic. I noted, then quickly made a point of not noting, that it was mostly made up of girls, a few of them crowded up close, next to the stage, holding their beers and swaying to the music.

The music, in fact, was a mix of covers and originals. The covers were, as Dexter put it, 'a necessary evil' – required at weddings, and useful at clubs, at least at the beginning of sets, to prevent being beaned with beer caps and cigarette butts. (This, apparently, had happened as well.) But Dexter and Ted, who had started the band during their junior year of high school, preferred their original compositions, the biggest and most ambitious of which were the potato songs.

By the time we sat down, the band was finishing the last verse of 'Gimme Three Steps' as the assembled girls clapped and whoo-whooed. Then there was a few seconds of practice chords, some conferring between Ted and Dexter, and then Dexter said, 'We're going to do an original song for you all now, an instant classic. Folks, this is "The Potato Song".'

More cheering from the girls, one of whom – a buxom redhead with broad shoulders I recognised from the perpetual lines for the ladies' room – moved closer to the stage, so that she was practically at Dexter's feet. He smiled down at her, politely.

'I saw her in the produce section,' he began, *'late last Saturday. It hadn't been but seven days since she went away . . .'*

Another loud whoop, from someone who was, apparently, already fond of 'The Potato Song'. *Good thing,* I thought. There were dozens where that came from.

'Once she'd loved my filet mignon, my carnivore inklings,' Dexter continued, *'but now she was a vegan princess, living off beans. She'd given up the cheese and bacon, sworn off Burger King, and when I wouldn't do the same she gave me back my ring. I stood there by the romaine lettuce, feeling my heart pine'* – and here he put a hand over his chest, and looked mournful, to which the crowd cheered – *'wishing that this meatless beauty still would be all mine. She turned around to go to checkout, fifteen items or less.*

And I knew this was the last go-round, so this is what I said . . .'

He stopped here, letting the music build, and John Miller drummed a bit faster, the beat picking up. I could see some people in the crowd already mouthing the words.

'*Don't you ever give me no rotten tomato, 'cause all I ever wanted was your sweet potato,*' Dexter sang. '*Mashed, whipped, creamed, smothered, chunked, and diced, any way you fix it baby sure tastes nice.*'

'This is a song?' Jess asked me, but Lissa was laughing now, clapping along.

'This is many songs,' I told her. 'It's an opus.'

'A what?' she said, but I didn't even repeat it, because now the song was reaching its climax, which was basically a recitation of every possible kind of vegetable. The crowd was shouting things out, and Dexter was singing hard, winding up the song: when they finished, with a crashing of cymbals, the crowd burst into loud applause. Dexter leaned into the microphone, said they'd be back in a few minutes, and then got down off the stage, grabbing a plastic cup off a speaker as he did so. I watched as the redheaded girl walked up to him, zeroing in, effectively cutting off his path as he started across the floor.

'Ooh, Remy,' Chloe said, noticing this too, 'your man has a groupie.'

'He's not my man,' I said, taking a sip of my beer.

'Remy's with the band,' Chloe told Jess, who snorted. 'So much for that no-musicians rule. Next thing you know she'll be on the bus and selling

T-shirts in the parking lot, showing off her boobs to get in the stage door.'

'At least she has boobs to show,' Jess said.

'I have boobs,' Chloe said, pointing to her chest. 'Just because they're not weighing me down doesn't mean they're not substantial.'

'Okay, B cup,' Jess said, taking a sip of her drink.

'I have boobs!' Chloe said again, a bit too loudly – she'd already had a couple of minibottles at the Spot. 'My boobs are great, goddammit. You know that? They're fantastic! My boobs are *amazing*.'

'Chloe,' I said, but of course then it was too late. Not only were two guys standing nearby now completely absorbed in checking out her chest, but Dexter was sliding in beside me, a bemused look on his face. Chloe flushed red – rare for her – while Lissa patted her sympathetically on the shoulder.

'So it is true,' Dexter said finally. 'Girls do talk about boobs when they're in groups. I always thought so, but I never had proof.'

'Chloe was just making a point,' Lissa explained to him.

'Clearly,' Dexter said, and Chloe brushed a hand through her hair and turned her head, as if she was suddenly fascinated by the wall. 'So anyway,' he said brightly, moving on, ' "The Potato Song" really went over well, don't you think?'

'I do,' I said, moving in closer as he slid his arm around my waist. That was the thing about Dexter: he wasn't totally touchy-feely, like Jonathan had been, but he had these signature moves that I liked. The hand around my waist, for one, but then there was this thing that made me crazy, the way he cupped his fingers around the back of my neck, putting them just so, so that his thumb touched a pulse point. It was so hard to explain, but it gave me a chill, every time, almost like he was touching my heart.

I looked up and Chloe had her eye on me, vigilant as ever. I shook off these thoughts, quick, and finished my beer just as Ted came up.

'Nice work on that second verse,' was the first thing he said, and not nicely, but in a sarcastic, snarky way. 'You know, if you butcher the words you do the song a disservice.'

'Butcher what words?' Dexter said.

Ted sighed, loudly. 'It's not that she was a vegan princess, living *off* beans. It's she's a vegan princess, living *off* of beans.'

Dexter just looked at him, completely nonplussed, as if he'd just given the weather report. Chloe said, 'What's the difference?'

'The entire world is the difference!' Ted snapped. '*Living off beans* is proper English, which brings with it the connotation of higher society, accepted standards, and the status quo. *Living off of beans*, however, is reminiscent of a more slang culture, realistic, and a lower class, which is indicative of both the speaker in the song and the music that accompanies it.'

'All this from one word?' Jess asked him.

'One word,' Ted replied, dead serious, 'can change the whole world.'

There was a moment while we all considered this. Finally Lissa said to Chloe, loud enough for all of us to hear (she'd had a minibottle or two herself), 'I bet he did really well on his SATs.'

'Shhh,' Chloe said, just as loudly.

'Ted,' Dexter said, 'I hear what you're saying. And I understand. Thanks for pointing out the distinction, and I won't make the mistake again.'

Ted just stood there, blinking. 'Okay,' he said, somewhat uneasily. 'Good. Well. Uh, I'm gonna go smoke.'

'Sounds good,' Dexter said, and with that Ted walked away, cutting through the crowd toward the bar. A couple of girls standing by the door eyed him as he passed, nodding at each other. God, this band thing was sick. Some women had no shame.

'Very impressive,' I said to Dexter.

'I've had a lot of practice,' he explained. 'You see, Ted is very passionate. And really, all he wants is to be heard. Hear him, nod, agree. Three steps. Easy cheesy.'

'Easy cheesy,' I repeated, and then he slid his hand up to my neck, pressing his fingers just so, and I got that weird feeling again. This time, it wasn't so easy to shake, and as Dexter moved closer to me, kissing my forehead, I closed my eyes and wondered how deep I'd let this get before ducking out. Maybe it wouldn't be the whole summer. Maybe I needed to derail it sooner, to prevent a real crash in the end.

'Paging Dexter,' a voice came from the front of the club. I looked up: it was John Miller, squinting in the house lights. 'Paging Dexter. You are needed on aisle five for a price check.'

The redheaded girl was back at the stage, right up close. She turned her head and followed John Miller's gaze, right to us. To me. And I looked right back at her, feeling possessive suddenly of something that I wasn't even sure I should want to claim as mine.

'Gotta go,' Dexter said. Then he leaned into my ear and added, 'Wait for me?'

'Maybe,' I said.

He laughed, as if this was a joke, and disappeared into the crowd. A few seconds later I watched him climb onstage, so lanky and clumsy: he tagged a speaker with one foot, sending it toppling, as he headed to the mike. One of his shoelaces, of course, was undone.

'Oh, man,' Chloe said. She was looking right at me, shaking her head, and I told myself she was wrong, so wrong, even as she spoke. 'You're a goner.'

9

'I thought this was a cookout. You know, dogs and burgers, Tater Tots, ambrosia salad.' Dexter picked up a box of Twinkies, tossing them into the cart. 'And Twinkies.'

'It is,' I said, consulting the list again before I picked a four-dollar glass jar of imported sun-dried tomatoes off the shelf. 'Except that it's a cookout thrown by my mother.'

'And?'

'And,' I said, 'my mother doesn't cook.'

He looked at me, waiting.

'At all. My mother doesn't cook at all.'

'She must cook sometimes.'

'Nope.'

'Everyone can make scrambled eggs, Remy. It's programmed into you at birth, the default setting. Like being able to swim and knowing not to mix pickles with oatmeal. You just *know*.'

'My mother,' I told him, pushing the cart farther up the aisle as he lagged along beside, taking long, loping steps, 'doesn't even like scrambled eggs. She only eats eggs Benedict.'

'Which is?' he said, stopping as he was momentarily distracted by a large plastic water gun that was displayed, right at kid's eye level, in the middle of the cereal section.

'You don't know what eggs Benedict is?'

'Should I?' he asked, picking up the water gun and pulling the trigger, which made a click-click-click sound. He pointed it around the corner, like a sniper, taking shelter behind a display of canned corn.

'It's a way of making eggs that is really complicated and fancy and involves hollandaise sauce,' I told him. 'And English muffins.'

'Ugh.' He made a face, then shuddered. 'I *hate* English muffins.'

'What?'

'English muffins,' he said, putting the water gun back as we started walking again. 'I can't eat them. I can't even think about them. In fact, we should stop talking about them right now.'

We paused in front of the spices: my mother wanted something called Asian Fish Sauce. I peered closely at all the bottles, already frustrated, while Dexter busied himself juggling some boxes of Sweet 'n Low. Shopping with him, as I'd discovered, was like having a toddler in tow. He was constantly distracted, grabbing at things, and we'd already taken on entirely too many impulse items, all of which I intended to rid the cart of at the checkout when he wasn't looking.

'Do you mean to tell me,' I said, reaching up as I spotted the fish sauce, 'that you can eat an entire jar of mayonnaise in one sitting but find English muffins, which are basically just bread, to be disgusting?'

'Ughhh.' He shuddered again, a full-body one this

163

time, and put a hand on his stomach. 'Icks-nay on the uffins-may. I'm serious.'

It was taking us forever. My mother's list only had about fifteen things on it, but they were all speciality items: imported goat's cheese, focaccia bread, an incredibly specific brand of olives in the red bottle, not the green. Plus there was the new grill she'd bought just for the occasion – the nicest one at the speciality hardware store, according to Chris, who didn't keep her from overspending as I would have – plus the brand-new patio furniture (otherwise, where would we sit?), and my mother was spending a small fortune on what was supposed to be a simple Fourth of July barbecue.

This had been all her idea. She'd been working away at her book ever since she and Don had returned from the honeymoon, but a few days earlier she'd emerged midday with an inspiration: a real, all-American Fourth of July cookout with the family. Chris and Jennifer Anne should come, and Don's secretary, Patty, who was single, poor thing, and wouldn't it be wonderful if she hit it off with my mother's decorator, Jorge, who we just had to have over to thank for all his hard work on the addition? And wouldn't it be such a great way for everyone to meet my new beau (insert me cringing here) and christen the new patio and our wonderful, amazing, beautiful lives together as a blended family?

Oh, yes. It would. Of course.

'What?' Dexter said to me now, stepping in front of the cart, which I'd been pushing, apparently, faster and faster as these stress thoughts filled my head. It knocked him in the gut, forcing him backward, and he put his hands on it, pushing it back to me. 'What's wrong?'

'Nothing,' I said, trying to get the cart going again. No luck. He wasn't budging. 'Why?'

'Because you just got this look on your face like your brain was caving in.'

'Nice,' I said. 'Thanks ever so much.'

'And,' he continued, 'you're biting your lip. You only do that when you're about to shift into superobsessive, what-if mode.'

I just looked at him. As if I was that easy to figure out, a puzzle that could be cracked in, how long had it been, two weeks? It was insulting.

'I'm fine,' I said coolly.

'Ah! The ice queen voice. Which means, of course, that I'm right.' He came around the cart, holding the edge, and stood behind me, putting his hands over mine. He started pushing and walking in his goofy way, forcing me to fall into his rhythm, which felt as awkward as it looked, like walking with a shoeful of marbles. 'What if I embarrass you?' he said, as if posing a theory, like, say, quantum physics. 'What if I break some heirloom family china? Or talk about your underwear?'

I glared at him, then pushed the cart harder, making him stumble. But he hung on, pulling me back against him, his fingers spreading across my stomach. Then he leaned down and whispered, right in my ear, 'What if I throw down a challenge to Don, right there over dinner, daring him to eat that entire jar of sun-dried tomatoes and chase it with a stick of margarine? And what if' – and here he gasped, dramatically – 'oh my God, he *does* it?'

I covered my face with my hand, shaking my head. I hated it when he made me laugh when I didn't want to: it seemed some huge loss of control, so unlike me, like the most glaring of character flaws.

'But you know,' he said, still in my ear, 'that probably won't happen.'

'I hate you,' I told him, and he kissed my neck, finally letting go of the cart.

'Not true,' he replied, and started down the aisle, already distracted by a huge display of Velveeta cheese in the dairy section. 'Never true.'

'So, Remy. I hear you're going to Stanford!'

I nodded and smiled, shifting my drink to my other hand, and felt with my tongue to see if I had spinach in my teeth. I didn't. But Don's secretary, Patty, who I hadn't seen since her tearful bit at the wedding reception, was standing in front of me expectantly, with a nice big piece wedged around an incisor.

'Well,' she said, dabbing at her forehead with a napkin, 'it's just a wonderful school. You must be really excited.'

'I am,' I told her. Then I reached up, nonchalantly, and brushed at one of my teeth, hoping that somehow she would subconsciously pick up on this, like osmosis, and get the hint. But no. She was still smiling at me, fresh sweat beading her forehead as she gulped down the rest of her wine and glanced around, wondering what to say next.

She was distracted suddenly, as was I, by a small commotion over by the brand-new grill, where Chris had been assigned to prepare the incredibly expensive steaks my mother had special-ordered from the butcher. They were, I'd heard her tell someone, 'Brazilian beef', whatever that meant, as if cows from below the equator were of greater value than your average Holstein chewing cud in Michigan.

Chris wasn't doing well. First he'd burned off part of an eyebrow and a fair amount of arm hair lighting the grill. Then he'd had some trouble mastering the complicated spatula in the top-of-the-line accessories set the salesman had convinced my mother she absolutely had to have, resulting in one of the steaks being flung across the patio, where it landed with a slap on one of the imported loafers of our decorator, Jorge.

Now the flames on the grill were leaping as Chris struggled with the gas valve. All of us assembled stood there, holding our drinks as the fire shot up, making the steaks scream and sizzle, then died out completely, the grill making a gurgling noise. My mother, deep in conversation with one of our neighbours, glanced over in a disinterested way, as if this methodic burning and destruction of the main course was someone else's problem.

'Don't worry!' Chris called as the flames shot up again and he batted at them with the spatula, 'it's under control.' He sounded about as sure of this as he looked, which was to say, with half a right eyebrow and the smell of singed hair still lingering, not very.

'Everyone, please!' my mother called out, covering

167

gamely by gesturing at the table where we'd set up all the cheeses and appetisers. 'Eat, eat! We've got so much food here!'

Chris was waving smoke out of his face while Jennifer Anne stood off to his left, biting her lip. She'd brought several side dishes, all in plastic containers with matching, pastel-coloured lids. On the bottom of each lid, in permanent marker, was written PROPERTY OF JENNIFER A. BAKER, PLEASE RETURN. As if the whole world was part of an international conspiracy to steal her Tupperware.

'Barbara,' Patty called out, 'this is just wonderful.'

'Oh, it's nothing!' my mother said, fanning her face with her hand. She was in black trousers and a lime green tank top that showed off her honeymoon tan, her hair pulled back in a head-band: she looked the picture of suburban entertaining, as if at any moment she might light a tiki torch and spray some Cheez Whiz onto crackers.

It was always interesting to see how my mother's relationships manifested themselves in her personality. With my dad she was a hippie – in all the pictures I'd seen she looked so young, wearing gauzy skirts or frayed jeans, her hair long and black and parted right down the middle. During the time she was married to Harold, the professor, she'd gone academic, sporting a lot of tweed and wearing her reading glasses all the time, even though she saw well enough without them. Once married to Win, the doctor, she'd gone country club, in little sweater sets and tennis skirts, though she couldn't play to save her life. And with Martin, the golf pro – who she'd met, of course, at the country club – she went into a young phase, since he was six years her junior: short skirts, jeans, little flimsy dresses. Now, as Don's wife, Barb, she'd gone subdivision on us: I could just see them, years from now, wearing matching jogging suits and riding around in a golf cart, en route to work on their back swing. I really did hope this was my mother's last marriage: I wasn't sure she, or I, could take another incarnation.

Now I watched as Don, wearing a golf shirt and drinking a beer in the bottle, helped himself to another of the crostini, popping it into his mouth. I'd expected him to be the grill master, but he didn't even seem to be that fond of food at all, in fact, judging by the vast quantities of Ensure that he consumed, those little cans of liquid diet that claim to have all the nutritional value of a good meal with the convenience of a pop-top. He bought them by the case at Sam's Club. For some reason, this bothered me even more than my now breasty breakfasts, seeing Don walking through the house reading the newspaper, in his leather slippers, a can of Ensure seemingly affixed to his hand, the *fffftttt* sound of him popping the top now signalling his presence.

'Remy, honey?' my mother called out. 'Can you come here a second?'

I made my excuses to Patty and walked across the patio, where my mother slid her hand around my wrist, pulled me gently close to her, and whispered, 'I'm wondering if I should be worried about the steaks.'

I glanced over at the grill, where Chris had

positioned himself in such a way that it was difficult –
but not impossible – to see that the prime Brazilian
beef cuts had been reduced to small, black objects
resembling lava rocks.

'Yes and no,' I told her, and she absently brushed
her fingers over my skin. My mother's hands were
always cool, even in the hottest of weather. I suddenly
had a flash of her pressing a palm to my forehead
when I was a child, checking for fever, and me thinking
this then too. 'I'll deal with it,' I told her.

'Oh, Remy,' she said, squeezing my hand. 'What am
I going to do without you?'

Ever since she'd come home it had been like this,
these sudden moments when her face changed and I
knew she was thinking that I might actually go to
Stanford after all, that it was really about to happen.
She had her new husband, her new wing, her new book.
She'd be fine without me, and we both knew it. This is
what daughters did. They left, and came home later
with lives of their own. It was a basic plot in any number
of her books: girl strikes out, makes good, finds love,
gets revenge. In that order. The making good and
striking out part I liked. The rest would just be bonus.

'Come on, Mom,' I told her. 'You won't even know
I'm gone.'

She sighed, shaking her head, and pulled me close,
kissing my cheek. I could smell her perfume, mixed
with hair spray, and I closed my eyes for a second,
breathing it in. With all the changes, some things
stayed the same.

Which is exactly what I was thinking as I stood in

the kitchen, pulling the hamburgers I'd bought out of the back of the refrigerator, where I'd camouflaged them behind a stack of Ensures. At the supermarket, when Dexter had asked why I was buying this stuff even though it wasn't on the list, I'd just told him that I liked to be prepared for any eventuality, because you just never knew. Could be I was too cynical. Or maybe, unlike so many others who moved in my mother's orbit, I had just learned from the past.

'Okay, so it is true.' I turned around to see Jennifer Anne standing behind me. In one hand, she had two packs of hot dogs: in the other, a bag of buns. She half-smiled, as if we'd both been caught doing something, and said, 'Great minds think alike, right?'

'I am impressed,' I told her as she came over and opened one of the packs, arranging the dogs on a plate. 'You know her well.'

'No, but I do know Christopher,' she said. 'I had my reservations about that grill from the day we brought it home from the store. He went in there and just got bedazzled. As soon as the guy started talking about convection, he was gone.'

'Convection?' I said.

She sighed, pushing her hair out of her face. 'It has to do with the heating process,' she explained. 'Instead of the heat just rising up, it surrounds the food. That's what got Christopher in. The guy just kept saying it, like a mantra. It *surrounds* the food. It *surrounds* the food.'

I snorted, and she glanced over at me, then smiled, almost tentatively, as if she had to check first to make sure I wasn't making fun of her. Then we just stood there, both of us stacking meat products, for a second, until I decided we were on the verge of a Hallmark moment and had to take action.

'So anyway,' I said, 'I'm wondering how we're going to explain this last-minute menu substitution.'

'The steaks were bad,' she said simply. 'They smelled off. And this is just so kitschy, all-American, burger and dogs. Your mom will love it.'

'Okay,' I said, picking up my plate of patties. She grabbed the buns and her plate, then started toward the door to the patio. I followed behind, glad to let her handle it.

We were halfway out the door when she turned her head, nodding to the front yard, and said, 'Looks like your guest has arrived.'

I glanced out the window. Sure enough, there was Dexter, coming down the sidewalk, a good half hour late. He was carrying a bottle of wine (impressive) and wearing jeans and a clean white T-shirt (even more so). He was also holding a leash, the other end of which was attached to Monkey, who was charging ahead, tongue out, at a speed that seemed impressive considering his old age.

'Can you take this?' I asked Jennifer Anne, handing over my plate of patties.

'Sure,' she said. 'See you outside.'

As I came down the driveway, the screen door slamming behind me, Dexter was tying Monkey's leash to our mailbox. I could hear him talking to the dog as I came up, just as you would talk to anyone, and

Monkey had his head cocked to the side, still panting, as if he was listening carefully and waiting for his turn to respond.

'. . . might not be into dogs, so you'll just stay here, okay?' Dexter was saying, tying the leash into a knot, then another knot, as if Monkey, whose back leg was trembling even as he sat down, possessed some form of superhuman strength. 'And then later, we'll go find a pool so you can take a dip, and then maybe, if we're really feeling crazy, we'll take a ride in the van and you can put your head out the window. Okay?'

Monkey kept panting, closing his eyes as Dexter scratched under his chin. As I came closer he saw me and started wagging his tail, the sound a dull thump against the grass.

'Hey,' Dexter said, turning around. 'Sorry I'm late. Had a little problem with the Monkster here.'

'A problem?' I said, squatting down beside him and letting Monkey sniff my hand.

'Well,' Dexter said, 'I've been so busy with work and the gigs and all that, you know, I've kind of neglected him. He's lonely. He doesn't know any other dogs here, and he's really quite social. He's used to having a whole network of friends.'

I looked at him, then at Monkey, who was now busy chewing his own haunch. 'I see,' I said.

'And I was getting ready to leave this afternoon, and he was following me around, all pathetic. Whining. Scratching at my shoes.' He rubbed his hand over the top of Monkey's head, pulling on his ears in a way that looked painful but that the dog seemed to love, making a low, happy noise in his throat. 'He can just stay out here, right?' Dexter asked me, standing up. Monkey wagged his tail hopefully, perking up his ears, the way he always seemed to do at the sound of Dexter's voice. 'He won't cause any trouble.'

'It's fine,' I said. 'I'll bring him some water.'

Dexter smiled at me, a nice smile, as if I'd surprised him. 'Thanks,' he said, and then added, to Monkey, 'See, I told you. She likes you.'

Monkey was back to chewing his haunch now, as if this last fact didn't concern him much. Then I got him some water from the garage, Dexter double-checked the leash knot again, and we headed around the side of the house, where I could already smell hot dogs cooking.

My mother was deep in conversation with Patty when we walked up, but at the sight of Dexter she stopped talking, put a hand to her chest – a trademark fluttering gesture – and said, 'Well, hello. You must be Dexter.'

'I am,' Dexter said, taking her hand as she extended it and shaking it.

'I recognise you from the wedding!' she said, as if just now putting this together, even though I'd told her at least twice about the connection. 'What a wonderful singer you are!'

Dexter seemed pleased and somewhat embarrassed at this. My mother was still holding his hand. 'Great wedding,' he said finally. 'Congratulations.'

'Oh, you must have something to drink,' my mother said, glancing around for me, and of course, I was right

174

there between them. 'Remy, honey, offer Dexter a beer. Or some wine? Or a soft drink?'

'Beer would be fine,' Dexter said to me.

'Remy, sweetie, there's some more cold in the fridge, okay?' My mother put a hand on my back, effectively steering me toward the kitchen, then hooked her arm in Dexter's and said, 'You have to meet Jorge, he's just this brilliant decorator. Jorge! Come here, you absolutely have to meet Remy's new boyfriend!'

Jorge started across the patio as my mother kept trilling about how fabulous everyone within a five-foot radius was. Meanwhile, I headed into the kitchen to fetch Dexter a beer, like hired help. By the time I brought it back out to him Don had joined the conversation and now everyone was discussing, for some weird reason, Milwaukee.

'Coldest weather I've ever felt,' Don was saying, popping a handful of imported nuts into his mouth. 'The wind can rip you apart in five minutes there. Plus it's murder on cars. Salt damage.'

'Great snow, though,' Dexter said, taking the beer as I handed it to him and managing, very subtly, to brush his fingers with mine as he did so. 'And the local music scene is really coming on there. It's early, but it's there.'

Don huffed at this, taking another swig of his beer. 'Music is not a real career,' he said. 'Up until last year this boy was majoring in business, can you believe that? At UVA.'

'Well, isn't that interesting,' my mother said. 'Now, tell me again how you two are related?'

'Don is my father's brother-in-law,' Dexter told her. 'His sister is my aunt.'

'That's just wonderful!' my mother said, a bit too enthusiastically. 'Small world, isn't it?'

'You know,' Don went on, 'he had a full scholarship. His way paid. Dropped out. Broke his mother's heart, and for what? Music.'

Now, even my mother couldn't come up with anything to say. I just looked at Don, wondering where this was coming from. Maybe it was the Ensures.

'He's a brilliant singer,' my mother said again to Jorge, who nodded, as if he hadn't already heard this several times. Don seemed to be distracted now, looking out across the patio, holding his empty beer. I glanced at Dexter and realised that I'd never seen him like this: a bit cowed, uncomfortable, unable to come up with the quick funny retort that always seemed so close at hand. He ran a hand through his hair, tugging at it, then glanced around the yard, taking another sip of his beer.

'Come on,' I said, and slipped my hand around his. 'Let's get some food.' Then I pulled him away, gently, over to the grill, where Chris seemed very happy to be poking at the hot dogs, back in his element.

'Guess what,' I said, and he glanced up, eyebrows raised. 'Don's an asshole.'

'No, he isn't,' Dexter said. He smiled, as if it wasn't any big deal, then put an arm over my shoulders. 'Every family has a black sheep, right? It's the American way.'

'Tell me about it,' Chris said, flipping a burger. 'At least you weren't in jail.'

Dexter took a big swig of his beer. 'Only once,' he said cheerfully, then winked at me. And that was it: so quickly, he was back to his old self, as if all that had just happened was a big joke, one that he was in on, and didn't bother him in the least. I, however, kept looking at Don, my stomach burning, as if I now had a score to settle. Seeing Dexter so quiet, if only for a second, had somehow made him more real to me. As if for those few moments, he wasn't just my summer boyfriend but something bigger, something I had a stake in.

The rest of the evening went well. The burgers and dogs were tasty, and most of the expensive olive-and-sun-dried-tomato spread went uneaten, while Jennifer Anne's devilled eggs and three-bean salad were a hit. I even saw my mother licking her fingers after consuming a second piece of Jennifer Anne's chocolate pudding pie, which was garnished with a healthy scoop of Cool Whip. So much for gourmet.

By dark everyone was saying their good-byes, and my mother disappeared to her room, claiming to be completely wiped out from the party because entertaining, even when other people do most of the work, can be so exhausting. So Jennifer Anne and Chris and Dexter and I stacked the dishes and wrapped things up, tossing most of the gourmet crap and the burned steaks, saving only one, with the blackened stuff trimmed off, for Monkey.

'He'll love it,' Dexter said, taking it from Jennifer Anne, who had wrapped it up in foil, the edges folded neatly. 'He's really a Dog Chow kind of guy, so this is like Christmas to him.'

'What an interesting name he has,' she said.

'I got him for my tenth birthday,' Dexter told her, glancing outside. 'I really wanted a monkey, so I was kind of disappointed. But he's turned out to be much better. Monkeys get really mean, apparently.'

Jennifer Anne looked at him, somewhat quizzically, then smiled. 'I've heard that,' she said, not unkindly, and went back to covering leftover pitta bread with Cling Wrap.

'So if you've got a minute,' Chris said to Dexter, wiping the counter down with a sponge, 'you should come up and see my hatchlings. They're amazing.'

'Oh, yeah,' Dexter said enthusiastically. Then he looked at me. 'You okay?'

'Go ahead,' I said, as if I was his mom or something, and they took off up the stairs, feet clumping, on the way to the lizard room.

Across the kitchen, Jennifer Anne sighed, shutting the fridge. 'I will never understand this hobby of his,' she said. 'I mean, dogs and cats you can cuddle. Who wants to cuddle a lizard?'

This seemed like a difficult question to answer, so I just pulled the plug on the drain, where I was washing dishes, and let the water gurgle down noisily. Upstairs, it sounded like the honeycomb hideout: giggling, various oohs and ahhs, and the occasional skittering noise, followed by uproarious laughter.

Jennifer Anne cast her eyes up at the ceiling, obviously unnerved. 'Tell Christopher I'm in the den,' she said, picking up her bag from the sideboard, where it was parked next to her plastic containers, now cleaned, lids accounted for. She drew out a book and headed into the next room, where a few seconds later I heard the TV come on, murmuring softly.

I picked up the foil-wrapped steak and walked outside, flicking on the porch light. As I came down the front walk Monkey got to his feet and started wagging his tail.

'Hey buddy,' I said. He poked at my hand, then got a whiff of the steak and started nudging my fingers with his nose, snuffling. 'Got a treat for you here.'

Monkey wolfed down the steak in about two bites, almost taking part of my little finger with it. Well, it was dark. When he was done he burped and rolled over onto his back, sticking his belly in the air, and I sat down on the grass beside him.

It was a nice night, clear and cooler, perfect Fourth of July weather. A few people were popping off firecrackers a couple of streets over, the noise pinging in the dark. Monkey kept rolling closer to me, nudging my elbow, until I finally relented and scratched the matted fur on his belly. He needed a bath. Badly. Plus he had bad breath. But there was something sweet about him, nonetheless, and he was practically humming as I moved my fingers across him.

We sat there like that for a while until I heard the screen door slam and Dexter call out my name. At the sound of his voice, Monkey instantly sat up, ears perked, and then got to his feet, walking toward it until the leash was stretched to the limit.

'Hey,' Dexter said. I couldn't see his face, just his outline in the brightness of the porch light. Monkey barked, as if he'd called him, and his tail wagging grew frenzied, like intense windmill action, and I wondered if he'd knock himself down with the sheer force of it.

'Hey,' I said back, and he started down the steps toward us. As he came closer across the grass, I watched Monkey, amazed at his full-body excitement to see this person he'd only been away from for an hour or so. What did it feel like, I wondered, to love someone that much? So much that you couldn't even control yourself when they came close, as if you might just break free of whatever was holding you and throw yourself at them with enough force to easily overwhelm you both. I had to wonder, but Monkey clearly knew: you could see it, feel it coming off him, like a heat. I almost envied him that. Almost.

It was late that night, when I was lying in Dexter's room on his bed, that he picked up the guitar. He wasn't much of a player, he told me, as he sat across the room, shirtless, barefoot, his fingers finding the strings in the dark. He played a little riff of something, a Beatles song, then a few lines of the latest version of 'The Potato Opus'. He didn't play like Ted, of course: his chords seemed more hesitant, as if he was plucking by sheer luck. I leaned back against the pillows and listened as he sang to me. A bit of this, a bit of that. Nothing in full. And then, just as I felt I might be drifting off to sleep, something else.

'This lullaby is only a few words, a simple run of chords—'
'No.' I sat up, now wide awake. 'Don't.'

Even in the dark, I could see he was surprised. He

dropped his hands from the guitar and looked at me, and I hoped he couldn't see my face either. Because it was all fun and games, so far. Just a few moments when I worried it might go deep enough to drown me. Like now. And I could pull back, would pull back, before it went that far.

I'd only told him about the song in a moment of weakness, a time of true confessions, which I usually avoided in relationships. The past was so sticky, full of land mines: I made it a point, usually, not to be so detailed in the map of myself I handed over to a guy. And the song, that song, was one of the biggest keys to me. Like a soft spot, a bruise that never quite healed right. The first place I was sure they would strike back, when the time came for them to do so.

'You don't want to hear it?' he asked now.

'No,' I said again. 'I don't.'

He'd been so surprised when I told him. We'd been having our own challenge of sorts, a kind of Guess What You'd Never Know About Me. I found out that he was allergic to raspberries, that he'd busted out his front tooth running into a park bench in sixth grade, that his first girlfriend was a distant cousin of Elvis. And I'd told him that I'd come this close to piercing my belly button before fainting, that one year I'd sold more Girl Scout cookies than anyone else in my troop, and that my father was Thomas Custer, and 'This Lullaby' had been written for me.

Of course he knew the song, he said, and then hummed the opening chords, pulling the words out of thin air. They'd even sung it a couple of times at weddings, he said: some brides picked it for the dance with their father. Which seemed so stupid to me, considering the words. *I will let you down*, it says, right there in the first verse, plain as day. What kind of father says such a thing? But that, of course, was a question I'd long ago quit asking myself.

He was still strumming the chords, finding them in the dark.

'Dexter.'

'Why do you hate it that much?'

'I don't hate it. I just . . . I'm sick of it, that's all.' But this wasn't true either. I did hate it sometimes, for the lie that it was. As if my father had been able, with just a few words scribbled in a motel, to excuse the fact that he never bothered to know me. Seven years he'd spent with my mother, most of them good until one last blowout, resulting in him leaving for California, with her pregnant, although she didn't find that out until later. Two years after I was born, he died of a heart attack, never having made it back across the country to see me. It was the ultimate out, this song, admitting to the world that he'd only disappoint me, and didn't that just make him so noble, really? As if he was beating me to the punch, his words living for ever, while I was left speechless, no rebuttal, no words left to say.

Dexter strummed the guitar idly, not picking out any real melody, just messing around. He said, 'Funny how I've heard that song all my life and never knew it was for you.'

'It's just a song,' I said, running my fingers over the

windowsill, easing them around those snow globes. 'I never even knew him.'

'It's too bad. I bet he was a cool guy.'

'Maybe,' I said. It was weird to be talking about my father out loud, something I hadn't done since sixth grade, when my mother found therapy the way some people find God and dragged us all in for group, individual, and art until her money ran out.

'I'm sorry,' he said softly, and I was unnerved by how solemn he sounded, how serious. As if he'd found that map after all and was dangerously close, circling. 'It's nothing,' I said.

He was quiet for a second, and I had a flash of his face earlier that night, caught unaware by Don's pronouncements, and the vulnerability I'd seen there. It had unsettled me, because I was used to the Dexter I liked, the funny guy with the skinny waist and the fingers that pressed against my neck just so. In just seconds I'd seen another shade of him, and if it had been light where we were now, he'd have seen the same of me. So I was grateful, as I had been so often in my life, for the dark.

I rolled over and pressed myself into the pillow, listening to the sound of my own breathing. I heard him move, a soft noise as the guitar was put down, and next his arms were around me, circling my back, his face against my shoulder. He was so close to me in that moment, too close, but I had never pushed a guy away for that. If anything I pulled them nearer, taking them in, as I did now, sure in my belief that knowing me that well would easily be enough to scare them away.

10

'I mean, God,' Lissa said, stopping in front of a huge display of bedsheets, 'who knows the difference between a duvet and a comforter?'

We were in Linens Etc., armed with Lissa's mom's gold card, the list of items that the university suggested for all incoming freshmen, and a letter from Lissa's future room-mate, a girl named Delia from Boca Raton, Florida. She'd already been in contact so that she and Lissa could colour-coordinate their bed linens, discuss who should bring what in the way of televisions, microwaves, and wall hangings, and just to 'break the ice' so that by August, when classes started, they'd already 'be like sisters'. If Lissa wasn't already glum about starting college post-Adam, this letter – written on pink stationery in silver ink, and spewing forth glitter when she pulled it from the envelope – had pretty much done her in.

'A duvet,' I told her, stopping to eye a stack of thick purple towels, 'is a cover for a comforter, usually a down comforter. And a comforter is just a glorified quilt.'

She crossed her eyes at me, sighed, and pushed some hair out of her face. Lately she'd just seemed cranky all the time, defeated, as if at the age of eighteen life already sucked beyond any hope of improvement.

'I'm supposed to get a comforter in a purple/pink hue,' she said, reading off Delia's letter. 'And sheets to match. And a bed ruffle, whatever the hell that is.'

'It goes around the base of the bed,' I explained. 'To cover the legs and provide a sort of colour continuity, all the way to the floor.'

She looked at me, eyebrows raised. 'Colour continuity?' she asked.

'My mother bought a new bedroom suite a few years back,' I said, taking the list out of her hand. 'I got an entire education in thread count sheets and Egyptian cotton.'

Lissa stopped the cart next to a display of plastic wastebaskets, picking up a lime green one with blue trim. 'I should get this,' she told me, turning it in her hands, 'just because it will so clash with her predetermined scheme. In fact, I should pick the most butt-ugly furnishings as a complete protest against her assumption that I would just go along with whatever she said.'

I glanced around: butt ugly was entirely possible at Linens Etc., which carried not only lime green trash cans but also leopard-patterned tissue holders, framed prints of kittens frolicking with puppies, and bath mats shaped like feet. 'Lissa,' I said gently, 'maybe we shouldn't do this today.'

'We have to,' she grumbled, grabbing a pack of sheets – the wrong size, and bright red – off a nearby shelf and tossing them into the cart. 'I'm seeing Delia at orientation next week and I'm sure she'll want a freaking update.'

I picked up the red sheets and put them back on the shelf while she pouted around the toothbrush holders, completely unenthused. 'Lissa, is this really how you want to start college? With a totally shit attitude?'

She rolled her eyes. 'Oh, yeah, well that's easy for you to say, Miss Going-across-the-Country-Free-and-Clear-No-Problems. You'll be out in sunny California, windsurfing and eating sushi while I'm stuck here in the same place I've always been, watching Adam date his way through the entire freshman class.'

'Windsurfing and sushi?' I said. 'At the same time?'

'You know what I mean!' she snapped, and a woman pricing a stack of washcloths glanced over at us. Lissa lowered her voice and added, 'I might not even go to school anyway. I might defer and join the Peace Corps and go to Africa and shave my head and dig latrines.'

'Shave your head?' I said, because, really, this was the most ludicrous part of the whole thing. 'You? Do you have any idea how ugly most people's bare heads are? They've got all kinds of bumps, Lissa. And you won't know until it's too late and you're flat-out bald.'

'You're not even listening to me!' she said. 'It's always been so easy for you, Remy. So gorgeous and confident and smart. No guy ever dumped you and left you shattered.'

'That's not true,' I said in a level voice. 'And you know it.'

She paused at this, as our shared history caught up with her. Okay, so maybe I was known for having the upper hand in my relationships, but there was a reason for that. She didn't know what happened that night at Albert's, within shouting distance of her own bedroom window. But since then, I'd been stomped on my fair share. Even Jonathan had caught me unawares.

'I planned my whole future around Adam,' she said now, quietly. 'And now I have nothing.'

'No,' I told her, 'now you just don't have Adam. There's a big difference, Lissa. You just can't see it yet.'

She harrumphed at this, yanking a cow-print Kleenex box cover off the shelf and adding it to the cart. 'I can see that everyone else is doing exactly what they wanted with the rest of their lives. They're all at the gate, pawing the dirt and ready to run, and I've already got a lame leg and am this close to being taken around back of the stable to be put out of my misery.'

'Sweetie,' I said, trying to be patient, 'we've only been out of high school a month. This isn't even the real world yet. It's just in-between time.'

'Well, I hate it here,' she snapped, gesturing all around her, including not only Linens Etc. but the world itself, 'in between or not. Give me high school any day. I'd go back in a second, if I could.'

'It's too early for nostalgia,' I told her. 'Really.'

We walked along the main aisle toward the mini-blind section, not talking. As she grumbled over curtains I walked over to the clearance section, where summer picnic ware was on special, one day only.

There were plastic plates in all colours, and cutlery with clear handles, forks with metallic prongs. I picked up a set of tumblers decorated with pink flamingoes: definitely butt ugly.

But I was thinking of the yellow house, where the only dishware consisted of one ceramic plate, a few mismatched forks and knives, some gas-station freebie coffee mugs, and whatever paper goods Ted had managed to score from the damaged bin at Mayor's Market. It was the only time I'd ever heard someone ask, 'Can you grab me *the* spoon?' as opposed to 'a spoon', which at least connoted there was more than one. And here, on bargain special, was an entire plastic, blue-handled set of cutlery – a virtual plethora of flatware – for only $6.99. I picked them up and put them in the cart without even thinking.

About ten seconds later, it hit me. What was I doing? Buying flatware for a guy? For a *boyfriend*? It was as if I, like my brother, had been suddenly brainwashed by aliens. What kind of girl purchases houseware for someone she has hardly been dating for a month? Psycho desperate-to-get-married-and-pop-out-babies types, that's who, I told myself, shuddering at the thought. I threw the cutlery set back onto the table with such speed it crashed into a stack of dolphin-patterned plates, causing a commotion loud enough to distract Lissa from the reading lamps.

Calm down, I told myself, taking in a deep breath, then promptly spitting it out, since everything in Linens Etc. stank of scented candles.

'Remy?' Lissa said. She was holding a green lamp. 'You okay?'

I nodded, and she went back to browsing. At least she was feeling better: the lamp did match the trash can.

I pushed the cart through hand towels, storage supplies, and halfway into candles – where the smell became a stench – all the while reminding myself that everything does not necessarily have a Greater Meaning. It was just a bargain set of plastic ware, for God's sake, not a promise ring. This settled me somewhat, even as the more rational part of my mind reminded me that never, in the course of oh, say, fifteen relationships since junior high school, had I ever had the urge to buy a boyfriend anything more permanent than a Zip Coke. Even at birthdays and Christmas I kept to my basic gifts, stuff like shirts and CDs, things that would eventually go out of style. Not like plastic picnic ware, which would probably be around to greet the roaches after the final nuclear holocaust. Plus, if you really went deep into the meaning of gifts, dishes equalled food, food equalled sustenance, and sustenance equalled life, which meant that by giving even one plastic fork I was basically saying I wanted to take care of Dexter for ever and ever, amen. Yikes.

On the way to the checkout, Lissa and I passed the clearance table again. She picked up a retro-looking alarm clock. 'This is cute,' she said. 'And look at those plastic plates and silverware. Maybe I could use those for when we fix stuff in the room.'

'Maybe,' I said, shrugging and ignoring the table as if it was someone I'd dated.

'But what if I didn't use it?' she went on, in the voice I recognised as Lissa entering Prime Indecisive Mode. 'I mean, it's only seven bucks, right? And it's cute. But I probably don't have room for it, anyway.'

'Probably not,' I said, starting to push the cart again.

She didn't move, the alarm clock in one hand, fingering the cute plastic pouch the cutlery came in. 'It's really cute, though,' she said. 'And it would be better than using takeout stuff all the time. But still, it's a lot of silverware, I mean it'll only be me and Delia . . .'

This time I didn't say anything. All I could smell were those candles.

'. . . but maybe we'd have other people in sometimes, you know, for pizza or whatever?' She sighed. 'No, forget it, it's just an impulse thing, I don't need it.'

I started to push the cart again, and she took a couple of steps. Two, to be exact.

'On the other hand,' she said, then stopped talking. A sigh. Then, 'No, forget it—'

'God!' I said, reaching behind me and grabbing the plastic pouch, stuffing it into the cart. 'I'll buy it. Let's just go, okay?'

She looked at me, wide-eyed. 'Do you want it, though? Because I'm not really sure I'll use it—'

'Yes,' I said loudly. 'I want it. I *need* it. Let's go.'

'Well, okay,' Lissa said, somewhat uncertainly. 'If you really need it.'

Later, when I dropped her off, I told her to make

sure she took everything, even the plastic ware. But in typical fashion, she cleaned out every bag from my trunk except one. I promptly forgot about it, that is until a few nights later, when Dexter and I were unloading some groceries he'd bought for the yellow house – peanut butter, bread, orange juice, and Doritos – from my car. He grabbed all his bags, then was about to shut the trunk when he stopped and leaned over.

'What's this?' he asked, pulling out a white plastic shopping bag, knotted neatly at the top – I'd taught Lissa well – so that its contents wouldn't spill.

'Nothing,' I said quickly, trying to take it from him.

'Wait, wait,' he said, holding it out of my reach. The peanut butter fell out of one of his other bags, rolling across the yard, but he ignored this, too intrigued by what I didn't want him to see. 'What is it?'

'Something I bought for myself,' I said curtly, grabbing for it again. No luck. He was too tall, and his arms too long.

'Is it a secret?'

'Yes.'

'Really?'

'Yes.'

He shook the bag slightly, listening to the sound it made. 'Doesn't *sound* secret,' he decided.

'What does *secret* sound like?' I asked. Idiot. 'Give it here.'

'Like tampons,' he told me, shaking it again. 'This doesn't sound like tampons.'

I glared at him, and he handed it over, as if now he

didn't want to find out. He walked across the grass to pick up the peanut butter, wiping it on his shirt – of course – and chucking it back into the bag.

'If you must know,' I said, as if it was absolutely no big deal whatsoever, 'it's just this plastic ware I bought at Linens Etc.'

He thought about this. 'Plastic ware.'

'Yes. It was on sale.'

We stood there. From inside the yellow house, I could hear the TV, and someone laughing. Monkey was standing on the other side of the screen door, watching us, his tail going full speed.

'Plastic ware,' he said slowly, 'like knives and forks and spoons?'

I brushed a bit of dirt off the back of my car – was that a scratch? – and said casually, 'Yeah, I guess. Just the basics, you know.'

'Did you need plastic ware?' he asked.

I shrugged.

'Because,' he went on, and I fought the urge to squirm, 'it's so funny, because I need plastic ware. *Badly.*'

'Can we go inside, please?' I asked, slamming the trunk shut. 'It's hot out here.'

He looked at the bag again, then at me. And then, slowly, the smile I knew and dreaded crept across his face. 'You bought me *plastic ware,*' he said. 'Didn't you?'

'No,' I growled, picking at my licence plate.

'You did!' he hooted, laughing out loud. 'You bought me some forks. And knives. And spoons. Because . . .'

'No,' I said loudly.

'. . . you love me!' He grinned, as if he'd solved the puzzler for all time, as I felt a flush creep across my face. Stupid Lissa. I could have killed her.

'It was on sale,' I told him again, as if this was some kind of an excuse.

'You love me,' he said simply, taking the bag and adding it to the others.

'Only seven bucks,' I added, but he was already walking away, so sure of himself. 'It was on clearance, for God's sake.'

'Love me,' he called out over his shoulder, in a singsong voice. 'You. Love. Me.'

I stood there in the front yard, at the bottom of the stairs, feeling for the first time in a long while that things were completely out of my control. How had I let this happen? Years of CDs and sweaters, interchangeable gifts, and now one set of picnic ware and I totally lose the upper hand. It seemed impossible.

Dexter walked up the front steps to the door, Monkey bursting forth and bustling around, sniffing at the bags, until they both went inside and the door slammed shut behind them. Something told me, as I stood there, that I should just turn around, go back to my car, and drive home as fast as possible, then lock every door and window and hunker down to protect my dignity. Or my sanity. So many times it seemed like there were chances to stop things before they started. Or even stop them in midstream. But it was even worse when you knew at that very moment that there was still time to save yourself, and yet you couldn't even budge.

The door swung open again, and there was Monkey, panting. Above him, dangling past the doorframe from the left, was one hand, fingers gripping a bright blue fork, wiggling it around suggestively, as if it was some kind of signal, spelling out messages in supersecret spy code. What was it saying? What did it mean? Did I even care any more?

The fork kept wiggling, beckoning. Last chance, I thought.

I sighed out loud, and started up the steps.

There were certain ways to tell that my mother was getting close to finishing a novel. First, she'd start working at all hours, not just her set schedule of noon to four. Then I'd start waking up in the middle of the night to the sound of her typewriter, and look out my window to see the light spilling in long, slanting squares from her study onto the side yard. She'd also start talking to herself as she wrote, under her breath. It wasn't loud enough to really make out what she was saying, but at times it sounded like there were two people in there, one dictating and one just rushing to get it down, one clackety-clacking line at a time. And finally, the most revealing sign of all, always a dead giveaway: when she hit her stride, and the words came so easily she had to fight to hold them back long enough to get them on the page, she always put on the Beatles, and they sang her to her epilogue.

I was on my way down for breakfast in the middle of July, rubbing my eyes, when I stopped at the top of the stairs and listened. Yep. Paul McCartney, his voice high, something from the early years.

The lizard room door opened behind me and Chris came out, in his work uniform, carrying a few empty jars of baby food, one of the daily diet staples of the lizards. He cocked his head to the side, shutting the door behind him. 'Sounds like that album with the Norwegian song on it,' he said.

'Nope,' I told him, starting down the stairs. 'It's that one where they're all in the window, looking down.'

He nodded, and fell into step behind me. When we reached the kitchen we saw the bead curtain was drawn across the entrance to the study, and beyond it Paul's voice had given way to John Lennon's. I walked over and peered through the curtain, impressed by the stack of paper on the desk beside her and one burned-out candle. She had to have had two hundred pages, at least. When she was rolling, nothing could stop her.

I turned back into the kitchen and pushed aside two empty cans of Ensure – I was determined not to clean up after Don, although I was tested daily – before fixing myself a bowl of oatmeal with bananas and a big cup of coffee. Then I sat down, my back to the naked woman on the wall, and pulled the family calendar – a freebie from Don Davis Motors, featuring Don himself smiling in front of a shiny 4Runner – off the wall.

It was July 15th. In two months, give or take a few days, I would be packing up my two suitcases and my laptop and heading to the airport, and seven hours later I would arrive in California to begin my life at Stanford. There was so little written between now and then; even the day I left was hardly marked, except for a simple circle in lipstick I'd done myself, as if it was a big deal only to me.

'Oh, man,' Chris grumbled from in front of the fridge. I glanced over to see him holding an almost empty bag of bread: all that was left were the two end pieces, which I suppose have a real name, but we'd always called the butts. 'He did it again.'

Don had lived alone so long that he was having trouble grasping the concept that other people actually came after him and, sometimes, used the same products he did. He thought nothing of finishing off the last of the orange juice, then sticking the empty carton back in the fridge, or taking the last of the usable bread and leaving the butts for Chris to deal with. Even though Chris and I had both asked him, oh so politely, to write things down when he used them up (we kept a list on the fridge, labelled GROCERIES NEEDED) he either forgot or just didn't care.

Chris shut the fridge door a bit enthusiastically, shaking the rows of Ensures that were stacked there. They clanked against one another, and one toppled off, falling back between the fridge and the wall with a thunk.

'I hate those things,' he grumbled, stuffing the bread butts into the toaster. 'And, God, I just bought this bag. If he's sucking down those Ensures, why does he need to eat my bread anyway? Isn't that a complete meal in itself?'

'I thought so,' I said.

'I mean,' he went on as the music picked up in the next room, all yeah-yeah-yeahs, 'all I'm asking for is a little consideration, you know? Some give-and-take. It's not too much to ask, I don't think. Is it?'

I shrugged, looking again at that lipstick circle. Not my problem.

'Remy?' My mother's voice drifted from the study, the typewriter noises stopping for a second. 'Can you do me a favour?'

'Sure,' I called back to her.

'Bring me some coffee?' The typewriter started up again. 'With milk?'

I got up and poured a cup almost to the top, then dumped in skimmed milk until it reached the rim: one of the only things that we had in common, completely, was taking our coffee the same way. I walked over to the entrance to the study, balancing her cup and mine, and pushed aside the curtain.

The room smelled like vanilla, and I had to move a row of mugs – most half full, their rims stained with the pearly pink that was her 'house lipstick' – aside to make room. One of the cats was curled up on the chair next to her, and hissed at me halfheartedly as I slid it out of the way so I could sit down. Next to me was a stack of typewritten pages, neatly aligned. I was right: she was really cooking. The number of the page on the top was 207.

I knew better than to start talking until she was done

with whatever sentence, or scene, she was in the midst of writing. So I pulled page 207 off the stack and skimmed it, folding my legs beneath me.

'Luc,' Melanie called to the other room in the suite, but there was only silence beyond. 'Please.'

No answer from the man who just hours earlier had kissed her under a shower of rose petals, claiming her in front of all Paris society as the one he loved. How could a marriage bed be so cold? Melanie shivered in her lace gown, feeling tears fill her eyes as she caught sight of her bouquet, white roses and purple lilies, lying where the maid had left it on the bedside table. It was still so fresh and new, and Melanie could remember pressing her face to the full blossoms, breathing them in as the realisation that she was now Mrs Luc Perethel washed over her. Once, the words had seemed magical, like a spell cast in a fairy tale. But now, with the city lit up through her open window, Melanie ached not for her new husband but for another man, in another city. Oh, Brock, she thought. She didn't dare to say the words aloud for fear that they would be carried away, soaring out of her reach, to find the only one true love she'd ever had.

Uh-oh. I glanced up at my mother, who was still typing away, her brow furrowed, lips moving. Now, I knew that what she wrote was pure fiction. After all, this was a woman who'd been constructing stories about the lives and loves of the rich while we were clipping coupons and having our phone cut off on a regular basis. And it wasn't like Luc, the cold new husband, had a fondness for Ensures or anything. I hoped.

'Oh, thank you!' My mother, spying her fresh cup of coffee, stretched her fingers and picked it up, taking a sip. She had her hair pulled back in a loose ponytail, no make-up, and was wearing pyjamas and the leopard-print bedroom slippers I'd got her for her last birthday. She yawned, leaning back in her chair, and said, 'I've been going all night. What time is it?'

I glanced at the clock in the kitchen, visible through the curtain, which was still swaying slightly. 'Eight-fifteen.'

She sighed, putting the cup to her lips again. I glanced over at the sheet in the typewriter, trying to make out what happened next, but all I could see was several lines of dialogue. Apparently, Luc did have something to say after all.

'So it's going well,' I said, nodding toward the stack next to my elbow.

She flopped her hand at me in a so-so kind of way. 'Oh, well, it's smack in the middle, and you know there's always a dull spot. But last night I was just about asleep when I had this inspiration. It had to do with swans.'

I waited. But that appeared to be all she would tell me, as now she'd grabbed a nail file from the mug stuffed with pens and pencils and was at work on a thumbnail, shaping it deftly.

'Swans,' I said finally.

She chucked the nail file down on the desk and stretched her arms over her head. 'You know,' she said, tucking a stray hair behind her ear, 'they're dreadful creatures, really. Beautiful to look at but mean. The Romans used them instead of guard dogs.'

I nodded, drinking my coffee. Across the room, I could hear the cat snoring.

'So,' she went on, 'it got me thinking about what cost beauty. Or for that matter, what cost anything? Would you trade love for beauty? Or happiness for beauty? Could a gorgeous person with a mean streak be a worthy trade? And if you did make the trade, decide you'd take that beautiful swan and hope it wouldn't turn on you, what would you do if it did?'

These were rhetorical questions. I thought.

'I just couldn't stop thinking about it,' she said, shaking her head. 'And then I couldn't sleep, either. I think it's that ridiculous tapestry Don insisted we hang on the wall. I can't relax looking at all these carefully stitched depictions of military battles and people being crucified.'

'It is a little much,' I agreed. Every time I went into her room to get anything I found myself somewhat transfixed by it. It was hard to tear your eyes away from the panel that illustrated the beheading of John the Baptist.

'So I came down here,' she said, 'thinking I'd just tinker, and now it's eight in the AM and I'm still not sure what the answer is. How can that be?'

The music faded out now, and it was very, very quiet. I was sure I could feel my ulcer stirring, but it might have just been the coffee. My mother was always very dramatic when she was writing. At least once during every novel she'd fling herself into the kitchen, near tears, hysterical that she'd lost any talent she ever possessed, the book was a quagmire, a disaster, the end of her career, and Chris and I would just sit there, silent, until she wailed out again. After a few minutes, or hours, or – in bad times – days, she'd be right back in the study, curtain closed, typing away. And when the books arrived months later, smelling so new with their smooth, not-yet-cracked spines, she always forgot about the breakdowns that played a part in creating them. If I reminded her, she said writing novels was like childbirth: if you truly remembered how awful it got, you'd never do it again.

'You'll work it out,' I said now. 'You always do.'

She bit her lip and glanced down at the page in the typewriter, then out the window. The sunlight was spilling in, and I realised she did look tired, even sad, in a way I hadn't noticed before. 'I know,' she said, as if only agreeing with me to move past this. And then, after a quiet second or two, she switched gears completely and asked, 'How's Dexter?'

'Okay, I guess,' I said.

'I like him very much.' She yawned, then smiled at me apologetically. 'He's not like the other boys you've dated.'

'I had a no-musician rule,' I explained.

She sighed. 'So did I.'

I laughed, and she did too. Then I said, 'Okay, so why'd you break it?'

'Oh, the reason anyone does anything,' she said. 'I was in love.'

I heard the front door swing shut as Chris left for work, yelling a good-bye behind him. We watched as he walked down the driveway to his car, a Red Bull – his version of coffee – in one hand.

'I think he's going to buy her a ring, if he hasn't already,' my mother said thoughtfully. 'I just have this feeling.'

Chris started the engine, then pulled out into neighbourhood traffic, turning around slowly in the cul-de-sac. He was swigging the Red Bull as he drove past.

'Well,' I said, 'you would know.'

She finished her coffee, then reached over and brushed her fingers over my cheek, tracing the shape of my face. A dramatic gesture, like most of hers, but it was comforting in that she'd done it for as long as I could remember. Her fingers, as always, were cool.

'Oh, my Remy,' she said. 'Only you understand.'

I knew what she meant, and yet I didn't. I was a lot like my mother, but not in ways I was proud of. If my parents had stayed together and grown to be old hippies singing protest songs as they washed dishes after dinner, maybe I would have been different. If I'd ever seen what love really could do, or was, maybe I'd have believed in it from the start. But too much of my life had been spent watching marriages come together and then fall apart. So I understood, yes. But sometimes, like lately, I wished that I didn't, not at all.

* * *

'But it's filling up.'

'Filling up but not full.' I took the Tide from him and unscrewed the cap. 'It has to be full.'

'I always put the soap in right when it starts,' he said.

'Which is why,' I said, pouring a bit of detergent in as the water level rose, 'your clothes don't ever get truly clean. There is a chemistry involved here, Dexter.'

'It's laundry,' he said.

'Exactly.'

He sighed. 'You know,' he said as I poured in the rest of the Tide and eased the lid shut, 'the rest of the guys are even worse. They hardly ever even do laundry, much less separate their colours and brights.'

'Colours and whites,' I corrected him. 'Colours and brights go together.'

'Are you this anal about everything?'

'Do you want everything to be pink again?'

That shut him up. Our little laundry lesson this evening had been precipitated by his throwing a new red shirt into the hot water cycle, which left everything he'd been wearing lately with a rosy tinge. Since the plastic ware incident I'd been doing all I could to be the very opposite of domestic, but I couldn't abide a pink boyfriend. So here I was, in the laundry room of the yellow house, a place I normally steadfastedly avoided because of the enormous pile of unwashed underwear, socks, and various T-shirts that dwelled there, often spilling out into the hallway. Which was not surprising, considering that hardly anyone ever bought detergent. Just last week, John

Miller had apparently washed all his jeans in Palmolive.

Once the cycle started, I stepped carefully over a pile of nasty socks, back out into the hallway, and eased the door shut as far as it would go. Then I followed Dexter into the kitchen, where Lucas was sitting at the table, eating a tangerine.

'You doing laundry?' he asked Dexter.

'Yep.'

'Again?'

Dexter nodded. 'I'm bleaching out my whites.'

Lucas looked impressed. But then, he was wearing a shirt with a ketchup stain on the collar. 'Wow,' he said. 'That's—'

And then, suddenly, it was dark. Totally dark. All the lights cut off, the refrigerator whirred to a stop, the swishing of the washing machine went quiet. The only brightness anywhere left that I could see was the porch light of the house next door.

'Hey!' John Miller yelled from the living room, where he was absorbed, as usual about this time each night, in *Wheel of Fortune*. 'I was just about to solve the puzzle, man!'

'Shut up,' Lucas said, standing and walking over to the light switch, which he flipped on and off a couple of times, click-clack-click. 'Must be a blown fuse.'

'It's the whole house,' Dexter said.

'So?'

'So, if it was just one fuse something would still be on.' Dexter picked up a lighter from the middle of the table and flicked it. 'Must be a power outage. Probably the whole grid's out.'

'Oh.' Lucas sat back down. In the living room, there was a crash as John Miller attempted to navigate the darkness.

This wasn't my problem. Surely it wasn't. Still, I couldn't help but point out, 'Um, the lights are on next door.'

Dexter leaned back in his chair, glancing out the window to verify this. 'So they are,' he said. 'In-teresting.'

Lucas started to peel another tangerine as John Miller appeared in the kitchen doorway. His pale skin seemed even brighter in the dark. 'Lights are out,' he said, as if we were blind and needed to be told this.

'Thank you, Einstein,' Lucas grumbled.

'It's a circuitry problem,' Dexter decided. 'Bad wiring, maybe.'

John Miller came into the room and flopped down on the couch. For a minute, no one said anything, and it became clear to me that this, to them, wasn't really that big a problem. Lights, schmights.

'Did you not pay your bill?' I asked Dexter, finally.

'Bill?' he repeated.

'The power bill.'

Silence. Then, from Lucas, 'Oh, man. The freaking power bill.'

'But we paid that,' John Miller said. 'It was right there on the counter, I saw it yesterday.'

Dexter looked at him. 'You saw it, or we paid it?'

'Both?' John Miller said, and Lucas sighed, impatiently.

'Where was it?' I asked John Miller, standing up. Someone had to do something, clearly. 'Which counter?'

'There,' he said, pointing, but it was dark and I couldn't see where. 'In that drawer where we keep the important stuff.'

Dexter picked up a lighter and lit a candle, then turned to the drawer and began to dig around, sorting through what, to the guys, was deemed Important. Apparently, this included soy sauce packets, a plastic hula girl toy, and matchbooks from what looked like every convenience store and bar in town.

Oh, and a few pieces of paper, one of which Dexter seized and held aloft. 'Is this it?'

I took it from him, squinting down at the writing. 'No,' I said, slowly, 'this is a notice saying if you didn't pay your bill by – let's see – *yesterday*, they were going to cut the power off.'

'Wow,' John Miller said. 'How did that slip past us?'

I turned it over: stuck to the back was a set of pizza coupons with one ripped off, all of those left still a little greasy. 'No idea,' I said.

'Yesterday,' Lucas said thoughtfully. 'Wow, so they gave us, like, a half day over that. That's mighty generous of them.'

I just looked at him.

'Okay,' Dexter said cheerfully, 'so whose job was it to pay the power bill?'

Another silence. Then John Miller said, 'Ted?'

'Ted,' Lucas echoed.

'Ted,' Dexter said, reaching over to the phone and yanking it off the hook. He dialled a number, then sat there, drumming his fingers on the table. 'Hi, hey, Ted. Dexter. Guess where I am?' He listened for a second. 'Nope. The dark. I'm in the dark. Weren't you supposed to pay the power bill?'

I could hear Ted saying something, talking fast.

'I was about to solve the puzzle!' John Miller yelled. 'I only needed an *L* or a *V*.'

'Nobody cares,' Lucas told him.

Dexter continued to listen to Ted, who apparently had not taken a breath yet, making only hmm-hmm noises now and then. Finally he said, 'Okay then!' and hung up the phone.

'So?' Lucas said.

'So,' Dexter told us, 'Ted has it under control.'

'Meaning?' I asked.

'Meaning that he's royally pissed, because, apparently, I was supposed to pay the power bill.' Then he smiled. 'So! Who wants to tell ghost stories?'

'Dexter, honestly,' I said. This kind of irresponsibility made my ulcer ache, but apparently Lucas and John Miller were used to it. Neither one of them seemed particularly fazed, or even surprised.

'It's fine, it's fine,' he said. 'Ted's got the money, he's going to call them and see what he can do about getting it on tonight or early tomorrow.'

'Good for Ted,' Lucas said. 'But what about you?'

'Me?' Dexter seemed surprised. 'What about me?'

'He means,' I said, 'that you should do something nice for the house by way of apology for this.'

'Exactly,' Lucas said. 'Listen to Remy.'

Dexter looked at me. 'Honey, you're not helping.'

'We're in the dark!' John Miller said. 'And it's your fault, Dexter.'

'Okay, okay,' Dexter said. 'Fine. I'll do something for the house. I'll—'

'Clean the bathroom?' Lucas said.

'No,' Dexter said flatly.

'Do a load of my laundry?'

'No.'

Finally, John Miller said, 'Buy beer?'

Everyone waited.

'Yes,' Dexter said. 'Yes! I will buy beer. Here.' He reached into his pocket and came up with a crumpled bill, which he held up for all of us to see. 'Twenty bucks. Of my hard-earned money. For you.'

Lucas swiped it off the table, fast, as if expecting Dexter to change his mind. 'Wonderful. Let's go.'

'I'll drive,' said John Miller, jumping to his feet. He and Lucas left the kitchen, arguing about where the keys were. Then the screen door slammed, and we were alone.

Dexter reached over the kitchen counter and found another candle, then lit it and put it on the table as I slid into the chair opposite him. 'Romantic,' I told him.

'Of course,' he said. 'I planned all of this, just to get you alone in a dark house in the candlelight.'

'Chee-sy,' I said.

He smiled. 'I try.'

We sat there for a second, in the quiet. I could see him watching me, and after a second I pushed out my chair and walked around the table to him, sliding into his lap. 'If you were my room-mate and pulled this kind of crap,' I said as he brushed my hair off my shoulder, 'I'd kill you.'

'You'd learn to love it.'

'I doubt that.'

'I think,' he said, 'that you are actually, secretly attracted to all the parts of my personality that you claim to abhor.'

I looked at him. 'I don't think so.'

'Then what is it?'

'What is what?'

'What is it,' he said, 'that makes you like me?'

'Dexter.'

'No, really.' He pulled me back against him, so my head was next to his, his hands locked around my waist. In front of us the candle was flickering, sending uneven shadows across the far wall. 'Tell me.'

'No,' I said, adding, 'it's too weird.'

'It is not. Look. I'll tell you what I like about you.'

I groaned.

'Well, obviously, you're beautiful,' he said, ignoring this. 'And that, I have to admit, was what first got my attention at the dealership that day. But then, I must say, it's your confidence that really did me in. You know, so many girls are always insecure, wondering if they're fat, or if you really like them, but not you. Man. You acted like you couldn't have given less of a shit whether I talked to you or not.'

'Acted?' I said.

'See?' I could feel him grinning. 'That's what I mean.'

'So you're attracted to the fact that I'm a bitch?'

'No, no. That's not it.' He shifted his weight. 'What I liked was that it was a challenge. To get past that, to wriggle through. Most people are easy to figure out. But a girl like you, Remy, has layers. What you see is so far from what you get. You may come across hard, but down deep, you're a big softie.'

'What?' I said. Honestly, I was offended. 'I am *not* soft.'

'You bought me plastic ware.'

'It was on sale!' I yelled. 'God!'

'You're really nice to my dog.'

I sighed.

'And,' he continued, 'not only did you volunteer to come over here and teach me how to properly separate my colours from brights . . .'

'Colours from *whites*.'

'. . . but you also stepped up to help solve our power bill problem and smooth over the differences with the guys. Face it, Remy. You're sweet.'

'Shut up,' I grumbled.

'Why is that a bad thing?' he asked.

'It's not,' I said. 'It's just not true.' And it wasn't. I'd been called a lot of things in my life, but sweet had never been one of them. It made me feel strangely unnerved, as if he'd discovered a deep secret I hadn't even known I was keeping.

'Okay,' he said. 'Now you.'

'Now me what?'

'Now, you tell me why you like me.'

'Who says I do?'

'Remy,' he said sternly. 'Don't make me call you sweet again.'

'Fine, fine.' I sat up and leaned forward, stalling by pulling the candle over to the edge of the table. Talk about losing my edge: this was what I'd become. True confessions by candlelight. 'Well,' I said finally, knowing he was waiting, 'you make me laugh.'

He nodded. 'And?'

'You're pretty good-looking.'

'*Pretty* good-looking? I called you beautiful.'

'You want to be beautiful?' I asked him.

'Are you saying I'm not?'

I looked at the ceiling, shaking my head.

'I'm kidding, I'll stop. God, relax, would you? I'm not asking you to recite the Declaration of Independence at gunpoint.'

'I wish,' I said, and he laughed, loud enough to blow out the candle on the table, leaving us again in total darkness.

'Okay,' he said as I turned back to face him, sliding my arms around his neck. 'You don't have to say it out loud. I already know why you like me.'

'You do, huh?'

'Yep.'

He wrapped his arms around my waist, pulling me closer. 'So,' I said. 'Tell me.'

'It's an animal attraction,' he said simply. 'Totally chemical.'

'Hmm,' I said. 'You could be right.'

'It doesn't matter, anyway, why you like me.'

'No?'

'Nope.' His hands were in my hair now, and I was leaning in, not able to totally make out his face, but his voice was clear, close to my ear. 'Just that you do.'

11

'This,' Chloe said as another bubble rose up and popped in her face, 'is disgusting.'

'Stop,' I told her. 'He can hear you, you know.'

She sighed, wiping her face with the back of her hand. It was hot, and the black asphalt of the driveway made things seem positively steamy. Monkey, however, sitting between us in a plastic baby pool up to his haunches in cold water, was totally content.

'Get his front feet,' I said to Chloe, squeezing more shampoo into my hand and lathering it up. 'They're really dirty.'

'All of him is dirty,' she grumbled as Monkey stood up and shook again, sending soap suds and dirty water over both of us in a wave. 'And have you looked at these nails? They're longer than Talinga's, for God's sake.'

Monkey stood up suddenly, barking, having spied a cat working its way through a row of hedges on the edge of Chloe's yard. 'Down boy,' Chloe said. 'Hello? Sit, Monkey. *Sit*.'

Monkey shook again, dousing us both, and I pushed down on his butt. He sat with a splash, his tail flopping over the side. 'Good boy,' I said, even though he was already trying to stand up again.

'You know, if my mother were to show up now I'd

be homeless,' Chloe said, spraying Monkey's chest with the hose. 'Just the sight of this mangy beast within spitting distance of her prized Blue Category Chem Special would give her an aneurysm.'

'Blue Category What?'

'It's a kind of grass,' she explained.

'Oh.'

Chloe had first given me a flat-out no when she opened the door to see me on her front porch, shampoo and dog in hand, before I'd even begun my hard sell. But after a few minutes of wheedling, plus a promise to buy her dinner and whatever else she wanted to do that night, she'd relented, and even seemed to warm to Monkey a bit, petting him cautiously as I got the baby pool – a Wal-Mart bargain at a mere nine bucks – out of my car. I'd planned to wash the dog at my house, but Chris had co-opted our hose to rig up an elaborate watering system for the lizards, which left me with few options.

'I still can't believe how low you've stooped,' she said now as I finished the final rinse, then let Monkey leap from the pool and do a series of full-body shakes up and down the driveway. 'This is total girlfriend behaviour.'

'No,' I said, steering Monkey away from the grass before Chloe had a chance to freak out. 'This is a humanitarian act. He was miserable.'

Which was true. Plus, I'd been spending a fair amount of time with Monkey lately, and okay, there was a certain odour to him. And if all it took to fix things was a five-dollar bottle of dog shampoo, some nail clippers, and a quick trim, what was the harm in taking action? It wasn't for me, anyway. It was for Monkey.

'I thought you weren't getting attached,' she said as I pulled the clippers out of my pocket and sat the dog down again.

'I'm not,' I told her. 'It's just for the summer. I told you that.'

'I'm not talking about Dexter.' She nodded at Monkey, who was now trying to lick my face. He stank of citrus now: all they'd had left was an orangey citrus scent. But we'd trimmed the hair over his eyes and around his feet, which made him look five years younger. It was true what Lola said: a good haircut changed everything. 'This is an additional level of commitment. And responsibility. It's going to make things complicated.'

'Chloe, he's a dog, not a five-year-old with an abandonment complex.'

'Still.' She squatted down beside me, watching as I finished up one paw and switched to the other. 'And anyway, what happened to our wild and carefree summer? Once you dumped Jonathan I thought we'd just date our way to August. No worries. Remember?'

'I'm not worried,' I said.

'Not now,' she said darkly.

'Not ever,' I told her. I stood up. 'There. He's done.'

We stood back and surveyed our work. 'A vast improvement,' she said.

'You think?'

'Anything would have been,' she said, shrugging.

But then she bent down and petted him, running her hand over the top of his head as I spread a few towels across the back seat of my car. I liked Monkey, sure, but that didn't necessarily mean I was up for picking dog hair out of my upholstery for the next few weeks.

'Come on, Monk,' I called out, and he sprang up, trotting down the driveway. He just hopped in, then promptly stuck his head out the back window, sniffing the air. 'Thanks for the help, Chloe.'

As I slid into the front seat, the leather hot under my legs, she stood and watched me, her hands on her hips. 'You know,' she said, 'it's not too late. If you go ahead and break up with him now you'd still have a good month's worth of quality single-girl time before you leave for school.'

I stuck my key in the ignition. 'I'll keep that in mind,' I said.

'See you around five-thirty?'

'Yeah,' I told her. 'I'll pick you up.'

She nodded, then stood there, one hand shielding her eyes as I backed out into the street. Of course it would be that cut-and-dried for her, how I could end things with Dexter. It was the way we'd always operated. Chloe was, after all, my twin in all things concerning boys and relationships. Now, I was throwing her a curve, veering off in a way she couldn't understand. I knew how she felt. Ever since I'd met Dexter, things weren't making much sense to me either.

* * *

The collage was on the wall in the kitchen of the yellow house, right over the sofa. It started innocently enough, with just a couple of snapshots tacked up; at first glance, I'd assumed they were of the guys' friends. But upon closer inspection, I'd realised that the pictures, like the ones Dexter had given me weeks earlier, were of customers of Flash Camera.

Dexter and Lucas had both been hired there to run the photo machine, which basically consisted of sitting on a stool and peering through a little hole at the images, marking them and adjusting them, if possible, for optimum colour and brightness. This wasn't rocket science, but it did involve a bit of skill, a good eye, and most of all an attention span that could focus on one, sometimes monotonous activity for an hour or two at a time. This meant, pretty much, that Dexter was out. After Dexter had ruined an entire set of once-in-a-lifetime Hawaiian vacation pictures and twenty disposable wedding cameras, the owner of Flash Camera gently suggested that he might be happier using his strong customer service skills by taking a counter position. And because he was so charming, she'd kept him on at a technician's salary, which Lucas was always quick to bitch about when given the chance.

'My job involves so much more responsibility,' he'd sniff every payday, snatching up his cheque. 'All you have to do is basic maths and be able to alphabetise.'

'Ah,' Dexter always said, smartly adjusting his name tag in a model employee fashion, 'but I alphabetise very, very well.'

Actually, he didn't. He was constantly losing

people's pictures, mostly because he'd get distracted and stick the *R*s in with the *B*s, or sometimes glance at the labels wrong and put them under people's first names. If he worked for me, I wouldn't have trusted him with anything more complicated than sharpening pencils, and even that only when supervised.

So while Ted, working at Mayor's Market, could score some bruised but edible produce, and John Miller was jacked up on coffee constantly from his job at Jump Java, Dexter and Lucas were left with little to contribute. That is, until they started making doubles of the pictures that intrigued them.

They *were* boys, so of course it started with a set of dirty pictures. Not X-rated, exactly: the first one on the wall that I saw was of a woman in her bra and panties, posing in front of a fireplace. She wasn't exactly pretty, however, and it didn't help that right in the back of the shot, clearly visible, was a huge bag of cat litter with the words KITTY KLEAN! splashed across the front of it, which took away from that exotic, *Playboy*-esque quality that I assumed she and whoever took the picture had been going for.

As the weeks passed, more and more pictures were added to the collage. There were vacation snapshots, a family posing en masse in front of the Washington Monument, everyone smiling except for one daughter who was scowling darkly, her middle finger clearly displayed. A few more nudie shots, including one of a very fat man spread out in black underwear across a leopardskin bedspread. All of these people had no idea that in a little yellow house off Merchant Drive their personal memories were being slapped up on the wall and showcased as art for strangers.

The day I washed Monkey, Chloe and I brought him back about six, and Dexter was already home, sitting in the living room watching PBS and eating tangerines. Apparently they were on special at Mayor's Market, and Ted was getting a discount. They came about twenty-five to a case and, like Don's Ensures at home, were everywhere.

'Okay,' I said, pushing open the screen door and holding Monkey back by the collar. 'Behold.'

I let him go, and he skittered across the floor, tail wagging madly, to leap on the couch, knocking a stack of magazines to the floor. 'Oh, man, look at you,' Dexter said, scratching Monkey behind his ears. 'He smells different,' he said. 'Like you washed him in Orange Crush.'

'That's the shampoo,' Chloe said, flopping into the plastic lawn chair next to the coffee table. 'It'll stop stinking in, oh, about a week.'

Dexter glanced at me and I shook my head to show him she was kidding. Monkey hopped off the couch and went into the kitchen, where we heard him gulping down what sounded like about a gallon of water without stopping.

'Well,' Dexter said, pulling me into his lap, 'those makeovers sure make a man thirsty.'

The screen door opened and John Miller walked in, tossing the van keys onto a speaker by the door. Then he walked to the middle of the room, held up his hands to stop all conversation, and said, very simply, 'I have news.'

We all looked at him. Then the door opened again, and Ted came in, still wearing his Mayor's Market green smock, and carrying two boxes of tangerines.

'Oh, God,' Dexter said, '*please* no more tangerines.'

'I have news,' Ted announced, ignoring this. 'Big news. Where's Lucas?'

'Work,' Dexter said.

'I have news too,' John Miller said to Ted. 'And I was here first, so—'

'This is important news,' Ted replied, waving him off. 'Okay, so—'

'Wait just a second!' John Miller shook his head, his face incredulous. He had been born indignant, always convinced that he was somehow being wronged. 'Why do you always do that? You know, my news could be important too.'

It was quiet as Ted and Dexter exchanged a sceptical look, not unnoticed by John Miller, who sighed loudly, shaking his head.

'Maybe,' Dexter said finally, holding up his hands, 'we should just take a moment to really think about the fact that we've gone a long time with no big news at all, and now here, simultaneously, we have two big newses all at once.'

'Newses?' Chloe said.

'The point is,' Dexter went on smoothly, 'it's really impressive.'

'The point is,' Ted said loudly, 'I met this A&R chick

today from Rubber Records and she's coming to hear us tonight.'

Silence. Except for Monkey walking in, dripping water from his mouth, his newly clipped nails tippy-tapping very quietly on the floor.

'Does anyone smell oranges?' Ted asked, sniffing.

'That,' John Miller said darkly, glaring at him, 'was totally unfair.'

'A and R?' Chloe said. 'What's that?'

'Artists and Repertoire,' Ted explained, taking off his smock and balling it up in one hand, then stuffing it into his back pocket. 'It means if she likes us she might offer us a deal.'

'I had news,' John Miller grumbled, but it was over. He knew he'd been beaten. 'Big news.'

'How serious is this?' Dexter asked Ted, leaning forward. 'Just-making-conversation-I'll-show-up-to-see-you, or definitely-I-have-pull-at-the-label-I'll-come-see-you?'

Ted reached into his pocket. 'She gave me a card. She's got a meeting tonight, but when I said we usually started the second set by ten-thirty she said she'd make it by then, no problem.'

Dexter slid me off his lap, then stood up, and Ted handed him the card. He squinted at it for a good while, then handed it back. 'Okay,' he said. 'Find Lucas. We have to talk about this.'

'You know this could be nothing,' John Miller said, still smarting a bit. 'It could be a bunch of smoke up your ass.'

'And it probably is,' Ted replied. 'But it also could

be that she likes us and we get a meeting and before the summer's out we're in a bigger place, bigger venue, bigger town. It happened to Spinnerbait.'

'Hate Spinnerbait,' John Miller said, and they all three nodded, as if this was clear fact.

'Spinnerbait has a deal, though,' Dexter added. 'And a record.'

'Spinnerbait?' I said.

'They were this band that started playing the bars near Williamsburg when we did,' Dexter said to me. 'Total assholes. Frat rats. But they had this really good guitar player . . .'

'He wasn't that good,' Ted said indignantly. 'Totally overrated.'

'. . . and their original stuff was tight. They got signed last year.' Dexter sighed, then looked up at the ceiling. 'We hate Spinnerbait.'

'Hate Spinnerbait,' John Miller repeated, and Ted nodded.

'Okay, get ahold of Lucas,' Dexter said, slapping his hands together. 'Emergency session. Band meeting!'

'Band meeting!' Ted yelled, as if everyone who was in the band and could feasibly hear it wasn't within a two-foot radius. 'I'm gonna go scrub up and we reconnoitre in the kitchen, twenty minutes.'

Dexter grabbed the cordless phone off the top of the TV, jabbed in some numbers, and then left the room with it pressed against his ear. I could hear him ask for Lucas, then say, 'Guess what Ted scored at work today?' Then a pause, as Lucas offered a theory. 'No, not tangerines . . .'

John Miller sat down on the couch, crossing one leg over another and leaning back so that his head hit the wall behind him with a thunk. Chloe looked at me, raising her eyebrows, then shook a cigarette out of her pack and lit it, dropping the spent match in an ashtray already overflowing with tangerine peels.

'Okay, I'll bite,' I said finally. 'What's your news?'

'No, now it's completely anti-climactic,' he grumbled. He still looked so much like a little kid to me, all red haired and freckled, like a grade schooler you might see on TV in a peanut butter commercial. It didn't help that he was pouting.

'Suit yourself,' I said, and picked up the remote, turning the TV on. It wasn't like I was about to beg him or anything.

'My news was,' he said slowly, lifting his head off the wall, 'that she agreed to come to Bendo tonight.'

'She did.'

'Yes. Finally. I've only been asking her for *weeks*.' He reached up and scratched his ear. 'And it was a very big deal because I was beginning to think I was going to make no progress at all with her.'

I said to Chloe, 'John Miller is in love with his boss.'

Chloe exhaled loudly. 'At Jump Java?'

John Miller sighed again. 'She's not really my boss,' he told us. 'She's more of a co-worker. A friend, really.'

Chloe looked at me. 'This is Scarlett Thomas?'

I nodded, but John Miller's eyes shot open. 'You know her?'

'I guess,' Chloe said, shrugging. 'Remy knows her better, though. She and Chris go way back, right?'

I swallowed, concentrating on flipping the channels on the TV. I'd known about John Miller's infatuation with Scarlett back when it was just curious interest, then watched – along with the rest of the employees at various Mayor's Village businesses – as it progressed to puppy-dog-esque devotion before finally reaching the ridiculous level of romantic pining that was its current state. Scarlett was the manager of Jump Java, and she'd only hired John Miller because of Lola, who she still owed a favour to for her last cut and colour. And while I'd listened to John Miller sing her praises, I'd managed to keep it quiet that I knew her more than just in passing. Until now.

I could feel John Miller looking at me, even as I pretended to be completely engrossed in a news story about structural problems with the new county dam. He said, 'Remy? You know Scarlett?'

'My brother dated her,' I said, in what I hoped was a no-big-deal kind of voice. 'It was ages ago.'

He reached over and took the remote, hitting the mute button. The dam remained on the screen, holding water back just fine, it seemed to me. 'Tell me,' he said. 'Now.'

I looked at him.

'I mean,' he said quickly, 'can you tell me? Anything?'

Across the room, Chloe laughed. I shrugged and said, 'My brother dated her toward the end of their senior year. It wasn't serious. Chris was still in his pot-head thing, and Scarlett was way too smart to put up with it. Plus she already had Grace, then.'

224

He nodded. Grace was Scarlett's daughter, who was three now. She'd been born when Scarlett was a junior, causing a minor neighbourhood scandal. But Scarlett had stayed in school, finishing during a summer session the credits she'd missed, and now was taking classes part-time at the university while managing Jump Java and, apparently, putting up with the besotted John Miller passing longing glances over the muffins about twenty hours a week.

'Isn't Scarlett a little out of your league?' Chloe asked him, not unkindly. 'I mean, she's got a kid.'

'I am wonderful with children,' he said indignantly. 'Grace loves me.'

'Grace loves everybody,' I told him. *Just like Monkey*, I thought. *Kids and dogs. It's just too easy.*

'No,' he said, 'she especially likes me.'

Dexter stuck his head through the doorway and pointed a finger at John Miller. 'Band meeting!' he said.

'Band meeting,' John Miller repeated, standing up. Then he looked at me and said, 'A little help tonight would be greatly appreciated, Remy. A good word, maybe?'

'I can't promise anything,' I said. 'But I'll see what I can do.'

He seemed happier, hearing this, as he headed into the kitchen. I got up and grabbed my bag, finding my keys. 'Let's go,' I said to Chloe. 'Band meeting and all.'

She nodded, stuffing her smokes in her pocket and walking to the front door, pushing it open. 'I'll call

Lissa from the car. See if she wants to meet us at the Spot.'

'Sounds good.'

As the screen door slammed behind her, Dexter walked over to me. 'This is big,' he said, smiling. 'I mean, maybe it isn't. Maybe it'll be a crushing disappointment.'

'That's the right attitude.'

'Or maybe,' he went on, pulling his hands through his hair the way he always did when just barely able to contain himself, 'it's the beginning of something. You know, when Spinnerbait got that meeting with the label, they immediately got an in to the bigger clubs. We could be in Richmond, or D.C., easy. It could happen.'

He was just standing there, grinning, and I made myself smile back. Of course this was good news. Wasn't it me who wanted everything to be transitory, anyway? It was the best-case scenario, really, for him to get some great chance and ride off in the dirty white van into the sunset, tailpipe dragging. In time he'd just be some story I'd tell, about the crazy musician I'd spent the last days of my senior summer with, just the way Scarlett Thomas was only a footnote now to Chris. *They had these stupid songs about potatoes*, I could hear myself telling someone. *A whole opus*.

Yes, definitely. It was best this way.

Dexter leaned down and kissed my forehead, then looked at me closely, cocking his head to the side. 'You okay? You look weird.'

'Thanks,' I said. 'God.'

'No, I mean, you just seem—'

'Band meeting!' Ted yelled from the kitchen. 'We're reconnoitring right now!'

Dexter glanced toward the doorway, then back at me.

'Go,' I said, pressing my palms to his chest and pushing him backward, gently. 'Band meeting.'

He smiled, and for a second I felt a tug, some alien feeling that made me, for an instant, want to pull him back within arm's length. But by then he was already walking backward, toward the kitchen, where the voices of his band mates were now building as they made their plans.

'I'll see you at Bendo around nine,' he said. 'Right?'

I nodded, cool as ever, and he turned the corner, leaving me standing there. Watching him go. What a weird feeling that was. I decided I didn't like it. Not at all.

By ten-thirty, as Truth Squad's second set was about to get under way, the A&R chick still hadn't shown up. The natives were getting restless.

'I say we just go on and forget about her,' Lucas said, spitting some ice back into his cup of ginger ale. 'All this worrying is making us suck anyway. Ted was off key the whole last set.'

Ted, sitting next to me and carving lines into the table, glared at him darkly. 'I,' he said, 'am the only reason she's coming. So get off my goddam back.'

'Now, now.' Dexter tugged at his collar, something he'd been doing all night long: it was completely stretched out of shape, hanging lopsided. 'We need to go up there and do the best job we can. A lot is riding on this.'

'No pressure, though,' Lucas grumbled.

'Where the hell is John Miller?' Ted said, pushing up from the table and craning his neck around the room. 'Isn't this a band meeting?'

'It's impromptu,' Dexter told him, tugging at his collar again. 'Plus he's over there with what's-her-name. The coffee boss.'

We all looked at once. Sure enough, at a booth by the stage, John Miller was sitting with Scarlett. He had his drumsticks on the table and was talking animatedly, using his hands. Scarlett was drinking a beer and listening, a polite smile on her face. Every once in a while she'd glance around the room, as if she'd expected this to be more of a group thing and was wondering where everyone else was.

'Pathetic,' Ted said. 'Totally blowing us and the band's future off for a chick. That's Yoko Ono behaviour, man.'

'Leave him alone,' Dexter said. 'Okay, so I'm thinking we should start with "Potato Song Two", then do the kumquat version, and then . . .'

I tuned them out, drawing my finger through the circle of water under my beer. Off to my left, I could see Chloe, Lissa, and Jess talking to a group of guys at the bar. At the Spot earlier, Chloe had decided they all needed to 'get back out there' and make the most of the 'summer single-girl thing', appointing herself ringleader for the effort. So far there had been progress: she was sitting on a barstool next to a blond guy with surfer looks. Lissa was talking to two guys, one really cute, who was still scoping the room as if in search of an upgrade (bad sign), and one not-so-cute-but-decent who seemed interested and not completely offended that he was most likely an also-ran. And then there was Jess, trapped by the beer taps by a short, wiry guy who was talking so excitedly that she kept having to lean back, which could only have meant he was spitting out more than words.

'. . . decided that we'd do no covers. That was the entire upshot of yesterday's meeting,' Dexter said.

'I'm just saying that if the potato songs don't go over well we need a back-up plan,' Lucas argued. 'What if she hates potatoes? What if she thinks the songs are, you know, infantile, frat-party crap?'

There was a moment of astonished silence as Dexter and Ted absorbed this. Then Ted said, 'So that's what you think?'

'No,' Lucas said quickly, glancing at Dexter, who was now tugging his collar hard enough that I had to reach up and unlatch his fingers, bringing down his hand. He hardly noticed. Lucas said, 'I'm just saying we don't want to come across as derivative.'

'And doing covers isn't derivative?' Dexter said.

'Covers will get the crowd going and show our range,' Lucas told him. 'Look, I've been in a lot of bands . . .'

'Oh, God,' Ted said, throwing up his hands dramatically. 'Here we go. Educate us, oh wise one.'

'. . . and I know from experience that these reps like

229

a tight set that gets the crowd going and showcases our potential as a band. Which means a mix of our own stuff and songs that we cover, yeah, but with our own take on them. It's not like we do "I've Got You Babe" just the way Sonny and Cher do. We give it a twist.'

'We are *not* doing a Sonny and Cher song here tonight!' Ted yelled. 'No way, man. I am not going to be the G Flats for this chick. That's wedding crap. Forget it.'

'It was just an example,' Lucas said flatly. 'We can do another song. Calm down, would you?'

'Hey,' Robert, the owner of Bendo, yelled from behind the bar, 'you guys planning on actually *working* tonight?'

'Let's go,' Ted said, standing up and finishing his beer.

'Did we even decide anything?' Lucas asked, but Ted ignored him as they made their way to the stage.

Dexter sighed, running his fingers through his hair. I'd never seen him like this, so on edge. 'God,' he said softly, shaking his head. 'This is so freaking stressful.'

'Stop thinking about it,' I told him. 'Just go up there and play the way you always do. Thinking about it is throwing you off.'

'We sounded like shit, didn't we?'

'No,' I said, which wasn't entirely a lie. But Ted had been off-key, John Miller was showboating outrageously – tossing drumsticks in the air, missing them – and Dexter had mangled the words to 'Potato Song Three', a song that I knew he could, literally, sing in his sleep. 'But you sounded unsure of yourself.

Wobbly. And you're not. You've done this a million times.'

'A million times.' He still didn't sound convinced, however.

'It's like riding a bike,' I told him. 'If you actually think about it too much, you realise how complicated a concept it actually is. You have to just hop on and go, and not worry about the mechanics. Let it run itself.'

'You,' he said, kissing my cheek, 'are so right. How can you always be so right?'

'It's a curse,' I said, shrugging. He squeezed my leg and slid out of the booth, still tugging at his collar, and I watched him weave through the crowd, stopping to flick John Miller, who was still chatting up Scarlett, on the head as he passed. Ted put on his guitar, played a few random chords, and then he, Lucas, and Dexter exchanged glances and head nods, setting the game plan.

The first song was a bit unsteady. But then, the next was better. I could see Dexter relaxing, easing into it, and by the third song, when I saw the A&R chick come in, they sounded tighter than they had all evening. I recognised her immediately. First, she was a little old for Bendo, which catered to a college and younger crowd, and second, she was dressed entirely too fashionably for this small town: black trousers, silky shirt, small black glasses just nerdy enough to be cool. Her hair was long and pulled back loosely at the base of her neck, and when she walked up to the bar for a drink, every one of the guys chatting up my girlfriends stopped to stare at her. By the time the song wound down, the crowd on the floor was thickening, and I saw Ted glance at the bar, see her, and then say something, quietly, to Dexter.

After the applause and hooting died down, Dexter tugged at his shirt collar and said, 'Okay, we're going to do a little number for you now called "The Potato Song".'

The crowd cheered: they'd been playing Bendo long enough now that 'The Potato Song', and its many incarnations, was known. Ted started the opening bridge, John Miller picked up his sticks, and they launched into it.

I kept my eyes on the girl at the bar. She was listening, beer in hand, taking a sip now and then. She smiled at the line about the vegan princess, and again when the crowd chimed in and yelled, 'sweet potato!' And when it was over, she clapped enthusiastically, not just politely. A good sign.

Feeling confident, they continued with another 'Potato Song'. But this one wasn't quite so strong, and the crowd didn't know it as well. They gave it a good shot, the best they could, but it sounded flat, and at one point John Miller, who'd only recently learned the new part, screwed up and lost the beat for a second. I saw Dexter flinch at this, then tug his collar. Ted was looking everywhere but at the bar. They launched right into another original song, one not even about potatoes, but it too sounded off, and they cut it short after two verses, ditching the third.

By now the A&R girl seemed distracted, almost bored, looking around the club and then – very bad sign – at her watch. Ted leaned over and said something to Dexter, who shook his head quickly. But then Lucas stepped forward, nodding, and Ted said something else, and Dexter finally shrugged and turned back to the microphone. John Miller tapped out a beat, Ted picked it up, and they launched full force into an old Thin Lizzy song. And suddenly the crowd was right with them again, pressing up closer. And after the first verse, the A&R chick ordered another beer.

When the song was over, Ted spoke to Dexter, who hesitated. Then Ted said something else, and Dexter made a face, shaking his head.

Just do it, I thought to myself. *Another cover won't kill you.*

Dexter looked at Lucas, who nodded, and I relaxed. Then the first chords began. They sounded so familiar, somehow, as if I knew them in a different incarnation. I listened for a second, and the realisation grew stronger, as if it was just at the tip of my mind, close enough to touch. And then, I got it.

'*This lullaby*,' Dexter sang, '*is only a few words . . .*'

Oh, my God, I thought.

'*A simple run of chords . . .*'

It sounded more retro and lounge-singer-esque, the maudlin aspect that had made it a wedding and lite FM favourite now twisted into something else, something self-mocking, as if it was winking at its own seriousness. I felt a drop in my stomach: he knew how I felt about this. He knew. And still, he kept singing.

'Quiet here in this spare room, but you can hear it, hear it . . .'

The crowd was loving it, cheering, some girls along the back row singing along, hands on their hearts, like washed-up divas on the Labor Day telethon.

I looked over at the bar, where Chloe was staring right at me, but she didn't have a smug look, instead something even worse. It might have been pity, but I turned my head away before I could know for sure. And a few seats down from her, the A&R chick was swaying, smiling. She loved it.

I got up from the booth. All around me the crowd was singing along to the song, one they'd heard all their lives too, but never quite in the context that I had. To them it was just old and sappy enough now to be nostalgic, a song their parents might have listened to. It was probably played at their bar mitzvahs or sisters' weddings, trotted out about the same time as 'Daddy's Little Girl' and 'Butterfly Kisses'. But it was working. The appeal was obvious, the energy coming through the crowd so strongly, the kind of response that Ted, in a million potato dreams, wouldn't even have hoped for.

'I will let you down,' Dexter sang as I pushed my way toward the bar. *'But this lullaby plays on . . .'*

I went to the bathroom, where for once there was no line, and shut myself into a stall. Then I sat down, pulled my hands through my hair, and told myself to calm down. It meant nothing, this song. All my life I'd let other people put so much weight to it, until it was heavy enough to drown me, but it was just music. But even there, locked in the stall, I could still hear it going, those notes I'd known by heart for as long as I could remember, now twisted and different, with another man I hardly knew who had some claim to me, however small, singing the words.

What had my mother always said when we listened to it on the one scratchy album she owned of my dad, back when we still had a record player? *His gift to you,* she'd tell me, idly brushing my hair back from my forehead with a dreamy expression, as if someday I'd truly understand how important this was. By then, she had already forgotten the bad times with my father, the ones I heard secondhand: how they were dirt-poor, how he'd hardly spent any time with Chris when he was a baby, and only married her – not even legally, it turned out – in a last-ditch attempt to save a relationship already beyond repair. What a legacy. What a gift. It was like a parting prize in a game show where I'd lost big, a handful of Rice-A-Roni and some cheap luggage thrust upon me as I left, little consolation.

The final note sounded: the drum cymbals hummed. Then, huge applause, cheering. It was over.

Okay then. I walked out of the bathroom and headed straight to the bar, where Chloe was sitting on a stool with a bored expression. Truth Squad was still going, playing a medley of camp songs – played Led Zeppelin style, with crashing guitars and a lot of whooping – that I recognised as being a set-ender. The guy Chloe had been talking to was gone, Lissa was still talking to the not-cute-but-decent one, and Jess, I assumed, had used one of her regular excuses and was either 'at the pay phone' or 'getting something from the car'.

'What happened to the surfer boy?' I asked Chloe as she scooted over, making room for me on her stool.

'Girlfriend,' she said, nodding to a booth off on our left, where the guy was now nuzzling a redheaded girl with a pierced eyebrow.

I nodded as Ted did a few windmill guitar moves, John Miller going all out on a drum solo, his face almost as red as his hair. I wondered if Scarlett was impressed, but she'd left the booth where she'd been sitting, so I couldn't know for sure.

'Interesting song choice earlier, didn't you think?' Chloe asked me, pushing off the floor with her foot so that we twisted slightly in the stool, to one side and then back again. 'Couldn't help but feel that I had heard it somewhere before.'

I didn't say anything, instead just watching as John Miller continued to battle his drum set while the crowd clapped along.

'Of all the things he should know,' she went on, 'that you hate that song is a freaking given. I mean, God. It's *basic*.'

'Chloe,' I said softly, 'shut up, okay?'

I could feel her looking at me, slightly wide-eyed, before going back to stirring her drink with her finger. Now there was only one person between me and the A&R chick, who was jotting something down with a pencil she'd borrowed from the bartender, who was watching her write with great interest while ignoring a whole slew of people waving money for beers.

'We're Truth Squad!' Dexter yelled, 'and we're here every Tuesday. Thank you and good night!'

The canned dance music came on, everyone pushed toward the bar, and I watched as Dexter hopped off the stage, conferred with Ted for a second, and they both began heading toward us, Lucas in tow. John Miller was already making a beeline for Scarlett, who I now saw standing by the door, as if trying to ease herself out gradually.

The A&R chick was already holding out her hand to Dexter as they came up. 'Arianna Moss,' she said, and Dexter pumped her hand a bit too eagerly. 'Great set.'

'Thanks,' he replied, and she kept smiling at him. I glanced across the room, looking toward the door, wondering where Jess was.

Ted, pressing closer, added, 'The acoustics in here are terrible. We'd sound much better with decent equipment, and the crowd kind of sucks.'

Dexter shot him a you-aren't-helping kind of look. 'We'd love to hear what you think,' he said to her. 'Can I buy you a beer?'

She glanced at her watch. 'Sure. Let me just make a call first.'

As she walked away, pulling a cell phone out of her pocket, Dexter saw me, waved, and mouthed that he'd be just a minute. I shrugged, and he started to move toward me, but Ted pulled him back.

'What the hell are you doing?' he demanded. 'She's here to talk to all of us, Dexter, not just you.'

'He said we wanted to hear what she thinks,' Lucas told him. 'Calm down.'

'He's buying her a beer!' Ted said.

'That's called public relations,' Dexter told him, glancing back in my direction. But now Arianna Moss was already coming back, tucking her phone in her pocket.

'And what was up with that song?' Ted shook his head, incredulous. 'Sonny and Cher would have been better. God, *anything* would have been better. We might as well have had on leisure suits and been playing dinner theatre with that crappy song.'

'She loved it,' Dexter said, trying to catch my eye, but I let a burly guy wearing a baseball cap step into my line of vision.

'She did,' Lucas agreed. 'Plus it got us out of the bottomless pit into which "The Potato Song" had flung us.'

' "The Potato Song",' Ted huffed, 'was doing just fine. If John Miller had bothered to make it to the last band practice on time—'

'Oh, it's always somebody else, isn't it?' Lucas snapped.

'Shut up, you guys,' Dexter said under his breath.

'Ready to talk?' Arianna Moss asked as she walked up. She asked Dexter. I noticed, and so did Ted. But only he, of course, was truly bothered.

'Sure,' Dexter said. 'Over here okay?'

'Sounds good.'

They started walking and I turned my back again, waving down the bartender for a beer as they passed.

By the time I'd paid they were sitting in a booth by the door, she and Dexter on one side, Lucas and Ted on the other. She was talking: they were all listening.

Jess appeared next to my elbow. 'Is it time to go yet?' she asked me.

'Where have you been?' Chloe said.

'I had to get something from the car,' Jess said flatly.

'Remy, hey, there you are.' John Miller popped up beside me. 'You seen Scarlett?'

'She was over by the door last I saw her.'

He jerked his head around, eyes scanning the wall. Then he started waving his arms. 'Scarlett! Over here!'

Scarlett looked up, saw us, and smiled in a way that made me think I'd been right on in assuming she'd been hoping to leave inconspicuously. But John Miller was waving her over, oblivious, so she had no choice but to work her way through the crowd to us.

'You were great,' she said to John Miller, who beamed. 'Really good.'

'We're usually a lot tighter,' John Miller told her with a bit of a swagger, 'but Ted was off tonight. He was late for the last practice, didn't know the new arrangements.'

Scarlett nodded and glanced around her. The crowd at the bar was thickening, now about three deep, and people kept jostling us.

Lucas came up behind John Miller and managed to flick him on the back of the head while balancing two beers. 'Hey, in case you, you know, have a minute, we're talking to this A&R woman over here and she's probably getting us a great gig in D.C. if, you know, you care in the *least*.'

John Miller rubbed the back of his head. 'D.C.? Really?'

'That big theatre, the one where we saw Spinnerbait that time.' Lucas grimaced. 'Hate Spinnerbait, though.'

'Hate Spinnerbait,' John Miller agreed, taking one of the beers. 'That's a band,' he explained to Scarlett.

'Ah,' she said.

'Come on,' Lucas said. 'She needs to talk to all of us. This could be big, man.'

'I'll be back in a minute,' John Miller said to Scarlett, squeezing her arm. 'This is just, you know, official band business. Management decisions and all that.'

'Right,' Scarlett said as he followed Lucas over to the booth, where Ted made room for both of them. I could see Dexter sitting in the corner, against the wall, folding a matchbook and listening intently as Arianna Moss spoke.

'Poor you,' Chloe said to Scarlett. 'He's obsessed.'

'He's very nice,' Scarlett said.

'He's pathetic.' Chloe hopped off the barstool. 'I'm going to the bathroom. You coming?'

I shook my head. She bumped a couple of guys aside and disappeared into the crowd. As the bodies around us shifted I could catch the occasional glance of Dexter. He looked like he was explaining something while Arianna Moss nodded her head, taking a sip of her beer. Ted and Lucas were talking, and John Miller seemed totally distracted, glancing over at us every few seconds to make sure Scarlett hadn't made a break for it.

'John Miller's very nice,' I said, feeling obligated to do so just because he kept looking at me.

'He is,' Scarlett agreed. 'A little young for me, though. I'm not sure he's really parent material, if you know what I mean.'

I wanted to tell her that this, at least in my experience, wasn't as big a factor in a relationship as you'd think, but decided against it.

'So how long have you been dating Dexter?' she asked me.

'Not long.' I glanced over again at the booth. Dexter was waving his hands around while Arianna Moss laughed, lighting a cigarette. You would have thought they were on a date. If you didn't know better.

'He seems really great,' she said. 'Sweet. And funny.'

I nodded. 'Yeah. He is.'

Ted suddenly appeared next to me, bursting through a crowd of large girls in tight shirts who seemed to be celebrating a bachelorette: one of them was wearing a veil, the rest Barbie hats. 'Two beers!' he shouted at the bartender in his typical vexed way, then stood there and seethed for a second before noticing us.

'How's it going?' I asked him.

He glared back at the booth. 'Fine. Dexter will probably be in her trousers within the hour, not that it's gonna help the band any.'

Scarlett looked at me, raising her eyebrows. I said, 'Really.'

'Well,' he shrugged, as if only now realising that

maybe I wasn't the best person to say this to. Not that it stopped him: this was Ted, after all. 'It's just how he is, you know. He hooks up, things end badly, and we're out a gig, or a place to live, or a hundred bucks in grocery money. He always does this.'

Now, standing there, I felt so stupid I was sure it showed on my face, if that was possible. I picked up Chloe's drink – now all ice – and took a gulp from it, just to do something.

'The point is,' he growled as the beers were dropped in front of him, 'if we're going to work as a group, we have to think as a group. Full stop.'

And then he was gone, bumping the girls behind us hard enough to trigger a wave of curse words and lewd gestures. I was stuck there with Scarlett, looking like Band Floozy Number Five.

'Well,' Scarlett said uneasily. 'I'm sure he didn't really mean that.'

I hated that she felt sorry for me. It was even worse than feeling sorry for myself, but not by much. I turned my back to the booth – damned if I cared what happened over there now – and sat back on the stool, crossing my legs. 'Whatever,' I told her. 'It's not like I don't know the deal about Dexter.'

'Oh. Really?'

I picked up Chloe's straw, twisting it between my fingers. 'Just between you and me,' I said, 'it's kind of why I picked him in the first place. I mean, I'm off to school in the fall. I can't have any big commitments. That's why it's perfect, you know. A set ending. No complications.'

'Right,' she said, steadying herself as a stray elbow bumped her from behind.

'I mean, God. All relationships should be this easy, you know? Find a cute guy in June, have fun till August, leave scot-free in September.' This was so easy to say, I realised, that it had to be the truth. Wasn't this always what I'd said about Jonathan, and any other of my seasonal boyfriends? Of course this wasn't different.

She nodded, but something in her face told me she wasn't the kind of girl to believe this, much less do it herself. But then again, she had a kid. It was different when other people were at stake. I mean, in normal families.

'Yep,' I said, 'just a summer boyfriend. No worries. No entanglements. Just the way I like it. I mean, it's not like Dexter's husband material or anything. He can't even keep his *shoes* tied.'

I laughed again. God, this was so true. So true. What had I been thinking?

We stood there for a second, in a silence that was not exactly awkward but not altogether comfortable either.

She looked at her watch, then behind me, into the crowd. She seemed surprised for a second, and I figured John Miller must have given her another one of his hold-on-honey-I'm-almost-done-here waves. 'Look,' she said, 'I really have to go, or my sitter's going to kill me. Can you tell John Miller I'll see him tomorrow?'

'Sure,' I told her. 'No problem.'

'Thanks, Remy. Take care, okay?'

'You too.'

I watched her walk to the door, then cut out quickly just as John Miller turned his head, looking over at us again. *Too late*, I thought. *I scared her off.* Big, bad Remy, cold bitch, was back.

'Now,' Jess said, appearing next to me, 'it has *got* to be time to go.'

'I'm in,' Chloe said, plopping down beside me. 'No decent prospects here.'

'Lissa's doing okay,' Jess told her.

Chloe bent forward, peering down the bar. 'That's the first guy that spoke to her when she got here, so yes, we should go. If we don't she'll be engaged to him by last call. Lissa!'

Lissa jumped. 'Yes?'

'We're going!' Chloe slid off the stool, pulling me with her. 'There's got to be something better to do tonight. *Got* to be.'

'You guys,' Lissa said as she came up, fluffing her hair, 'I'm *talking* to somebody.'

'He's subpar,' Chloe told her, glancing at him again. He waved and smiled, poor guy. 'You can do better.'

'But he's nice,' Lissa protested. 'I've been talking to him all night.'

'Exactly,' Jess said. 'You need a variety of guys, not just one. Right, Remy?'

'Right,' I agreed. 'Let's go already.'

We were almost to the door when I saw Jonathan. He was standing by the juke-box, talking to the bouncer. I'd seen him from a distance a few times since we'd broken up, but this was the first official drive-by, so I slowed down.

'Hey Remy,' he said as we passed, reaching out, in typical fashion, to brush my arm. Normally I would have sidestepped, out of range, but this time I didn't. He didn't look much different, his hair a bit shorter, his skin tanned. Typical summer changes, all easily undone by September. 'How've you been?'

'Good,' I said as Chloe and Lissa walked past me, out the door. Jess I could feel hovering closer by, as if I needed reminding not to waste too much breath here. 'How about you?'

'Freaking great,' he said, smiling big, and I wondered what I'd ever seen in him, with his slick looks and touchy-feely ways. Talk about subpar. I'd been bottom fishing and hadn't even known it. Not that Dexter was much of an improvement, apparently.

'Oh, Jonathan,' I said, smiling at him and moving just a bit closer as two girls passed behind me. 'You always were so modest.'

He shrugged, touching my arm again. 'I was always great too. Right?'

'I wouldn't say that,' I told him, but I kept smiling. 'I gotta go.'

'Yeah, I'll see you around,' he called after me, too loudly. 'Where you gonna be later? You going to that party in the Arbors?'

I reached over my head with my hand and waggled my fingers, then walked out into the thick, humid night air. Lissa had already pulled her car around, and she

245

and Chloe were waiting, engine idling, as Jess and I came down the stairs.

'Classy,' she said to me as we slid into the back seat.

'I was just talking,' I told her, but she only turned her head, rolling down her window, and didn't say anything.

Lissa put the car in gear and we were off. I knew Dexter would wonder where I'd gone, just like he'd probably wonder who I'd been talking to and, whoever he was, why I'd been smiling at him that way. Boys were so easy to play. And if nothing else, I gave as good as I got. He could cosy up with some chick all he wanted, but I'd be damned if I'd sit and wait while he did it.

'Where we going?' Lissa asked, turning her head and glancing back at me.

'The Arbors,' I said. 'There's a party there.'

'Now we're talking,' Chloe said. She reached forward and cranked up the radio. And just like that, it could have been old times: the four of us, on the prowl. Earlier I'd been the odd girl out, Miss Committed, having to warm the bench while they set out into the game. But no more. And there was still so much of summer left.

We were almost out of the parking lot when I heard it. A voice, yelling after us. Chloe turned down the radio as I twisted in my seat, already wondering what I'd say when Dexter asked why I was leaving, what was the deal, how exactly I could refute that automatic assumption that this was just jealous girlfriend behaviour. Which it wasn't. Not at all.

The voice yelled again, just as I peered through the back window. But it wasn't Dexter. It was the guy Lissa had been talking to. He called her name, looking confused as we pulled out into traffic and drove away.

It was after one when Lissa dropped me off at the end of my driveway. I took off my shoes and started across the grass, taking a sip of the Diet Zip I'd got on the way home from the party in the Arbors, which had turned out to be a total bust. By the time we'd got there the cops had already been and gone, so we'd headed to the Quik Zip to sit on the hood of Lissa's car, talking and sharing a big bag of buttered popcorn. A good way to end what had been, for the most part, a crap night.

It was nice outside now, though. Warm, the crickets chirping, and the grass cool under my bare feet. There was a sky full of stars, and the whole neighbourhood was quiet, except for a dog barking a few yards over and the soft clackety-clacking of my mother's typewriter, drifting out of her study window, where the light, as was the norm lately, was bright and burning.

'Hey!'

There was someone behind me. I felt my whole body tense, then run hot, as I turned around. My full Diet Zip left my hand before I even realised it, sailing through the air at warp speed toward the head of the person who was standing in the middle of the lawn. It would have hit square on, perfect target, except that he moved at the last second, and it flew past, crashing against the mailbox and bursting open, showering the kerb with Diet Coke and ice.

'What is your problem?' Dexter shouted.

'My problem?' I snapped. I could feel my heart beating, thunk thunk thunk, in my chest. Who lurks around neighbourhoods past midnight, sneaking up on people? 'You scared the *shit* out of me.'

'No.' He walked up to me, shoes leaving a trail across the damp grass, until he was right in front of me. 'At the club. When you just took off, no explanation? What was that all about, Remy?'

I had to take a moment to collect myself. And mourn for my Diet Zip, which I had refilled just minutes earlier. 'You were busy,' I said, shrugging. 'And I got tired of waiting.'

He stuck his hands in his pockets and looked at me for a second. 'No,' he said. 'That's not it.'

I turned my back to him and dug out my keys, shaking them until I found the one that fitted the front door. 'It's late,' I said. 'I'm tired. I'm going inside to go to bed.'

'Was it the song?' He stepped up even closer to me as I stuffed the key in the lock. 'Is that why you freaked out and left?'

'I did not freak out,' I said flatly. 'I just figured you had your hands full with that girl, and—'

'Oh, God,' he said. He stepped back, down the steps, and laughed. 'Is that what this is about? You're jealous?'

Okay. Those, as far as I was concerned, were fighting words. I turned around. 'I don't get jealous,' I told him.

'Oh, right. So you're not human, then.'

I shrugged.

'Remy, for God's sake. All I know is that one minute I'm telling you I'll be done in a second and the next you just vanish, and the last I see is you talking to some old boyfriend about meeting him later. Which was kind of surprising, considering we're seeing each other. Or so I thought.'

There was so much erroneous information in this statement that it honestly took me a second to decide, outline style, what to address first. 'You know,' I said finally, 'I waited around, Ted said you were deep in negotiations with this girl, my friends were ready to leave. So I left.'

'Ted,' he repeated. 'What else did Ted say?'

'Nothing.'

He reached up and pulled his hand through his hair, then let his hand drop to his side. 'Okay, then. I guess everything's fine.'

'Absolutely,' I said and turned around again, turning the key in the lock.

And then, just as I was about to push the door open, he said, 'I heard you, you know.'

I stopped, pressing my palm against the wood of the door. I could see myself in the small square of glass there, and him reflected behind me. He was kicking at something in the grass with his toe, not looking at me.

'Heard me what?' I said.

'Talking to Scarlett.' Now he did look up, but I couldn't turn around. 'I wanted to tell you I'd be done in a minute and to wait, if you could. So I walked over, and I heard you. Talking about us.'

So that had been what had surprised Scarlett. I reached up and tucked my hair behind my ear.

'It's nice to know where I stand, I guess,' he said. 'Summer boyfriend and all. Set ending. No worries. A bit surprising, I have to admit. But maybe I should just admire your honesty.'

'Dexter,' I said.

'No, it's okay. My mother did always say I'd make a lousy husband, so it's good to get a second opinion. Plus I like knowing you don't see us going anywhere. Takes the guesswork out of it.'

I turned around and looked at him. 'What did you expect? That we'd stay together forever?'

'Are those the only options? Nothing or forever?' He lowered his voice. 'God, Remy. Is that what you really believe?'

Maybe, I thought. *Maybe it is.*

'Look,' I told him, 'honesty is good. I'm going away to college, you'll be gone by the end of the summer, or maybe, after tonight, even sooner. Ted made it sound like you were leaving tomorrow.'

'Ted is an idiot!' he said. 'Ted probably also told you I sleep with every girl we meet, didn't he?'

I shrugged. 'It doesn't—'

'I knew it,' he said. 'I knew there was some Ted factor involved in this. The Ted curve. What did he say?'

'It doesn't matter.'

He sighed, loudly. 'A year ago I got involved with the girl who booked bands for this club in Virginia Beach. It ended badly and—'

I held up my hand, stopping him. 'I don't care,' I told him. 'I don't. Let's not do the true confessions thing, okay? Believe me, you don't want to hear mine.'

He looked surprised at this, and for a second I realised he didn't know me at all. Not at all.

'I do, though,' he said, and his voice was softer now, conciliatory, as if all this was fixable in some way. 'That's the difference. I'm not in this just for a week, or a month, Remy. I don't work like that.'

A car drove by, slowing down as it passed. The guy behind the wheel was blatantly staring at us. It took all I had not to flip him the finger, but I resisted.

'What are you afraid of?' he asked, coming closer. 'Is it that bad that you might actually really like me?'

'I'm not afraid,' I said. 'That's not it. It's just simpler this way.'

'So you're saying we should just decide now that this summer doesn't mean anything? Just use each other and then when you go or I go it's over, see you later?'

It sounded so bad when he said it that way. 'I have worked all my life to get out of here scot-free,' I said. 'I can't take anything else with me.'

'This doesn't have to be a burden,' he said. 'Why do you want to make it one?'

'Because I know how things end, Dexter.' I lowered my voice. 'I've seen what commitment leads to, and it isn't pretty. Going in is the easy part. It's the endings that suck.'

'Who do you think you're talking to?' he said incredulously. 'My mother's had six husbands. I've been related to half the country at one time or another.'

'It's not a joke.' I shook my head. 'This is how it has to be. I'm sorry.'

For a minute neither of us said anything. After so many years of only thinking these things, saying them out loud felt so strange, as if now they were officially real. My cold, hard heart exposed, finally, for what it truly was. *Fair warning*, I thought. *I should have told you from the start. I will let you down.*

'I know why you're saying this,' he said finally, 'but you're missing out. You know, when it works, love is pretty amazing. It's not overrated. There's a reason for all those songs.'

I looked down at my hands. 'They're just songs, Dexter. They don't mean anything.'

He walked over and stood right in front of me, taking my hands in his. 'You know, we only sang that tonight because we were dying up there. Lucas heard me humming it the other day and got all inspired and came up with that arrangement. They don't know it has anything to do with you. They just think it's a good crowd pleaser.'

'I guess it is,' I said. 'Just not for me.'

I felt it then. That strange settling feeling that meant the worst part of breaking up was over, and now there were only a few pleasantries to exchange before you were done for good. It was like the finish line coming up over the hill, and knowing that what lies ahead is all within your sight.

'You know,' he said, rubbing my thumb with his, 'it

could have gone either way with us. All those marriages and everything. Another day, you'd be the one who believed, and I'd be sending you away.'

'Maybe,' I replied. But I couldn't even imagine believing in love the way he did. Not with the history we shared. You had to be crazy to come out of it and think forever was still possible.

He leaned forward, still holding my hand, and kissed my forehead. I closed my eyes as he did so, pressing my toes into the grass. I took in everything about him that I'd grown to like: the smell of him, his narrow hips, the smoothness of his skin against mine. So much in so little time.

'I'll see you around,' he said, pulling back from me. 'Okay?'

I nodded. 'Okay.'

He squeezed my hand one last time, then let it drop and started across the grass. His feet left fresh tracks: the ones from earlier were gone, already absorbed, as if nothing had happened up to here.

Once inside I went up to my bedroom and got undressed, pulling on an old pair of boxers and a tank top and crawling under the sheets. I knew this feeling, the 2 AM loneliness that I'd practically invented. It was always worse right after a break-up. In those first few hours officially single again the world seems like it expands, suddenly bigger and more vast now that you have to get through it alone.

That was why I'd started listening to the song, in the beginning: it took my mind off things. It was the one constant in my life, however I felt about it, the one thing that had remained a part of me as stepfathers and boyfriends and houses shifted in and out. The recording never changed, the words staying the same, my father's voice taking the same breaths between lines. But now I couldn't even do that. It was now stuck in my mind the way Dexter had sung it: mocking and sweet and different, carrying a heavier and stranger weight than it ever had before.

I kept thinking about how he'd kissed my forehead as we said good-bye. It had to be the nicest break-up ever. Not that it made it any easier. But still.

I rolled over and pulled the pillow tight under my head, closing my eyes. I tried to distract myself with other songs: the Beatles, my current favourite CD, old 1980s hits from my childhood. But Dexter's voice kept coming back, slipping easily over the words I knew too well. I fell asleep with it still playing in my mind, and the next thing I knew it was morning.

August

12

'Come on! Who wants to KaBoom?'

I looked at Lissa. It was over ninety degrees out, the sun was blasting hot, and somewhere over to my left, a barbershop quartet was singing 'My Old Kentucky Home'. It was official: we were in hell.

'Not me,' I said. Again. Two weeks into her job marketing a new sports drink/caffeine jolt soda, and Lissa still couldn't accept that I didn't like the taste of it. And I wasn't alone.

'It's . . . it's like . . . fizzy lemonade,' Chloe said delicately, swirling the tiniest sip of it around in her mouth. 'With a weird cheap cola aftertaste.'

'So what do you think?' Lissa asked her, refilling the row of plastic cups on the table in front of her.

'I think . . .' Chloe said. Then she swallowed, and made a face. '*Eeeech.*'

'Chloe!' Lissa hissed, glancing around. 'Honestly.'

'I told you, it tastes like crap,' I said, but she just ignored me, piling more KaBoom merchandise – plastic Frisbees, T-shirts, and plastic cups all emblazoned with the same swirling yellow sunshine logo – onto the table. 'You know that, Lissa. You don't even drink this stuff.'

'That is not true,' she said, adjusting her KaBoom name tag, which said *Hi, I'm Lissa! Want to Boom?* I'd tried to point out that this could be taken in other ways than sampling products, but she'd only waved me off, so self-righteous in her quest to spread the KaBoom message to cola drinkers everywhere. 'I drink this stuff like water. It's amazing!'

I turned around and looked behind me, where a family of four was passing by, hands already full of Don Davis Toyotafaire freebie merchandise. They didn't stop, though. In fact, the KaBoom table was pretty much deserted, even with all the free stuff Lissa and her co-worker, PJ, were giving away.

'Balloons, everyone! Who wants a KaBoom balloon?' Lissa shouted out into the crowd. 'Free samples, folks! And we've got Frisbees!' She picked up one of the Frisbees and hurled it across the parking lot. It sailed evenly for a little way before banking off and missing one of the new Land Cruisers by about a foot before crashing to the pavement. Don, who was talking up some customers by a row of Camrys, glanced over at us.

'Sorry!' Lissa said, covering her mouth with her hand.

'Easy on the Frisbees, slugger,' PJ told her, picking up one of the plastic sample cups and downing it. 'It's still early.'

Lissa smiled at him gratefully, blushing, and I realised Chloe's hunch about her feelings for PJ were, in fact, correct. KaBoom, indeed.

The Don Davis Motors Toyotafaire had been in the works for weeks. It was one of the biggest sales bonanzas of the year, with games for the kids, fortune-tellers, Slurpee machines, even one very tired looking pony that was walking circles around the auto bays.

And, right this way, in the shade by the showroom, local author and celebrity Barbara Starr.

Normally my mother never did publicity except when she had a new book out, and she now was at a point in her writing when she didn't even want to leave her study, much less the house. Chris and I had been used to her schedule for years and knew to keep quiet when she was sleeping – even if it was at four in the afternoon – to stay out of the way when she passed through the kitchen mumbling to herself, and to understand that we'd know when she was done when she pushed the typewriter carriage to the left one last time, clapped her hands twice, and let out a loud, very emphatic, 'Thank you!' It was the closest she came to religion – this one, final expression of gratitude.

But Don didn't get it. First, he had no respect for the beaded curtain. In he'd walk, without hesitation, putting his hands on her shoulders even as she was still typing. When he did this, my mother's keystrokes grew speedier: you could hear it, as if she was rushing to get out what was in her head before he broke her train of thought entirely. Then he'd go to take a shower, asking her to bring him a cold beer in a few minutes, would you, darling. Fifteen minutes later he'd be calling for her, wondering where that beer was, and she'd type fast again, pounding out the last lines she could before he padded back in, smelling of aftershave and asking what they were having for dinner.

The weird thing was that my mother was going along with it. She seemed totally smitten, still, with Don, to the point that she saw creeping around in the wee hours to write as a completely fair trade. With all her other husbands and boyfriends, she'd always stuck to her schedule, lecturing them, as she had us, about her 'creative needs' and the 'disciplinary necessity' of her time spent in the office. But she seemed more willing to compromise now, as if this was, indeed, going to be her last marriage.

Now, Chloe headed to the bathroom as I walked over to the table Don had set up for my mother next to the showroom. MEET BEST-SELLING AUTHOR BARBARA STARR! was painted on the banner that hung behind her, in big red letters framed by hearts. She was wearing sunglasses, fanning herself with a magazine while she talked to a woman wearing a bum-bag who had a toddler on her hip.

'. . . that Melina Kennedy was just the best character ever!' the woman was saying, switching the baby to her other side. 'You know, you just really felt her pain when she and Donovan were separated. I couldn't stop reading, I really couldn't. I just *had* to know if they got back together.'

'Thank you so much,' my mother said, smiling.

'Are you working on something new?' the woman asked.

'I am,' my mother said. Then she lowered her voice and added, 'I think you'll like it. The main character is a lot like Melina.'

'Oooh!' the woman said. 'I can't wait. I honestly can't.'

'Betsy!' a voice shouted from over by the popcorn machine. 'Come here a second, will you?'

'Oh, that's my husband,' the woman said. 'It was just so nice to finally meet you. Really.'

'Same to you,' my mother replied as the woman walked away, over to where her husband, a shorter man wearing a bandanna around his neck, was scrutinising the mileage on a minivan. My mother watched her go, then glanced at her watch. Don wanted her to stay for the full three hours, but I was hoping we'd get to go soon. I wasn't sure how much more barbershop music I could take.

'Your public loves you,' I said as I walked up.

'My public is not really *here*, I don't think. I've already had two people ask me about financing, and I've mostly just directed people to the bathroom,' she said. Then, more brightly, she added, 'But I have really enjoyed that wonderful barbershop quartet. Aren't they charming?'

I plopped down on the kerb beside her, not even bothering to answer this.

She sighed, fanning herself again. 'It's very hot,' she said. 'Could I have some of your drink?'

I looked down at the bottle of KaBoom Lissa had forced on me. 'You don't want this,' I said.

'Nonsense,' she said easily. 'It's scorching out here. Just let me have a sip.'

I shrugged and handed it over. She screwed off the top, tipped it to her lips, and took a decent-size mouthful. Then she made a somewhat uneasy face, swallowed, and handed the bottle back to me.

'Told you,' I said.

Just then the white Truth Squad van bumped into

the parking lot, pulling into a space by the auto bay. The back door opened and John Miller jumped out, his drumsticks tucked under his arm, followed by Lucas, who was eating a tangerine. They started unloading equipment and stacking it as Ted climbed out of the driver's side, slamming the door behind him. And then, as I watched, Dexter got out of the van, pulling a shirt on over his head. He checked his reflection in the side mirror, then ducked around the side of the van, out of my sight.

It wasn't the first time I'd seen him, of course. The morning after we broke up, in fact, I'd been standing in line at Jump Java for Lola's morning mocha when he walked in, crossed the room in a most determined fashion, and came right up to me.

'So I'm thinking,' he said, no hello or hi or anything, 'that we need to be friends.'

Instantly, my internal alarms went off, reminding me of the break-up logic I'd been preaching for almost as long as I could remember. *Not possible*, I thought, but out loud I said, 'Friends?'

'Friends,' he repeated. 'Because it would be a shame if we did the whole awkward, ignoring-each-other, pretending-nothing-ever-happened thing. In fact, we could just jump right in and deal with it right now.'

I looked at the clock next to the espresso machine. It was 9:05. 'Isn't it a little early,' I said slowly, 'to take that on?'

'That's just the point!' he said emphatically as a man talking on his cell phone glanced over at us. 'Last night we broke up, right?'

'Yes,' I said, in a quieter voice than he was using, hoping he'd catch the hint. No luck.

'And today, here we are. Meeting up, as we are bound to do endless other times between now and when the summer ends. We do work across from each other.'

'Agreed,' I said as I finally got up to the front of the line, nodding as the guy behind the counter asked if I wanted Lola's usual.

'So,' he went on, 'I say that we just admit that things may be a little strange, but that we won't avoid each other or allow things to be awkward at all. If anything feels weird, we acknowledge it straight up and move on. What do you think?'

'I think,' I said, 'that it won't work.'

'Why not?'

'Because you can never go from going out to being friends, just like that,' I explained, grabbing some napkins out of the dispenser. 'It's a lie. It's just something that people say they'll do to take the permanence out of a break-up. And someone always takes it to mean more than it does, and then is hurt even more when, inevitably, said "friendly" relationship is still a major step down from the previous relationship, and it's like breaking up all over again. But messier.'

He considered this, then said, 'Okay. Point taken. And in this scenario of yours, since I'm the one pursuing the idea of a friendship, then it would be me who would get hurt again. Correct?'

'Hard to say,' I said, taking Lola's coffee and mouthing a thanks to the counter guy as I stuffed a dollar bill into the tip box. 'But if this followed the formula, yes.'

'Then I,' he said, 'will prove you wrong.'

'Dexter,' I said softly as we walked to the door, 'come on.' It seemed surreal to be discussing the previous night in such analytical terms, as if it had happened to someone else and we were just off to the side, doing the running commentary.

'Look, this is important to me,' he said as he held the door open and I ducked beneath his arm, keeping the cup in my hands level. 'I hate bad break-ups. I hate awkwardness and those weird stilted conversations and feeling like I can't go somewhere because you're there, or whatever. For once I'd like to just skip all that and agree to part as friends. And mean it.'

I looked at him. Last night, as we'd stood in my front yard, I'd dreaded this, seeing him again. And I had to admit I kind of liked that it was already pretty much over with, the first awkward Ex Sighting. Check it off the list, move on. Break up efficiently. What a concept.

'It would be,' I said, brushing a hair out of my face, 'the challenge of all challenges.'

'Ah,' he agreed, smiling. 'Indeed. You up for it?'

Was I? It was hard to say. It sounded good on paper, but when actually put into practice I suspected there would be a few variables that would really screw up the numbers. But I hadn't backed down from a challenge yet.

'Okay,' I said. 'You're on. We're friends.'

'Friends,' he repeated. And then we shook on it.

That had been two weeks ago, and since then we'd

talked several times, sticking to neutral topics like what was happening with Rubber Records (not much yet, but there was talk of A Meeting) and how Monkey was (good, but suffering through an infestation of fleas that had left everyone at the yellow house scratching and cranky). We'd even eaten lunch together once, sitting on the kerb outside of Flash Camera. We'd decided there had to be rules, and established two so far. Number one: no unnecessary touching, which could only lead to trouble. And number two was if anything happened or was said that felt strange or awkward, there could be no strained silences: it had to be acknowledged as quickly as possible, brought out in the open, dealt with and dismantled, like diffusing a bomb.

Of course my friends all thought I was crazy. Two days after we'd broken up, I'd gone with them to Bendo, and Dexter had come over and chatted with me. When he'd left, I'd turned back to a row of sceptical, holier-than-thou faces, like I was drinking beer with a bunch of apostles.

'Oh, man,' Chloe said, pointing a finger at me, 'don't tell me you guys are going to be friends.'

'Well, not exactly,' I said, which only made them look more aghast. Lissa, who'd spent the better part of the summer reading the kind of self-help books I normally associated with Jennifer Anne, looked especially disappointed. 'Look, we're better friends than dating. And we hardly dated at all, anyway.'

'It won't work,' Chloe told me, lighting a cigarette. 'Crutch for the weak, the whole friends thing. Who used to say that?'

I rolled my eyes, staring up at the ceiling.

'Oh, that's right!' she said, snapping her fingers. 'It was you! You always said that, just like you always said that you should never date a guy in a band . . .'

'Chloe,' I said.

'. . . or give in to a guy who really pursues you, since they'll just lose interest the moment the chase ends . . .'

'Give it a rest.'

'. . . or fall for someone with an ex-girlfriend who is still hanging around, because if she hasn't got the message he probably isn't sending it.'

'Wait a second,' I said. 'That last one has nothing to do with this.'

'Two out of three,' she replied, waving her hand. 'My point is made.'

'Remy,' Lissa said, reaching over and patting my hand, 'it's okay. You're human. You make the same mistakes as any of us. You know, in that book I was reading, *Coming to Terms: What Love Can and Can't Do*, there's a whole chapter on how we break our rules for men.'

'I am not breaking my rules,' I snapped, hating that I'd ended up on the advice-receiving end of things, jumping from Dear Remy to Confused in Cincinnati all in one summer.

Now, at Toyotafaire, Chloe and I left my mother chatting with another fan and headed over to a patch of grass for some shade. At the microphones, Truth Squad was almost totally set up. Don had told us over dinner a few days earlier that he'd hired them to play an hour-long set of nothing but car-related songs to really push the idea of fun, freewheeling summer driving.

'Okay, so I've got some prospects for us,' Chloe said as Truth Squad launched into 'Baby You Can Drive My Car'.

'Prospects?'

She nodded. 'College guys.'

'Hmm,' I said, fanning myself with one hand.

'His name is Matt,' she continued, 'and he's a junior. Cute, tall. He wants to be a doctor.'

'I don't know,' I said. 'It's too hot to date.'

She looked at me. 'I knew it,' she said, shaking her head. 'I *knew* it.'

'Knew what?'

'You,' she said, 'are so not one of us any more.'

'What does that mean?'

She crossed her legs at the ankles, kicking off her shoes, and leaned back on her palms. 'You say that you're single and ready to be out there with us again.'

'I am.'

'But,' she went on, 'every time I've tried to set you up or introduce you to anyone, you beg off.'

'It was just the one time,' I told her, 'and that was because I'm not into skaters.'

'It was twice,' she corrected me, 'and the second time he was totally cute and tall, just the way you like them, so don't give me that crap. We both know what the problem is.'

'Oh, we do? And what is that?'

She turned her head and nodded toward where Truth Squad was in full swing, while two little kids in

267

KaBoom T-shirts were dancing, jumping around. 'Your "friend" over there.'

'Stop,' I said, waving this off as ridiculous, which it was.

'You still see him,' she said, holding up a finger, counting this off.

'We work two feet from each other, Chloe.'

'You're talking to him,' she said, holding up another finger. 'I bet you even have driven past his house when it wasn't even on your way home.'

That I wasn't even going to honour with a response. God.

For a minute or two we just sat there, as Truth Squad played a rousing medley of 'Cars', 'Fun, Fun, Fun', and 'Born to Be Wild'. There were only a certain number of songs related to automobiles, but already they seemed to be grasping a bit.

'So, fine,' I said finally. 'Tell me about these guys.'

She cocked her head to the side, suspicious. 'Don't do me any favours,' she said. 'If you're not ready to be out there, it'll show. We both know that. It's not even worth the trouble.'

'Just tell me,' I said.

'Okay. They're all going to be sophomores, and . . .'

She kept talking, and I half listened, noticing at the same time that Truth Squad was stretching the theme considerably as they started playing 'Dead Man's Curve', not exactly the kind of song that fired anyone up to plunk down five figures on a shiny new car. Don picked up on this too, glaring at Dexter until the song was cut short, just as the curve was about to get really deadly: instead, they segued, a bit clumsily, into 'The Little Old Lady from Pasadena'.

I could see Dexter rolling his eyes, between verses, back at John Miller, and felt that twinge again, then quickly shook it off, not wanting to risk another set of told-you-sos from Chloe. It was time to get back on that horse, before I'd done permanent damage to my reputation.

'. . . so we set it up for tonight, seven o'clock. We're all meeting at Rigoberto's for dinner. It's free breadstick night.'

'Okay,' I said. 'Count me in.'

The thing about Out There that you always forget is how, at times, it can really suck.

This is what I was thinking that night around eight-thirty, as I sat at a table at Rigoberto's, chewing on a stale breadstick and wishing my date, Evan, a chunky guy with tangled shoulder-length hair that desperately needed washing, would shut his mouth when he chewed.

'Tell me again,' I said under my breath to Chloe, who was already cuddled up close with her date, the only good-looking one in the bunch, 'where you found these guys?'

'The Wal-Mart,' she said. 'They were buying trash bags, and so was I. Can you believe it?'

I could. But this was because Evan had already told me that the day they'd met Chloe they had been on their way to pick up litter. Their fantasy game club had adopted a stretch of highway and spent one Saturday a month cleaning it up. The rest of their time, apparently, was spent drawing up sketches of their game 'alter egos' and combating strange trolls and demons by rolling dice in somebody's basement. In just an hour, I'd already learned more about Orcs, Klingons, and some master race invented by Evan himself called the Triciptiors than I ever cared to know.

Chloe's date, Ben, was cute. It was clear, however, that she had not taken the trouble to look past him when making these plans: Evan was, well, Evan, and the twins David and Darrin both were sporting *Star Wars* T-shirts and had spent the entire dinner so far ignoring Lissa and Jess completely while discussing Japanese animation. Jess was shooting Chloe death looks, while Lissa just smiled politely thinking, I knew, about her KaBoom co-worker, PJ, and the crush she had on him that she thought wasn't obvious. This, basically, was Out There, and I realised in the last four weeks I'd not missed it one bit.

After dinner the brothers Darrin and David headed home with Evan in tow, clearly as smitten with us as we had been with them. Jess begged off by saying she had to put her little brothers to bed, and Chloe and Ben stayed at the table, feeding each other tiramisu, leaving just me and Lissa.

'What now?' she asked me as we climbed into my car. 'Bendo?'

'Nah,' I said. 'Let's just go to my house and watch movies or something.'

'Sounds good.'

As we turned into my driveway, the headlights

curving across the lawn, the first thing I saw was my mother sitting on the front steps. She had her shoes off, her elbows on her knees, and when she saw me she stood up, waving her arms, as if she was in the middle of the ocean clinging to a life raft instead of twenty feet from me on solid ground.

I got out of the car, Lissa behind me. I hadn't taken two steps when I heard someone off to my left say, 'Finally!'

I turned around: it was Don, and he was holding a croquet mallet in one hand. His face was red, his shirt untucked, and he looked pissed.

'What's going on?' I asked my mother, who was now coming across the grass to us, quickly, her hands fluttering.

'What's going on,' Don said loudly, 'is that we have been locked out of the house for the last hour and a half with no way of gaining entry. Do you realise how many messages we've left for you on your phone? Do you?'

He was *yelling* at me. This took a moment to compute, simply because it had never happened before. None of my previous stepfathers had taken much interest in the parenting role, even when Chris and I were young enough to actually have tolerated it. Honestly, I was speechless.

'Don't just stand there. Answer me!' he bellowed, and Lissa stepped back, a nervous look on her face. She hated confrontations. No one in her family yelled, and all discussions and disagreements were held in controlled, sympathetic, indoor voices.

'Don, honey,' my mother said, coming up beside him. 'There's no need to be upset. She's here now and she can let us in. Remy, give me your keys.'

I didn't move, keeping my eyes on Don. 'I was at dinner,' I said in an even voice. 'I didn't have my phone with me.'

'We have called you six times!' he said. 'Do you have any idea how late it is? I have a sales meeting at seven AM tomorrow, and I don't have time to be standing around out here trying to break into my own house!'

'Don, please,' my mother said, reaching out a hand to touch his arm. 'Calm down.'

'How did you get home if you don't have your keys?' I asked her.

'Well,' she said. 'We—'

'We drove home one of the new year models,' Don snapped, 'and that's not the point. The point is that we have left messages for you and your brother which were not returned or acknowledged and we have been out here for over an hour, about to bust out a goddamn window—'

'But she's here now,' my mother said cheerfully, 'so let's just get her key and we'll get inside and everything will be—'

'Barbara, for Christ's sake, do not interrupt me when I'm talking!' he snapped, whipping his head around to look at her. 'Jesus!'

For a second, it was very quiet. I looked at my mother, feeling a pang of protectiveness that I hadn't experienced in years, since it was usually me either yelling at her or, more often, just wishing I could. But regardless of the anger my mother could flare in me, there had always been a clear line, at least in my mind, de-marking the short but always clear distance between the We that was my family and whatever man was in her life. Don couldn't see it, but I could.

'Hey,' I said to Don, my voice low, 'don't talk to her like that.'

'Remy, honey, give me your keys,' my mother said, reaching out to touch my arm. 'Okay?'

'You,' Don said, pointing right in my face. I stared at his fat finger, focusing only on it, while everything else – Lissa standing off to the side, my mother pleading, the smell of the summer night – fell away. 'You need to learn some respect, missy.'

'Remy,' I heard Lissa say softly.

'And you,' I said to Don, 'need to respect my mother. This is nobody's fault but your own and you know it. You forgot your keys, you got locked out. End of story.'

He just stood there, breathing hard. I could see Lissa shrinking down the driveway, bit by bit, as if with just another couple of steps she might be able to disappear completely.

'Remy,' my mother said again. 'The keys.'

I pulled them out of my pocket, my eyes still on Don, then handed them past him to her. She took them and started quickly up the lawn. Don was still staring at me, as if he thought I might back down. He was wrong.

The porch light snapped on suddenly, and my mother clapped her hands. 'We're in!' she called out. 'All's well that ends well!'

Don dropped the croquet mallet. It hit the driveway with a thunk. Then he turned his back to me and headed up the walk, taking long, angry strides. Once up the front steps, he pushed past my mother, ignoring her as she spoke to him, and disappeared down the hallway. A second later I heard a door slam.

'What a baby,' I said to Lissa, who was now down by the mailbox, pretending to be engrossed with reading the new letters STARR/DAVIS that had recently been affixed to it.

'He was really mad, Remy.' She came up the driveway carefully, as if expecting Don to throw himself back out the door, ready for round two. 'Maybe you should have just said you were sorry.'

'Sorry for what?' I said. 'For not being psychic?'

'I don't know. It just might have been easier.'

I looked up at the house, where my mother was standing in the doorway, hand on the knob, glancing down the hall to the darkened kitchen, the direction in which Don had stalked off. 'Hey,' I called out. She turned her head. 'What's his problem, anyway?'

I thought I heard him saying something from inside, and she eased the door shut a bit, turning her body away from me. And suddenly I felt completely strange, like the distance between us was much much greater than what I could see from where I was standing. Like that line, always so clear to me, had somehow shifted, or never even been where I'd thought it was at all.

'Mom?' I called out. 'You okay?'

'I'm fine. Good night, Remy,' she said. And then she shut the door.

'I'm telling you,' I said to Jess. 'It was totally messed up.'

Across from me, Lissa nodded. 'Bad,' she said. 'Like scary bad.'

Jess sipped on her Zip Coke, pulling her sweater tighter over her shoulders. We'd gone by and knocked on her window after leaving my mom's, when I decided I wasn't about to spend the evening under the same roof as Don and his temper. Plus there was something else: this weird feeling of betrayal, almost, as if for so long my mother and I had been on one team, and now suddenly she'd up and defected, pushing me aside for someone who would stick a finger in my face and demand respect he hadn't even begun to earn.

'It's really kind of normal behaviour,' Jess told me. 'This whole my-house-my-rules thing. Very male. Very Dad-esque.'

'He's not my dad,' I told her.

'It's a dominance thing,' Lissa chimed in. 'Like dogs. He was making clear to you that he is the alpha dog.'

I looked at her.

'I mean, you're the alpha dog,' she said quickly. 'But he doesn't know that yet. He's testing you.'

'I don't want to be the alpha dog,' I grumbled. 'I don't want to be a dog, full stop.'

'It's weird that your mom would put up with that,' Jess said in her thinking voice. 'She's never been the type to take much crap, either. That's where you get it from.'

'I think she's scared,' I said, and they both looked at

me, surprised. I was surprised myself; I didn't realise I thought this until I said it aloud. 'I mean, of being alone. This is her fifth marriage, you know? If it doesn't work out . . .'

'. . . and you're leaving,' Lissa added. 'And Chris is this close to being married himself . . .'

I sighed, poking at my Zip Diet with my straw.

'. . . so she thinks this is her last chance. She has to make it work.' Lissa sat back, ripping open the bag of Skittles she'd bought and popping a red one in her mouth. 'So maybe, she would pick him over you. Just for now. Because he's the one she has to live with, you know, indefinitely.'

Jess eyed me as I heard this, as if expecting some reaction. 'Welcome to adulthood,' she said. 'It sucks as much as high school.'

'This is why I don't believe in relationships,' I said. 'They're such a crutch. Why would she put up with his baby ways like this? Because she thinks she *needs* him or something?'

'Well,' Lissa said slowly, 'maybe she does need him.'

'Doubtful,' I said. 'If he moved out tomorrow she'd have a new prospect within a week. I'd lay money on it.'

'I think she loves him,' Lissa said. 'And love is needing someone. Love is putting up with someone's bad qualities because they somehow complete you.'

'Love is an excuse to put up with shit that you shouldn't,' I replied, and Jess laughed. 'That's how it gets you. It throws off the scales so that things that should weigh heavily don't seem to. It's a crock. A trap.'

'Okay, then,' Lissa said, sitting up straighter, 'let's talk about untied shoelaces.'

'What?' I said.

'Dexter,' she said. 'His shoelaces were always untied. Right?'

'What does that have to do with anything?'

'Just answer the question.'

'I don't remember,' I said.

'Yes, you do, and yes, they were. Plus he was clumsy, his room was a mess, he was completely unorganised, and he ate in your car.'

'He ate in your car?' Jess asked incredulously. 'No shit?'

'Just the one time,' I said, and ignored the it's-a-miracle-throw-up-a-hallelujah face she made. 'What's the point here?'

'The point is,' Lissa cut in, 'that these are all things that would have made you send any other guy packing within seconds. But with Dexter, you put up with them.'

'I did not.'

'You did,' she said, pouring more Skittles into her hand, 'and why, do you think, were you willing to overlook these things?'

'Don't say it was because I loved him,' I warned her.

'No,' she said. 'But maybe you *could* have loved him.'

'Unlikely,' I said.

'Extremely unlikely,' Jess agreed. 'Although, you did let him eat in your car, so I suppose anything's possible.'

'You were different around him,' Lissa said to me. 'There was something new about you that I'd never seen before. Maybe that *was* love.'

'Or lust,' Jess said.

'Could have been,' I said, leaning back on my palms. 'But I never slept with him.'

Jess raised her eyebrows. 'No?'

I shook my head. 'I almost did. But no.' The night he'd played the guitar for me, that first time, picking out the chords of my father's song, I'd been ready to. It had already been a few weeks, which at one time might have been considered a record for me. But just as we'd got close, he'd pulled back a bit, taking my hands and folding them against his chest, instead pressing his face into my neck. It was subtle, but clear. Not yet. Not now. I'd wondered what he was waiting for, but hadn't found a good time to ask him. And now I'd never know.

'That,' Lissa said, snapping her fingers as if she'd just discovered uranium, 'proves it. Right there.'

'Proves what?' I said.

'Any other guy you would have slept with. No question.'

'Watch it,' I said, pointing at her. 'I have changed, you know.'

'But you would have, right?' she asked. She was so insistent, this new Lissa. 'You knew him well enough, you liked him, you'd been hanging out for a while. But you didn't. And why is that?'

'I have no idea,' I said.

'It's because,' she said grandly, sweeping her hand, 'it meant something to you. It was bigger than just one guy and one night and out you go, free and clear. Part of the change I saw in you. That we all saw. It would mean more, and that scared you.'

I glanced at Jess but she was scratching her knee, choosing not to get into this. And what did Lissa know anyway? It was Dexter who'd stopped things, not me. But then again, I hadn't tried to push it further, and there had been other chances. Not that that meant anything. At all.

'See?' Lissa said, pleased with herself. 'You're speechless.'

'I am not,' I said. 'It's the stupidest thing I've ever heard.'

'Dexter,' she said quietly, 'was the closest you've come to love, Remy. Real love. And you dodged it, at the last second. But it was close. Real close. You could have loved him.'

'No way,' I said. 'Not a chance.'

When I got home later that night I realised, irony of ironies, that I was locked out. I'd given my key to my mother, and never thought to ask for it back. Luckily, Chris was home. So I just tapped on the window over the kitchen sink, making him jump about four feet vertically and shriek like a schoolgirl, which made having to forge through the dark and navigate around the pricker bushes in the backyard at least worthwhile.

'Hey,' he said nonchalantly as he opened the back door, all cool now, as if we both hadn't just witnessed this particularly spineless behaviour. 'Where's your key?'

'Here, somewhere,' I said, stopping the door before it slammed shut. 'Mom and Don were locked out earlier.' Then I filled him in on the gory details as he munched on a peanut butter sandwich – bread butts again – nodding and rolling his eyes in all the right places.

'No way,' he said as I finished. I shushed him, and he lowered his voice. Our walls, we both knew, were thin. 'What a chump. He was yelling at her?'

I nodded. 'I mean, not in a violent way. More in a pouty, spoiled brat kind of way.'

He looked down at the last remnants of bread butts in his hand. 'No surprise there. He's a total baby. And the next time I trip over one of those Ensures on the side porch someone's going down. *Down.*'

This made me smile, reminding me of how much I really liked my brother. Despite our differences, we did have a history. No one understood where I was coming from the way he did.

'Hey Chris?' I asked him as he pulled a carton of milk from the fridge and poured himself a glass.

'Yeah?'

I sat down on the edge of the table, running my hand over the surface. I could feel little pieces of sugar, or salt, fine but distinct beneath my fingers. 'What made you decide to love Jennifer Anne?'

He turned around and looked at me, then swallowed with a glunking noise my mother always screamed at him about when we were kids, saying it made him sound like he was drinking rocks. 'Decide to love?'

'You know what I mean.'

He shook his head. 'Nope. No idea.'

'What made you,' I expanded, 'feel like it was a worthwhile risk?'

'It isn't a financial investment, Remy,' he said, sticking the milk back in the fridge. 'There's no maths to it.'

'That's not what I mean.'

'What *do* you mean?'

I shrugged. 'I don't know. Forget it.'

He put his glass in the sink, then ran water over it. 'Do you mean what made me love her?'

I wasn't sure I could take further discussion of that question. 'No. I mean, when you thought about whether or not you wanted to open yourself up, you know, to the chance that you could get really hurt, somehow, if you moved forward with her, what did you think? To yourself?'

He cocked an eyebrow at me. 'Are you drunk?'

'No,' I snapped. 'God. It's a simple question.'

'Yeah, right. So simple I still don't even know what you're asking.' He flipped off the light over the sink, then wiped his hands on a dishtowel. 'You want to know how I debated about whether or not to fall in love with her? Is that even close?'

'Forget it,' I said, pushing off the table. 'I don't even know what I'm trying to find out. I'll see you in the morning.' I started toward the foyer, and as I got closer, I could see my keys laid out neatly on the table by the stairs, waiting for me. I slid them into my back pocket.

I was on the second step when Chris appeared in the kitchen doorway. 'Remy.'

'Yeah?'

'If what you're asking is how I debated whether or not to love her the answer is I didn't. Not at all. It just happened. I didn't ever question it; by the time I realised what was happening, it was already done.'

I stood there on the stairs, looking down at him. 'I don't get it,' I said.

'What part?'

'Any of it.'

He shrugged and flipped off the last kitchen light, then started up the stairs, brushing past me. 'Don't worry,' he said. 'Someday, you will.'

He disappeared down the hall, and a minute later I heard him shut his door, his voice low as he made his required good-night-again-this-time-by-phone call to Jennifer Anne. I washed my face, brushed my teeth, and was on my way to bed when I stopped by the half-open door of the lizard room.

Most of the cages were dark. The lights for the lizards were kept on timers, which clicked them on and off at just the right cycles to make the lizards believe, I supposed, that they were still sunning themselves on desert rocks instead of sitting in a cage in a converted linen closet. But at the far end of the room, on a middle shelf, one light was on.

It was a glass cage, and the floor of it was covered in sand. There were sticks crisscrossing it, and at the top of one stick were two lizards. As I came closer, I saw that they were entwined – not in a mating, nature-takes-its-course kind of way, but almost tenderly, if that was even possible, like they were holding each other. They both had their eyes closed, and I could see the pattern of their ribs, revealed and hidden with each breath they took.

I kneeled down in front of the cage, pressing my index finger against the glass. The lizard on the top opened his eyes and looked at me, unflinching, his pupil widening slightly as he focused on my finger.

I knew this meant nothing. They were just lizards, cold-blooded and probably no smarter than the average earthworm. But there was something so human about them, and for a minute all the things that had happened in the last few weeks blurred past in my mind: Dexter and I breaking up, my mother's worried face, Don's finger pointing at me, all the way up to Chris shaking his head, unable to put into words what seemed to me, at least, the most simple of concepts. And all of it came down to one thing: love, or the lack of it. The chances we take, knowing no better, to fall or to stand back and hold ourselves in, protecting our hearts with the tightest of grips.

I looked back at the lizard in front of me, wondering if I had finally gone completely crazy. He returned my gaze, now having decided I was not a threat, and then slowly closed his eyes again. I leaned in closer, still watching, but already the light was dimming as the timer kicked in, and before I knew it, everything was dark.

13

'Remy, sugar? Come here for a minute, will you?'

I got up from behind the reception desk, putting down the stack of body lotion invoices I'd been counting, and walked back into the manicure/pedicure room, where Amanda, our best nail girl, was wiping down her work space. Behind her was Lola, patting her scissors into her open palm.

'What's going on?' I asked, already suspicious.

'Just sit down,' Amanda told me, and the next thing I knew I *was* sitting: Talinga had snuck up behind me and pressed down on my shoulders, whipping a hair cape around me and snapping it at the neck before I even knew what was happening.

'Wait a second,' I said as Amanda grabbed my hands and planted them, quick as lightning, onto the table between us. She spread out my fingers and started filing my nails with quick, aggressive jerks of an emery board, biting her lip as she did so.

'Just a quick makeover,' Lola said smoothly, coming up behind me and lifting up my hair. 'A little manicure, a little trim, a little make-up—'

'No way,' I said, pulling free from her grip. 'You are not touching my hair.'

'Just a trim!' she replied, yanking me back into place. 'Ungrateful girl, most women would pay big money for this. And you get it for free!'

'I bet not,' I grumbled, and they all laughed. 'What's the catch?'

'Keep your hands still or I'll cut more than this cuticle,' Amanda warned me.

'No catch,' Lola said breezily, and I braced myself as I heard snipping behind me. God, she *was* cutting my hair. 'A bonus.'

I looked at Talinga, who was testing lipsticks on the back of her hand, glancing at me every so often as she gauged my colours. 'Bonus?'

'A plus. A gift!' Lola laughed one of her big laughs. 'A special present for our Miss Remy.'

'A gift,' I repeated, warily. 'What is it?'

'Guess,' Amanda said, smiling at me as she started applying smooth streaks of red polish to my fingernails.

'Is it bigger than a bread box?' I said.

'You wish!' Lola said, and they all started laughing hysterically, like this was the funniest thing ever.

'Tell me what's going on,' I said sternly, 'or I'm out of here. Don't think I won't do it.'

They were still tittering, trying to control themselves. Finally Talinga took a deep breath and said, 'Remy, honey. We found you a *man*.'

'A man?' I said. 'God. I thought maybe I was getting some free cosmetics or something. Something I *need*.'

'You need a man,' Amanda said, moving to my next nail.

'No,' Talinga said, '*I* need a man. Remy needs a boy.'

'A nice boy,' Lola corrected her. 'And today is your lucky day, because we happen to have one for you.'

'Forget it,' I said as Talinga bent down next to me, poking at my face with a make-up brush. 'Is this the one you tried to set me up with before? The bilingual one with nice hands?'

'He'll be here at six,' Lola went on, ignoring me completely. 'His name is Paul, he's nineteen, and he thinks he's coming to pick up some samples for his mother. But instead he'll see you, with your beautiful hair . . .'

'And make-up,' Talinga added.

'And nails,' Amanda said, 'if you stop wiggling around, goddammit.'

'. . . and be completely smitten,' Lola finished. Then she did two more small snips and ran a hand through my hair, checking her work. 'God, you had some split ends. Disgraceful!'

'What in the world,' I said slowly, 'makes you think I'll go through with this?'

'Because he's good-looking,' Talinga said.

'Because you should,' Amanda added.

'Because,' Lola said, whisking the cape off me, 'you can.'

I had to admit they were right. Paul *was* good-looking. He was also funny, pronounced my name right, had a firm handshake – and, okay, nice hands – and seemed to be a good sport about the fact that it was such an obvious set-up, exchanging a wary expression with me when Lola 'just happened' to have a gift certificate from my favourite Mexican place that she was suddenly sure she'd never use.

'Do you get the feeling,' Paul asked me, 'that this is out of our control?'

'I do,' I agreed. 'But it is a free dinner.'

'Yes,' he said. 'Good point. But really, don't feel obligated.'

'You either,' I told him.

We stood there for a second while Lola and Talinga and Amanda, in the next room, were so quiet I could hear someone's stomach growling.

'Let's just go,' I said. 'Make their day and all.'

'Okay.' He smiled at me. 'I'll pick you up at seven?'

I wrote down my address on the back of a Joie business card, then watched as he walked out to his car. He was cute, and I *was* single. It had been almost three weeks since Dexter and I had split, and not only was I dealing with it, we'd almost finessed the impossible: a friendship. And here was this nice guy, an opportunity. Why wouldn't I take it?

One possible answer to this question appeared as I was walking out to my car, digging in my bag for my keys and sunglasses. I wasn't looking where I was going, much less around me, and didn't even see Dexter come out of Flash Camera and cross the parking lot until I heard a loud clicking noise and looked up to see him standing there, holding a disposable wedding camera.

'Hey,' he said, winding the film with one finger. Then he put the camera back up to his eye and bent back a bit, getting me from another angle. 'Wow, you look great. Got a hot date or something?'

I hesitated, and he took the picture. Click. 'Well, actually . . .' I said.

For a second, he didn't move, not winding the film or anything, just looking at me still through the viewfinder. Then he took the camera away from his eye, then smacked his forehead with one hand and said, 'Ouch. Oh, man. Awkward moment time. Sorry.'

'It's just a set-up,' I said quickly. 'Lola did it.'

'You don't have to explain,' he said, winding the film, click-click-click. 'You know that.'

And then it happened. One of those too-long-to-just-be-a-regular-pause-in-conversation pauses, and I said, 'Okay. Well.'

'Oh, man, awkward. Double awkward,' he said. Then shrugged his shoulders briskly, as if shaking this off, and said, 'It's okay. It's a challenge, after all, right? It's not supposed to be easy.'

I looked down at my bag, realising my keys, which I'd been digging for this whole time, were in fact in my back pocket. I pulled them out, glad to have some kind of task, however stupid, to focus on.

'So,' he said casually, pointing the camera over my head and taking a picture of Joie's storefront, 'who's the guy?'

'Dexter. Really.'

'No. I mean, this is what friends discuss, right? It's just a question. Like asking about the weather.'

I considered this. We had known what we were getting into: eating ten bananas wasn't easy either. 'The son of a client here. I just met him twenty minutes ago.'

'Ah,' he said, rocking back on his heels. 'Black Honda?'

I nodded.

'Right. Saw him.' He wound the film again. 'Looked like a nice, upstanding guy.'

Upstanding, I thought to myself. As if he were running for student council president, or volunteering to help your grandmother across the street. 'It's just dinner,' I said as he snapped another picture, this one, inexplicably, of my feet. 'What's with the camera?'

'Defective shipment,' he explained. 'Somebody at the main office left the box out in the sun, so they're all warped. Management said we could have them, if we wanted them. Kind of like the tangerines, you know. Can't turn down free stuff.'

'But will the pictures even come out?' I asked, noticing now, as I looked closer, that the camera itself was bent, warped, like the VCR tape I'd accidentally left on my dash the summer before. It didn't look like you could even get the film out, much less develop it.

'Don't know,' he said, taking another picture. 'They might. Or they might not.'

'They won't,' I said. 'The film's probably ruined from the heat.'

'Or maybe,' he said, holding the camera out at arm's length and smiling big as he snapped a picture of himself, 'it isn't. Maybe it's just fine. We won't know until we develop it.'

'But it's probably a total waste,' I told him. 'Why bother?'

He put down the camera and looked at me, really looked at me, not through the lens, or from the side, just me and him. 'That's the big question, isn't it?' he said. 'That's the whole problem here. I think they just might come out. Maybe they won't be perfect – I mean, they could be blurred, or cut off in the middle – but I'm thinking it's worth a shot. That's just me, though.'

I just stood there, blinking, as he lifted the camera up and took one more shot of me. I stared straight at him as it clicked, letting him know I got his little metaphor. 'I have to go,' I said.

'Sure,' he said, and smiled at me. 'See you later.'

As he walked away, he tucked the camera into his back pocket, darting between cars as he headed back to Flash Camera. Maybe he would print out the pictures and find them perfect: my face, my feet, Joie rising up behind me. Or maybe it would just be black, void of light, not even an outline of a face or figure visible. That was the problem, after all. I wouldn't waste the time on such odds, while he jumped to them. People like Dexter followed risks the way dogs followed smells, thinking only of what *could* lie ahead and never logically of what probably did. It was good we were friends, and only that. If even that. We never would have lasted. Not a chance.

It had been two days since the scene with Don in the front yard, and so far I'd managed to avoid him, timing my trips to our common area, the kitchen, when I knew he was either out or in the shower. My mother was easier: she was completely immersed in her novel, pushing through the last hundred pages at breakneck speed, and hardly would have noticed a bomb going off in the living room if it meant pulling herself away from Melanie and Brock Dobbin and their impossible love.

Which was why I was surprised to find her sitting at the kitchen table, a cup of coffee beside her, when I came home to get ready for my date with set-up Paul. She had her head balanced on one hand and was staring up at Don's naked lady painting, so lost in thought that she jumped when I touched her shoulder.

'Oh, Remy,' she said, pressing a finger to her temple and smiling. 'You scared me.'

'Sorry.' I pulled out a chair and sat down across from her, dropping my keys on the table. 'What are you doing?'

'Waiting for Don,' she said, fluffing her hair with her fingers. 'We're meeting some Toyota VIPs for dinner, and he's a nervous wreck. He thinks if we don't impress them they'll cut back on his dealer perk allotment.'

'His what?'

'I don't know,' she said, sighing. 'It's dealership talk. This whole night will be dealership talk, and meanwhile I've got Melanie and Brock at a sidewalk café in Brussels with her estranged husband fast approaching and the *last* thing in the world I want to think about is sales figures and cut-rate financing techniques.' She cast a longing look into her study at her typewriter, as if being pulled there by some tidelike force. 'Oh, God, don't you sometimes wish you could live two lives?'

Inexplicably, or maybe not, Dexter suddenly popped into my head, watching me through a bent disposable camera. Click. 'Sometimes, yeah,' I said, shaking this off. 'I guess I do.'

'Barbara!' Don bellowed, opening the door to the New Wing. I couldn't see him, but his voice had no trouble carrying. 'Have you seen my red tie?'

'Your what, darling?' she called back.

'My red tie, the one I wore to the sales dinner? Have you seen it?'

'Oh, honey, I don't know,' she said, turning in her chair. 'Maybe if you—'

'Never mind, I'll just wear the green one,' he said, and the door shut again.

My mother smiled at me, as if he was just really something, then reached over and patted my hand. 'Enough about me. What's happening with you?'

'Well,' I said, 'Lola set me up with a blind date for tonight.'

'A blind date?' She looked at me warily.

'I already met him, at the salon,' I told her. 'He seems really nice. And it's just dinner.'

'Ah,' she said, nodding. 'Just dinner. As if nothing could happen within three courses and a bottle of wine.' Then she sat there, blinking. 'That's good,' she said suddenly. 'Oh, my. I should write that down.'

I watched as she picked up an envelope, an old power bill, and a pen. *Three courses – just dinner – nothing could happen* she scrawled on the side of it, capping it off with a big exclamation mark, then slid the envelope under the sugar bowl, where it would probably remain, forgotten, until one day when she was totally blocked and found it. She left these scribblings all around the house, folded into corners, on the backs of shelves, acting as markers in books. I'd once found one about seals, which later turned out to be a major plot point in *Memories of Truro*, sticking out of a box of tampons under my sink. I guess you just never knew when inspiration would strike.

'Well, we're going to La Brea,' I told her, 'so it'll probably just be the one course. Even less chance of it working out.'

She smiled at me. 'You never know, Remy. Love is so unpredictable. Sometimes you'll know a man for years and then one day, boom! Suddenly you see him in a different way. And other times, it's that first date, that first moment. That's what makes it so great.'

'I'm not falling in love with him. It's just a date,' I said.

'Barbara!' Don yelled. 'What did you do with my cuff links?'

'Darling,' she said, turning around again. 'I haven't *touched* your cuff links.' She sat there, waiting, and when he didn't say anything else she just shrugged, turning back to me.

'God,' I said, lowering my voice, 'I don't see how you put up with him.'

She smiled, reaching over to brush my hair out of my face. 'He's not so bad.'

'He's a big baby,' I said. 'And the Ensure thing would make me nuts.'

'Maybe it would,' she agreed. 'But I love Don. He's a good man, he's kind to me. And no relationship is perfect, ever. There are always some ways you have to bend, to compromise, to give something up in order to gain something greater. Yes, Don has habits that try my patience. And I'm sure I have plenty that do the same for him.'

'At least you act like an adult,' I said, although I knew myself this wasn't always true. 'He can't even dress himself.'

'But,' she went on, ignoring this, 'the love we have for each other is bigger than these small differences. And that's the key. It's like a big pie chart, and the love in a relationship has to be the biggest piece. Love can make up for a lot, Remy.'

'Love is a sham,' I said, sliding the saltshaker in a circle.

'Oh, honey, no!' She reached over and took my hand, squeezing my fingers. 'You don't really believe that, do you?'

I shrugged. 'I have yet to be convinced otherwise.'

'Oh, Remy.' She picked up my hand, folding her fingers around mine. Hers were smaller, cooler, the nails bright pink. 'How can you say that?'

I just looked at her. One, two, three seconds. And then she was with me.

'Oh, now,' she said, letting my hand go, 'just because a few marriages didn't last doesn't make it a total wash. I had many good years with your father, Remy, and the best part was that I got Chris and you out of it. The four years I was with Harold were wonderful, until the very end. And even with Martin and Win, I was happy for most of the time.'

'But they did end, all of them,' I said. 'They failed.'

'Maybe some people would say so.' She folded her hands in her lap and thought for a second. 'But I think, personally, that it would be worse to have been alone all that time. Sure, maybe I would have protected my heart from some things, but would that really have been better? To hold myself apart because I was too scared that something might not be for ever?'

'Maybe,' I said, picking at the edge of the table. 'Because at least then you're safe. The fate of your heart is *your* choice, and no one else gets a vote.'

She considered this, really thinking about it, then said, 'Well, it's true that I have been hurt in my life. Quite a bit. But it's also true that I have loved, and been loved. And that carries a weight of its own. A greater weight, in my opinion. It's like that pie chart we talked about earlier. In the end, I'll look back on my life and see that the greatest piece of it *was* love. The problems, the divorces, the sadness . . . those will be there too, but just smaller slivers, tiny pieces.'

'I just think that you have to protect yourself,' I said. 'You can't just give yourself away.'

'No,' she said solemnly. 'You can't. But holding people away from you, and denying yourself love, that doesn't make you strong. If anything, it makes you weaker. Because you're doing it out of fear.'

'Fear of what?' I said.

'Of taking that chance,' she said simply. 'Of letting go and giving into it, and that's what makes us what we are. Risks. That's living, Remy. Being too scared to even try it – that's just a waste. I can say I made a lot of mistakes, but I don't regret things. Because at least I didn't spend a life standing outside, wondering what living would be like.'

I sat there, not even sure what to say next. I realised I'd felt sorry for my mother for nothing. All these years I'd pitied her all her marriages, saw the very fact that she kept trying as her greatest weakness, not understanding that to her, it was the complete opposite. In her mind, me sending Dexter away made me weaker than him, not stronger.

'Barbara, we've got to be there in ten minutes so let's—' Don appeared in the kitchen doorway, tie crooked, his jacket folded over one arm. He stopped when he saw me. 'Oh. Remy. Hello.'

'Hi,' I said.

'Oh, look at your tie,' my mother said, standing up. She walked over to him, smoothing her hands down the front of his shirt, and straightened it, tightening the knot. 'There. All fixed.'

'We should go.' Don kissed her on the forehead and she stepped back from him. 'Gianni hates having to wait.'

'Oh, well, then let's get going,' my mother said. 'Remy, honey, have a wonderful time. Okay? And think about what I said.'

'I will,' I told her. 'Have fun.'

Don headed out to the car, keys in hand – which I noticed, of course – but my mother came over to me as I stood up, putting her hands on my shoulders. 'Don't let your mother's history make you a cynic, Remy,' she said softly. 'Okay?'

Too late, I thought as she kissed me. Then I watched

as she walked out to the car, where Don was waiting. He put a hand against the small of her back, guiding her into her seat, and in that one moment I began to think I just might understand what she was talking about. Maybe a marriage, like a life, isn't only about the Big Moments, whether they be bad or good. Maybe it's all the small things – like being guided slowly forward, surely, day after day – that stretch out to strengthen even the most tenuous bond.

My luck was continuing. Paul was actually not a bad set-up.

I'd been a little wary when he'd picked me up, but was surprised when, actually, we'd immediately fallen into talking about college. Apparently one of his best friends from high school was at Stanford, and he'd been there over Christmas to visit.

'Great campus,' he was saying as the mariachi band, a La Brea staple, started up yet another rendition of 'Happy Birthday' across the restaurant. 'Plus the ratio in the classes of professors to students is really good. You're not just dealing with a TA, you know?'

I nodded. 'I hear it's pretty rigorous academically.'

He smiled. 'Oh, come on. I know how smart you have to be to get in there. I doubt you'll have a problem. You probably, like, aced the SATs, right?'

'Wrong,' I said, shaking my head.

'I, however,' he said grandly, taking a sip of his water, 'scored in the moron category. Which is why I'll still be at my fine state school pulling the gentleman's C, while you head off to lead the free world. You can send me a postcard. Or, better yet, come see me at my postgraduate job, where I'll be happy to Supersize your order because, you know, we're friends and all.'

I smiled. Paul was a charmer, and a rich boy, but I liked him. He was the kind of guy where talking comes easily because he has something in common with everyone. Already, other than Stanford we'd discussed waterskiing (he was terrible, but addicted), the fact that he was bilingual (Spanish – his grandmother was Venezuelan), and the fact that once summer was over, he'd head back to school, where he was a brother at Sigma Nu, majored in psychology, and managed what he described as the 'all heart, no skills' men's basketball team. He wasn't goofy or uproariously hilarious, but then again, he wasn't clumsy either, and both his shoes were tied. Before I knew it, our food had come, we'd eaten, and we were still sitting there talking, even as they cleared every plate from around us in a subtle hint that we were lingering too long.

'Okay,' he said, as we made our waiter's day by finally leaving, 'in the interest of full disclosure, I have to say I was a little wary about this.'

'In the interest of full disclosure,' I replied, 'I would say that you were not alone in that feeling.'

As we reached the car, he surprised me by unlocking my door, then holding it open as I climbed in. *Nice*, I thought, as he walked around to the driver's side. *Very nice*.

'So, if this *had* been a total disaster,' he said as he got in, 'I'd tell you I had a great time, then take you home, walk you to your door, and run every stop sign on the way out of your neighbourhood.'

'Classy,' I said.

'But,' he went on, 'since it wasn't, I was wondering if you wanted to go to a party with me. Some friends of mine are having a pool thing. You interested?'

I considered my options. So far, it had been a good night. A good date. Nothing had happened that I would regret, or have to think about too much later. It was all going by the book, but for some reason I couldn't shake what my mother had said to me from my mind. Maybe I did hold the world at arm's length, and so far it had worked for me. But you just never knew.

'Sure,' I said. 'Let's go.'

'Great.' He smiled, then cranked the engine. As he started to back out, I caught him glancing over at me, and knew, right then, that already things were in motion. It was funny how easy it was to start again, after only three weeks. I'd thought Dexter would affect me more, change me, but here I was with another boy in another car, the cycle starting all over again. Dexter was the different one, the aberration. This was what I was used to, and it was good to be back on a sure footing again.

'Man,' Lissa said, dipping a fry into her ketchup, 'it's like you special-ordered him or something. How is that?'

I smiled, sipping on my Diet Coke. 'Just lucky, I guess.'

'He's totally cute.' Lissa stuffed another fry in her mouth. 'God, all the good ones are taken, aren't they?'

'So does this whining,' Jess asked Lissa, 'mean that KaBoom PJ has a girlfriend?'

'Don't call him that,' Lissa said sulkily, eating another fry. 'And they've already broken up once this summer. She hasn't come to a single event, either.'

'Bitch,' Jess said, and I laughed out loud.

'The point is,' Lissa continued, ignoring us, 'that it's just not fair that I've been dumped and now the guy I like is unavailable while Remy gets not only fun band boyfriend but now cute college boyfriend. It's not right.' She ate another fry. 'And, I can't stop eating. Not that anybody cares, since I'm completely unlovable anyway.'

'Oh, please,' Jess grumbled. 'Get out the violin.'

'Fun band boyfriend?' I said.

'Dexter was nice,' she told me, wiping her mouth. 'And now you have perfect Paul too. And all I've got is an endless supply of KaBoom and the appetite of a truck driver.'

'There's nothing wrong with a healthy appetite,' Jess told her. 'Guys like a few curves.'

'I have curves already,' Lissa replied. 'What's next? Clumps?'

Chloe, the thinnest of all of us, snorted at this. 'That's one word for it.'

Lissa sighed, shoving her tray away and wiping her hands on a napkin. 'I gotta go. I'm due at the Tri-Country track meet in fifteen minutes. We're KaBooming the all-state athletes.'

'Well,' Jess said dryly, 'be sure to wear protection.'

Lissa made a face. She was over the KaBoom jokes, but they were just too easy.

Back at work, Paul dropped by to see me on his way home from his life-guarding job at the Y. I couldn't help but notice a couple of bridesmaids waiting for prewedding manicures ogle him a bit as he came in, tanned and smelling like suntan lotion and chlorine.

'Hey,' he said, and I stood up and kissed him, very lightly, because that was about where we were at relationship-wise. It had been a week and a half, and we'd seen each other almost every day: lunches, dinners, a couple of parties. 'I know you're busy tonight, but I just wanted to say hello.'

'Hello,' I said.

'Hello.' He grinned at me. God, he was cute. I kept thinking that if only I'd gone out with him way back when Lola had first tried to set us up, the entire summer would have been different. Totally different.

After all, Paul met just about every criteria on my guy list. He was tall. Good-looking. Had no annoying personal habits. Was older than me but not by more than three years. Was a decent dresser but didn't shop more than I did. Fell within the acceptable limits in terms of personal hygiene (i.e., aftershave and cologne yes, mousse and fake tan, no). Was smart enough to carry on good conversation but not an eggbert. But the big whammy, the tipping point, was that he was leaving at the end of the summer and we'd already established that we would part as friends and go our separate ways.

Which left me with a nice, cute, courteous guy with his own life and hobbies who liked me, kissed very well, paid for dinner, and had no problem with any of the terms that so many before him had stumbled over. And all this from a blind date. Amazing.

'So I know tonight is girls' night,' he said as I slid my hands across the counter, over his, 'but I wondered what the chances were for catching up with you later?'

'Not good,' I told him. 'Only the lamest women bail their girlfriends for a guy. It's against the code.'

'Ah,' he said, nodding. 'Well. It was worth a shot.'

Across the parking lot, I could see the white Truth Squad van pulling up to Flash Camera. Ted parked in the loading zone and hopped out of the driver's side, slamming the door behind him, then disappeared inside.

'So what are you doing tonight?' I asked Paul. 'Boy stuff?'

'Yep,' he said as I looked across at Flash Camera again, watching as Dexter followed Ted back to the van. They were talking animatedly – arguing? – as they hopped in and drove off, running the stop sign that led past Mayor's Market, toward the main road.

'. . . some band the guys want to see is playing at that club over by the university.'

'Really,' I said, not exactly listening as the white van pulled out into traffic in front of a station wagon, which let loose with an angry beep.

'Yeah, Trey says they're really good . . . Spinnerbait, I think they're called.'

'Hate Spinnerbait,' I said automatically.

'What?'

I looked at him, realising I'd been in a complete fog for this entire conversation. 'Oh, nothing. I just, um, I heard that band kind of sucked.'

He raised his eyebrows. 'Wow. Really? Trey says they're great.'

'Oh, well,' I said quickly. 'I'm sure he knows better than me.'

'I doubt that.' He leaned across the counter and kissed me. 'I'll call you tonight, okay?'

I nodded. 'Sure.'

As he left, the two bridesmaids eyed me appreciatively, as if I was due respect simply because such a guy was with me. But for some reason I was distracted, ringing up Mrs Jameson's hair streaking as a bikini wax and then charging her fifty bucks instead of five for some cuticle cream. At least it was almost time to go home.

I was getting into my car when I heard someone tap on the passenger window. I looked up: it was Lucas. 'Hey Remy,' he said, when I rolled down the window. 'Can you give me a ride home? Dex already left with the van and otherwise I have to hoof it.'

'Sure,' I said, even though I was already running late. I was supposed to pick up Lissa, and the yellow house was entirely in the other direction. But it wasn't like I could just leave him there.

He climbed in, then immediately began to fiddle with the radio as I backed out of my parking spot. This, at one point, would have been grounds for instant ejection, but I let it slide because I was in a decent mood. 'What CDs you got?' he asked, flipping past my main preset to the lower end of the dial and cranking up some experimental-sounding, shrieking-ish noise on the college radio station.

'They're in the glove box,' I said, pointing. He opened it up and shuffled through them – they had been arranged alphabetically, but only because I'd had some extra time when stuck in a traffic jam a few days earlier. He kept making clucking noises, low sighs, and mumbles. Apparently my collection, like my presets, wasn't up to his standards. But I had no need to impress Lucas. Thanks to Dexter I knew not only that his given name was Archibald, but also that in high school he'd had long hair and played in a metal band called Residew. Apparently there was only one picture existing of Lucas wailing on his keyboard in full-hair-sprayed mode, and Dexter had it.

'So,' I said, feeling the need to mess with him a bit anyway, 'I hear Spinnerbait's playing tonight.'

He jerked his head around and looked at me. 'Where?'

'Murray's,' I told him as we cruised through a yellow light.

'Where's that?'

'Across town, by the university. It's a pretty big place.' I could see him in my peripheral vision; he was gnawing on the cuff of his shirt, looking irritated.

'Hate Spinnerbait,' he grumbled. 'Bunch of poser rock assholes. Totally manufactured sound, and their fans are a bunch of pretty-boy, frat-a-tat blondies with good hair driving Daddy's car with no taste *whatsoever*.'

'Ouch,' I said, unable to help but notice this description, while harsh, did somewhat describe Trey, Paul's best friend, as well as Paul himself, if you didn't know him better. Which, of course, I did.

'Well, this is big news,' Lucas said as I turned onto their street. 'But not as big as what else is going on.'

'What's that?' I said, immediately flashing back to the van speeding out of Mayor's Village earlier.

He glanced over at me, and I could tell by his face he was weighing whether it was even my business. 'High-level band stuff,' he said cryptically. 'We're on the brink. Basically.'

'Really,' I said. 'The brink of what?'

He shrugged as I slowed down, the yellow house coming up in sight. I could see Ted and Scary Mary in the front yard, sitting in lawn chairs: she had her feet in his lap, and they were sharing a box of Twinkies. 'Rubber Records wants to meet with us. We're going up to D.C. next week, to you know, talk to them.'

'Wow,' I said, navigating my way into the driveway, where the van was parked at an angle. Ted looked over at us, mildly interested, and Mary waved as Lucas popped open his door and got out. 'That's great.'

'Get this,' he yelled at Ted. 'Spinnerbait's playing tonight.'

'Hate Spinnerbait!' Mary said.

'Where at?' Ted asked as Lucas shut my door and walked around the front of the car.

'Thanks for the ride,' he said, knocking his hand on my half-open window. 'I appreciate it.'

'Man, what is that all about?' Ted yelled. 'They're invading our territory!'

'It's a turf war!' Lucas said back, and they both laughed.

He started to walk away, but I beeped the horn, and he turned around. 'Hey, Lucas.'

'Yeah?' He took a couple of steps back toward me.

'Good luck with everything,' I said, then felt somewhat awkward, seeing that I hardly knew him. Still, for some reason I needed to say something. 'I mean, good luck to you guys.'

'Yeah,' he said, shrugging. 'We'll see how it goes.'

As I pulled out, he was dragging up a milk crate to join Mary and Ted's outdoor picnic as Ted tossed him a Twinkie. I glanced back one last time at the house, where I could see Monkey sitting in the doorway, panting. I wondered where Dexter was, then reminded myself that it wasn't my concern any longer. But if he'd been home, he probably would have come out and said hello to me. Just because we *were* friends.

I started down the street, easing to a slow stop at the stop sign. In my rearview, I could see Ted, Mary, and Lucas still sitting there, talking, but now Dexter was with them, crouching down next to the makeshift table, unwrapping a Twinkie while Monkey circled them, tail wagging. They were all talking, and for a split second I felt a pang, as if I was missing out on something. Weird. Then, the car behind me beeped, impatient, and I jerked myself back to reality, shaking off this fog and moving forward again.

When I got home, the house was quiet. My mother

was out of town, at a writers' conference she attended every August, where she taught workshops to aspiring romance novelists, soaking up buckets of admiration for three days and two nights in the Florida Keys. As for Chris, he was basically living and sleeping at Jennifer Anne's, where the bread wasn't all butts and he could eat his breakfast staring at prints of cheerful flower gardens instead of fifteen-pound neoclassic breasts. Normally I liked having the house to myself, but things were still awkward with me and Don, so I'd taken Lissa up on her offer of sleeping at her house for the weekend, informing Don of my decision with a formal note I wedged under the growing pyramid of empty Ensure cans on the kitchen table.

Now I went into my mother's office, pushing the curtain aside. On the shelf next to her desk, there was a stack of papers: the new novel, or what there was of it so far. I pulled it into my lap and tucked my legs up underneath me, flipping the pages. When I'd last left Melanie, she'd been facing a cold marital bed with a distant husband, realising her marriage had been a mistake. That had been about page 200, and by 250, she had left Paris and was back in New York, working in fashion design for a nasty woman with villain written all over her. Apparently, coincidence of coincidences, Brock Dobbin was also back in New York, having been injured during some kind of third world riot while working in his prizewinning career as a photojournalist. At the fall shows, they'd caught each other's eye from across the runway, and a romance was reborn.

I skipped to page 300, where things had obviously gone bad: Melanie was in a mental hospital, doped up on painkillers, while her former boss took credit for her entire fall line. Her estranged husband, Luc, was also back in the picture, involved in some kind of elaborate financial scheme. Brock Dobbin seemed to have disappeared entirely, but I found him on page 374, in a Mexican prison, where he was facing dubious charges of trafficking drugs and falling for the charms of a local beggar girl named Carmelita. This, I figured, had to be where my mother was losing her train of thought, but by 400 she seemed to have her steam back, and everyone was in Milan preparing for the fall shows. Luc was trying to reconcile with Melanie, but his intentions weren't good, while Brock was back on the job, chasing a story about the dirty underside of fashion with his trusty Nikon and a sense of justice that no injury, not even a rock to the head in Guatemala, could quell.

The last sheet in my lap was numbered 405, and in it Melanie and Brock were drinking espresso at a café in Milan.

> *They only had eyes for one another, as if their time apart had made them hungry for each other in a way that could be conveyed solely by a glance, forbidden to be expressed in words. Melanie's hands were shaking, even as she wrapped them in her silk shawl, the fabric providing little comfort in the stiff breeze.*
>
> *'And you love him?' Brock asked her. His green*

eyes, so deep and probing, were watching her intently.

Melanie was shocked at his bluntness. But it seemed the time in prison had given him an urgency, a need for answers. He stared at her, waiting. 'He is my husband,' she said.

'That is not what I asked.' Brock reached over and took her hand, folding it within his. His fingers were calloused and thick, rough against her pale skin. 'Do you love him?'

Melanie bit her lip, forcing down the sob she feared would escape if she was pressed to tell the truth about Luc and his cold, cold heart. Brock had left her all those months ago with no other choice. She'd given him up for dead, their love as well. He had been like a ghost walking up to her as she sat at the café, crossing over from that world to her own.

'I do not believe in love,' she said.

Brock squeezed her hand. 'How can you say that, after what we had? What we still have?'

'We have nothing,' she said, and took her hand back. 'I am married. I will make my marriage work because . . .'

'Melanie.'

'Because this man loves me,' she finished.

'This man,' Brock said, his voice grave, 'loves you.'

'You are too late.' Melanie stood. She had put Brock Dobbin from her mind again and again, telling herself that she could make a life with Luc. Luc, so suave and debonair, so steady and strong. Brock was always coming in and out of her life,

309

making promises, the love they shared so passionate, and then just gone, leaving her behind in a cloud of memories and train smoke as he disappeared, heading across the world, chasing the story that would never be theirs. Maybe Luc wasn't ever going to love her the way Brock had, filling her body and mind with a joy that made the world fall away. But that joy never lasted, and she wanted to believe in a forever. Even one that sometimes left her wanting at night, dreaming of better things.

'Melanie,' Brock called after her as she started down the cobblestone street, wrapping her scarf around her. 'Come back.'

They were words she knew well. She had said them herself, at the station in Prague. Outside the Plaza, as he'd climbed into a cab. On the deck of the yacht, as his boat sped away, riding the waves. He always did the leaving. But not this time. She kept walking, and did not look back.

Go Melanie, I thought, turning the last page over on the stack on my lap. But I had to admit, it was not typical of my mother's heroines to turn from a man of passion to a faulty man who provided a steady hand, if not a passionate one. Was my mother preaching settling? It was a discomforting thought. She'd been so quick to tell me I was wrong about love. But it was too early to know: there were always more pages to go, more words to be written, before the story was over.

14

'Pull over at this store up here,' Paul called out to Trey, who was driving. 'Okay?'

Trey nodded and put on the turn signal. In the front seat, Lissa turned around to look at me, raising her eyebrows as she nodded toward the back seat console, where there was not only the standard ashtray and cup holder but also a separate CD player and a video screen.

'This car is amazing,' she whispered. I had to agree with her. Trey drove one of those huge Range Rovers, fully loaded. It reminded me of a spaceship, full of glowing buttons and levers, and I half expected that somewhere to the left of the steering wheel would be a small switch marked WARP SPEED.

We pulled up in front of the Quik Zip and Trey cut the engine. 'Who wants what?' he asked. 'It's a long ride ahead.'

'We definitely need provisions,' Paul told him, opening his door. A small, polite chiming noise sounded, bing bing bing. 'Beer and . . . ?'

'Skittles,' Lissa finished for him, and he laughed.

'One pack of Skittles,' he said. 'Okay. Remy?'

'Diet Coke,' I told him. 'Please.'

He hopped out of the car, shutting his door behind him. Trey jumped out as well, leaving the keys in and the radio on low. We were on our way to the drive-in one town over that played triple features on summer nights. It wasn't a double date, since Trey had a girlfriend at school, and we'd originally invited Chloe and Jess as well. But Jess had to baby-sit, and Chloe, having already dumped her nerd boyfriend, was now pursuing some guy she'd met at the mall.

'If I had a car like this,' Lissa said now, turning around completely in her seat, 'I would live in it. I *could* live in it. And still have room to rent.'

'It is huge,' I agreed, glancing behind me, where there were two more rows of seats before you even got close to the back door. 'It's kind of sick, actually. Who needs this much room?'

'Maybe he buys a lot of groceries,' Lissa suggested.

'He's a college student,' I told her.

'Well,' she said, shrugging, 'all I know is I wish he didn't have a girlfriend. I've decided I like cute rich boys.'

'What's not to like,' I said absently as I watched Paul and Trey eye the guy behind the counter – it was well-known underground information which Zip clerks checked IDs closely and which didn't – and make their way to the rear of the store, picking up not one but two packs of Skittles for Lissa on the way. These boys did nothing in a small way, or so I was learning. Everything Paul had bought me in the two weeks we'd been dating had been Supersized or Doubled, and he always reached for his wallet immediately, not even entertaining my efforts to go Dutch every once in a while. He was still Perfect Paul, the Ideal Boyfriend

Exhibit A. And yet something in me continued to nag, as if I just wasn't enjoying this – the fruit of so many years of hard dating work – enough.

I heard a rattling noise and glanced over to my left, startled to see the Truth Squad van pull up right beside us. I started to lean back, out of sight, before remembering that the windows were tinted so black you couldn't see in. Ted was behind the wheel, a cigarette poking out of his mouth, and John Miller was in the passenger seat. As we watched, he leaned down and pulled on his door handle, and it swung open, but for some reason he forgot to let go and was taken with it, quickly dropping out of sight, the door left ajar.

Ted glanced over at the empty seat, sighed in an irritated way, and got out of the van, slamming his door behind him. 'Idiot,' he said loud enough for us to hear as he rounded the front bumper, where we could still see him through the windscreen. He was looking down at the pavement. 'Are you hurt?'

We couldn't hear John Miller's reply. But by then I was distracted anyway, because I'd spotted Dexter climbing clumsily into the front seat of the van, tripping over the gearshift before tumbling into the driver's seat and then out the door, dropping to the pavement a bit more gracefully than John Miller but not by much. He had on the same orange T-shirt as the day I'd met him, with a white Oxford cloth shirt over it. Sticking out of the front pocket was another one of those warped wedding cameras. He looked in Lissa's window, peering close, but couldn't see anything. She just stared back, as if on the hidden side of a two-way mirror.

'Isn't that Dexter?' she whispered, keeping her voice low – Trey's window, on the driver's side, was open – as he pulled the camera out of his pocket and leaned in, taking a picture of her black window. The flash lit the whole inside of the truck for a second, and then he went to stick it back in his pocket, missing once, before fitting it back in.

'Yeah,' I said as we watched him stumble slightly as he rounded the front of the van, reaching out a hand to touch Trey's bumper for support. He was weaving, and not in the typical Dexter-clumsy way. He seemed drunk.

'Okay, look you two,' Ted announced as Dexter ambled up, 'I said I'd get you here and I did. But I've got a date with Mary and she's already pissed at me so this is the end of the line. I'm not a taxi service.'

'My good man,' I heard John Miller say, in a faux Robin Hood voice, 'you have done your duty.'

'Are you going to get up, or what?' Ted asked.

John Miller got to his feet. He was still in his work clothes but looked entirely wrinkled, as if someone had balled him up in a pocket for a couple of hours. His shirt was hanging out, his trousers totally creased, and he, too, had a disposable camera, sticking out of one of his trouser pockets. He had a scratch on his cheek, too, which looked fresh, probably the result of the tumble from the van. He reached up and touched it, as if surprised to find it there, then let his hand drop.

'My good man,' Dexter said, flopping an arm around Ted, who immediately made a face, clearly fed up, 'we owe you the greatest of favours.'

'My good man,' John Miller echoed, 'we will repay you with gold, and maidens, and our eternal allegiance to your cause. Huffah!'

'Huffah!' Dexter repeated, raising his fist.

'Will you two cut that shit out?' Ted snapped, shaking off Dexter's arm. 'It's annoying.'

'As you wish, comrade,' John Miller told him. 'Raise a glass and huffah!'

'Huffah!' Dexter said again.

'That's it.' Ted started back to the van. 'I'm gone. You guys can huffah all you want . . .'

'Huffah!' they yelled in unison. John Miller, throwing his arms into it, seemed close to tumbling over again.

'. . . but you get home on your own. And don't do anything stupid, okay? We don't have bail money right now.'

'Huffah!' John Miller said, saluting Ted's retreating back as he walked away. 'Thank you, oh kind sir!'

Ted flipped them the finger, obviously over it, then coaxed the van's engine to life and backed away, leaving them there in front of the Quik Zip, where they commenced taking pictures of each other posing by the newspaper racks. Inside, I watched as Paul and Trey chatted up the guy behind the counter as he slid their two six-packs into a paper bag.

'Okay, now give me some pout,' Dexter was saying to John Miller, who struck a model's pose, sticking out his chest and using a stack of coupon fliers as a prop, fanning them in front of his face and peeking over them, seductively. 'There, that's good! Great!' The flash popped, and Dexter wound the film, giggling. 'Okay, now do sombre. That's right. You're serious. You're hurt . . .'

John Miller looked out at the road, suddenly mournful, contemplating the Double Burger, which was across the street, with a wistful expression.

'Beautiful!' Dexter said, and they both busted out laughing. I could hear Lissa chuckling in front of me.

John Miller had struck his best pose yet, draping himself across the phone booth and fluttering his eyelashes, when Dexter popped one last flash and ran out of film. 'Damn,' he said, shaking the camera, as if that would suddenly make more pictures appear. 'Oh, well. So much for that.'

They sat down on the kerb. I kept thinking we should roll down the window, say something to let them know we were there, but already it seemed too late to do so without repercussions.

'Truth be told, my good man,' John Miller said solemnly, turning his own disposable camera in his hands, 'I am sombre. And serious. And hurt.'

'My good man,' Dexter told him, leaning back on his palms and stretching his feet out in front of him, 'I understand.'

'The woman I love will not have me.' John Miller squinted up at the sky. 'She thinks I am not husband material, and, in her words, a bit immature. And today, in defiance of this proclamation, I quit my very easy job in which I made nine bucks an hour doing not very much at all.'

'There are other jobs, my squire,' Dexter said.

'And, on top of that,' John Miller continued, 'the band will mostly likely be rejected by yet another record label because of the artistic integrity of Sir Ted, who will drive us all into retirement by stubbornly refusing to admit that his potato opuses are a bunch of crap.'

'Aye,' Dexter said, nodding. 'It is true. Young Ted may, indeed, shoot us all in the foot.'

This was news to me, but not entirely surprising. Dexter had told me that Ted's vehement insistence that they do no covers for a demo, ever, had worked against them in previous towns, with previous chances.

'But you, fine sir.' John Miller clapped Dexter on the shoulder, a bit unsteadily. 'You have problems of your own.'

'This is true,' Dexter replied, nodding.

'The women,' John Miller sighed.

Dexter wiped a hand over his face, and glanced down the road. 'The women. Indeed, dear squire, they perplex me as well.'

'Ah, the fair Remy,' John Miller said grandly, and I felt a flush run up my face. Lissa, in the front seat, put a hand to her mouth.

'The fair Remy,' Dexter repeated, 'did not see me as a worthwhile risk.'

'Indeed.'

'I am, of course, a rogue. A rapscallion. A *musician*.

I would bring her nothing but poverty, shame, and bruised shins from my flailing limbs. She is the better for our parting.'

John Miller pantomimed stabbing himself in the heart. 'Cold words, my squire.'

'Huffah,' Dexter agreed.

'Huffah,' John Miller repeated. 'Indeed.'

Then they just sat there, saying nothing for a moment. In the back of the Range Rover, I could feel my heart beating. Watching him, I knew there was nothing I could do now to take any of it back. And I felt ashamed for hiding.

'What kind of money you got?' John Miller said suddenly, digging into his own pocket. 'I think we need more beer.'

'I think,' Dexter said, pulling out a wad of bills and some change, which he promptly dropped on the ground, 'that you're right.'

Paul and Trey came out of the store then, and Paul yelled over at us, 'Hey, Remy – was that diet you wanted or regular? I couldn't remember.' He stuck his hand in the bag he was carrying and pulled out two bottles, one of each. 'I got you both, but . . .'

Lissa put her hand on the window button to lower it, then glanced back at me, not knowing what she should do. But I just froze, my eyes on Dexter. He looked at Paul, slowly comprehending the situation, and then over at the truck, at us.

'Diet,' he said out loud, looking right at me, as if suddenly he could see me.

Paul looked over at him. 'What's that?'

Dexter cleared his throat. 'She wants diet,' he said. 'But not in a bottle, like that.'

'Hey man,' Paul said, smiling slightly, 'what are you talking about?'

'Remy drinks Diet Coke,' Dexter told him, standing up. 'But from the fountain drink thing. Extra large, lots of ice. Isn't that right, Remy?'

'Remy,' Lissa said softly. 'Should we—'

I opened up my door and was out, dropping to the ground – it was unbelievable how high up the Range Rover was – before I even really knew what I was doing. I walked up to them. Paul was still smiling, confused, while Dexter just looked at me.

'Huffah,' he said, but this time John Miller didn't chime in.

'This is fine,' I said to Paul, taking the drinks from him. 'Thanks.'

Dexter was just staring at us and I could tell Paul was uneasy, wondering what was going on.

'No, it's okay,' Dexter said suddenly, as if someone had asked him. 'Not awkward at all. But we'd say if it was, right? Because that's the deal. The friends deal.'

By now, Trey had started toward the car, wisely knowing to keep out of this. John Miller walked into the Quik Zip. And then there were three.

Paul glanced at me and said, 'Everything okay?'

'Everything,' Dexter told him, 'is just fine. Fine.'

Paul was still watching me, waiting for verification. I said, 'It's fine. Just give me a minute, okay?'

'Sure.' He squeezed my arm – as Dexter watched, a pointed look on his face – then walked over to the

319

car, climbing in and shutting the door behind him.

Dexter looked at me. 'You know,' he said, 'you could have let me know you were there.'

I bit my lip, looking down at the Diet Coke. I lowered my voice, then said, 'Are you okay?'

'Fine,' he said, too quickly, then snapped his fingers, all happy-go-lucky. 'Absolutely-freaking-fantastic!' Then he looked at the car again. 'Man,' he said, shaking his head. 'That thing has a freaking Spinnerbait sticker on it, for God's sake. Better hurry, Remy, old Tucker and Bubba the third are probably getting impatient.'

'Dexter.'

'What?'

'Why are you acting like this?'

'Like what?'

Okay, so I knew why. This, in fact, was the standard post-break-up behaviour, the way he should have been behaving all along. But since it was starting now, instead of then, I was thrown a bit.

'You were the one who said we should be friends,' I said.

He shrugged. 'Oh, come on. You were just playing along with that, right?'

'No,' I said.

'This is all you,' he said, pointing one somewhat wobbly finger at my chest. 'You don't believe in love, so it just follows logic you wouldn't believe in like, either. Or friendship. Or anything that might involve even the smallest personal risk.'

'Look,' I said, and now I was starting to get a little pissed. 'I was honest with you.'

320

'Oh, well let's just give you a medal, then!' he said, clapping his hands. 'You break up with me because I might really like you, enough to look past just hooking up for the summer, and now *I'm* the bad guy?'

'Okay,' I said, 'so you would have rather I lied and said I felt the same way, then dumped you a month later instead?'

'Which would have been just so inconvenient,' he said sarcastically, 'making you miss Mr Spinnerbait and that opportunity.'

I rolled my eyes. 'Is that what this is about?' I asked him. 'You're jealous?'

'That would make it simple, wouldn't it?' he said, nodding. 'And Remy likes simple. You think you have everything figured out, that you can chart my reaction and what I'm saying on some little graph you keep tucked away. But life isn't like that.'

'Oh, really?' I said. 'Then what is it like? You tell *me*.'

He leaned in very close to me, lowering his voice. 'I meant what I said to you. I wasn't playing some kind of summer game. Everything I said was true, from the first day. Every goddamn word.'

My mind flitted back then, over the challenges, the jokes, the half-sung songs. What meaningful truth was there in that? It had only been that first day that he'd said anything big, and that was just—

There was a whirring noise behind me, and next Lissa's voice, slight and tentative. 'Um, Remy?' she asked, then cleared her throat, as if realising how she sounded. 'We're going to miss the beginning of the movie.'

'Okay,' I said, over my shoulder. 'I'll be right there.'

'We're done anyway,' Dexter explained, saluting the car. To me he added, 'That's what this has been all about for you, correct? Making it clear. That you and me – it was nothing more than what you'll have with Spinnerbait boy, or the guy after that, or the guy after that. Right?'

For one split second, I wanted to tell him he was wrong. But there was something in the way he said this, a cocky angriness, that stopped me. He'd said himself I was a bitch, and once I would have taken pride in that. So sure, okay. I'd play.

'Yeah,' I said, shrugging. 'You're right.'

He just stood there, looking at me, as if I had actually changed before his eyes. But this was the girl I'd been all along. I'd just hidden her well.

I started to walk away, toward the car. Paul opened the back door for me. 'Is he bothering you?' he asked, his face serious. 'Because if he is—'

'No,' I said, shaking my head. 'It's fine. We're done.'

'Young knight!' Dexter yelled at Paul, just as he was shutting the door. 'Be forewarned, when she does have the fountain drink, she has a vicious arm on her. She will peg you, my good man. When you least see it coming!'

'Let's go,' Paul said, and Trey nodded, starting to back up.

As we drove away I was determined not to look back. But in Lissa's side mirror, I could still see him standing there, shirt-tails flapping, arms spread, up in the air, as if waving us off on a grand trip while he stayed behind. *Bon voyage, take care. Go in peace. Huffah.*

The next day when I got back from spending the night at Lissa's, my mother was home. I dropped my keys on the side table, my bag on the stairs, and was just starting into the kitchen when I heard her.

'Don?' she called out, her voice bouncing down the hallway that led to the new wing. 'Honey? Is that you? I took an earlier flight, thought I could surprise—' She rounded the corner, the sandals she was wearing clicking across the floor, then stopped when she saw it was me. 'Oh, Remy. Hello. I thought you were Don.'

'Obviously,' I said. 'How was Florida?'

'Heavenly!' She walked over and hugged me, pulling me close against her. She had a nice tan and a new haircut, shorter and streaked with a bit of blonde, as if in Florida you are required by law to go tropical. 'Just wonderful. Invigorating. Rejuvenating!'

'Wow,' I told her as she released me, stepping back. 'All that in only three days?'

'Oh,' she sighed, walking ahead of me into the kitchen, 'it was just what I needed. Things have been so busy and stressful since the wedding, and then before the wedding with all the planning and organising . . . it was just too much, you know?'

I decided not to point out how little wedding planning *she* had actually done, figuring she was going somewhere with this. So instead I just leaned against the sink as she pulled an Ensure out of the fridge, popping the little tab top and taking a sip.

'But once I was there,' she said, pressing a hand to her heart and closing her eyes, dramatically. 'Sheer heaven. The surf. The sunsets. Oh, and my fans. I just felt like I was finally *myself* again. You know?'

'Yeah,' I agreed, although it had been a while since I'd felt anything like myself. All night I'd kept seeing Dexter in my mind, arms waving, calling after me.

'So I came home on an earlier flight, hoping to share this new feeling of contentment with Don, but – he's not here.' She took another sip of her Ensure, glancing out the kitchen window. 'I guess I was just feeling hopeful.'

'He hasn't been around at all,' I told her. 'I think he worked, like, all weekend.'

She nodded gravely, putting the Ensure down on the counter. 'It's been such a problem for us. His work. My work. All the details of each. I feel like we haven't even had a chance to really bond as husband and wife yet.'

Uh-oh, I thought again, as a warning bell sounded softly in my head. 'Well,' I began, 'you've only been married a couple of months.'

'Exactly,' she said. 'And while I was gone, I realised that we really have to focus on this marriage. The work can wait. Everything can wait. I think I've been guilty too long of putting other things first, but not this time. I just know things are going to be better now.'

Okay. So that sounded positive. 'That's great, Mom.'

She smiled at me, pleased. 'I really believe it, Remy. We may have had a bumpy adjustment, but this one's for good. I'm finally realising what it takes to really be a partner. And it just feels great.'

She was smiling so happily, with this new

conversion. As if somewhere high over the Southeast seaboard, she'd finally found the answer to the puzzle that had eluded her for so long. My mother always had ducked out of relationships when the going got tough, not wanting to dirty her hands with messy details. Maybe people could change.

'Oh, goodness, I just can't wait to see him,' she said to me now, walking to the table and picking up her bag. 'I think I'll just run down to the dealership and bring him lunch. He *loves* it when I do that. Honey, if he calls, don't let on, okay? I want it to be a surprise.'

'Okay,' I told her, and she blew me a kiss as she sailed out the door and across the lawn to her car. I had to admire it, that absolute kind of love that couldn't even wait a couple of hours. I'd never felt that strongly about anyone. It was nice, this rushing need to say something to someone right this very second. Almost romantic, really. If you liked that sort of thing.

The next morning I was in line at Jump Java, half asleep and waiting for Lola's morning mocha, when I saw the white Truth Squad van pull up outside, rattling to a stop in the fire lane. Ted hopped out and came into the store, pulling some wrinkled bills out of his pocket.

'Hey,' he said when he saw me.

'Hey,' I replied, pretending to be engrossed in a story on re-districting on the front page of the local newspaper.

The line for coffee was long, and full of cranky

people who wanted their drinks made with such intricate specifics that it gave me a headache just listening to the orders. Scarlett was working the espresso machine, trying to keep up with a slew of nonfat, soy-milk double-tall requests with a sour look on her face.

Ted was a bit behind me in line, but then the guy between us, disgusted by the wait, walked out. Which left us next to each other, so we had no choice but to talk to each other.

'So Lucas told me you guys have a meeting with Rubber Records,' I said.

'Yup. Tonight, in D.C. We're leaving in an hour.'

'Really,' I said as we slowly crept forward about an inch in the line.

'Yeah. They want us to play for them, you know, in the office. And then maybe at this showcase on Thursday, if they can get us a spot. Then, if they like us, it might get us something permanent up there.'

'That's great.'

He shrugged. 'It is if they like our stuff. But they're pushing for some stupid covers instead, which, you know, totally goes against our integrity as a band.'

'Oh,' I said.

'I mean, the other guys, they'd do freaking anything for a contract, but, you know, to me it's about more than that. It's about music, man. Art. Personal expression. Not a bunch of corporate, upper-management bullshit.'

A businessman holding the *Wall Street Journal* glanced back at us, but Ted just looked at him, indignant, until he faced forward again.

'So you're doing "The Potato Opus"?' I asked.

'I think we should. That's what I've been pushing all along. Like us for our original stuff, or not at all. But you know Lucas. He's never been behind the potato stuff at all. He's so freaking lowbrow, it's ridiculous: I mean, he was in a *hair-metal* band. What the hell does he know about real music?'

I wasn't sure what to say to this.

'And then there's John Miller, who'd play anything as long as he doesn't have to go back to school and push paper in his daddy's company some day. Which leaves us with Dexter, and you know how *he* is.'

I was startled, slightly, at this. 'How he is?' I repeated.

Ted rolled his eyes. 'Mr Positive. Mr Everything's-Gonna-Be-All-Right-I-Swear. If we left it up to him, we'd just go up there with no game plan, no set of demands, and just see how it goes.' He flipped his hand in a loose, silly way, punctuating this. 'God! No plan, no worries whatsoever. Ever! I hate people like that. *You* know what I'm talking about.'

I took in a breath, wondering how to respond to this. It was the same thing I'd always been so annoyed with about Dexter, as well, but coming from Ted it sounded so small-minded, and negative. He was so opinionated, so sure he knew everything. God. I mean, sure, maybe Dexter didn't think things through quite enough, but at least you could stand to—

'Next!' Scarlett yelled. I was at the front of the line. I stepped up and told her I wanted Lola's regular, then moved aside so Ted could get his extra-large, black coffee, no lid.

'Well,' I said, as he paid, 'good luck this week.'

'Yeah,' he replied. 'Thanks.'

We walked out together, him to the van, me starting down to Joie, where I was ticking down my last days as receptionist extraordinaire. It was August 20th, and I was leaving for school in three weeks. If we'd stayed together, I'd always assumed it would be me leaving Dexter behind. But now, I saw, it might have been me staying here, watching him go. Funny all the ways things could work out. But this was better, totally. Of course it was.

With Dexter gone for a full week, I didn't have to worry about chance encounters or awkward moments. It made life so much easier, and inspired me to really get things done, as if him being in my same area code was enough to affect my sense of equilibrium.

First, I cleaned. Everything. I detailed my car, Armor All-ing every inch of it, and had my oil changed. I shampooed the interior, realphabetised my CDs, and, yes, cleaned the windows and windscreen from the inside. This inspired me so much I tackled my room, stuffing four garbage bags with my closet discards for the thrift shop before hitting the clearance rack at the Gap, to stock up on new, college-me clothes. I was so industrious I shocked myself.

How had I got so disorganised? Once, keeping the vacuum cleaner lines even on my bedroom carpet was second nature. Now, struck with this sudden fervour, I found mud tracks in my closet, spilled mascara in my cosmetic drawer, one mismatched shoe – one! –

stuffed far underneath my bed. It made me wonder if I'd been in some sort of fugue state. Restoring order to my personal universe suddenly seemed imperative, as I refolded my T-shirts, stuffed the toes of my shoes with tissue paper, and arranged all the bills in my secret stash box facing the same way, instead of tossed in sloppy and wild, as if by my evil twin.

All week, I kept making lists and crossing things off them, ending each day with a sense of great accomplishment eclipsed only by complete and total exhaustion. This, I told myself, was exactly what I'd wanted: a clean exit, smooth and effortless, every *t* crossed and *i* dotted. There were only a few more loose ends, a couple of items to deal with. But I already had a game plan set, the steps numbered and outlined clearly, and there was still plenty of time.

'Uh-oh,' Jess said darkly as we sat at Bendo. 'I know that look.'

Chloe looked at her watch. 'Well,' she said, 'it is about that time. You leave in three weeks.'

'Oh no!' Lissa cried, finally catching on. 'Not Paul. Not yet.'

I shrugged, sliding my beer in a circle on the table. 'It makes sense,' I said. 'The time I have left, I want to concentrate on being with my family. And you guys. There's no point in dragging it out so there has to be some big airport scene with him.'

'Good point,' Chloe agreed. 'He definitely hasn't been of airport status.'

'But I like Paul,' Lissa said to me. 'He's so sweet.'

'He is,' I said. 'But he's also temporary. As I am for him.'

'And so, he joins the club,' Chloe said, holding up her beer. 'To Paul.'

We drank, but even as I did so I flashed back to what Dexter had said to me in the parking lot of the Quik Zip, about how he'd end up no different from the guy before, or the guy after. And he wasn't, really. Just a blip between Jerk Jonathan and Perfect Paul, one more summer boyfriend who was already fading from memory.

Or was he? Dexter had been on my mind. I knew it was because things had, in fact, ended badly, regardless of our efforts. *He* was one thing that didn't get done as planned, and I couldn't check him off the way I wanted to.

Paul, on the other hand, had been inching that way for the last few days. But honestly, I hadn't really been in it from the word go. It wasn't his fault. Maybe I was just tapped out and needed a break instead of starting something new. But so often I'd felt like I was going through the motions, moving mechanically as we talked, or went to dinner, or hung out with his friends, or even made out in the darkness of his room or mine. Sometimes, when we weren't together, I had trouble even picturing him clearly. It seemed, in light of this, the right time to end things neatly and totally.

'The boyfriend club,' Jess said now, leaning back in the booth. 'God. How many guys has Remy dated?'

'A hundred,' Lissa said instantly, then shrank back when I looked at her. 'I mean, I don't know.'

'Fifty,' Chloe decided. 'Not less than.'

They all looked at me. 'I have no idea,' I said. 'Why are we talking about this?'

'Because it's topical. And now, as you are about to leave to spread your dating experience across not only this town but also the *country* . . .'

Jess laughed out loud.

'. . . it's only fair that we run through a greatest hits, if you will, of your past just as you embark on your present.'

'Are you drunk?' I asked her.

'First!' she said, ignoring me. 'Randall Baucom.'

'Oh, Randall,' Lissa sighed. 'I loved him too.'

'That was sixth grade,' I pointed out. 'God, how far back are we going?'

'Next,' Jess said, 'seventh grade. Mitchell Loehmann, Thomas Gibbs, Elijah what's-his-bucket . . .'

'The one with the jug head,' Lissa added. 'What was his last name?'

'I never dated anybody with a jug head,' I said indignantly.

'Then we had the six months of Roger,' Chloe said, shaking her head. 'Not a good time.'

'He was an asshole,' I agreed.

'Remember when he cheated on you with Jennifer Task and the whole school knew but you?' Lissa asked me.

'No,' I said darkly.

'Moving on,' Chloe sang out, 'we get to ninth grade, and the triple whammy of Kel, Daniel, and Evan, as Remy methodically works her way through the offensive line of the soccer team.'

'Now, wait just a second,' I said, knowing I was getting defensive, but God, I had to stick up for myself sometime. 'You're making me sound like a total slut.'

Silence. Then they all burst out laughing.

'Not funny,' I grumbled. 'I've changed.'

'We know you have,' Lissa said earnestly, patting my hand in her sweet way. 'We're just talking about the old days here.'

'Why don't we talk about you guys, then?' I said. 'How about Chloe and the fifty-odd people she's dated?'

'I cheerfully claim every one of them,' she said, smiling at me. 'God, Remy. What's up with you? Lost your touch? Not proud of your conquests any more?'

I just looked at her. 'I'm fine,' I said.

The count continued, while I tried not to squirm. There were guys I didn't remember – Anton, who'd worked selling vitamins at the mall – and guys I wished I didn't, like Peter Scranton, who'd turned out to be not only a total jerk but also involved with a girl from a school in Fayetteville who'd made the two-hour trip to town specifically to kick my ass. *That* had been a fun weekend. And still the names kept coming.

'Brian Tisch,' Lissa said, folding down a finger. 'He drove that blue Porsche.'

'Edward from Atlantic Beach,' Jess added. 'The two-week required summer fling.'

Chloe took a deep breath, then said dramatically, one hand fluttering over her chest, '*Dante.*'

'Oh, man!' Jess said, snapping her fingers. 'The exchange student. Remy goes international!'

'Which leads us,' Chloe said finally, 'to Jonathan. And then Dexter. And now . . .'

'Paul,' Lissa said sadly, into her beer. 'Perfect Paul.'

Who was now, as I watched, walking in the door of Bendo, pausing to get his ID checked. Then he saw me. And smiled. He started across the room, the same way Jonathan had, unaware of what was about to happen. I took a deep breath, telling myself that by now this should be second nature, like falling into the water and instantly knowing to swim. But instead I just sat there as he approached.

'Hey,' he said, sliding in beside me.

'Hey.'

He took my hand, wrapping his fingers around mine, and suddenly I felt so tired. Another break-up. Another end. I hadn't even taken the time to figure out how, exactly, he'd react, the kind of prep work that had always come naturally before.

'You need a beer?' he asked me. 'Remy?'

'Look,' I said, and the words came on their own, no thought required. It was just process, cold and indifferent, like plugging numbers into an equation, and I could have been someone else, listening and watching this, for all I felt. 'We need to talk.'

15

'And for when she told that awful Mrs Tucker to sit
down and wait her turn . . .' Talinga said, her glass
wobbling.

'And for the time she untangled the judge's wife
from the overhead dryer . . .' Amanda chimed in.

'And,' Lola said, louder than either of them, 'for all
the days she just wouldn't put up with our mess . . .'

A pause. Talinga sniffled, then wiped her eye with
one very long, bright red, perfectly shaped nail.

'. . . To Remy,' Lola finished, and we let our glasses
knock together, champagne sloshing onto the floor.
'Girl, we're gonna miss you.'

We drank. It was all we'd been doing, toasting and
drinking, since Lola had officially closed down the
salon for appointments at four o'clock, two hours early,
so we could celebrate my leaving in high style. It had
hardly been a workday up until then, anyway. Talinga
brought me a corsage, which she insisted I wear, so I'd
spent the day answering the phone and looking as if I
was waiting for my prom date to pull up in his father's
car. But it was a sweet gesture, as was the cake, the
champagne, and the envelope that they'd given me,
which held five hundred bucks, all mine.

'For incidentals,' Lola had said as she pressed it into
my hand. 'Important stuff.'

'Like manicures,' Amanda added. 'And eyebrow waxing.'

It was almost enough to choke me up, but I knew that would only set them all off. Joie girls loved a good cry. But even more so, it reminded me that this was all really happening. Stanford. The end of the summer. The beginning of my real life. It was no longer just creeping up, peeking over the horizon, but instead lingering in plain sight.

The signs were everywhere. I was getting tons of stuff in the mail from school, forms and last-minute To Do lists, and my room was now lined with boxes, clearly labelled for what was going and what would stay behind. I did not entertain any notions about my mother keeping my room as some sort of a shrine to The Remy That Had Been. The minute my plane took off she'd be in there poking around, trying to figure out if the new bookshelves she'd been wanting to build a proper library around would fit within my walls. When I came home everything would be different. Especially me.

Everyone was getting ready to go. Lissa was the weepiest, even though her trip was only one across town, with the steeple of the church on her block visible from her dorm room window. Jess had a job lined up at the hospital, doing administrative stuff in the kids' ward, and started night classes right after Labor Day. And Chloe was busy with her own boxes, buying new stuff to take on her trip to a school just far enough away to provide new boys who didn't already know about her reputation as a pure-T heartbreaker.

Our in-between time, which had once seemed to stretch into forever, was ending.

The night before, I'd dug out my CD Walkman from the back of my closet, then sat down on my bed with it, carefully removing my father's CD from it and sliding it back into the case. The Walkman I was taking, but when I went to put the CD in the box with the others, something stopped me. Just because my father had left me a legacy of the expectation that men would let me down didn't mean I had to accept it. Or carry a reminder of it across the country. So instead I put it in a drawer in my now empty desk. I hadn't taped up the box yet, however, so there was still time to change my mind.

'Okay, ladies,' Lola said now, picking up the bottle of champagne, 'who wants a refill?'

'Me,' Talinga said, handing over her glass. 'And let's have more cake.'

'You don't need more cake,' Amanda told her.

'I don't need more champagne, either,' Talinga replied. 'But damned if that's going to stop me.'

They all laughed, and then the phone rang and Lola scurried off, still holding the bottle, to answer it. I picked a rose off the top of the cake and popped it into my mouth, feeling the sugar melt on my tongue. I was supposed to be saving my appetite for the dinner my mother was having tonight, one of the final family celebrations before I left. The mood she'd picked up in Florida still seemed to be lingering, making her work extra hard at playing Don's Wife. Her novel had clearly come to a lurching halt, and I wondered where

Melanie was now. It wasn't like my mother to walk away from a story, especially so close to the end. But each time I felt that anxious pull, I reminded myself that she would be okay. That she had to be.

I walked to the front window, sipping my champagne, and looked out at the parking lot. Across the way I could see the door to Flash Camera was open, and I was feeling the champagne as I leaned into the glass, pressing my forehead against it. Truth Squad had come back a couple of days earlier. I'd seen Lucas from a distance, eating a bag of crisps in front of Mayor's Market, but knew better than to go up and ask him how things had gone in D.C. Ever since the day I'd driven away from the yellow house, with them all out in the yard behind me, I'd felt more clearly than ever that their fate was in no way entwined with mine.

Still, I did keep thinking of Dexter. He was the one loose end that still remained, and I hated loose ends. Making things right wasn't an emotional thing. It was more that I didn't want to go across the country feeling like I had left the iron on or forgotten to turn off the coffeemaker. It was about my mental health, I told myself. As in, necessary.

Just as I thought this, I saw him move across the open doorway of Flash Camera, recognising him immediately from his gangly, crooked walk. *Well*, I thought. *Perfect timing*. I downed the rest of my champagne then checked my lipstick. It would be a good feeling to deal with this one last thing and still be home on time for dinner.

'Where you going?' Talinga called after me as I opened the front door. She and Amanda had now turned on the stereo we kept in the shampoo room and were dancing around the empty salon, both of them barefooted, while Lola helped herself to more cake. 'You need more champagne, Remy! This is a party, after all.'

'I'll be back in a sec,' I said. 'Pour me another glass, okay?'

She nodded, then poured herself one instead, while Amanda cackled, swaying her hips wide and bumping into a display of nail polishes. They all burst out laughing, the door falling shut on the sound when I walked out into the heat.

My head was buzzing as I crossed the parking lot to Flash Camera. When I came in, I saw Lucas behind the counter, working the developing machine. He glanced up at me and said, 'Hey. When's the prom?'

I started at this, then realised he was talking about my corsage, which was now hanging kind of limply, as if it, too, had consumed a bit too much champagne. 'Is Dexter around?'

Lucas pushed back his chair, which was on castors, and rolled a bit, sticking his head through a door in the back. 'Dex!' he said.

'What?' Dexter yelled back.

'Customer!'

Dexter came out, wiping his hands on his shirt, with an easy-going, can-I-help-you kind of smile. When he saw me it shifted, but just a bit. 'Hey,' he said. 'When's the homecoming dance?'

'Weak,' Lucas mumbled, pushing himself back to the machine. 'And late.'

Dexter ignored this, coming up to the counter. 'So,' he said, picking up a stack of snapshots and shuffling them, 'what can we do for you? Need some pictures developed? Perhaps an enlargement? We're running a special on four-by-sixes today.'

'No,' I said, talking over the sound of the machine Lucas was working, as it made chunk-chunk noises, spitting out someone's precious memories. 'I just wanted to talk to you.'

'Okay.' He kept messing with the pictures, not really looking at me. 'Talk.'

'How was D.C.?'

He shrugged. 'Ted threw a fit, the whole artistic integrity thing. Stormed out. We managed to sweet-talk them into another meeting, but for now we're stuck doing another wedding tonight while we're left hanging. In the lurch. Happening a lot lately, it seems.'

I just stood there for a second, gathering my words. He was being kind of a jerk, I decided, but pressed on anyway. 'So,' I said, 'I'm leaving soon, and—'

'I know.' Now he looked at me. 'Next week, right?'

I nodded. 'And I just wanted to, you know, make peace with you.'

'Peace?' He put the pictures down. The one on top, I saw, was of a group of women posing around a quilt, all of them smiling. 'Are we at war?'

'Well,' I said, 'we didn't exactly part well the other night. At the Quik Zip.'

'I was kind of drunk,' he admitted. 'And, uh . . .

maybe I wasn't dealing with your Spinnerbait relationship quite as well as I might have.'

'The Spinnerbait relationship,' I said slowly, 'has now been terminated.'

'Well. Can't say I'm sorry about *that*. They are, like the biggest suckjob band, and their fans—'

'Okay, okay,' I said. 'I know. Hate Spinnerbait.'

'Hate Spinnerbait!' Lucas mumbled.

'Look.' Dexter leaned across the counter at me, 'I liked you, Remy. And maybe we couldn't be friends. But, God, you sure didn't waste any time, you know?'

'I never wanted it to be ugly,' I told him. 'And I did want us to be friends. But it just never works. Never.'

He considered this. 'Okay. I think you're right. Maybe we're both a bit at fault here. I wasn't exactly honest when I said I could deal with us being friends. And you weren't exactly honest when you said, you know, that you loved me.'

'What?' I said, a bit too loudly. It was the champagne. 'I never said I loved you.'

'Maybe not in so many words,' he said, shuffling the pictures again. 'But I think we both knew the truth.'

'No way,' I said, but I could feel it now, that loose end slowly winding up, closer and closer to tied tight.

'In five more days,' he decided, holding up his open hand, 'you would have loved me.'

'Doubtful.'

'Well, it is a challenge. Five days, and then—'

'Dexter,' I said.

'I'm kidding.' He put the pictures down, and smiled

at me. 'But we'll never know, right? Could have happened.'

I smiled back. 'Maybe.'

And there we had it. Closure. The last item of so many, eliminated from my list with a big, thick check mark. I could almost feel the weight of it lifting, the slow, steady feeling as all my planets aligned and everything, at least for now, was right with the world.

'Remy!' I heard someone yell from outside, and then turned around to see Amanda standing in the doorway to Joie, wearing a dye cap on her head and snapping her fingers. 'You're missing the dance party!' Behind her, Talinga and Lola were laughing.

'Wow,' Dexter said as Amanda continued her bump-and-grind, unaware of the elderly couple passing, carrying a bag of birdseed and eyeing her disapprovingly. 'Looks like we work at the wrong place.'

'I should get back,' I said.

'Okay, but before you go, you should check these out.' He pulled out a drawer, then took out a stack of glossy prints, spreading them on the counter in front of me. 'The last and best shots for our wall of shame. Just look.'

They were pretty bad. One was of a middle-aged guy posing bodybuilder style, flexing his muscles while his potbelly pooched over a very small Speedo bathing suit. Another featured two people standing on the bow of a ship: the man was grinning, loving it, while the woman was literally *green*, and you just knew the next picture featured vomit. Depravity and embarrassment was pretty much the theme of the collection, each one sillier or more disgusting than the last. I was so caught up reacting to a shot of what looked like a cat trying to mate with an iguana that I almost skimmed past a picture of a woman in her bra and panties, posing seductively, entirely.

'Oh, Dexter,' I said. 'Honestly.'

'Hey.' He shrugged. 'You do what you gotta do. Right?'

I was about to answer this when I suddenly realised something. I *knew* this woman. She was dark-haired, lower lip pouting seductively, sitting on the end of a bed with her hands on her hips so that her cleavage was enhanced, considerably. But even more importantly, I knew what was behind her: a large, ugly tapestry, depicting biblical scenes. Right over her head, to the left, was John the Baptist's head being served on a plate.

'Oh, my God,' I said. It was my mother's room. And this woman on the bed was Patty, Don's secretary. I looked at the date stamp at the bottom of the picture: Aug 14th. The previous weekend. When I'd been staying at Lissa's and my mother was in Florida, deciding that everything was now going to be okay.

'Really something, huh?' Dexter asked me, peeking over the top of the picture. 'I knew you'd like that one.'

I looked up at him, everything now falling into place. Closure. Yeah, right. This was Dexter's little revenge scheme, his way of poking me back when I wasn't even protecting myself. Suddenly I was so mad I could feel the blood rising in my face, hot and flushed. 'You *asshole*,' I said.

'What?' His eyes widened.

'You think this is some little game?' I snapped, throwing the picture at him. It hit him in the chest, the corner poking, and he stepped back, letting it fall to the floor. 'You want to get back at me and you do *this*? God, I was trying to leave things right, Dexter. I was trying to be beyond this!'

'Remy,' he said, holding up his hands. Behind him Lucas had pushed his chair back and was just staring at me. 'What are you talking about?'

'Oh, yeah, right,' I said. 'All this talk about faith, and love. And then you do something like this, just to hurt me. And not even me! My family . . .'

'Remy.' He tried to reach out and grab my hand, to calm me, but I pulled back, my wrist smacking wildly against the register, as if it wasn't even under my control. 'Come on. Just tell me—'

'Go to hell!' I screamed, and my voice sounded so shrill.

'What is the problem?' he yelled back, then ducked down, picking the picture up off the floor. He stared at it. 'I don't—'

But I was already walking across the store, toward the door. I just kept seeing my mother in my mind, floating toward me on a wave of perfume and hopefulness, trying so hard to make this, of all marriages, work. She'd been ready to settle, to give it all up, even her own voice, just to stay with this man who would not only commit adultery but save the

343

evidence on film. Bastard. I hated him. I hated Dexter. I had come so close to wanting to be wrong about the possibilities of what the heart could really do. Give me proof, I'd said, and she had tried. It's not tangible, she'd said, you can't mark it so clearly. But against love, the case was solid. Easily argued. And you could, indeed, hold it in your hand.

Finding out about Don pretty much ended my party. Which was fine, actually, since Amanda had already fallen asleep on the table in the waxing room and Lola and Talinga were finishing off the cake and bemoaning whose love life was more pathetic. We said our final good-byes, and then I left, carrying the envelope they'd given me, a freebie case of my favourite conditioner, and the burden of knowing that my mother's latest husband was the worst of the lot. Which was saying quite a bit, considering.

My head was clear as I drove home, blasting my air conditioner and trying to calm down. The shock of seeing Patty on my mother's bed, in my mother's room, had sobered me up quick, the way only bad news can. I was so mad at Dexter for showing me the picture, and as I drove I wondered why I'd never seen this duplicitous, petty, evil side of him. He'd hid it well. And it was low-down, bringing my family into it. Hurt me, fine. I could handle it. But my mother was different.

I pulled into the driveway and cut the engine, then just sat there as the A/C whined to a stop. I was dreading what I had to do. I knew that someone else might not have said anything, just letting the marriage, sham that it was, take its course. But I couldn't allow that. I wouldn't have been able to leave knowing that my mother was stuck here, living with that kind of deception. As a firm believer in the rip-it-off-like-a-Band-Aid school of bad news, I had to tell her.

As I walked up the driveway to the front porch, however, something was off. I couldn't say exactly what: it was more of a hunch, unexplainable. Even before I came upon the Ensure cans, which were scattered across the front walk, some in the grass, some rolled under the bushes, one just sitting upright on the steps, as if waiting to be retrieved, I had a feeling I was too late.

I pushed open the front door, then felt it hit against something: another can. They were everywhere, scattered across the foyer as I crossed it, going into the kitchen.

'Mom?' I said, and listened to my voice bounce off the countertops and cabinets, back at me. No response. On the table, I could see the food stacked for our big family dinner: steaks, corn on the cob, most of it still in the plastic bags from the supermarket. Next to them, a stack of mail, with one envelope, addressed to my mother in clean block writing, ripped open.

I moved across the room, stepping over another Ensure, to the doorway of her study. The curtain was hanging down, the old busy-don't-bother-me sign, but this time I pushed it aside and walked right through.

She was sitting in her chair, in front of the typewriter. Sticking out of it was a copy of the picture

I'd thrown at Dexter. It was positioned the same way a sheet of paper would have been right before she rolled it in.

My mother, strangely, seemed very calm. Whatever fury had caused the explosion and scattering of Ensure cans had obviously passed, leaving her sitting there with a stoic expression as she considered Patty's face, so pouty and posed, staring back at her.

'Mom?' I said again, and then I reached out my hand and put it over hers, carefully. 'Are you okay?'

She swallowed, and nodded. I could tell she'd been crying. Her mascara was smeared, black smudgy arcs underneath both her eyes. This, I thought, was the most disturbing thing of all. Even in the worst of circumstances, my mother always looked put together.

'They took it in my own room,' she said. 'This picture. On my bed.'

'I know,' I said. She turned her head, looking at me quizzically, and I backtracked, knowing it was best to keep the fact that yet another copy existed to myself. 'I mean, that's the quilt, right? Behind her.'

She turned her gaze back to the snapshot, and for a second we both just looked at it, the only sound that of the refrigerator ice machine cheerfully spitting out a new batch of cubes in the next room. 'I *missed* him,' she said finally.

I put my hand over hers and sat down, pulling my chair closer. 'I know,' I said softly. 'You came back from Florida feeling really good, and then you find out he's such a rat bastard that he—'

'No,' she said distractedly, interrupting me. 'I *missed*

him. All those Ensures, and not a one made contact. I have terrible aim.' And then she sighed. 'Even just one would have made it better. Somehow.'

It took a second for this to sink in. 'You threw all those cans?' I asked her.

'I was very upset,' she explained. Then she sniffled, wiping her nose with a Kleenex she was gripping in her other hand. 'Oh, Remy. My heart is just breaking.'

Whatever humour I might have been able to see in her pelting Don with empty Ensures – and it was funny, no question – left me as she said this.

She sniffled again, and clenched her fingers around mine, holding on tight. 'What now?' she said, waving her Kleenex in a helpless way, the white blurring past my vision. 'Where am I supposed to go from here?'

My ulcer, long dormant, rumbled in my stomach, as if answering this call. Here I was, so close to my getaway, and now my mother was adrift again, needing me most. I felt another flash of hate for Don, so selfish, leaving me with a mess to deal with while he slipped away scot-free. I wished I had been here when it all came down, because I did have a good arm. I wouldn't have missed. Not a chance.

'Well,' I said to her, 'first, you should probably call that lawyer. Mr Jacobs. Or Johnson. Did he take anything with him?'

'Just one bag,' she said, wiping at her eyes again.

I could already feel it happening, the neat click as I shifted into crisis management mode. It wasn't like it had been that long since Martin left. The path might have grown over a bit, but it was still there. 'Okay,' I continued, 'so we'll need to tell him he has to set up a specific time to come back and get everything. He can't just come whenever he feels like it, and one of us should be here. And we should probably get in touch with the bank, just to be safe, and put a freeze on your joint account. Not that he doesn't have money of his own, but people do weird stuff in the first few days, right?'

She didn't answer me, instead just staring out the window at the backyard, where the trees were swaying, just slightly.

'Look, I'll find that lawyer's number,' I said, standing up. 'He's probably not in, with it being a Saturday and all, but at least we could leave a message, so he'd get back to you first thing—'

'Remy.'

I stopped, midbreath, and realised she'd turned her head to look at me. 'Yes?'

'Oh, honey,' she said quietly. 'It's okay.'

'Mom,' I said. 'I know you're upset, but it's important that we—'

She reached over for my hand, pulling me back into my chair. 'I think,' she said, and then stopped. A breath, and then she said, 'I think it's time I handle this myself.'

'Oh,' I said. Weird, but my first thought was that I was somewhat offended. 'I just thought . . .'

She smiled at me, very weakly, and then patted my hand. 'I know,' she said. 'But you've dealt with enough, don't you think?'

I just sat there. This was it, what I'd always wanted.

348

The official out, the moment I was finally set free. But it didn't feel the way I'd thought it would. Instead of a wash of victory, I felt strangely alone, as if everything fell away suddenly, leaving me with only the sound of my own heart beating. It scared me.

It was almost as if she sensed this, saw it on my face. 'Remy,' she said softly, 'it's all going to be all right. It's time you worry about yourself, for a change. I can take it from here.'

'Why now?' I asked her.

'It feels right,' she replied simply. 'Don't you feel it? It just feels . . . okay.'

Did I feel it? Everything seemed so tangled, all at once. But then in my mind, I saw something. The country, spread out so wide, with my mother and me separated not only by our difference of opinions, but also by miles and miles of space, too far to cross with just a look or a touch. My mother was down, but not out. And she might have denied me some of my childhood, or the childhood I'd thought I deserved, but it wasn't too late for her to give something in return. An even trade, years for years. Those passed for those to come.

But for now, I scooted closer, until we were touching. Knee to knee, arm to arm, forehead to forehead. I leaned into her for once, instead of away, appreciating the pull I felt there, something almost magnetic that held us to each other. I knew it would always be there, no matter how much of the world I put between us. That strong sense of what we shared, good and bad, that led us to here, where my own story began.

16

In the hour before Chris and Jennifer Anne were due to show up for dinner, I gathered all the Ensure cans from the front yard and various spots in the house, depositing them with a satisfying clank in the recycling bin. My mother was taking a shower, having insisted we go ahead with our family dinner, despite what had happened. While I was doing my best to adjust to my new hands-off role in this separation, some habits died hard. Or so I told myself as I took down the big naked woman off the kitchen wall, sliding it behind the refrigerator.

After our talk, my mother had filled me in on the gruesome details. Apparently the Patty thing had been going on for a while, since even before my mother and Don met. Patty had been married, and the affair had been a series of break-ups and make-ups, ultimatums and backsliding, finally ending with Don saying if she wasn't serious enough to leave her husband, he was moving on. Don's marrying my mother, however, was a catalyst for her subsequent separation, and while they'd tried to stay apart they couldn't, in Don's words, 'fight the feeling'. My mother winced as she repeated this phrase: I was sure I winced hearing it. It was Patty who'd sent the picture, fed up with waiting. Don, according to my mother, hadn't even denied it, instead sighing and walking into the bedroom to pack a bag. This, I felt, said a lot. What kind of car salesman doesn't at least try to talk his way out of things?

'He couldn't,' my mother said when I asked her this. 'He loves her.'

'He's an asshole,' I said.

'It was unfortunate,' she agreed. She was taking it so well, but I wondered if she was just still in shock. 'Everything, in the end, comes down to timing.'

I considered this as I piled the steaks onto a plate, then went out to the fancy new grill, opening it up. After struggling for about fifteen minutes with the high-tech, supposed-to-be-moron-proof ignition system, I decided I liked having my eyebrows intact and instead dug out our old Weber grill from behind a stack of lawn chairs. A few handfuls of charcoal, some fluid, and I was in business.

As I poked at the coals, I kept thinking about Dexter. If once he had been a loose end, now it was a full hanging string, capable of pulling everything apart with one good tug. Chalk it up to another bad boyfriend story, one more added to the canon. It was where I'd intended him to be, all along.

I was in the kitchen, arranging some tortilla chips and salsa on a plate, when Chris and Jennifer Anne pulled up. They came across the lawn, carrying her trademark Tupperware, and they were holding hands. I could only imagine how Jennifer Anne, who'd found my cynicism about this marriage to be completely abhorrent, would react to this latest family news. Chris,

I figured, would instantly move into protective mode for my mother's sake while privately feeling grateful to have his bread back, butts and all.

They came in the front door, chatting and laughing. They sounded positively giddy, in fact. As they got closer to the kitchen. I looked up, noticing they were both flushed, and Jennifer Anne was as relaxed as I'd ever seen her, as if she'd had a double dose of self-esteem affirmations that day. Chris looked pretty happy too, at least until he saw the empty space on the wall over the breakfast table.

'Oh, man,' he said, his face falling. Next to him, Jennifer Anne was still grinning. 'What's going on?'

'Well,' I said. 'Actually . . .'

'We're engaged!' Jennifer Anne shrieked, thrusting her left hand out in front of her.

'. . . Don's got a mistress, and he's left to be with her,' I finished.

For a minute, there was total silence as Jennifer Anne caught up with what I'd said, and I backtracked, clumsily, finally hearing her news. Then, at the same time, we both blurted out, 'What?'

'Oh, my God,' Chris groaned, stumbling back against the fridge with a thud.

'You're engaged?' I said.

'It's just . . .' Jennifer Anne said, putting a hand to her face. Now I could see a ring on her finger: a good-size diamond, so sparkly as it caught the light shining from over the sink.

'Wonderful,' I heard my mother say, and turning around I saw she'd come in behind me, and was now standing there, her eyes a bit watery, but smiling. 'Oh, my. It's just *wonderful*.'

It says something about my mother, and her utter and total belief in the love stories she not only wrote but lived, that she was able to say this then, not two hours after her fifth marriage had dissolved in a puddle of deceit, bad clichés, and discarded Ensure cans. As I watched her move across the room, pulling Jennifer Anne into her arms, I felt an appreciation for her I would not have been capable of three months earlier. My mother was strong, in all the ways I was weak. She fell, she hurt, she felt. She lived. And for all the tumble of her experiences, she still had hope. Maybe this next time would do the trick. Or maybe not. But unless you stepped into the game, you would never know.

We ate at the table in the backyard, off paper plates. My mother's contribution: Brazilian beefsteaks, imported artichoke salad, and fresh Italian bread, baked just that day. Jennifer Anne's: macaroni and cheese, salad with iceberg lettuce and Thousand Island dressing, and a jelly mould with whipped cream. Worlds may have been colliding, but as the conversation began to roll around to wedding plans and preparations, it was clear there was a common ground.

'I just have no idea where to start,' Jennifer Anne said. She and Chris held hands all through dinner, which was somewhat disgusting but a bit tolerable, considering the newness of their engaged status.

'Reception halls, cakes, invitations . . . the whole thing. It's overwhelming.'

'It's not that bad,' I told her, spearing a bit of lettuce with my fork. 'Just get a folder, a notebook, and get second estimates on everything. And don't use the Inverness Inn because they overcharge and never have toilet paper in the bathrooms.'

'Oh, weddings are always fun!' my mother chirped, sipping on her glass of wine. And for a second I caught her as a wave of sadness crossed over her face. But she shook it off, smiling at Chris instead. 'Anything you two need, help, money . . . let me know. Promise you will.'

'We will,' Chris said.

I gathered up the plates as they kept talking, discussing possible dates, places, all the things that I'd been starting to think about this time last year, when my mother was the bride-to-be. There was something incongruous about one marriage ending the same day another began, as if there was an exchange programme in the universe or something, a trade required in order to keep the numbers even.

As I pulled open the screen door, I turned around, looking again at the backyard, where the dark was now coming on. I could hear their voices rising and falling, and for a second I closed my eyes, just listening. Times like this it did seem real I was leaving, and even more that my family, and this life, would go on without me. And again I felt that emptiness rise up, but pushed it away. Still, I lingered there, in the doorway, memorising the noise. The moment. Tucking it away out of sight, to be remembered when I needed it most.

After dinner and dessert, Jennifer Anne and Chris packed up the Tupperware and went home, armed with all the crap I'd kept from planning my mother's wedding to Don – brochures, price lists, and phone numbers of everything from limo services to the best make-up guy in town. In my typical cynical fashion, I'd had no doubt we would need it again, and I was right. Just not in the way I'd thought.

My mother kissed me and headed off to bed, a bit teary but okay. I went up to my room and double-checked some of my boxes, reorganising a few more items and packing up a few last things. Then I sat on my bed, restless, listening to the whir of the air-conditioning until I couldn't take it any more.

When I pulled up to the Quik Zip, heeding the call of that Extra Large Zip Diet, I was surprised to see Lissa's car parked in front of the pay phones. I snuck up behind her in the candy section as she stood debating whether to get Skittles or Spree. She had one in each hand, and when I poked her in the small of her back, she jumped, shrieking, sending both flying.

'Remy!' She swatted at my hand, the colour rising in her face. 'God, you scared me.'

'Sorry,' I told her. 'Couldn't resist.'

She bent down, collecting the candy. 'Not funny,' she grumbled. 'What are you doing out, anyway? I thought you were having a big family night.'

'I was,' I said, heading over to the Zip Fountain

station. It was weird how even the smallest things were making me nostalgic now, and I had a moment of quiet respect as I picked a cup off the stack, then filled it with ice. 'I mean, I did. Bigger family night than you would even believe. You having a Zip?'

'Sure,' she said, and I handed her a cup. We didn't talk for a second as I filled mine, stopping at the right intervals to allow the fizz to die down. Plus, sometimes you got a new shot of syrup when you pushed in the Diet Coke button, which made them extra wonderful. Then I got a lid and a straw, as Lissa did the same with the 7UP. As I sipped mine, testing it for full flavour, I noticed that she looked very nice; she appeared to be wearing a new skirt, and had painted her toenails. Plus she smelled good, a light floral scent, and I was almost positive she had curled her eyelashes.

'Okay,' I said. 'Confess. What are you doing tonight?'

She smiled slyly, dropping the candy by the register. As the guy ran it up, she said, offhandedly, 'Got a date.'

'Lissa,' I said. 'No way.'

'Three seventy-eight,' the guy said.

'I'll get hers too,' Lissa told him, nodding at my Diet Zip.

'Thanks,' I said, surprised.

'No problem.' She handed the guy a couple of folded bills. 'Well, you know that PJ and I have been kind of circling lately.'

'Yeah,' I said as she took her change and we headed for the door.

'And the summer is close to over. And today, when we were at this craft festival KaBooming, I just decided the hell with it. I was tired of waiting around, wondering if he was ever going to make a move. So I asked him out.'

'Lissa. I'm impressed.'

She stuck her straw in her mouth and took a dainty sip, shrugging. 'It wasn't as hard as I thought, actually. It was even . . . kind of nice. Empowering. I liked it.'

'Watch out, PJ,' I said as we came up to her car, both of us climbing up to sit on the bonnet. 'It's a whole new girl.'

'I'll drink to that,' she replied, and we pressed our cups together.

For a minute we just sat there, watching the traffic pass on the road in front of us. Another Saturday night at the Quik Zip, one of so many in the years we'd been friends.

'So,' I said finally, prompted by this, 'my mom and Don are over.'

She jerked her straw out of her mouth, turning to look at me. 'No.'

'Yep.'

'No way! What happened?'

I filled her in, going all the way back to seeing the picture at Flash Camera, stopping at certain intervals so she could shake her head, request specific details, and call Don all the names I already had that day, which didn't exactly stop me from chiming in again, for good measure.

'God,' she said, when it was all done. 'That sucks. Your poor mom.'

'I know. But I think she'll be okay. Oh, and Chris and Jennifer Anne are engaged.'

'What?' she said, shocked. 'I can't believe that you stood there calm and cool, fixing a Diet Zip, and had an entire conversation with me when you had such big information, Remy. God!'

'Sorry,' I said. 'It's just been a long day, I guess.'

She sighed loudly, still upset with me. 'What a summer,' she said. 'It's hard to believe that just a few months ago your mom and Don were getting married and I was getting dumped.'

'It's been a shitty season for relationships,' I agreed. 'Enough to make you give up on love altogether.'

'Nah,' she said easily, not even considering this. 'You can never really do that.'

I took a measured sip of my drink, pulling my hair out of my face. 'I don't know,' I said to her. 'I did. I mean, I don't believe things can really work out. And this latest with Don just confirms it.'

'Confirms what?'

'That relationships suck. And that I was right to break things off with Dexter, because it never would have worked. Not in a million years.'

She thought about this for a second. 'You know what?' she said finally, crossing her legs. 'Frankly, I think that's a bunch of *shit*.'

I almost choked on my straw. 'What?'

'You heard me.' She pulled a hand through her hair, tucking a mass of curls behind one ear. 'Remy, as long as I've known you, you always thought you had it all figured out. And then something happened this summer that made you wonder if you were right after all. I think you always believed in love, deep down.'

'I did not,' I said firmly. 'Things have happened to me, Lissa. I've seen stuff that—'

'I know,' she said, holding up her hand. 'I am new to this, I'm not disputing that. But if you truly didn't believe in it, why did you keep looking all this time? So many boys, so many relationships. For what?'

'Sex,' I said, but she just shook her head.

'Nope. Because a part of you wanted to find it. To prove yourself wrong. You had that faith. You know you did.'

'You're wrong,' I told her. 'I lost that faith a long time ago.'

She looked at me as I said this, an expression of quiet understanding on her face. 'Maybe you didn't, though,' she said softly. 'Lose it, I mean.'

'Lissa.'

'No, just hear me out.' She looked out at the road for a second, then back at me. 'Maybe, you just misplaced it, you know? It's been there. But you just haven't been looking in the right spot. Because lost means for ever, it's gone. But misplaced . . . that means it's still around, somewhere. Just not where you thought.'

As she said this, I saw a blur in my mind of the faces of all the boys I'd been with, literally or just figuratively. They passed quickly, their features melting into one another, like the pages in one of my old Barbie dream date books, none of them truly distinct. They had certain things in common, now that I thought about it: nice faces, good bodies, so many of the qualities I'd drawn up in my mind on yet another checklist. In fact, I'd always approached boys this way, so methodically, making sure before I took even one step that they fitted the profile.

Except, of course, for one.

I heard a horn beep, loud, and looked up to see Jess pulling in beside us. To my shock, Chloe was in the passenger seat.

'Hey,' Jess said as they got out, doors slamming, 'nobody said anything to me about a meeting. What gives?'

Lissa and I just sat there, staring at them. Finally she said, 'What on earth is going on tonight, anyway? Has everyone gone crazy? What are you two doing together?'

'Don't get too excited,' Chloe said flatly. 'My car got a flat over at the mall, and neither one of you was answering the phone.'

'Imagine my surprise,' Jess added drolly, 'when I was her last resort.'

Chloe made a face at her, but it wasn't a mean one, more just rankled irritation. 'I said thank you,' she told Jess. 'And I will buy you that Zip Drink, as promised.'

'The deal was Zip Drinks for life,' Jess said, 'but for now I'll just take one Coke. Extra large, light on the ice.'

Chloe rolled her eyes and headed into the store.

Lissa slid off the bonnet, shaking her own cup. 'Refill time,' she said. 'You?'

I handed over my drink, and she followed Chloe in, one in each hand. Jess came over and sat on the bumper, smiling to herself. 'I love it that she owes me,' she said, watching as Chloe fixed the drinks, with Lissa chattering away beside her. From the way Chloe kept glancing at her, her mouth dropping open, aghast, I knew she was getting the full story about my mother and Don. So I filled Jess in, getting much of the same reaction, and by the time they returned and we all had our drinks, everyone was more or less on the same page.

'Asshole,' Chloe said decisively, taking a sip of her drink. Then she made a face, coughed, and said, 'Yuck. This is regular Coke.'

'Thank God,' Jess said as they traded, both of them wincing now. 'Because this stuff I'm drinking tastes like shit.'

'So let me get this straight,' Chloe said, ignoring this. 'Patty sent the picture to your mom?'

'Yep,' I replied.

'But she got the pictures developed at Flash Camera.'

'Correct.'

Chloe swallowed, considering this. 'And Dexter knew it was her, and what the implications were, so he showed it to you to get you back for dumping him.'

'Exactly.'

There was a moment of silence, during which all I could hear was the sloshing of ice, creaking of straws, and a few doubtful murmurings. Finally Jess said, 'I'm not getting the logic of that, exactly.'

'Me neither, now that I think about it,' Lissa agreed.

'There is no logic,' I said. 'He was just being a jerk. He knew it was the one way he could really hurt me, so he did it, just when I'd tried to make amends and had my guard down.'

More silence.

'What?' I said, irritated.

'I think,' Chloe began tentatively, 'that there's really no proof that he even knew that you knew her.'

'Wrong. He met her at my mother's cookout. And she was at Toyotafaire too.'

'Not naked,' Lissa pointed out.

'What does that have to do with it? Naked or not she still had the same face.'

'But,' Chloe said, 'how could he have known it was Don that took the picture? Or even that it was in your mom's room? I mean, I haven't even been in there. Has he?'

Now, I was the quiet one, as this logic – if it was even that – suddenly began to click together in my head. I'd just assumed, in my shock, that Dexter had seen my mother's bedroom, and especially that ugly biblical tapestry. But had he? For all he knew, it was just a picture of a woman who worked for my stepfather getting her kicks taking nudie lingerie pictures in someone's bedroom. Anyone's bedroom.

'I'm all for you being pissed at Dexter,' Chloe said, tapping her nails on the bonnet of the car. 'But it should be for a good reason. Face it, Remy Starr. You're in the wrong here.'

And I was. I'd been so ready to blame Dexter for everything, from my mother's marriage dissolving to making me trust him in a way I hadn't anyone else in a long time. But none of it was his fault.

'Oh, my God,' I said softly. 'What now?'

'Go find him and apologise,' Lissa said decisively.

'Admit it was a mistake, don't find him, move on,' Chloe countered.

I looked at Jess, but she just shrugged and said, 'I have no idea. It's all you.'

I'd yelled at him. Told him to go to hell, thrown the picture at him, and stalked out even as he was trying to explain. I'd dumped him because he'd wanted more from me than to be a faceless, smelling-of-sunshine-and-chlorine summer boyfriend, made to order.

So what had changed? Nothing. Even if I did go to him, we'd already be too late, no time left to make a foundation before we were flung to opposite coasts, and everyone knew that kind of relationship *never* worked.

It was just like my mother said. Everything, in the end, comes down to timing. One second, one minute, one hour, could make all the difference. So much hanging on just these things, tiny increments that together build a life. Like words build a story, and what had Ted said? One word can change the entire world.

Hey, Dexter had said that first day he sat down beside me. That was one word. If I'd talked one minute longer with Don in the office, Dexter might already have been called away and gone when I came out. If my mother and I waited maybe another hour, Don might not have been at the dealership the day we went shopping for her new car. And if Jennifer Anne hadn't needed that oil change on that particular day of that particular week, maybe she wouldn't have ever looked over a garage counter and seen Chris at all. But something, somehow, had made all these paths converge. You couldn't find it on a checklist, or work it into the equation. It just happened.

'Oh, man,' Jess said suddenly, tugging at the cuff of my jeans. 'Check *this* out.'

I looked up, my mind still reeling. It was Don. He was driving a shiny, brand-new dealer-tagged Land Cruiser, which he parked on the other side of the Quik Zip. He didn't see us as he got out, hitting the remote door lock, and went inside, smoothing a hand over the thinning hair on the back of his head as he did so.

'God,' I said. 'Talk about timing.'

'What?' Lissa whispered.

'Nothing.' We all watched as he moved down the aisle of the Quik Zip, picking up a bottle of aspirin and a bag of crisps, which, I figured, was the chosen meal of adulterers. Even when he was checking out he didn't look at us, glancing instead at the headlines of the newspapers stacked by the register. Then he walked out, fiddling with the lid of the aspirin, and got back into his car.

'Asshole,' Chloe said.

It was true. He'd hurt my mother badly, and there wasn't much I could do to make her feel better. Except maybe one thing.

Don started the car and headed toward us. I lifted up my Diet Zip, feeling the weight in my hands.

'Oh, yes,' Lissa whispered.

'On three,' Jess said.

He didn't see us until he was right next to Lissa's car, and by then I'd already put my whole arm into it, my cup sailing through the air and smacking right against the windscreen, exploding soda all over the shiny bonnet. He hit the brakes, swerving slightly, as two other cups crashed against the back door and sunroof, respectively. But it was Lissa's, surprisingly, that had the best hit. It nailed his half-open window perfectly, the lid breaking off on impact, sending a wave of ice and 7UP smack in his face and down his shirt. He slowed down but didn't stop, the cups sailing off as he jerked into traffic, the car leaving a wet trail as it drove away from us.

'Nice shot,' Jess said to Lissa. 'Great arc.'

'Thanks,' Lissa said. 'Chloe's was good too. Did you see that impact?'

'It's all in the wrist,' Chloe said, shrugging.

Then we just sat there. I could hear the buzz of the Quik Zip sign overhead, that constant hum of fluorescence, and for a minute I lost myself in it, remembering Dexter standing in this same place not too long before, waving after me. Arms open. Calling me back, or saying good-bye. Or maybe a little bit of both.

He'd always had that fearless optimism that made cynics like me squirm. I wondered if it was enough for both of us. I would never know from here, though.

And time was passing. Crucial minutes and seconds, each one capable of changing everything.

I drove off, with my friends watching me go, all of them grouped on Lissa's bonnet. As I pulled onto the road, I glanced into the rearview and saw them: they were waving, hands moving through the air, their voices loud, calling out after me. The square of that mirror was like a frame, holding this picture of them saying good-bye, pushing me forward, before shifting gently out of sight, inch by fluid inch, as I turned away.

17

I knew from experience that there were nine decent
reception halls in town. At the fifth one, I found Truth
Squad.

I saw the white van as soon as I pulled into the
parking lot of the Hanover Inn. It was parked around
back, by the service entrance, next to a catering van.
As I got out of my car, I could hear music, the faint
beat of bass guitar. Through the long windows that
broke up the building, I saw people dancing. The bride
was in the centre, a blur of white, trailing tulle, leading
a conga line around in a wide, lopsided circle.

In the lobby, I passed some girls in hideous
baby blue bridesmaids dresses, complete with big bows
on the back, as well as someone wheeling a big ice
sculpture depicting wedding bells. The sign next to
the door said MEADOWS-DOYLE RECEPTION, and I slipped
in the far door and moved along the back wall, trying
to stay hidden.

The band was onstage, in their G Flats garb. Dexter
was singing an old Motown song, which I recognised
as one of their regular covers, and behind him
Ted was strumming his guitar with a bored, irritated
expression, as if just standing there was paining him.

The song ended with a flourish, provided by John
Miller, who then stood up for applause. It came, but

barely, and he sat back down again with a sigh.

'Hello everyone,' Dexter said into the microphone in his game show host voice. 'Let's give another big congratulations to Janine and Robert, the Doyles!'

Now, a big cheer as the bride beamed, blowing kisses at everyone.

'This next song is a special one from the bride to her groom,' Dexter went on, glancing at Lucas, who nodded. 'But the rest of you, feel free to sing along.'

The band launched into the opening chords of a song I barely recognised as one from a recent blockbuster movie. It was a power ballad, totally schmaltzy, and even Dexter, who was usually the best sport of the bunch, seemed to deflate when he had to deliver a line about *loving you till the stars are gone / and the heart I have just turns to stone* . . . Around the second chorus, Ted actually started gagging, stopping only when he had to concentrate hard on the guitar solo that wound up the final verse. The bride and groom, however, seemed oblivious to this, staring into each other's eyes as they danced, their bodies pressed together so closely they were hardly moving.

The song finished and everyone clapped. The bride was crying, her new husband reaching up to wipe her eyes while everyone made ain't-it-sweet noises. Truth Squad left the stage squabbling, Ted and Lucas already at each other, with Dexter and John Miller lagging behind. They all disappeared out a side door as the canned music came on and the staff wheeled the cake, four tiered and covered with roses, onto the dance floor.

As the door shut behind them I moved to follow, but something stopped me, and I took a step back, pressing myself against the wall and closing my eyes. God, it was one thing to come over here on a wave of post-Don-soakage euphoria, but another thing entirely to actually *do* this crazy thing. It was like driving on the wrong side of the road, or letting my gas gauge get down to flat empty before refilling, something that went completely against my nature and everything I had, up until this point, believed in.

But what had that got me so far, anyway? A string of boyfriends. A reputation as a cold, bitter bitch. And a secure bubble that I'd drawn so tightly around myself that no one, not even someone with the best of intentions, could get in, even if I wanted them to. The only way to truly reach me was to sneak up, crash in, bust past the barricades on the equivalent of a kamikaze mission, end result unknown.

That night at the Quik Zip he'd told me, so angrily, that everything he'd said to me, from the first day, was true. Then, I had blanked, not remembering anything. But now, as I pressed my back into the wall, it came to me.

I just thought to myself, all of a sudden, that we had something in common, he'd said. *A natural chemistry, if you will.*

That had been right after he'd crashed into me. My arm had been still buzzing at the funny bone.

And I just had a feeling that something big was going to happen.

I remembered, suddenly, how ridiculous this had

sounded. A car dealership soothsayer, telling my fortune.

To both of us. That we were, in fact, meant to be together.

Meant to be. He hadn't known me at all. Just seen me from across a room.

You didn't feel it?

Not then. Or maybe, deep in some hidden, misplaced spot, I had. And when I couldn't find it later, it came looking for me.

'They're about to cut the cake!' some woman in a green, shimmery dress was calling out as I pushed away from the wall, headed to that side door. Halfway there I got lost in a mass of people, all depositing their empty drinks on tables and pressing toward the dance floor. I navigated through them, past suits and tuxedos, crinkly dresses and a thick cloud of mixed perfumes before finally coming out on the other side. The door to the parking lot was open now, and as I stepped through it I saw the band had disappeared, with only a few tangerine peels remaining, scattered around the kerb.

From behind me, I heard a drum roll, followed by a crash of cymbals, and the best man was at the microphone, holding his glass aloft. John Miller was behind his drum set, picking at his teeth, while Lucas snuck some more beer into a cup off to the side of the stage. Ted was standing glumly next to his amp, as if he'd lost a bet. I craned my neck, looking for Dexter, but then a large woman in a pink dress stepped in front of the door, blocking my view. And suddenly I just knew I was too late.

I stepped back out into the fresh air, crossing my arms over my chest. Bad timing, again. It was hard not to think this was some kind of cue from the universe, letting me know that this wasn't the right thing to do. I tried, and failed. There. It was over.

But God! Who could live like this, anyway, with the kind of guesswork that was enough to make a person *crazy*, just sailing along, taking the bumps here and there, no course navigated whatsoever, with any big wave capable of just tipping and sinking you entirely. It was madness, stupidity, and—

Then I saw him. Sitting there on the kerb, under a streetlight, knees pulled up to his chest. And for one second, it was like I could feel the timing clicking together, finally, pieces falling into place. Behind me, the best man was winding up his toast, his voice sounding tight, emotional. *To the happy couple*, he said, and everyone repeated it, their voices blending as one. *To the happy couple.*

And then I was walking toward Dexter, folding my fingers tight into my hands. I could hear the cheers as the bridal couple cut their cake. So I took the last few steps of this long journey fast, almost running, before plunking myself down and knocking into Dexter, just enough to tip his balance for a second. Because I knew, now, this was how it had to begin. The only way was to crash in.

I knocked him sideways, startling him. But once he got his equilibrium, and his wits, back, he just looked at me. Not even one word. Because we knew it had to come from me this time.

'Hey,' I said.

'Hey.'

I took in his dark curls, the smell of his skin, that cheap tuxedo with the loose threads on the cuff. He was just looking at me, not pulling back, but not moving closer either. And I felt a sudden whirl in my head, knowing this leap was now inevitable, that I wasn't just on the cliff, toes poking over, but already in mid-air.

'Did you really believe, that first day, that we were meant to be together?' I asked him.

He looked at me and then said, 'You're here, aren't you?'

There was only so much space between us, not even a real distance if measured in miles or feet or even inches, all the things that told you how far you'd come or had left to go. But this was a big space, if only for me. And as I moved forward to him, covering it, he waited there on the other side. It was only the last little bit I had to go, but in the end, I knew it would be all I would truly remember. So as I kissed him, bringing this summer and everything else full circle, I let myself fall, and was not scared of the ground I knew would rise up to meet me. Instead, I just pulled him closer, my hand sliding up around his neck to find that one place where I could feel his heartbeat pulsing. It was fast, like my own, and finding it, I pressed down hard, as if it was all that connected us, and kept my finger there.

November

18

Melanie knew she had a choice. There was a time when she would have run after Luc, and the security he'd provided. And in another, more distant past, Brock would have seemed like the answer to all the questions that still woke her in the night, heart racing, wondering how she'd got here. The choice was clear, and yet not clear at all. As Melanie boarded the train that would take her to the station in Paris, she picked a window compartment and sank into the seat, pressing one hand against the glass. The countryside would soon slip away, replaced by the beautiful skylines that were the backdrop for so much of her past. She had the entire trip to figure out what her next step should be. And as the train pulled away, gaining speed, she settled back into her seat, relishing only the forward motion, as it pulled her toward her destiny.

'Remy?'

I looked up to see my room-mate, Angela, standing in the open doorway of our room. 'Yeah?'

'Mail call.' She came over and sat down beside me, dealing out envelopes into two piles. 'School crap. Credit card offer. Something from the Jehovah's Witnesses . . . that must be yours . . .'

'Finally,' I said. 'I've been waiting for that for ever.' Angela was from LA, taught aerobics part-time, and never made her bed. She wasn't a perfect match for me, but we got along okay.

'Oh, and this big one's yours,' she said, sliding a large manila envelope out from under the calculus textbook she was carrying. 'How's the book?'

'It's good,' I said, marking my page and shutting it. It was only a bound galley of Barbara Starr's newest, *The Choice*, but already three girls on my hall had asked me to borrow it when I was done. I was thinking, though, that they would be surprised by the ending, just as my mother's editor and publisher had been. I'd been a little shocked myself, reading the manuscript on the plane on the way out to school. I mean, in romance novels you just expected the heroine to end up with a man, some man, at the end. But Melanie, instead, made the choice of no choice, packing up her Paris memories and heading across the world to start anew with no lingering loves to hold her back. Not bad for an ending, I thought. It was, after all, the one I'd planned for myself, not too long ago.

Angela left the room, headed to the library, as I picked up the manila envelope and opened it, dumping its contents into my lap. The first thing I saw was a bunch of pictures, bound with a rubber band: the one on the top was of me, squinting, the sun bright in my face. There was something wrong with the picture, though: it seemed out of balance. There was also a blurred edge on the top, and a weird kind of after-image splayed across the left side. They were all a bit off, I realised, as I flipped through them. Most of them were of Dexter, and a few of me, with several featuring John Miller. Some were of inanimate objects, like a tyre or a tangerine, with the same defects. Finally, I realised what they were, remembering all those warped wedding cameras Dexter and the rest of them had been toting around most of the summer. So the pictures had come out, after all, just as Dexter had predicted. They weren't perfect, though, as I'd maintained. In the end, like so much else, they were good enough.

The other thing in the envelope was a CD wrapped in cardboard, taped carefully. The label on it said RUBBER RECORDS, and, beneath that, in smaller letters, TRUTH SQUAD. I knew the first cut well: it was called 'Potato Song, Part One'. I knew the second song even better.

I picked up my Walkman and slid on the headphones, pressing the CD in and hitting play. It made that little whirring sound, finding the tracks, and then I pressed past cut one, as I knew most people would eventually do, to call up the second song. Then I lay back across my bed, hearing the opening chords, and picked up the last picture in the stack.

It was of Dexter and me, at the airport, the day I'd left for school. The top edge was a bit blurry, and there was a weird sunburst of colour in the bottom right corner, but otherwise it was a good shot. We were standing in front of a window, and I had my head on his shoulder, both of us smiling. I'd been sad that day, but not in a final, end-of-story way. Like Melanie, I was heading off to my new world. But I was taking a part of my past, and the future, along with me for the ride.

The song was building in my headphones, the first words about to begin over the new, jazzy, retro-style start. I turned the picture over, and saw there was something on the back. Scrawled in black ink, smeared (of course), it said, *D.C., Baltimore, Philadelphia, Austin . . . and you. I'll be there soon.*

I reached over and turned up the volume, letting Dexter's voice fill my ears, smooth and fluid. And even though I had heard it so many times already, I still felt that little catch of breath as it began.

> *This lullaby is only a few words*
> *A simple run of chords*
> *Quiet here in this spare room*
> *But you can hear it, hear it*
> *Wherever you may go*
> *Even if I let you down*
> *This lullaby plays on . . . .*

I knew that there were no guarantees. No way of knowing what came next for me, or him, or anybody. Some things don't last for ever, but some things do. Like a good song, or a good book, or a good memory you can take out and unfold in your darkest times, pressing down the corners and peering in close, hoping you still recognise the person you see there. Dexter was a whole country away from me now. But I had a good feeling he would get to me, one way or another. And if not, I'd already proved I could meet him halfway.

But for now, I just sat there on the bed and listened to my song. The one that had been written for me by a man who knew me not at all, now sung by the one who knew me best. Maybe it would be the hit the record company predicted, striking a chord in our collective past, prompting a wave of nostalgia that would carry Dexter and the band everywhere they'd ever dreamed. Or maybe, no one would hear it at all. That was the thing: you just never knew. Right now, though, I wanted not to think forward or backward, but only to lose myself in the words. So I lay back, closing my eyes, and let them fill my mind, new and familiar all at once, rising and falling with my very breath, steady, as they sang me to sleep.

As a writer,
I'd always wanted to write a true
love story. With Remy, I got that and more.
What started out as a novel about one girl
falling in love became a story about love and
everything it can and can't be. Also, I think, This
Lullaby is about faith, and what it takes to truly
believe in something – or someone – even if it scares
you. Of all my narrators, Remy is my favourite.
You just have to love a girl who thinks she knows
everything and finds out, at least where her
heart is concerned, that she couldn't
be more wrong.